praise for

WORK OF THE ANGELS

"Kat Goldring has done it again! She has managed to weave a web of mystery, this time with a mixture of ancient Celtic lore and American Indian spiritualism that will keep her readers turning pages. If there is one uniqueness about her writing, it is the ability to mix just the right amounts of humor, melancholy and joy to take her readers on an exciting and believable journey . . . [She] whisks her readers off to the small Texas town of Nickelberry and keeps them there." —*The Cleburne Eagle News*

"A novel steeped in traditional lore." —*The Mystery Reader*

"A highly entertaining read with a funny and down-to-earth heroine. Don't miss this angelic read." —*Rendezvous*

"Delightful and well-written . . . some very unusual twists."
—*mysterylovers.com*

"Thoroughly entertaining . . . really does keep you guessing to the very end. . . . With a wonderful blend of the charm of the Irish and the wisdom of the Indian, this is a delightful book. . . . With a heroine as fey and whimsical as Willi is, all I can say is, write some more, Ms. Goldring!" —*Roundtable Reviews*

continued . . .

The Eye That Is Divine

☿✳

Kat Goldring

BERKLEY PRIME CRIME, NEW YORK

THE BERKLEY PUBLISHING GROUP
Published by the Penguin Group
Penguin Group (USA) Inc.
375 Hudson Street, New York, New York 10014, USA
Penguin Group (Canada), 10 Alcorn Avenue, Toronto, Ontario M4V 3B2, Canada
(a division of Pearson Penguin Canada Inc.)
Penguin Books Ltd., 80 Strand, London WC2R 0RL, England
Penguin Group Ireland, 25 St. Stephen's Green, Dublin 2, Ireland (a division of Penguin Books Ltd.)
Penguin Group (Australia), 250 Camberwell Road, Camberwell, Victoria 3124, Australia
(a division of Pearson Australia Group Pty. Ltd.)
Penguin Books India Pvt. Ltd., 11 Community Centre, Panchsheel Park, New Delhi—110 017, India
Penguin Group (NZ), Cnr. Airborne and Rosedale Roads, Albany, Auckland 1310, New Zealand
(a division of Pearson New Zealand Ltd.)
Penguin Books (South Africa) (Pty.) Ltd., 24 Sturdee Avenue, Rosebank, Johannesburg 2196,
South Africa

Penguin Books Ltd., Registered Offices: 80 Strand, London WC2R 0RL, England

THE EYE THAT IS DIVINE

A Berkley Prime Crime Book / published by arrangement with the author

PRINTING HISTORY
Berkley Prime Crime mass-market edition / February 2005

ISBN: 0-425-20199-6

Berkley Prime Crime Books are published by The Berkley Publishing Group,
a division of Penguin Group (USA) Inc.,
375 Hudson Street, New York, New York 10014.
The name BERKLEY PRIME CRIME and the BERKLEY PRIME CRIME design
are trademarks belonging to Penguin Group (USA) Inc.

PRINTED IN THE UNITED STATES OF AMERICA

10   9   8   7   6   5   4   3   2   1

ACKNOWLEDGMENTS

Special thanks goes to S.J. MacKenzie, who generously shared her tales, her materials, and her insights about her time living among the monks. She exemplifies the idea of balance: always sweet-spirited, always compassionate, always joyful.

Big hugs go to those who helped me keep my "balance" during the rougher waters in the manuscript, dear friends Claudia Francis Bennett, Peggy Sotelo, and Shirley McKee. I am so thankful for your keen critique, your gentle prodding, and your insistent statements such as, "Yes, you can do that. Of course, you have the ability and intelligence to complete this section. Just do it." Extra kudos to Neil Ross—he of the persevering nature, he of the poetic lilt, he who encourages with humor. I'm sure these are four of the folks who will always hear "the bells."

Hugs,
Kat G.

DEDICATION

Many fine men and women have been affected by tremendous pressures of difficult times, and although they've gone on afterward with rewarding lives away from the tumult, they do not forget their part in the pivotal moments in history. This is dedicated to two such people:

First, to my father, Phidias Arden (Pete) Goldring (1910–2001) who, as a civilian, played an important part in helping to serve the military during WW II. Pete led truck caravans from Texas to California, at night across the desert, and, due to blackouts, without headlights on, to take much needed supplies to the coast. In a time when trucks lacked the amenity of air conditioning, he said it wasn't much pay and a lot of heat and dust, but it was the least he could do to help the troops.

Second, to my uncle, Second Lieutenant Charles L. Stevens of the Army Aircorp, who was a navigator aboard a B29. Stationed at Tinnian in the Marrianas Islands, he flew fifteen combat missions to Japan and back. Flying low at 5,000 feet, his plane luckily never suffered from the giant thermal flareups that resulted from those close-to-the-earth fire bombs. During a daylight raid on a Japanese airfield, the B29 lost two engines and received fifty-seven flack holes. Gas poured out and against the navigator's window. Steve was ready to bail out, but since the bomber was over the ocean and he couldn't swim, he opted to stay and nurse the plane to the halfway point of Iwo Jima.

CHAPTER
I

Willi Gallagher sighed for the third time, not at her high school students, but at her childhood friend, MacKenzie Francis. Kenzie, blond tufts of her hair blowing in the summer breeze, stood in front of the Nickleberry Pharmacy Apothecary Shoppe. The window display advertised a Texas Wildflower committee meeting in the back booth on Wednesday, a checkers club get-together on Sunday, and a free blood-pressure clinic next week. Willi pushed her own dark tendrils off her shoulders and said, "Kiddo, we go back a long ways, but—"

"Since eleven years old, and—"

"And this retreat might be great for you, Kenzie, but for me? No."

Kenzie said, "Don't 'no' me, friend. This will be super. Just like when your grandmama used to take us on trips to Galveston. Only difference, this time I'll foot the whole bill."

"You always paid your way, Kenzie, so you don't have to—"

"I know, but I want to do this, and I'm not above using any means to sway you. If you didn't have that stubborn English teacher streak about you, you'd not need so much convincing."

Willi frowned, which made her heart-shaped face look more like a snarling cat—she'd been told. She pushed open the door to the Apothecary Shoppe. "I hate to tell Quannah after only two weeks together that oh, by the by, I'm going off to a Zen retreat for enlightenment and balance with my childhood friend."

Kenzie peered into the pharmacist's window.

Willi reached over and patted Kenzie's arm. "Not that he would care. He and I both know you've been through torture, what with the battering, the divorce, the stalking. Hells Bells, if anyone needs and deserves a break, it's you."

Willi shoved open the door and they entered the ice-cold shop. She shoved the retreat brochure into her purse. "Sure he cares! Like all tight-butted, control freaks of a man!"

"Kenzie!" Willi cringed at her sharp tone. "Sorry." She said more calmly, "You don't mean that. You're consumed with anger for that stupid—ex. Understandable and justifiable after what he's put you through, but not all men—"

"Not all men are like him? Yeah, right. Look. That's his pickup. He's waiting for us."

Willi peered outside. Sure enough. Jerry Cormack's dented brown Chevy pickup sat right beside Willi's Ford Focus. She rubbed her arms. "Why do they keep it so cold in here year round?"

A stock boy—one of Willi's sophomore English students—working with a display of bug sprays for delicate skin types, said, "Supposed to help kill the germs. But if we complain, it gets colder; if a customer does, it's turned to a more bearable level. Would you . . . ?"

Willi winked at him. "Sure, Leonard, no problem. By the by, since your braces are off, that smile is sure something."

"Aww, thank you, Ms. Gallagher."

When they reached the counter, she rubbed her arms again and said, "Could you get the cool down to a decent decibel, please? Must be fifty degrees in here." Mr. Umphrey peered at her, then at Leonard who hastily rearranged the Off bug sprays.

Kenzie asked for her thyroid prescription.

The pharmacist shook his head, turned away from the counter, and walked behind some of the stocked medicine shelves.

Kenzie leaned forward. "Mr. Umphrey, I called it in yesterday."

"Yes, well that's as it may be, yes, uh-huh." He rubbed his hands down the front of his smock, reached behind to the thermostat, and pushed the lever to the seventy mark. Immediately, the hum of the AC unit stopped, which made Willi suddenly seem like she was shouting.

Willi asked, "Is there a problem?"

Mr. Umphrey glowered in her direction, turned to Kenzie, and cleared his throat. "I don't believe I can fill . . . uh . . . no, I can't fill it today."

Kenzie smiled. "I'm sure it's okay. Check the computer. There are three more refills remaining."

"That's as it may be, yes ma'am, but Jerry doesn't think—"

"Jerry! Jerry?" Kenzie barely whispered the second utterance and swayed.

Willi grabbed for her friend's elbow. She glared at Mr. Umphrey. "Are you referring to her *former* spouse, Jerry Cormack?"

Umphrey wiped his hands down his white tunic again. "Jerry is real concerned, and has convinced me you might ought to have a full check-up, considering how . . . how you've been acting lately."

Willi shook a finger in his face. "He's the crazy one, not her. How dare you do this. He has no say in her life, and last I checked you weren't Kenzie's medical doctor, and the only damn thing you ought to do is follow the doctor's directions."

Kenzie seemed to gain strength from Willi's support and squared her shoulders. "Are you going to fill my prescription?"

Umphrey patted his pocket of pens. "You get checked by your doctor. Have him call me."

With a glare that would have melted kryptonite, Willi narrowed her eyes. "Oh, I'll check with her doctor all right and have you taken off the recommended list for patients. And while I'm at it, you'll have some questions to answer for the Better Business Bureau."

"Now, wait just a minute." He pulled a pen out of his pocket, dropped it, and swallowed. He chased the clattering pen with a sweaty palm. "When you talk to him, you might—"

Willi and Kenzie both leaned into Umphrey's personal space. "It's a *she*."

Kenzie ended with, "I'll never bring my business to you again."

"You only have one other place, the Mega Mart out by the college."

Willi guided Kenzie to the door and said over her shoulder, "Any place is preferable to this."

Outside, Kenzie sighed as if all her innards had just suffered through an elevator drop. "Oh, God, it's . . . it's just never-ending stuff. I feel like worms and spiders and scorpions are crawling on me. Not literally, girl, just that I never feel totally comfortable. About the time I get calmed down about one thing, he crawls from beneath the underside of a rock and pulls more crud from underneath it."

A shadow loomed over them. Kenzie gasped.

Jerry Cormack looked scruffy, despite his gray dress slacks and white shirt with cuff links and tie clasp. He worked a toothpick between his teeth and grinned as if expecting a warm welcome. "How are you two sweethearts? I been over to Pulido's Restaurant fixing their software problem."

"Who cares?" Kenzie said. "I've a restraining order. Now get away from me."

He ran his fingers down his tie before reaching up and plucking the toothpick from his five-thousand-dollars' worth of dental work. "Oh, honeychile, I'll never go away. I'll always be in your life, sweet *thang*."

"Don't call me that!"

Willi walked toward the phone booth in front of the Apothecary Shoppe. "I'm calling 911 now."

"No problem, darlings, I'm going. But go ahead and call. Tell the deputies I'm on my way over to fix their machines. All them good ol' boys and me, we're going fishing this weekend. It's good to have friends all over town, you know?"

Willi raised an eyebrow. "You *think* you have friends. You? Ha! Keep the hell away from her and from me. Go crawl under a rock with your so-called friends. Don't believe for a minute, Kenzie, he has any real ones. He's so full of hot air, one wrong prick with that wood in his mouth and he'd burst. And I know right where to stick it!"

He narrowed his eyes while his face turned red, but

placed the toothpick back between his teeth and sauntered to the pickup door. "Nasty mouth for an upstanding teacher. Might have to report that to my buddies on the school board. Yep, sure is good to have folks who trust and know me for the upstanding citizen and churchgoing deacon that I am."

He got in and leaned out the open window. "Have any problems with your prescriptions, sweet *thang?* Not to worry. I had a little talk with your doctor, too. Might have to spend some money and time on tests before you can get any more filled. Enough things like this happen and you'll have to claim bankruptcy. Be running right back to your Jerry; you bet on it, darling. Have a great day."

After he roared down the street, Willi sat on the bench beneath the huge oak in front of the Apothecary Shoppe. "So, has this happened at a lot of businesses?"

"Yeah, and I usually skedaddle like a whipped dog. And that's spelled d-a-w-g."

"That low, huh?"

"Yeah."

"Damn."

"I get my spirits up after a few days. Then he blindsides me. And—"

"And it preys on your mind. Typical guerrilla warfare tactics. Wasn't he big into those war games?"

"Yeah. I'm so tired of watching my back, bracing myself for the next snub, the innuendo that's going to tear me down, and make him *present* in my life again."

"You've really got a restraining order?"

"Best friend, you know it, but he's smart. Remember he's a Microsoft and general computer tech, and people think he's a god for that. Never breaks the order when there are eyewitnesses, other than his three geeky buddies, and they lie for him. One is that Vietnam vet who came back nasty and mad at his lady for leaving him. Second one is just as bad. Holes up in an Arlington duplex with a store-house of guns. Scary man."

"As in be very, *very* afraid?"

"You got that right. And the third one is a CEO. He's been arrested but never had to serve time. Twice. For flash-ing, once at the Bass Hall in Fort Worth, another time at a Sheriff's Posse Rodeo in Cleburne."

"Where in the yahoo is Cleburne?"

"Next county or so over; Johnson, I think. Nice little town. Stay focused, girl. Anyway, men with just enough power to commit crimes and and get away with them. Jerry and his buddies broke into my home three times." Kenzie ruffled her short blond curls with shaking fingers.

"But you can't prove it's him?"

"No. After the deputy sheriff almost got him for that fire he set at my folks' place, he started playing it close to his chest. I never said he wasn't intelligent."

"Oh, he may be cunning, Kenzie, but he'll fall on his face one of these days."

"I just hope it's before they're dusting mine with grave-yard dirt."

Willi shivered. The more she heard, the more frightened she became on Kenzie's behalf. Unreasonably, this trans-lated into her wanting to be home with Quannah even more, to be safe within his embrace, to sigh and tell him of her fears. Just one of his hugs could calm her far better than music, wine, or bath beads.

Kenzie looked up into the top of the tree and pointed to a squirrel on a branch. "I guess I'm looking for some peace of mind more than spirituality, if you will. The retreat just feels right. First thing I've been excited about since all this started. Please, reconsider. You have to have a Zen partner, or they won't allow you to take the seminar."

"I admit it seems a good idea to put distance between you both, especially if he's about to do a mental kamikaze scenario. I'll ask Quannah tonight."

"Ask him? Can't you just tell him this is what you want to do?"

"Yes, but we'll discuss it. I'm sure he'll think it's fine."

"And if not?"

"What do you mean?"

"You know what I mean, Willi. If he says, no I don't want my little woman out of the tipi, what will you do?"

Willi sighed. Hmm. Quannah had just moved in with her at the farmhouse. They were—*poco a poco, paso a paso*—little by little, step by step making her house *their* home. Each day brought something new to the forefront in their relationship. She figured they'd never be able to complain about having a humdrum day. However, she neither wanted uncomfortable conversations nor out-and-out fights.

"What will I do?"

Willi whipped mustard and mayo into the cooked yolks for the deviled eggs while eyeing the broad, strong back of Quannah Lassiter, who was cutting up orange slices for the fruit salad. She said, "It's been wonderful."

He turned and winked at her swinging his ponytail. "It's been okay."

"Just okay, Big Chief?"

"See, I knew you'd be teasing me about my Indian blood, but you remember, you have some, too." The twinkle in his eye warmed her. He said, "Hot Indian blood."

"Hmm. We'll see. I went out to lunch with Kenzie today."

"Little woman changes subject fast. It's that Tweetybird medicine in you—flighty."

"That's hummingbird, thank you very much, and I'm not flitting, but before we get into hot and heavy and other *H* words which usually describe you, I need to ask . . . I mean . . . let you know about an upcoming commitment I've let myself in for."

Quannah finished with the oranges and switched to opening and slamming drawer doors.

"What *are* you looking for?"

"Paring knife."

She pointed to the block of knives on the counter. "To the right of the stovetop."

"Ugh. Okay, *Winyan,* tell me." He chopped the apples.

"You know that ranch in the Guadalupe River area, the one you've cleared horse trails for in the past?"

He nodded. "The one with Serenity Island in the middle of it used as a retreat where the monks live?"

"Uh-huh. That's the one." She grinned.

He popped a bite of apple into his mouth. "So, what about Serenity Island?"

"It's not far away, I mean, It won't be like . . . like it's in another country or state, even."

"Back up, Gallagher. Take a deep breath."

Her heart was suddenly up in her throat, her tongue dry, she paused. This really was an important step in their relationship. She could not become a weak Stepford Wife, saying only what she thought he wanted to hear. So, why was she quaking at the idea of speaking her mind as she always had? Because if he disagreed, he might . . . he might be out the door? At that sudden cold image, her tongue stuck to the roof of her mouth.

He crossed his arms in his Big Chief Stance. "Spit it out, Gallagher."

She licked her lips. "I . . . a lady does not spit, thank you very much."

He reached behind him, picked up a juicy orange slice, and squeezed it between his fingers. "I have ways of *making* you talk."

"What?" She scooted away, hitting the edge of the table full of deviled eggs. "I am trying . . . to have an adult conversation . . . about . . ."

"About?" He flung open his fingers.

Orange juice sprayed in her face, light and tangy and cold on her lips. "You insufferable man. You expect me to be able to talk while you threaten me with . . ."

He grabbed a slice, reached over quickly, and dropped it down her blouse, then pushed it into a juicy pulp with his hand. "What about the island? What's on the island that interests you?"

"Ahhhhhh! Uck! I don't believe you just did that! Now, you back off of this silliness right now, Quannah Big Chief Lassiter, and I mean . . . ahhhh!"

With both hands he had squeezed two succulent pieces on top of her head. "The *island?*"

"The island offers a Zen retreat, and it's looking better every damned minute."

"Oh? Zen?"

"Kenzie needs the time away from the world."

He dribbled juice into one of her ears and whispered. "And how does that involve you?"

She shivered. "Well, she wants me to go with her. She has to have . . . now, stop that. Oh my Lordy, don't stop *that,* though . . ."

He drew back from her earlobe and stared into her eyes. "Has to have?"

"Who?" she squeaked out.

"Kenzie has to have . . . ?" He dove down toward the

sweet curve of her neck and nuzzled to lick off the drip-ping juice. "Kenzie has to have what?"

"Me . . . uh . . . me there, a partner to go through the week-long retreat, and I know if you don't back off right now, I'm going to do something . . . now, just stop it."

"And, if I don't?"

"I'll . . . I'll egg you."

"Naw, you're too much of a Stepford lady to do that."

"Oh." *Get out of my head, Lassiter.*

She pushed him away. "Oh, really?" She grabbed two deviled eggs and smashed them in the middle of his face. "I . . . I can't believe I did that . . . oh my gosh."

"Turn about is fair play, *Winyan.*" He grabbed the bowl of Cool Whip and doused her nose, neck, and between her breasts. He growled, "I guess you think you're going to traipse off into this wilderness without me."

Grabbing the bottle of canola oil, she squirted his shirt-front. When he ripped it off with an evil grin, she squealed and landed another onslaught of oil onto his chest. "I most certainly will go where I want to, you . . . you"— she gig-gled —"you savage."

Just before he laid her atop the egg-, orange-, and cream-covered kitchen floor, he whispered into her ear. "Now, what was so hard about saying that, Gallagher?"

He didn't really allow her to answer, since his lips were in the way. When he withdrew, he said, "I don't think we'll forget the first meal we made together. Oh, and by the way, I will be going to the island with you."

"I can't believe we arrived late," willi said, throwing her knapsack back over her shoulders as she climbed into one of the last canoes—old wooden skiffs with painted red designs—leaving the mainland of the ranch to head off for

Serenity Island some seven miles around meandering curves and inlets. "I've seen those designs before. Eyes. Humm. These are not fiberglass, are they?"

Kenzie, ramrod straight, hands clutching the sides of the canoe, said, "Don't hop around. You're the one that doesn't want water over your head, you know. Sit, girl, and sit still. I thought when they said we'd boat over to the island they meant motorboat. These look like children's camp rejects. Those designs are depictions of the Third Eye. They'll explain those in the classes."

Willi grinned and bounced from one foot to the other.

"Ornery!" Kenzie shot her a glance that would have stopped thunderbolts from on high. "Okay, when you bounce overboard and can't breathe when that water closes over you, don't blame me."

Willi sighed, settled, and punched her friend's arm. "Hey, what better way to get into balance than to start out on a slow paddle through the lake."

"It'll be great. The sun is wonderful, the wind perfect, the air . . . delicious," Kenzie said.

Willi wanted to say something about the scorching heat, the mugginess of the air, but she opted for, "Your blond hair is like a halo, Kenzie. And you're the only grown woman I know who has a beautiful dusting of freckles. You'd look angelic if you didn't have that constant frown."

She stared into Kenzie's terrified blue eyes. Okay, she'd have to figure out a way to get Kenzie to calm down, at least long enough to make it to Serenity Island. "Turn loose of the sides. I won't jump around anymore. Take a couple of deep breaths. There. Much better. We haven't even left the dock, and you're about to turn as white as a ghost."

Kenzie smiled. "This *will* be good for me. I'm more tense than a landlubber in a wild hurricane, but I can see the water *is* calm. I don't have to be afraid. It's not like we

have to hurry, either. No time check-ins like at work. Free
as those birds swooping by."

"Yeah, just common swallows I think, but so graceful."

Kenzie glanced around at the canoes remaining at the
dock. "Oh my gosh, girl, what happened to our luggage? I
knew something would go wrong. Move. We have to get
off right now. Someone has stolen our bags. I do not live
without my makeup kit, my vitamins, my—"

Willi grabbed onto Kenzie's shoulders and pushed her
down hard. "The luggage is already on the island. Quannah
took it over this morning when he went to give the first half-
day trail ride to early arrivals and start the *Inipi* lodge."

"Oh, yeah, yeah. I knew that. I just . . . forgot." She
rubbed her temples. "Why aren't we paddling out with the
others?"

"Kenzie?"

"What?"

"Where have you been the last couple of hours?"

"What do you mean?"

Willi sighed at the distraught face before her. "Remember? When we got to the ranch they told us to come down
to the pier and wait for the last two arrivals for today?
They're supposed to be experienced canoeists, which is
why we were paired with them. You'll be in one canoe, me
in another. You truly are stressed, aren't you?" That probably wasn't the best way to convince a friend to relax. Willi
grimaced. That island was some seven miles away. Oh,
Great Spirit better lend a helping hand today.

"You're right." Kenzie said. "I am. I'm so paranoid.
Seems like I'm always planning how I'm going to react to
something horrible before it happens. Do you think *he*
could have found out, followed us?"

"Of course not. Stop borrowing trouble." Willi flushed
at her lie of omission. She could not—would not—tell

Kenzie of the threatening call she'd received moments before leaving. After all, she could not prove it was Jerry Cormack, since it came from a pay phone.

She shut her eyes and recalled his words: *You could both end up at the bottom of the lake. That's what happens to women who think they run things. They become fish food. Bloated fish food.*

If it were him, he could have been on an info-fishing trip; maybe he had gotten an idea from someone that they were going to a lake; the call didn't mean he knew of their exact plans. No, she'd not bother Kenzie. She'd simply watch her friend's back until Quannah could help decide what to do. She said, "If Elba and Agatha were here, they'd be drowning you in herbal teas and telling you to trust in your own strength, your own right-to-be."

Kenzie's face beamed up at her. "You're so lucky to have the Kachelhoffer sisters as neighbors. Their good advice and lots of other teachings from my past have just gone . . . like I've metamorphosed into some alien creature with no ties . . . no human ties."

Willi leaned over and hugged her friend and patted her on the back. "That's about to change. We're going to get you in touch with your maker, yourself, and the world around you."

"Maybe it's an impossible feat to come back after being alienated so long."

"Nonsense. You've almost suffered a nervous breakdown, and no wonder. Now, It's time to heal wounds. You decided that, or you wouldn't have wanted to come on this Zen retreat so badly. You're doing a lot better than you think."

"Where in heck are those last arrivals? They're slower ladies than we are!"

"Patience, *k'ola,* patience."

Kenzie smiled. "That's nice."

"What?"

"You and Quannah, how you influence each other, the sharing of the small things. That word—that's something you learned from him, right? So what did you just call me?"

" 'K'ola?' Friend. That's all. Friend."

"Well, K'ola, where are the other ladies?"

Willi held up a hand, palm forward. "It's two fellows."

"Oh, great. *Men.*"

Willi laughed. "I recall a time when they were on a certain female's mind constantly. I knew you in college, remember."

"Well, that was then, and this is now, and—"

"And you're going to follow my lead and be pleasant to them. Give them a chance to prove that not all are knuckle-dragging Neanderthals. A Mr. Tulsa and a Mr. Rowley will be paired as partners."

"Yeah, right."

Willi glared.

"Okay, okay. I'll try."

Willi eyed Kenzie. Oh, Great Spirit and a couple of special Totems were going to be needed today in order to reach Serenity Island in a peaceful frame of mind.

The boat wavered as a foot descended into it. "Ladies." The quiet voice continued. "Paul Rowley." He leaned over to grab a paddle. Two sets of dog tags clanked around his neck. Willi guessed him to be in his mid-fifties.

She reached a hand forward. "Willi Gallagher and Kenzie Francis."

"Step back a pace, ma'am, step back a pace." Again he spoke quietly but with an intensity that bespoke leadership.

Kenzie gave Willi one of those told-you-so looks as Willi lowered her hand.

Paul Rowley bent over to pick up a curled line that

would have caught around Willi's legs and tripped her if she'd moved another step. Then he shot out his hand. "Try that again, now. Paul Rowley, Willi."

She smiled, including Kenzie in the wide grin.

"Didn't think you'd want to end up in the water," he said. "One of you will have to move over into this other canoe in a minute, by the by." He shook hands with Kenzie.

She said, "How can you see through those glasses?"

Willi rolled her eyes upward. She'd wondered the same thing, but wouldn't have been so blunt.

Paul took off his bifocals. "Are they dirty? You think they're dirty?"

Kenzie grabbed them and a soft tissue from her pocket and worked magic. "Here. And I'll make the move. Willi jumps around and jiggles the boat."

"That's canoe, ma'am, and thanks. Appreciate the clean lenses, I do. Might help this headache some to be able to see through them."

"So," Willi said, "you're a bit tense, too? Guess everyone who's going on this retreat is a little stressed."

"And you all aren't helping any, nope not helping any."

"Beg your pardon?" Willi and Kenzie both said, leaning toward him.

"Keep your distance. Just meant . . . I'm here to learn . . . uh . . . to let people like you all—"

"Like us?" asked Willi.

"You mean, *women?*" Kenzie chimed in as she stepped over to the other canoe.

"Yeah, women. I'm here to learn to let ladies into what my shrink calls, my emotional space." He smiled sheepishly. "Worked too many years with men, I guess. Yeah, never learned to . . . be comfortable around other . . . people."

"The dog tags? Those yours?" Willi asked.

"One set is mine. Vietnam. Other was my dad's. He died at Pearl Harbor," Rowley said.

A bull-elk voice on the pier said, "Lots of good men died at Pearl Harbor. Hell, I almost did. And I was only fifteen. Sneaked into the Navy. You could get away with things like that in those days, you know what I mean? Hell, you can't wipe your nose without two forms of picture ID anymore." He lowered himself into the boat. Despite his seventy-plus years he moved nimbly and comfortably. "Nestor D. Tulsa here. I'm an old newshound. Might as well warn you now, and I aim to win."

"What's to win on a Zen retreat?" Willi asked. She frowned. She just wanted to get to the island to see Quannah. That's what would get her back in balance.

"Just an expression, ma'am. Same thing with 'the mission, that's what's important.' "

Kenzie wadded the tissue into a minuscule ball, "This is supposed to be a retreat, for God's sake, not some interrogation camp. I don't want to have to watch over my shoulder for some camera to sneak pictures. The reason I came was to avoid being constantly under surveillance, constantly stalked. Let me out of this boat. I should have known once jerky men got involved—"

Both men held up their hands. Paul Rowley said, "Step back a pace. Keep your distance. Hear him out, hear him out." He glanced at Willi as if to ask for help.

She motioned for Kenzie to sit down on the canoe seat. "I'd like to have an answer to those questions, too," Willi said, while watching tremors go through Kenzie's frame. By Hades, she was tighter strung than a viola string with lit dynamite tied to it. She ought to have a sign: DANGER. DO NOT PLUCK. Maybe they wouldn't make it to the island. Willi shook that notion out of her head. "So? Are you here to get a scoop?"

Paul sat down and looked up at Nestor D. Tulsa. "I'll support a vet in any way, but I came here for like reasons. Are you here to relax or report?"

Nestor hitched his khaki pants up around his still slender waist. "You all are wilder than a flock of geese just been buckshot. I'm at the Zen retreat—this Serenity Island—for my own reasons, none of which have to do with reporting. But . . . I can't just turn off those instincts—the curiosity—so if I come out with questions, you mark it up to that. In other words, don't be fretting what you say or do will end up in black-and-white in any magazine or paper. That's not the way I work, and ma'am"—he peered at Kenzie—"I didn't even bring a camera." He patted her on the shoulder. "That's one of the things I want to escape."

"Okay," Kenzie said. "Sorry about the outburst."

Like a great elk stepping back from a fight, Nestor D. shook himself, peered at the sky, and nodded. "We best get rowing. Weather's about to change on us."

"Sunshine, not a cloud anywhere," Willi said, "and we thought you, Kenzie, were the one always looking for Eeyore's little blue rain cloud. If the good weather holds, I'll get one wish today: to get to Serenity Island before darkfall."

Paul Rowley took hold of a set of paddles, just as a fifth person joined them. Obviously one of the seven monks who worked on Serenity Island. He wore a red wraparound over a golden shirt and he had sandals on his feet. His shaved head glistened like a bronze apple beneath the hot sun. He bowed to each and said, "Ms. Willi Gallagher, Ms. MacKenzie Francis, Mr. Nestor D. Tulsa, Mr. Paul Rooster Rowley."

Paul cleared his throat. "Sort of appreciate it, if we could drop the Rooster. Name my friends gave me years ago, and I don't think it's done me any favors through the years, nope, no favors at all. That name is something I want to leave behind me. Just Paul Rowley, please."

The monk nodded. "All names have good side, bad side. But we honor what you say, Mr. Paul Rowley." He smiled at all, took one of the paddles, and handed one to Willi and another to Kenzie. "All will row." He gingerly seated himself in the middle of Willi and Paul's canoe, leaving Nestor and Kenzie to manage the other one.

Nestor and Paul both glared. Paul said, "Now, see here, no sense these ladies having to—"

Nestor pulled his pants up and put his head down as if he might have useable antlers on his great frame. "Might be seventy-five, but I can still do a thirty-year-old's workout."

"Understood," the monk said. He smiled. "All row. I show way."

Willi sighed and offered the paddle back to him. "I don't know how to—"

"Neither do I, and I don't mind if they want to—" Kenzie said.

The monk merely pushed the paddles back toward them.

"Now?" Willi asked.

"Now?" Kenzie growled out. "Who says?"

The monk placed a hand on his chest. "Jamyang. Means *Gentle Voice*. Jamyang says."

"Uh, well . . ." Kenzie said, "just wanted to know."

By the time they'd learn to row in opposite sequence to keep the canoes from doing circles, Willi had a scraped knuckle, Paul's glasses were covered with water droplets, Nestor was out and out laughing, and Kenzie exclaimed, "Hey, this isn't bad. We can do this."

Nestor said, "The mission, that's what's important. We *can* do it, maybe even by sundown, and I'll be ready for a rest and a whiskey on the rocks by then."

Seeing the way Jamyang looked at Nestor, Willi figured the reporter would discover no liquor on the island. Well, maybe that was something else he needed to escape.

An hour later, the sky supported Nestor's earlier prognostication. The cloudbank rolled in upon the horizon like a menacing devil deciding whether to burst or pass by, but sunshine still beat upon their backs. Surely, that particular malfeasance of nature would drift away from them. Willi smiled at Kenzie, who seemed to be getting comfortable with the rowing and with the men. They just might, after all, make it to the island retreat without one of Kenzie's panic attacks. After another half hour, Willi sighted the island. "Whoo—hoo!"

"Land ahoy," chimed in Paul Rowley and Nestor D.

"How long before we touch land?" asked Kenzie.

Jamyang said, "We are *here* now. *This* moment is what we live in."

"I know, but—"

Willi nodded. "I think we're getting a first lesson in Zen philosophy."

"Ah-ha. Okay." Kenzie agreed.

Paul's quiet voice broke in. "He's right. We're where we are in time and place, nowhere else, and can't be until the next moment. How could he tell us how long it would take; how could he tell us? The rain clouds could open and slow us down, the wind could pick up and help us row faster, the—"

"I see what you mean," Willi said.

"Got it," Kenzie said. She set her paddle down. "Enjoy *this moment*. The water lapping, the clouds pressing, the sun's heating rays."

Willi said, "The splinters on the canoe seat, knuckles burning, blisters forming, back muscles protesting." At

Kenzie's glare, she added. "Uh-oh, didn't mean to ruin the moment."

She bent her sore back to the task as all rowed again. Willi sighted something wiggling in the water. "What is that? Ahhhhhhhhh! Damn!" She pulled her paddle out of the water and with it came a writhing watersnake. Shining and quicksilver fast it landed on her legs. She screamed again, stood, and swiped at it. It flew through the air to land on Kenzie's back. Screeching, Kenzie jumped up. As Paul leaned from the opposite canoe to pull the snake off her shoulder, his Nestor's and Willi's canoe capsized, sending Willi and Jamyang's into the brackish water. No idea where the others were, she floundered while trying to move up to the surface. There she met the resistance of the canoe on top of her.

Oh, God. And where was that snake?

She couldn't push the canoe out of the way. Her lungs strained with the little air left to her. She dove and reached the side of the canoe just as it was being pushed right side up.

She exploded from the water and yelled, "Kenzie! Kenzie!"

Each of her soaked sneakers seemed to weigh fifty pounds. Something—the snake?—wrapped around her ankles and moved on. When she resurfaced, she could barely move her legs, but managed to grab hold of the edge of the canoe. No, it wasn't the canoe, but a paddle. Someone was trying to hit her with the damned paddle.

CHAPTER
2

Quannah paused to wipe sweat from his neck and chest with a towel provided by the silent monks. Scents of the humidity-soaked island invaded his nostrils: dirt, rocks, thick foliage, hot sun, and ozone arriving in the cloudbank in the distance. He rubbed his temples. Hmm. An uneasy prickling ran down his spine, and a picture of Willi came to mind. She was topless and the rest of her was a mermaid. Quannah whistled and grinned before shaking the vision from his head.

No telling what that woman was up to, but he'd not worry. He knew for a fact she was coming across the lake with two trained Navy men, participants in the retreat. After raising his head, flaring his nostrils to catch scents of fish and debris from the Guadalupe River below, he changed his mind. Something didn't *smell* right. He considered putting his shirt on and racing back to the mainland of the ranch. No, no. No way to tell whether she and her friend Kenzie had gotten to the ranch yet, much less boarded the canoes for the river and lake crossing.

He returned to the task at hand. The three International Organization of Diverse Development businessmen wanted a multi-experience during their week of serenity seeking. After the IODD men learned Quannah was going to be the lead trail rider, they also wanted him to help them participate in the sacred ritual of the Native American *Inipi* ceremony. Quannah prepared the sweat lodge with the help of two of the monks. At the moment, Rimshi and Rabten, also naked to the waist, bent the saplings together and tied them with twine at the top to form a half sphere disappearing into *Maka,* or as some referred to her, *Ina Maka*—Mother Earth.

This was to be a colorful sweat lodge, for the monks had come up with heavy brocaded rugs when Quannah asked for blankets to cover the round hutch. The things weighed more than truck tarps and were of a nap to be waterproof, although Quannah took the extra precaution of layering the lodge with heavy construction plastic beneath the rugs. He smiled and patted the curve they had just covered. It was a good Inipi lodge. Strong enough to last for many seasons with little maintenance.

He rubbed his temples again. That dang woman had to be into something she wasn't supposed to be doing, and he had an idea that he should feel sorry for the two Navy men.

Rimshi noticed his frown and raised an eyebrow.

Quannah said, "Oh, just worried about Willi, my lady. She has a talent for getting into things she shouldn't. I wish I understood what the message meant of her flashing through my mind as a mermaid. Probably that she's diving into somebody's business instead of minding her own." Of course, that ability to blithely fly in the face of social expectations was one of the reasons he loved her. He never doubted her bravery and courage, but that same quality often sent shivers of worry over him. His frown deepened.

For the first time during the hot work, Rimshi spoke. "Ah. If you understand, things are just as they are; if you do not understand, things are just as they are. Your Miss Willi *is* what and where she is whether you understand or not. She is doing what she is doing whether you understand or not. Ah-ha."

Quannah pondered that Zen saying as he, Rimshi, and Rabten hoisted the bright orange, red, and blue rugs into a cozy cover. Rimshi said, "Explain, please. This is one of your ways of meditating?"

"The Inipi ceremony is a way we cleanse ourselves physically and spiritually to prepare us for some further task or higher ceremony. Those who practice the Sun Dance, the *Wiwanyag Wachipi,* prepare themselves by first performing the Inipi. Those who go on the Vision Quest, the *Hanblecheya,* cleanse heart, mind and soul before seeking needed wisdom during their quest."

"Ah. So, it is like small temple . . . like—" Rimshi searched for the words. "—Like church."

"Yes, somewhat." Quannah retied a bandanna around his forehead and tightened the leather tie holding back his ponytail. "Many say it's similar to a little nave."

He drew in a deep breath and stopped to down a sixteen-ounce bottle of Deja Blue water. "The ceremony has been shared and taught to many races, creeds, and nationalities. Within the Inipi, many find a close connection to their maker and to all the Great Spirit has made, including Mother Earth and Father Sky, the four-leggeds, the crawlers, those with feathers, those with fins."

Fins.

That vision of Willi flashed before him again, and he peered through the copse of trees toward the lake, but he only saw peacefulness of clouds and waving tree branches. He *would* finish the task at hand, but then he would go check. He'd have to, just for his peace of mind.

He swallowed and continued. "Within the womblike church, a natural bonding comes about. You have a close encounter with your own concept of God, the Creator, and that which He created for us to thrive upon—*Unci* or *Maka.*"

"Or *Ina Maka*?"

Quannah nodded. "Yes."

"Ah . . . Mother Earth?"

"Yes, Mother Earth."

Rabten brought a huge laundry basket full of grass, sage, flowers, and flat cedar shingles cut in thin strips. He nodded toward the flap of bright blue that would serve as the door. Rabten had smiled and gestured through the hard work, but had not spoken even once.

Quannah said, "You may go ahead and cover the floor with the sweet smells. We will need another basketful just before the ceremony tomorrow morning."

. He stretched and walked through a bramble of bushes to look out over the butte, one of the many that had a picture-card depiction of the Guadalupe River on one side, the crevices and crannies of hills on the other, and a copse of comforting trees on the third and fourth sides. Secluded. Peaceful. A good *medicine* place. *Lila Waste. Lila Waste.* Very good.

Now, he could really enjoy the finishing touches of building the Inipi lodge if one sweet, heart-shaped face would stop grinning through dark tendrils of wet hair, and stop waving that infernal mermaid flipper. *By Great Eagle's tail feathers, please let her not be in real trouble.*

Rimshi smiled. "Ah. If you understand, things are just as they are; if—"

"If you do not understand, things are just as they are. If you had a lady like Willi in your life, Rimshi, you might very well change that to something closer to 'If you understand Willi, you're crazy, too.' "

Rimshi smiled. "Your Miss Willi be fine. Ah-ha." He helped Quannah with the last tie downs, ones strong enough that high winds would not affect the cozy womb near Mother Earth's heartbeat. Quannah kept a watchful eye on the Guadalupe on one side, the trees behind which lay the lake on the other side.

Gallagher. Winyan. What are you up to now?

He hurried with the work and rushed Rimshi and Rabten back toward the Zen complex of pagodas. Finally, he'd be able to figure out what Gallagher was doing. The elderly monk, Samdup, stepped into their pathway before they reached the border of trees. He gently turned Quannah back toward the cliff, while signaling Rimshi and Rabten on down the trail.

Samdup's wrinkled face, brown and weathered as a gnarled oak tree's bark, broke into a smile. "We must talk of things best said in this open cleared space, yes?"

"I know there's much information you need to let me in on considering—"

"Considering your undercover work for us."

"Yes, but perhaps it could wait until Willi and Kenzie arrive safely."

"We discussed this earlier. She is within good hands. Mr. Tulsa, Mr. Rowley. They will protect her and her friend with diligence."

Samdup sat in lotus position with the edge of the cliff to his left, which meant Quannah had no choice but to place his right shoulder toward the Guadalupe's curves and face the wise man of Serenity Island.

After a few moments of relaxed breathing, Samdup quietly spoke. "I choose here, because we can discern anyone around us. No one shall know these words I lay on your shoulders. Your superiors informed me that you above all other Texas Ranger employees would understand what I'm to impart."

Quannah also drew in deep breaths. With great emotional effort, he pushed Willi's finned appearance to the far recesses. His hooded eyes searched around them. It seemed suddenly as if no hot Texas wind blew; the trees stilled, the very sweat on his back dried, the scuttling of small creatures ceased while the liquid hum of the Guadalupe receded. From past experience he knew the goosebumps rising on his arms and neck were merely confirmation that what he was about to hear was not only to be approached with serious intent, but with sacred awareness. He nodded his head to indicate he was ready to be open and listen.

"You must understand that the one whose honored name we do not speak and only refer to as the Eye That Is Divine or the Divine One is of great importance to our spiritual life, and is to be protected."

"Texas being a far ways from his homeland and yours, I'd think no one would consider the possibility of him being here."

"Here, yes."

"Somewhere on the island or the ranch mainland?"

"On our island enclave."

"So, you want me to guard him?"

Samdup shook his head. "No, we will guard. You will find out which of the participants is trying to locate and harm him."

Quannah sighed. "That's good. So, I ask again: How am I supposed to lead the trail rides for the guests, take care of the horses, and one by one eliminate the participants from

the list of evildoers? And then you tie my hands more by
not revealing to me which one of your monks is this . . .
what do you call him?"

"We do not use his real name for now. You may refer to
him as the Eye That Is Divine."

"Isn't that a reference to the sacred third eye within the
middle of the forehead?"

"True. So if it is mentioned and anyone is nearby, they
will misunderstand our reference and think it is the third
eye of which we speak."

"I feel like we might want one or two others in to help
guard him."

Samdup smiled. "We guard, but we do not guard. He is
in our very bosom, but he's hidden. He's where we can say
prayers to him each day and honor him at any time."

"So, what do you need me for if you've got that so well
in hand?" Quannah flared his nostrils, but could pick up no
scents on the stilled breeze, no smells from the very earth
he sat upon. All senses focused only on the meaning behind the old monk's information.

"Word from superiors in Tibet, Japan, and the Eastern
United States indicate somehow that information has been
leaked. There are those among the visitors this week who
have been known to ask questions, communicate in various
ways about he whose name we do not speak but honor."

Quannah waited.

Samdup looked out toward the Guadalupe. He sighed.
With eyes shut, he said, "Men's hearts are sometimes as
muddy and debris-ridden as the slow-moving one there.
Such men and women do not focus on beauty and honor,
but control, not realizing that such action does not bring
them riches nor peace nor enlightenment. Those things are
gained in other ways, in other routes that keep them on the

brown river, never letting them debark on clear waterways until lessons are learned."

Samdup opened his eyes, eyes unlike the Guadalupe, that shone with an intense love for all humankind, even those on the muddy waters. "He who is here with us is to be honored. His presence teaches the lessons of higher planes. We lovingly watch over one of the most revered of all monks of Tibet. This is, as the world at large says, a twenty-four-seven duty. We take it on gladly, but fear that something will happen on our watch if we are not diligent."

"Any particular reason you think there is danger of this now, other than the information mentioned earlier?" Quannah asked.

Samdup said, "I'm told you understand what is meant by *inner knowing,* and that you trust this, shall we call it, sixth sense?"

"So, you have this awareness that he's in danger."

Samdup bowed his head. "Not only me. Many of the monks at different times have come to me the last six months with troubling dreams, visions during their prayers, frightful thoughts when they are in the silent time."

"I understand. Too many confirmations to deny that there is a danger. Then you received more validation from your sources."

"Yes. He has been with us for twelve years. Our enclave is trained and all have been destined to serve for our twenty-five years. We do not wish him to be whisked from us into obscurity again. We do not want bloodshed to occur and therefore want you to discover who is here to either do this horrible deed or to reconnoiter for someone else to come later. While some may want to take him to a private place for their own spiritual gratification, there are those who would merely want to destroy him, not understanding his sacredness, nor caring. There are few we could trust with this knowledge, few who would step forward and understand our sacred calling in this matter."

"And you think I'm the one?"

"Indeed, Mr. Quannah Lassiter, many have praised your skills and training to protect Native American burial grounds. You, at least, have the moral and spiritual training to honor those who, as you say, 'Walk the Good Red Road toward the Blue Road,' those who lead a spiritual life. Whether it is in your means to extend this same feeling to another culture, we will find out. Either way, your superiors said you would not let one drop of information leave this place, however you choose to act upon the information."

"I will act, sir. First, I've been given this as an assignment. Secondly, of course, I understand. In all beliefs there are special shamans, revered priests or leaders to be honored. Please do not concern yourself with that."

"Thank you." From the folds of his red robe, Samdup extracted a three-by-five spiral notecard book. On each card was a name of a participant with particulars. "You will need this information. Also, I'm the only one who knows your real purpose here, so the other monks will just continue as normal. They and the participants will consider you as the trail ride leader and the caretaker for the horses on the island."

"That's best," Quannah said.

"We will provide anything you need, but not anything that breaks the living laws governing the island."

Quannah pursed his lips. "So, no cell phones, no computers, no—"

"Exactly so." Samdup looked him squarely in the eye. "Only on the mainland of the ranch can you use those if needed. Also, here is a key to the motorboat, so you may use it anytime, even in the middle of the night, which might be best. That boat and the electricity and plumbing are our concessions to comfort for our guests. And . . ."

"And?"

"One cell phone. Kept in a locked box, only brought out to occasionally recharge. Only . . . absolutely *only* for medical emergencies."

Quannah loosened his hair, used the leather thong to tie the key, and then placed it around his neck underneath a second bandanna. "I understand. I'll read the notes. I've already had one trail ride with the three IODD Japanese-American businessmen. I'll make sure to have contact with all the participants and peruse this immediately."

Samdup rose as gracefully as if he were twenty instead of sixty-two years old. "We have chosen you well, Quannah Lassiter. Stop worrying about Miss Willi."

"You mean Miss Marple of the Range?"

Samdup smiled. "Yes, I've looked into her more interesting mystery exploits, too. Well, you should certainly not have a dull seven days with us, investigator."

"Certainly not." Quannah rose. "No more titles, though. I'm on a vacation, doing this just to please Willi. She has no idea I'm on a case. And we don't want her cute little turned-up nose into things. Trust me on that one, Samdup."

They both laughed and headed down the pathway. Quannah, out of respect, did not hurry the monk, but he wanted to fly with the wind, which now blew hot across his back, wanted to leap through the underbrush and across the island to see what that crazy Gallagher woman had gotten herself into.

Fins. That's what she'd gotten herself into, some fishy-smelling situation. Oh, Great Coyote's Balls and damn.

CHAPTER
3

"Grab it!" Kenzie's voice floated somewhere above her. Willi grasped the paddle and pulled herself hand over hand along its length until many arms reached out to clasp and haul her aboard.

Jamyang, red robes in a wet mass, smiled at the bedraggled group. "And all goes well. All together row now."

Willi kept expecting outbursts from the others about her reaction to the snake and her overturning the wooden canoe, but no one said anything. Jamyang never gave them a chance. He kept a quiet patter going about the rules to be followed once they reached Serenity Island. Despite the musky stench the encounter left in her clothes, she tried to pay attention.

He said, "No phones, including cell. No cameras, here, please."

Kenzie's eyes opened wide and she tucked a small

flower-covered bag underneath her. Willi gave her the look, the one that said, *I know what's in that bag, bad girl.* Kenzie shrugged and whispered, "I forgot."

Jamyang said, "Those, of course, have been handed over at ranch." He smiled benignly and stated, "All gentlemen stay in one pagoda house, ladies another."

Kenzie said, "But some, like Willi and Quannah, are couples."

Jamyang nodded. "Gentlemen in one pagoda, ladies in other."

Willi narrowed her eyes.

Kenzie shrugged. "Who knew? Sorry, really."

The gentle Jamyang continued. "After dark, no one on beach; all stay in recreation rooms. Or dining areas of Mimosa Pagoda. Maybe island gardens if you wish to walk or meditate outdoors. These are defined by prayer cloths on posts along borders."

Willi leaned toward Kenzie. "Gee, bad as college days. Hope the monks aren't into midnight panty raids."

Paul Rowley overheard and laughed. When he did, Willi thought she understood the nickname Rooster, because that's how the laughter erupted: in a cock-a-doodle-doo type of guffaw. Paul turned bright red.

"That's why you're called Rooster. That is so cool. Do it again," said Kenzie.

Paul ducked his head, took off his glasses, and glanced back up. "Guess that's a better reason than some. Not making fun of me now, are you?"

"No way," Kenzie said. "Distinctive laugh you have, yes, and a fun one."

"Laughter good, very good," intoned Jamyang. "Ah, here we are. As you explore you see three gates holding all in balance. They symbolize heaven, man, and earth."

Kenzie said, "Yes, and I read in your brochure that each part of the garden was specially designed by famous gardeners from Nagaoka, Japan."

Jamyang nodded. "Some areas, yes, and others from our Tibetan designers."

When Willi looked over her shoulder, the lowered section of dock wavered before her. Nestor D. and Paul "Rooster" Rowley jumped out and tied the canoes next to half a dozen others. Three other men waited above them.

Men of Japanese descent. Both Nestor D. and Paul stiffened. Jamyang made introductions by saying, "These fine *American* gentlemens are with IODD Company of electronics and land development. Mr. Nara Inoshi, Mr. Yataro Yodo, and Mr. Mike Toru. Like you fine gentlemens"—he turned toward Nestor D. and Paul—"they are here for same reasons of enlightenment and balance in busy lives."

Nestor D. swallowed and managed a nod.

Paul cleared his throat and picked up a knapsack. "Right. Which way is this garden area and the hospitality room, this Mimosa Pagoda?"

Mr. Nara Inoshi, a tall and handsome man, offered his arm to Kenzie. Kenzie shied away from his touch. "I can do it my—"

Willi elbowed her friend until Kenzie took the proffered support. "How kind of him to help. Right, Kenzie?"

Kenzie grimaced as a way of a smile, but nodded and grabbed hold of Inoshi's hand. "Oh, yes, very . . . kind."

Whereas Inoshi was stately in height, Mr. Yodo was rather stout, with a distinctive Charlie Chan profile accentuated by the white hat and suit he sported. He had a friendly smile and a mustache that barely twirled at each end. Willi grinned.

He grinned back and winked. Okay, maybe he was a combination of Hercule Poirot and Charlie Chan. He said,

"Most lovely island now has most lovely ladies as final touch. So glad to meet you, Willi Gallagher, and you, Kenzie Francis." He touched the brim of his white hat toward Rowley and Nestor D.

The third, Mike Toru, quite obviously a bodybuilder, remained quiet during the introductions, merely nodding his head in response to greetings. He offered a hand out of the canoe to Nestor D. Tulsa, who glared at him, and moved away, muttering under his breath. Mike Toru's face reddened, but he kept silent. When all of them followed Nestor D. and Paul, Willi was left on the dock with Jamyang.

"Do you know if Quannah has arrived back from the trail ride he led this morning?"

"Yes, Missy Willi, he must have. Those three men are ones he took."

"Why *Missy* Willi for me and Ms. Francis for my friend?"

The monk looked at the storm clouds gathering faster. "Somehow seemed right. No offense taken I hope."

"None at all. In fact, Sheriff Tucker calls me Miss Willi at home. Missy Willi will be fine, Jamyang. One more question."

"Why I feel you are lady with many questions?" His smile took any sting from the words.

"Why is the beach off limits at night? Seems like a lovely place to stroll."

"Garden better. This is not beach resort. Many dangerous rocks and here at docks and boathouses there are—"

"Yes? What?"

"Scorpions. Many copperheads, water moccasins. Snakessssss." He drew out the last word.

Willi gasped. Darn Jamyang. She'd swear he grinned as he scurried ahead of her toward the beautiful gardens and series of pagodas. Willi took a moment to retrieve Kenzie's camera bag still tucked into a corner of the canoe. The camera was a no-no, but Kenzie had forgotten. Luckily, the monks thought it was just another makeup bag. Thank goodness for waterproofing. As she bent over she squinted at the wooden floor.

What in Hades? Two small holes—well, no—more than half a dozen stood out like pimples in the wood-crafted canoe. In fact, one had a tiny filler. Willi scraped at it with her fingernail. "Ouch. Great, the first nail disaster of the week." Shaped like a small cork, but with a more solid consistency, the tiny piece came out easily.

The plug popped out much like a cork would though. "Uh-oh. That can't be good, that I could remove this with bare fingers. Hmm." She tried to push the filler back in, but now the hole was too big. "Why?" She lay flat on her stomach in order to lean over closer. She rubbed her small finger inside the hole.

"How odd. Seems like some sort of hardened mud."

When the plug came out, the water could reach and dissolve the adhesive. Then it became impossible to fit the piece back in. Scooching back with rear farther in the air, then back until her buttocks rested on her legs, she trembled. If someone had accidentally pushed those plugs out while the boat capsized, they might have been unable to make it back to shore before being swamped. Already, with the movement of the lake upon the canoe, water trickled in a few drops at a time. She'd have to tell Jamyang immediately. Surely, there was a better way to repair than with such a weak adhesive. A swish of red robe blew out in front of her; she looked up into one of the kindest faces she'd ever seen. Another of the monks, this one with a face as wrinkled as a Sharpei, beamed upon her.

"You are the curious Missy Willi?"

"You've talked to Jamyang."

He smiled and nodded. "And to Quannah. Would you allow Samdup to guide you to the first class, please?"

"Yes, that's very kind uh . . . Samdup, but first let me show you something."

Throughout the explanation, his expression faltered only a moment, in one fleeting frown etched so quickly, Willi figured she was mistaken about seeing it. After her explanation, he pulled the canoe around to the other side of the dock and into a large boathouse. Willi peeked at a motorboat and a pontoon boat inside before helping him to close the heavy double doors.

Samdup said, "We must be more vigilant and check our repair schedule. I do not recall holes in that canoe before. Also, you know, these wooden canoes we love, but now have some new canoes that are impossible to sink. Those should arrive this week. It would be an exercise in futility for someone to try to swamp those, if that was something worrying you."

"Of course not." Willi smiled at him. *Jerry Fartleberry Cormack loved mind games though. Wouldn't matter if the boat sank as long as there was a possibility of her or Kenzie discovering and worrying themselves sick about who might have drilled and filled the holes with a weak adhesive.* "Not worried at all. No unauthorized person could get past that main ranch security check, right?"

"No, none. Only participants and the monks who work on the island are here. Nine-eleven left many of us living a more watchful life, yes?" Samdup said.

"You have such a kind way of saying paranoid, and yes, you're right." However, Cormack's phone threat came clearly to mind. *You could both end up at the bottom of the lake.*

Willi shivered. "Switching subjects for a moment. You

speak English so well. Much better than most Americans and certainly better than Jamyang who leaves out all his articles—those *a*'s and *the*'s and *an*'s."

"That is possible. I was educated here at the University of Texas, in fact, before returning home and studying for this final calling. Jamyang has learned only through a few basic ESL classes. You are an English teacher, Missy Willi, yes?"

"Yes. Guess you all do read those forms, huh? Then you'll know I don't teach English as a Second Language classes, but rather high school sophomores. English, usually. *Romeo and Juliet*. Different types of writing. Vocabulary *ad nauseum*."

"Not to mention dealing with all those hormonal challenges that age offers. I admire what you do for the young people. Teachers never receive enough accolades."

"Thank you. And I'm looking forward to learning what you all do here on Serenity Island. I love to be the student now and again."

"Ah, good." Without more fuss, he guided her along the winding paths. "Quannah was worried about you, and did come to the lake edge many times to check on your arrival in between his many duties."

"Thank you for letting me know."

Willi gazed with open admiration at the broad expanse of heavy-beamed wooden walkways edged by lush foliage— azaleas here, clusters of bamboo, surprising nookeries of Texas bluebonnet groupings around giant oaks, stately pines, elms, and cottonwoods. Always at unexpected junctures, the walkways turned into bridges, some curved, others with steps, with a flowing riverway winding beneath. Pools of water lilies nestled in the middle of the calmer areas. Within crannies, wooden benches welcomed a person to sit forever. A night heron landed on a branch barely a foot away. Willi gasped at the wise clearness of his eyes contemplating her.

"Oh, I could just stay here the whole week and not move," she said.

Samdup, his Sharpei features soft, nodded his understanding. "I imagine you would like a little time with Quannah before the sun goes down, yes? I think he was showering when I left him. He should be at the Mimosa Pagoda."

"You *are* a wise man." Willi abandoned the night heron and kept in sync with Samdup's steps.

At a Y in the foliage, he pointed down one path, with orange and yellow brick. "You continue on this one. You will find the Mimosa Teahouse where everyone is gathered. I must part with you for a few moments and get ready for the first classes."

"I'll just follow the yellow brick road." Willi skipped along a few steps. Why, not, she mused. Hmm. This island didn't even feel like the usual Texas waterway haunts, not that she'd been on many other than Galveston Bay. She shivered at that thought. Two of her students died on a trip to the island. During that case, she and Quannah Lassiter had met. She sighed. Where was that infuriating but wonderful man?

Ah, voices up ahead. Must be close to the teahouse. She brushed at an overhanging frond and came face-to-face with a couple. For a moment the shadows played over the man's features.

Oh my God, Cormack.

She blinked and was about to scream, but the breeze blew the fronds away, and she took a deep breath and faced the complete stranger. "Oh, excuse . . . excuse me."

"I believe," the man said, "we're the ones who should apologize for frightening you. I'm Halliwell Pate. Most folks call me Preacher Pate. This is my lovely wife Juna Marie."

"Willi Gallagher." Her heart did a couple of cha-cha measures and calmed down. She licked her lips. She tried to ease by the couple, both in matching white knee-shorts and pullovers with blue sweaters tied around their hips.

"And by profession you are—?"

"Halliwell," Juna Marie Pate said, "not everyone likes to do an on-spot autobiography."

"It's okay." Willi smiled and shook their hands. "I'm a high school English teacher. And you, Mrs. Pate?"

"Just call her Juna Marie, everybody does. Beautiful name, Juna Marie."

"Uh . . . yes, it is. And you do what, uh . . . Juna Marie?"

Preacher Pate took his wife's elbow. "Juna Marie helps the shepherd—that's me—lead my flock of the Nightingale Baptist Church in Springtown, Texas. She's wonderful with the Sunday school classes, the ladies' quilt group, and she's my right hand. Couldn't do without her."

"I imagine not," Willi said and strained to hear the growling tones of Quannah's deep voice. How far was it to this teahouse?

"Wait up, now, Willi. You have a partner here? Everyone has to have a partner for the activities, right?"

"Halliwell, that's intrusive . . . I'm sure—"

"Not at all; just interested in my fellow participants."

Willi said, "Yes, as a matter of fact, two partners. One is my best girlfriend, MacKenzie Francis. My heartmate, Quannah Lassiter, is also here. He's helping with some of the horseback outings and such. Kenzie and I partner up for the Zen studies. I'm on my way to the Mimosa Teahouse to find them." With that said loudly, Willi tromped in a no-nonsense manner across the wooden bridge at the end of the yellow bricks. She'd soon leave the Pates behind and find a few moments for a much-needed hug.

Preacher Pate came up beside her, and with his free arm, grabbed her elbow. "We'll just mosey along with you. Glad to hear your Mr. Lassiter is spoken for. Don't like those single young men around my Juna Marie. She catches the eye, you know."

"Halliwell, now stop it. There's no one we know on this island, so there's no reason to get into that."

"Oh, sweet Juna Marie, not getting into anything, pet. Just teasin' you."

With the pretext of bending down and tying her shoe, Willi pulled her arm from his sweaty grasp. Her stomach sort of roiled at his touch. She shook her head. He was just a typical over-friendly minister, and blue blazes, she'd practice what she'd preached to Kenzie and be friendly back. "You've nothing to worry about from Quannah. He's more fond of horses and chasing his villains than anything."

"Villains?" Juna Marie said, wiping her forehead clear of the blond curls created by the humidity. Not like Kenzie's perky champagne tint, Juna Marie's hair was the pure white blond of childhood. Despite the effect of the heat, she resembled the elegance one thinks of when swans shake their head feathers. "Villains?" she repeated.

Willi grimaced, and a warning light went off. Quannah, when on vacation, didn't want folks to know his real identity unless necessary. She had to honor that, so she gave a truthful answer, but not about his job. "He's a comic-book aficionado. Into Batman, Superman, and all those villains they fight." She hoped that was enough to cover her possible faux pax.

"He's also working the trail rides and some of the hikes

for the retreat this week, so we won't have much time to be together, which is why I was in a rush."

Hint. Hint. Not to mention that Willi needed to confide in him about the call from one particular villain—Kenzie's stalker; tell him about a possible creep slithering through Serenity Island; inform him that he may have a case of attempted murder on his agenda soon. An attempt was all that damned Jerry Cormack would get because she was going to be watching Kenzie's back every minute.

Juna Marie smiled in such a way to rival an angel. Preacher Pate was definitely right. She was gorgeous, and that seemed to be from the inside out as she said to Willi, "I understand perfectly. There's nothing like the spark of romance to put a glow to the cheek and warmth in your heart. Don't let us keep you. We have to write our council report, part of our job on the retreat, to bring back the possibilities of sharing other cultures within our Outreach Community."

Halliwell said, "The cross-denominational sharing is one of the reasons we chose this retreat. They also serve wonderful meals, unlike so many other similar groups."

Willi smiled, "It's a gentle introduction to what can be an austere type of life in full practice."

"Exactly," Juna Marie said.

"Thanks. I'll hoof it along then. Nice to have met. See you all later." She raced over the bridge, down a quarter mile of tarmac that wound in and out of azaleas and a huge growth of wisteria that climbed over a wall. Good Lord have mercy, how far could this place be? After she passed a cluster of oaks, someone's hand grasped her hard, turned her down another trail, and pushed her along.

"What?" She yelped.

"We're off to see the Wizard, the wonderful Wizard of Zen," Kenzie said. "Don't you love these yellow bricks?

First class right down this path. See? They're marked with quaintly carved signs."

Willi did an about-face. "As soon as I find the Mimosa Pagoda teahouse and see if all is okay with Quannah."

"No time. Hear those chimes?"

"Kenzie, don't start that rhyming game."

"Sorry. Those are like the tardy bells, they said, to class. My shoulder muscles are already sore from today's little row. When do we get those promised massages?"

"Not a clue, oh friend and itinerary keeper," Willi said. "You go ahead. I'll just be a few more minutes late." As she recalled Cormack's call, she said, "No, wait a minute. No, you have to go with me. What was I thinking?"

"No idea, girl. Quannah's not there."

Willi swallowed and shut her eyes "But I need to talk to him, and tell him about—" *Careful. Careful.* She could not let this possibility of Cormack's presence ruin this retreat for Kenzie. Nothing less likely to end any feelings of balance to let her know, Oh by the way, your jerk of an ex is hightailing it here to trim your neck down to size.

Kenzie repeated, "Quannah's not at the Mimosa Pagoda."

"Samdup said he was."

"Who?"

Willi sighed. "One of the monks. Sweet old fellow. Face like a Sharpei. All wrinkles and kindness."

"Well, Samdup was right. Quannah's on the island, but he left the teahouse about five minutes ago. Seemed to be frantic about you at first, until I told him you were fine, even after a dunking in the lake. Said something about, 'Ah, that explains the fins.' He looked disappointed you hadn't hurried along with us to see him, but he had to go back to the mainland ranch compound before dark for the last supplies. One of the IODD businessmen went with him. You probably passed each other a few minutes ago. Why didn't you hurry?"

"But I did try to hurry. I was stopped by some folks." She pouched out her bottom lip. "Across the lake. That's two hours, at least, then they reach the mainland. Were they going to meet up with horses or wheels, there?"

Kenzie, palms up, said, "He didn't say. Why?"

"Why? Because if they're going by horseback, they'll be another three hours; if they have a pickup by the docks, won't take maybe a half hour. And then the time back, of course."

Kenzie patted her arm. "This is a huge and meandering ranch, some twenty-thousand acres, not counting the Guadalupe tributaries that wander in and out and around Serenity Island. Hmmm. How big is the island?" She searched through her information packet. "Ah, doesn't give acres, but says it's eight miles long, fifteen miles wide, with the Zen compound taking up about five by two miles of that."

"Yeah. Big. And lonely." Willi looked down at the yellow bricks, which now seemed tarnished and merely more steps between her and Quannah.

"Hey, girl, I'm here."

Willi swallowed. "And thank goodness for that. Okay, my pity party is over. I've no one to blame but my own slow-pokey self."

"Quannah mentioned something about getting your fool curious nose into things already. Snooping. Yes, that's the word he used. Hey, what did you say kept you so long?"

Willi poked Kenzie in the side. "Thought you were in a hurry. Let's get on to this class."

"You know it, but you talk as we walk."

"You're doing it again. That rhyming."

Kenzie grinned. "Wanna stop this sap; gotta get on with the rap."

Willi grimaced and told her about the canoes and the repairs needed, trying to keep the info in the general maintenance-of-water-craft category. She also mentioned they were to use the fiberglass boats when they arrived, not the wooden ones, for any more excursions. She couldn't tell her about her horrible theory, since she also couldn't reveal the threatening phone call. This was Kenzie's downtime, her moment to get back into balance and to rest. Willi sighed and rubbed her nose. By damned if she were going to ruin this week for Kenzie. Of course, she herself would be ready for another type of retreat after seven days of watching the bushes, a retreat with a title like La-La Land, a retreat with lots of folks in white coats with hypodermics full of soothing meds.

"Willi? Willi!"

"What?"

"So, you were snooping?" Kenzie asked.

Ignoring that, Willi told her about Preacher Halliwell Pate and his Juna Marie. She left out the part about thinking she had at first run into the piece of fartleberry known as Jerry Cormack. *Fartleberry* being an apt description of him, as it referred to the dried dung on the back end of sheep and cattle.

"Wow, not half an hour on the island and you've already met most of the folks here."

"So what," Willi asked, eyeing the brochure in Kenzie's hand, "is this first class about?"

Kenzie held up fingers as she listed items. *"History of Zen Buddhism. We Are Each Others' Mother. First Meditation."* Kenzie smiled. "We get to do that on a grassy knoll overlooking the Guadalupe River if we want. Come on."

Willi followed Kenzie around a curve where the yellow brick gave way to laid macadam near the beach area that was about to lead them back into dense foliage and up the hillside. Willi grabbed Kenzie's shoulder. "Look. What is that?"

"Duh-uh." Kenzie raised an eyebrow. "That would be your basic motorboat. Why didn't we get to use one? Who do you suppose those people are?"

The boat whizzed by them. A scruffy-bearded gnome waved at them. Beside him a buxom curly-haired brunette saluted. Kenzie punched Willi's shoulder. "Wonder what the monks are gonna think of that?"

"Ouch."

"So, you're sore, too. Come on." They wound around and up a hill and then up another. Every path was a surprise of colorful foliage and restful greenery. Beautiful, but as humid as a sauna. Both she and Kenzie were soaked through. Abruptly, Kenzie stopped and Willi crashed into her back.

Kenzie said, "Shush," and pointed.

In a sun-dappled half moon sitting area on a bench of the same shape sat two figures, intertwined in an embrace steamier than that created by the growth around them. Willi did a backward tiptoe routine, pulling Kenzie along with her.

When she could she turned around and raced back down the trail until she was sure they were out of earshot of the lovers.

Kenzie said, "Guess you and Quannah aren't the only couple on this retreat."

Willi nodded. "I told you about Preacher Pate and his wife."

"So that was them? Whoo-hoo!"

"No. Yes. Well, not exactly." Willi wiped sweat off her

brow with her shirttail. Seeing as it was wet, it did little good. She tried again with her forearm. "Now I know why the monks wear those headbands. I'll have to get some of those out that Sheriff Tucker made me pack. You know, some of his giant ones?"

Kenzie pulled Willi's arm down. "Yeah, his nose-honkers. Forget those. What do you mean, no-yes-not exactly?"

"That woman back there?"

"Yeah, Mrs. Pate?"

"Yes, Juna Marie, the beloved and protected one of Preacher Pate. Or else someone else has white shorts and baby blue sweater tied around her hips. No wonder she went on and on about romance and being in love."

"Yeah, boy, and it looked like the preacher was doing the loving part right then." Kenzie smiled and pointed to an alternate path. "I think this will get us past them."

"That wasn't," Willi said, "Halliwell Pate."

Kenzie stumbled, but righted herself by grabbing onto Willi's arm. "Girlfriend, for real? The preacher's wife, but not the preacher?"

"You got it. I think it was one of the businessmen we met at the dock. I couldn't tell which one."

"Oh my gosh."

Willi nodded. "Talk about needing to get in balance. This should be a real test for Jamyang, Samdup, and the rest of the monks."

A space opened before them, one of a rolling hill—cropped grass as soft as a spring blanket—with a huge pagoda to one side. Off the edge of the cliff and below, a tributary of the Guadalupe River surged past. When they went into the cool interior, Willi gasped. "My goodness, there must be a dozen or more rooms here. Which one do we—?"

Samdup, his wrinkled face in a smile, quietly came up beside her. "Welcome to the Lotus Pagoda. The schoolhouse, if you will. This room on the left is first. You will then travel around to each room as the week progresses. At the end of a day, you may choose to do communal meditation outside on the cliff or meditate alone in one of the rooms."

He opened a door and led them to a grouping of rugs. Others were there already in cross-legged or legs-to-the-side positions. "Choose what is comfortable for you. Pillows are there to help."

The scent of sandalwood incense filled the air as Willi chose a rug between Nestor D. and Paul Rowley. Kenzie sat in the row behind Willi and beside Juna Marie, whose face was flushed. Willi exchanged a knowing glance with Kenzie. *Flushed indeed.* Preacher Halliwell Pate came in and sat cross-legged beside his wife. He patted her knee. Juna Marie's response was like a startled swan, eyes rolling back, as if she were about to splash madly to an escape.

Willi peered over her shoulder. Right then, Yataro Yodo and Mike Toru took positions behind the Pates. Kenzie tilted her head and raised her eyebrows in the silent question: *One of them?*

Willi shrugged. She really couldn't tell. It could have been Nara Inoshi, the third one of that business group, stopping by for a quick nuzzle before racing back to the canoes to help Quannah. It could even have been Mr. Yodo. From the distance from which the couple was viewed, Mr. Yodo's more stocky figure would not have registered in one quick glance. The same for Mike Toru's muscle-bound body. Or . . . hmm . . . there could be another on the island they had not yet met. Kenzie was pointing toward the front in a frantic manner, and Willi frowned, but turned around to blink at Samdup's gentle features.

"If curious Missy Willi is ready, we will start with a

very short history of Zen Buddhism and how it might enlighten some parts of your lives."

So for a quarter hour, Samdup used his lilting voice to explain and soothe. Listening to him was like getting a mental massage. After a while, Willi's shoulder muscles relaxed. *Ahh, this is good.* Her mind focused, and Willi managed to take in at least one of Samdup's tales.

In his mesmerizing tones, he spoke of the bells. "A person walking along hears three bells distinctly. Immediately, the walker determines the sound to be strange, awesome, beautiful and lilting, frightening, or many other things. The listening one may decide they are church bells or merely outdoor chimes."

Willi shifted on the pillows. Ah, outdoor chimes. She loved those.

Samdup continued, "Ideas associated in the past with bell ringing intrude upon the mind. With each mental judgment the untainted listening experience becomes fainter and fainter. Only thoughts about the ringing sound come to the mind's forefront. So the lone walker has gone from concrete to abstract in a few flashes of thought. Once this happens, he lives no longer in the present, but in a chaotic maelstrom. In these modern times, there are, of course, moments when we wish to brainstorm, but this week I challenge you to listen for the bells and nothing but the bells around you. Be in balance with your moment of living."

Hmm. Willi peered back at Kenzie, who had a hungry look on her features. She truly was trying to soak it in, to learn, to become more balanced. Willi nodded. She had done a good thing to come with her friend. She hoped Kenzie would walk away a week from now with a restful glow about her, a renewal of her own wonderful spirit, and a strength to withstand without upset the machinations of Jerry Fartleberry Cormack.

Thoughts of him brought those of Preacher Halliwell Pate and his almost smothering attentions to *his* Juna Marie. Well, maybe that was what had sent *her* into the arms of whomever.

Samdup waved a trio of bells in her face and smiled. Willi blushed. She'd definitely have to work on that bit of philosophy this week if she were to help Kenzie. She was rather proud of her progress when she and Kenzie stepped toward the second room. There everyone had a quiet break, with *quiet* being the operative word. All sat in a circle and drank sweet tea and had light teacakes, but they were not supposed to talk during their repast.

As soon as the monk left them alone, Willi leaned over and whispered. "Meet you back at our pagoda or the big teahouse. I'm so tired. You'll be okay for the next hour with these folks?"

Preacher Halliwell Pate glowered at her. Paul Rowley made some sort of rumbling sound of disapproval. Mike Toru and Yataro Yodo peered up from their cups, looked through her as if she were some bothersome whiff of soured beans, and again contemplated their green tea.

Willi shivered. "Gee. Tough room. Sorry. Kenzie, okay if I leave?"

To Willi's surprise, Kenzie put a finger over her own lips and nodded. She patted her heart and then Willi's, but she didn't break the silence.

Willi said, "You're welcome. Love you, too. Later."

Juna Marie Pate glanced up quickly as Willi passed through. Her eyes were filled with unshed tears. She ducked her head over her cup and shook her head as if to say: *Please, don't notice. Please pass on.* Despite what Willi had earlier witnessed, she took pity on Juna Marie, now merely a melting version of an ice swan, her white feathery hair matted above an almost invisible face. Her elegant neck bent as if under a yoke pulling far too heavy a load.

Willi stepped outside the room, down the steps of the Lotus Pagoda, across two or three bridges, and finally ended up along the lake shore. Here she was already breaking one of the requests. Darkness had settled in, and she was supposed to stay on the bordered paths of gardens. Ah, well, no monks were here to chastise her. She breathed in deeply while wondering why in blue blazes she was drawn to the lake again. Perhaps the answer might simply lie in the fact that Quannah was on the other side. She wandered along the banks for a good half hour, enjoying the play of the evening palette of purples and pinks against a growing black velvet sky. Yet, she was restless above and beyond missing Quannah. Why? Moonlight now guided her steps, steps that brought her closer and closer to the boathouse, steps that carried her right up to the door, now slightly ajar.

Uh-oh.

Willi slowed her breathing, inched her way across the wooden planks, and paused. That night heron swooped past her head, then dove for something in the water before flying up into the branches to enjoy his meal. Willi pulled in a ragged breath while she smoothed hair strands lifted by the bird's passing flight.

She whispered, "Dang bird, I'm sure Quannah would tell me there's a message in you flying twice right in my face. Probably something about not sticking my nose where it doesn't belong."

That thought dissolved when the breeze caught the door, slamming it shut and then blowing back through to creak open the door again. Willi held her breath. Sweat trickled down her spine, turned cold in the breeze, and she shivered before leaning back against the wall to try and make herself invisible. The night heron's eyes glinted, blinked in her direction, and seemed to open wider. When no sounds came from inside the boathouse, she maneuvered closer to the opening.

Maybe the wind had just opened the door. Yeah, sure, that could be the problem, nothing sinister at all. Wouldn't hurt to just crack it open even wider and peek in. Holding her breath, she stepped upon a creaky board. At the same time, someone's cold fingers touched her wrist. Blood rushed from her head. Willi screamed and turned with hand raised to defend herself.

"You!"

"Damn, girlfriend. Who did you think I was? The bogeyman? Get a grip, girl. What are you doing down here?"

"Uh—"

"You weren't at the teahouse. Not at our room, either."

"Just taking a walk, Kenzie, and uh . . . saw the door open here. Samdup closed it earlier, so—"

"So Miss Marple of the Range had to investigate?"

"One of these days I'm going to think of a suitable payback for one Texas Ranger pinning me with that name."

"Oh, girl, I think it's cute. So does he."

"Yeah?"

"Yeah."

Willi grinned. "Maybe."

"So, let's go see what the problem is." Kenzie and Willi both faced the double door, and each grabbed one side.

Willi counted, "One, two . . . three."

She swung open her side in unison with Kenzie. No one jumped out at them. Wood scraped against wood as the waves washed the canoes gently in their berths. The newer canoes were moored up on the walls. Musty scents of oiled tools, fish nets and buckets, wet ropes and pots of worms vied with the scent of lilacs drifting down the hillside.

Willi said, "There's the explanation. The canoe that had

leaks has been taken out and set up on those sawhorses. Someone must have come in, done some work, and had to leave quickly, forgetting to close the door."

"There you go, girl. Simple."

Willi paced toward the back of the huge shed. "But—"

"But?"

"Kenzie, where's the motorboat?"

"Quannah and the IODD CEO took it for the trip to the mainland probably."

"Yeah, you're right. Sure." She tapped the end of her retroussé nose. "Something's not right, though, but I don't know what. Seems like there was something else . . ." She snapped her fingers. "The pontoon boat. One of those was here, too."

"Girl, you are always seeing a mystery in every nook and cranny. How about we make a deal? I won't look over my shoulder for jerk-face Jerry, and you don't go out of your way to find murder and mayhem."

"Listen to the three bells?"

"There you go. Listen to the three bells." Kenzie stepped outside.

Willi followed and helped her push the heavy doors closed. A slip of paper the size of a three-by-five index card slithered out, caught in the breeze, and wafted back down between them. Both bent down to retrieve it, bumped heads, and giggled, while each held a corner.

As Willi maneuvered to let the moonlight illuminate the printing, Kenzie yelped and turned loose. Willi frowned. "What?"

"No, no, not here. No." Kenzie's breathing was faster than a spin-wash cycle. She leaned back against the door, peered to the left, then right. Her bottom lip trembled.

Willi squinted at the card. Plastic-coated, it was one of a half-dozen such cards that every Microsoft employee carried as identification. This one also had the name of the employee—JERRY CORMACK. Three bells chimed out from the Mimosa Teahouse, distant and sweet, yet their sound sent a shiver through Willi, and, she noted, also through Kenzie. So much for staying calm and living in the absolute moment.

Willi said, "By Texas longhorns and jackalopes, this is not good."

CHAPTER
4

Willi grabbed her friend's arm to guide her away from the boathouse, up the trail, and back toward Lotus Pagoda. She had to calm Kenzie before she had a panic attack and shut down. Kenzie had broken out in a sweat and kept a strangle hold on Willi's denim vest.

Willi said, "We'll go sit a few minutes above the river. That will calm us both. I'm not ready to settle in for the evening." She sighed. She better find some way of helping Kenzie gain back her balance and quickly, or the first day of the retreat would be for naught.

Kenzie screeched. "He's *here*. How could *he* be here? I didn't breathe a word to anyone but you and Quannah. He didn't tell Jerry, did he? Oh my God."

"Quannah? No, no."

"Of course not. You all wouldn't have done that to me. Not on purpose, but maybe you said something in front of the pharmacist or someone somewhere? How else would the sorry bastard know?" Kenzie blubbered until Willi finally pulled her inside the Lotus Pagoda, now deserted and quiet.

Willi swallowed. She shut her eyes for a moment. A feather of fear tickled her throat. She placed cool fingertips against her neck to calm herself. She must not let Kenzie have an inkling of the phone call and implied threat. Oh God, how she needed to talk to Quannah.

Trust all your senses.

Yeah, sure, that's what Big Chief would say. Willi tilted her head. Well, her instincts told her that the call was definitely from the jerk-face stalker, but they also told her that Jerry Cormack didn't know squat. He was just trying to ferret out exact details. So, so . . . really, it was best not to panic and hold her own counsel for now.

Willi opened a door of a meditation room. One of the IODD men, head bowed, sang a soft mantra. In silence, Willi guided Kenzie to the room across the hallway where she shoved her friend down on a grouping of pillows.

"Get a grip, MacKenzie Francis. This may not be an indication of his presence at all. Lots of other ways one of these parking tags could have gotten here."

Willi lit a few of the candles. An undulating glimmer surrounded them along with the muted electrical lighting. She repeated, "Lots of explanations are possible."

"I'm trying to think." Kenzie swiped at her eyes and took deep breaths. "He has left stuff, even putting these and letters in my mailbox outside. Just one of his nasty little reminders that he's around."

"There you go." Willi snapped her fingers. "Card drops on your porch where you set your luggage before we loaded it into the car. It sticks to your duffel bag, and here it is."

"Maybe."

"Maybe, and most likely, since Quannah has tighter lips than any of his Texas Ranger buddies, and I didn't even tell the Kachelhoffer sisters, my neighbors."

And yet somehow that sorry bastard had discovered Kenzie's plans. Willi shook her head. The persistent mental nagging didn't waver. *He might have broken in, seen the brochures, and left the damned business card accidentally or on purpose.* She patted Kenzie's shoulder.

"And the arrangements weren't made in Nickleberry, even," Kenzie said. "I got all the info northwest of us in Cleburne, so there's no way he could know." She shook her head. "You see how little it takes to set me off? I thought I was relaxing today, getting my act together, enjoying the quiet, the peace, and the people here."

"You most certainly were and will again. What's important is that you recovered so much more quickly from this supposed attack. You didn't operate in total fear, were able to help reason the situation out, and without having to go hide from the world. I'm proud of you."

Willi rubbed her fingers along her scalp, through her hair. *Now, if she could just get herself calmed down, all would be fine in the Lone Star State along with cold long-necks, longhorns, and the long reach of the law.* Where in the heck was that lawman anyway?

"Girlfriend, at times like these I can see the teacher in you."

"What? Huh?"

"You were daydreaming again?"

"I do not daydream. Now what were you saying?"

"I was complimenting you, teach. You give a lot of credit for work you mostly did, not me."

"Oh, Hells Bells, I've done nothing of the sort. Now, I'm starving. Let's get our happy buns going, and we'll whistle a happy tune."

Kenzie giggled, locked arms with Willi, and together they began whistling. As they headed down the hall, Willi realized they might be disturbing the one across the way; she grimaced at Kenzie and both stopped simultaneously. Like guilty schoolgirls, Kenzie sighed and Willi put her hands over her mouth.

Kenzie whispered, "Guess you wouldn't want Quannah to know about this lapse into childhood, huh?"

Willi noted the twinkle in her friend's eyes and played along. "No way; it's one of those things brawny men don't understand." Her cheeks pinked up at the remembrance of a few playful moments with orange slices and whipped cream, but she didn't think that was something she wanted to share. Willi opened the outside door to the Lotus Pagoda just as a loud thump sounded, followed by a crash of glass.

A door on their left, the one next to the room they had vacated, opened up and Paul Rowley came out. "Uh . . . step back a pace now, ladies. You all are aware that this is the meditation and teaching pagoda, right?"

"Hiya, Rooster Rowley."

Paul grimaced and finally smiled at Kenzie's use of *Rooster*. "Sounds like your meditations must have made you happy, considering the whistling and clanging instruments, yes, very happy. And that's fine by me. Just a-kidding with you, yes, just a-teasing."

Willi smiled. Obviously, something he wasn't used to doing, but he was trying. "We were acting like junior high kids at lunch. Sorry. But we can only lay claim to the off-tune whistling. The other noise came from there." She pointed to where the IODD rep had been earlier.

"Seems like we'd hear him straightening things if he was still there."

"You saw him, too?" Kenzie asked. "No way, Rooster, not through those lenses."

Paul sighed. "Guess you're going to continue using that name."

Kenzie said, "Not if you really don't want me to, but it is a cool name."

"It's not bad coming off your lips. I guess it'll be okay." He grinned and pulled off his glasses; a mistake, since Kenzie immediately grabbed them to work her Miss Clean magic.

Rooster said, "Caught a glimpse as he went in a half minute before I decided to make use of this cubicle." He frowned and replaced his glasses while he nodded his thanks in Kenzie's direction. "You ladies step back a pace, now, and I'll just go peek. Yeah, I better peek."

Somewhere in the rear rooms, a door opened, creating a draft that sucked the front door from Willi's grasp and slammed it shut. Only an eerie breeze wafted through to raise hairs on her arms. She shivered. "We'll follow behind you."

He raised a hand, palm upward. "Just you ladies wait a moment. Probably him going out the back way, but you never know, you never know."

"Who else would be on the island?" Willi asked, ignoring his request to wait.

Kenzie followed to whisper in her ear, "Surely . . . surely not . . . not Jerry, right?"

"No. We covered that possibility." Willi sighed.

This balance Kenzie sought was not going to be achieved in one day. Her friend was emotionally fragile. Kenzie needed constant positive reinforcement and a feeling of being protected. If she could just get her back to the Mimosa Teahouse and have a good meal, they'd have achieved that for one day.

Rooster Rowley opened the door to meditation room number three, stood a moment like a golden retriever on point, and entered. Willi shifted to his left, Kenzie to his right.

Hmm. Willi said, "It's okay. Take deep breaths. It'll be fine."

Willi knelt down beside the prone figure in front of them. She swallowed back the waves in her stomach and said, "Mr. Yodo? I *think* he's Mr. Yodo. Mr. Yataro Yodo?" She grasped his shoulder. Rooster helped turn him over. Willi said, "He must have fainted. Maybe he's one of those that also fasts while he's here and went too far."

Rooster backed away. "Well, good riddance. One more Jap gone. We shouldn't ever forget, shouldn't ever . . ."

Kenzie pressed his arm. "Paul Rooster Rowley, you don't mean that. Mr. Yodo wasn't part of 1941. He didn't kill your father. He's an American citizen; probably his father was, too."

Rooster sighed. "I know. I know." He shook his head. "I want to get rid of this hate, I do; it's one of the reasons I came. I'm tired of hating."

"A good way to start down that path," Willi said, "is to help him now."

"Okay, but"—he bent over, took a pulse reading and shook his head—"can't nobody help. Mr. Yodo meditated his way right into the next realm. Heart attack, I'd guess. Yeah, most likely a heart attack."

Willi shivered. "Poor man."

Kenzie stepped back outside the door. "He's . . . he's dead?"

Willi frowned. The way he'd fallen over . . . hmm . . . didn't look like he'd clutched at his heart but more like he'd tried to grasp something just beyond his reach. "What's this?" She picked up a golden-handled contraption.

Kenzie swallowed and peered closely, but she wouldn't step back in the room. "A prayer wheel."

"Looks like an elaborate and oversized baby's rattle," Rooster said. "The top gyrates when you swing the handle."

"Now I remember." Willi nodded. "Inside are tiny pieces of paper with special prayers on them. Each time you swing it, the prayers are sent upward. At least he was in a heavenly state of mind when he keeled over."

"Let's go let the monks know," Rooster said. He picked up some things that obviously had fallen out of Mr. Yodo's pockets but were visible once they had turned him over.

Willi peered up at two packs of spearmint gum, a small notepad and pen, a slim folder of business cards, and a couple of receipts. "Guess since their company sent them, they get to take everything off as an expense."

Rooster said, "We better turn these over to the monks, too."

Willi glowered in his direction. "You shouldn't have touched them. Set them down."

He did and ducked his head. "You're right; yeah, you're right." He handed the things to Willi, who placed them neatly with the prayer wheel behind the shelf of votive candles.

Kenzie pulled him back beside her. "Let's go."

"Just a minute." Willi took one of the candles from the prayer wall and studied every inch of Mr. Yodo.

Kenzie said, "Forgive her. Insatiable curiosity. She's helped solve a couple of Texas murders. That just fueled her need to know more and more."

"Really?" Rooster said, standing with Kenzie and checking his watch. "Ten-fifteen. Thereabouts. That's when we found him." He cleared his throat and repeated, "Really?"

"Yeah, she helped our Nickleberry Sheriff and his nephew solve the Wicked Wiccan murders. Later, she and Quannah—that's the nephew—hunted down the Snow Snake killer."

Paul snapped his fingers. "I remember that. Happened in the ungodly ice and snow blizzard we had six, maybe seven months ago. Texas weather; it's something, all right." He stepped back into the room, crossed behind Willi, lowered the window and snapped the lock on the wooden shutter. "Guess this is what created the draft."

Willi said, "Quannah would prefer while on vacation not to have his occupation known, so you two be mum about that, okay?"

She then ignored the murmuring voices and concentrated on Mr. Yodo. He wore a purple kimono. He smelled as if he had just bathed, the scent of expensive soap reeling off his skin. One hand lay underneath his leg. She pulled it out and noticed it seemed swollen, but some older folks often had swollen joints in hands or legs by the evening time. Well, that would lend even more credence to the heart attack theory. She bent closer still. A musky scent—not human—seemed to emanate from his sleeve, which was moist with a water stain on the edge.

A slug in her memory banks stirred. She knew that scent from somewhere, somehow . . . but . . . couldn't quite grasp it. She leaned toward the floor. The odor there was stronger. Pictures of rain-drenched woods, musty mold, rotting grass came to mind. She laid her head down on the cold floor, an angle that allowed her to see a faint moist trail to Mr. Yodo's robe. She blinked, not sure it was there and not her imagination, so slight was the impression of moisture.

"Willi, come *on*." Kenzie backed farther into the hallway. "Let's go."

"Right. Right." She got up and brushed off her hands.

"There's nothing you can do, girlfriend."

"So tragic. His friends might not stay for the entire week's retreat now, I guess. I hate to tell them," Willi said.

"We're not going to say a word," Rooster said. "We'll just inform Jamyang or Samdup. They can be the bearers of bad tidings. Yes, they can tell the sad news."

Willi led the way outside and down the path. The day was beginning to catch up with her. She rubbed her gritty eyes. The waves in her stomach had subsided, but the musky scent stayed embedded in her nostrils. Ten minutes later, halfway to the teahouse, they practically stumbled over the older monk.

Samdup sat on a wooden bench in a cluster of wisteria. "You all are out late, but on the paths. That is fine. Night-time is a soothing part of the twenty-four to meditate."

"Mr. Yataro Yodo was meditating, too," Willi said.

The moonlight reflected off his soft Sharpei features as he listened to their tale. "So sad, yes. Come and show me, please."

After one more climb up the hillside, willi groaned. Her back muscles and arms already ached from the canoe trip. Now she added protesting legs to the list. She returned to the room with Samdup, Kenzie, and Rooster right behind her. Willi stared at the bare floor.

She shook her head and said, "We're in the wrong room."

"Nope, girl, this is the one."

Willi stepped out the doorway to the next cubicle over.

Rooster said, "This *is* the correct one. Yes, it's the right one."

Kenzie's eyes were bigger than Texas sunflower centers, the whites showing around the iris. "He was deader than a choked possum. He was so . . . so how . . . did he—?"

Willi patted her arm. "This . . . this *could* be good news. Guess we were mistaken. He must have rallied and gotten up."

Paul Rooster Rowley squatted on his haunches and scratched his head. He stared at the area where Yataro Yodo had been fifteen minutes ago. "I've seen lots of dead bodies, and I could have sworn. Yep, I could have sworn he was one of them."

Samdup said, "I shall go check the private pagoda of the IODD men, just to make sure all is well. You all are hungry and tired. Go to the Mimosa Teahouse and have sustenance. If there is bad news, I will inform you. Otherwise, you will know all is well."

"Suits me," Kenzie said, already out of Willi's grasp and out the front door. Rooster stood to follow closely on her heels. Samdup, too, went down the hall.

Willi said, "Be right there. I'll just go ahead and blow these candles out."

As she bent near the bunched grouping, candlelight flitted over the prayer wheel and other items placed behind the glass votives. She grabbed and stuffed them in her denim vest. Catching up to the others, she said, "Guess I'll mosey along to the women's pagoda just to freshen up a bit before eating. Check you all later."

She rushed ahead, scrambled to the side at a Y, and knelt within the overhanging shadows of wisteria. When Kenzie and Rooster went off to the left fork toward the Mimosa Teahouse, Samdup chose the right fork toward the area where there stood a men's-only pagoda and a number of small bungalows, one of which sheltered the IODD fellows. Willi allowed him to get several feet ahead before following. When she rounded a corner, she almost ran into his back. He'd stopped so suddenly.

She held her breath. If he turned now, he'd be able not only to see her, but also to touch her. He merely nodded and walked up the trail around the bungalow that led in a circle and back to the eatery and lounge—the Mimosa Teahouse. This time, Willi waited until his red robe no longer caught any moonlight. She stepped forward to his vacated spot and stared at the private bungalow.

In the bright lights shining outward, two figures sat across a table from each other having a glass of tea and conversation. The silhouette on the left, even from this distance, could easily be discerned as Mr. Yataro Yodo. When his head turned a certain way, she could see the tips of his mustache. She stayed long enough to see him move an arm out for his glass of tea before she sighed and followed Samdup's trail. She peered back over her shoulder once. The lights went out. Wow, didn't take them long to change and get into bed.

She yawned. Not a bad idea, except that she'd had nothing to eat since breakfast this morning, and she needed to at least locate the lounge and find a sandwich. Fifteen steps up, she was inside the Mimosa Teahouse. She always counted steps, one of the superstitious quirks inherited from her father, Phidias Gallagher, an otherwise quite rational lawyer. Thirteen would not have been good. Fifteen, great. Polished wood and brass lamps surrounded her. A dining area of mixed regular tables and sit-around low tables offered a welcome respite. Ceiling fans overhead stirred cool breezes.

She walked to the left of a heavy beam dividing the reception area. In front of the floor-to-ceiling windows was a huge sandbox with a gold-leafed fence about one foot off the ground surrounding the perimeter. An inner edging of some two feet of stonework encircled the actual seven-foot-by-five-foot workspace of colored sands.

Breathtaking.

She could think of no other word more appropriate for it. A depiction of a quiet monk beneath a spreading willow tree, birds flocked around him, glittered under the gentle directed light.

How absolutely exquisite.

Ah, must be the work of the monks. She'd love to see them while doing this artwork.

Awesome.

Okay, so she could come up with a few more adjectives. Between the bank of floor-to-ceiling windows a six-foot waterfall cascaded, its muted noise adding a relaxed feeling to the softly lit area.

"Back here," Kenzie said.

Willi jumped.

"Didn't mean to startle you, girl."

"Not a problem. Just sounded loud in this space. Beautiful, isn't it?"

"Yes, very restful. They change the sand picture every couple of days. Can you believe that? Each one is a work of art. *National Geographic* did a spread on it once, Samdup said. Come on back to the less formal sunroom. We've got fruit and sandwich plates; ice-cold tea and almond cookies. Got someone for you to meet, too."

Willi grinned. "Quannah's back? Yes, yes, yes."

Kenzie put an arm around her. "Sorry, no. Come on."

"Fine, but first point me in the direction of the soda machines."

"Not any," Kenzie said with palms upward.

"No Dr Pepper? Are you saying I'm on this deserted island without Quannah or Dr Pepper?"

"Hardly deserted. Twelve participants and seven or so monks; let's see—close to twenty folks. Nope, not deserted, but there is no caffeine. Even the tea is herbal. Hey, the good news is, there is a monk on duty at all times here to serve us no matter the hour."

"Great. Iced tea it is."

Seated within a rounded banquette in one corner was Rooster Rowley with the two Willi had seen earlier: the gnome with the white beard and his buxom companion. Paul offered introductions. "Willi Gallagher, meet Banjo Joe Skeeter and Miss Doretta Cameo."

She shook hands with both. "Banjo Joe, huh? You play?"

"Yes, ma'am, I do, the banjo and guitar. My cousin here, Doretta, can pick a little guitar and sing along when she's of a mind to, and when I can keep her out of the strip bars."

"He's teasing," Doretta said, slapping him on the shoulder. "Better be nice to me, old cuz, or I'll leave you high and dry on this old retreat."

As a concession to the heat, Doretta had a claw clamp holding her voluminous dark tendrils off her neck. A few escaped, giving her the appearance of a Venus. Other ample attributes added to that picture. With a napkin, she wiped perspiration from a cleavage worthy of Dolly Parton. Despite the age and gender differences, the familial resemblance showed in small noses, thick brows, and almost perfectly matched eye shape and chocolate color.

"So Skeeter is the family name?" Willi asked.

"Right you are," Doretta answered. "My mom and his are sisters. Were sisters. Both passed on. We're the only two left in the family. What a legacy that is." She laughed and patted her cousin's brown-splotched hand.

"Well now, there are legacies and there are legacies," Banjo Joe Skeeter added. His cousin glared at him, and he ducked his nose back into a frosty glass of tea.

Willi sighed. "Oh, that looks good."

No sooner were words out in the air than another of the monks placed a cold one on the table beside her, along with a plate of two types of sandwiches and a cluster of sugar-coated frozen grapes. "Thank you . . . I'm sorry, I don't know your name."

He smiled and waved away her thanks. He pointed to a tiny bell on the table.

Skeeter said, "That's to use when you want more."

Doretta added, "Yes, he won't talk to us, even though we've been a little evil in our efforts to get him to do so."

"But they don't maintain silence here with us." Willi frowned.

Kenzie scooted in beside her. "During the day, they'll talk to us, or most will, anyway. But at eleven o'clock at night, they keep a vow of silence until daylight. This guy's name is Rimshi, and no—most curious one—I don't know what it means."

"My understanding," Rooster said, "is that two of them each day keep completely silent. Guess they switch their days around. Except for Jamyang and Samdup."

Willi tasted the grapes. "Ahhh, talk about hitting the spot. Wonderful."

She listened to the talk around her while inhaling the two sandwiches. Sheepishly, she picked up the small dinner bell. One ring and Rimshi quietly came to the table.

She said, "I'd love some more grapes and maybe one more sandwich . . . uh . . . the chicken salad one would be great, and another glass of tea."

"You don't think," Kenzie said, "we're going to wait until you finish all that before finding out."

"Finding out what?"

Kenzie grinned. "Let me ask you a question. Do you know where our pagoda is—the women's pagoda?"

"No, not exactly, what does that have to do with anything?" Willi shut her eyes as soon as the sentence escaped her mouth. She knew why.

Kenzie raised an eyebrow and did a high-five slap with Paul Rooster Rowley. "Told you." Back at Willi she said, "So you didn't run by and freshen up, did you?"

Willi hung her head. "Busted."

Skeeter said, "Not to worry. Doretta's been there many times."

Doretta punched her cousin on his round shoulder. "Gonna hurt you in a moment. Stop that; they're gonna think all kinds of terrible things."

"So?" Kenzie insisted.

Rooster leaned across the table, too. "We caught up Skeeter and Doretta on the scare we had. You followed Samdup, didn't you?"

Willi thanked Rimshi as he slid the second helpings in front of her. "I would not have called it *following*, that's akin to stalking, and I abhor such goings-on," she said with her nose in the air. "I may have taken the wrong trail by *accident*, that's all."

"Yeah, yeah, girlfriend. That's all you're admitting to. So, what happened when you took off on the wrong trail?"

"I ended up, somehow, facing the private bungalow of the IODD men. Two of them were having tea in the living area, lit up inside like a store display."

"And?" All four asked in unison. They laughed and said, "And then? And then?"

"Nothing." Willi munched on her sandwich. "Nothing except Mr. Yataro Yodo was sitting up having tea and talking with that muscled-up fellow . . . uh—"

"Mike Toru?" Kenzie asked.

"Yes, he's the one. So, I guess Mr. Yodo just had a momentary collapse."

"All's well that ends well, as they say," Skeeter intoned. "Best be getting my old bones to bed. Been a long day."

"Cuz, you've been saying that since you were thirty. You're not much over fifty now. Good grief. And, you're crazy if you think you're gonna leave me as the only surviving family at that unripe age. Stop talking like that. And shave that beard. That'll take years off, right there."

"Doretta, now, don't get that pretty head in a dither. She can do that, you know, faster than any woman I know. You best be getting some sleep, too, if we're gonna be up two, three hours before those classes start."

Willi blinked. "Are you all early morning joggers?"

"No," Doretta said, glaring with teeth bared at her cousin. "We just want to take a leisurely boat trip around the island."

Willi snapped her fingers. "That's what's bothering me about the boathouse. The pontoon was gone, too. Quannah and Inoshi took the motorboat to the ranch mainland, but you all's should have been in dock."

Kenzie said, "They took both. Too many supplies to haul in just one." To the cousins, Willi said, "So why isn't your boat there?"

"Mr. Yancy, the ranch foreman, sort of gave us permission to have the boat just for our own purposes, but the participants in the retreat aren't supposed to use such things. So he told the monks to turn a blind eye to it as long as we don't use the main dock, so we got it tethered up around a bend farther down." Doretta explained.

Rooster Rowley leaned forward, muscular arms on the table. "What are those purposes?"

"We're bounty hunters. Looking for someone special," Skeeter said and pulled on his beard.

"Oh, you old fart, stop fibbing to these nice folks." Doretta slapped him on the arm. "Doctor's orders, but he just doesn't want to admit the fact. Told him to just get out in that old boat for an hour or two a day. Sometimes we fish, sometimes just picnic. Seems like his blood pressure comes right down, and that's better than taking pills."

Skeeter stretched and yawned. "Well, it's better than what you do to relax."

Doretta got up and walked with him to the entryway. "Don't you start that now."

"Belly dancing," Skeeter turned back and bellowed to make sure they all heard. "Belly dancing and sometimes with a snake."

"I tell you what, I'm gonna kill you before any high blood pressure has a chance. Get out of here. I'll set my clock. See you at daylight, you ornery no-good-for-nothing thing."

"All right, Cousin Doretta, hon. If Gabriel don't blow no horns, I'll be seeing you."

She returned to the table. "Guess I'll call it an evening, too. See you ladies at our cabin, pagoda, whatever. Hey, where'd that Rowley fellow go?"

"Nestor D. came in from the outdoor dining area and pulled him away to talk," Willi said.

"And," Kenzie added, pointing out the windows, "it doesn't seem to be a friendly encounter."

Nestor D. was up in Rowley's face. Both men's fists knotted, ready to swing.

Doretta, already standing, beat Kenzie and Willi to the door by seconds. Willi pushed through first, though.

Nestor D. snarled, "Boy, a vet like you ought to understand we can't let this go on. Damned Japs. They couldn't beat us one way, but they're going to try another. Technology war. Land deals. Then what we saw happening tonight. They're up to no good. And this is home ground. Texas ground. Hallowed ground, by damn."

Rowley pushed the older man back. "No, it's none of our business. I came here to find closure for Vietnam, my war, and my dad's death at Pearl Harbor. Peace. I've nothing against any of *these* men. Forget it, Nestor. Forget all of it. Let ghosts sink as they should have years ago. I'm gonna pretend you never said squat to me. If you're smart, you'll forget what you saw, and keep your reporter's nose out of others' personal business." He took off his glasses to rub his eyes. He pinched the bridge of his nose. With shoulders slumped and his bifocals hanging loosely from his fingers, he wandered toward the men's pagodas.

Nestor D. twirled him around. "Glad you took those glasses off, you damned turncoat of a sorry son-of-a-gun." He punched Rowley on the chin so powerfully the younger man staggered backward.

Rowley came up with the swiftness of a snarling tiger. Veins in his head bulged. His face reached volcano red. He grabbed Nestor around one arm to grapple him into a headlock.

Teeth gritted, he said, "Damn you, old man. What the hell were you thinking? Are you crazy pulling something like that? You got a death wish? Is that what you got, a death wish?"

Doretta and Kenzie both held one of Willi's arms. She pulled in air, something she'd not done since seeing the confrontation. "What are you all up to? What happened earlier, Nestor D.? Whatever it is, we can talk it out."

Like a SWAT team had sent a stream of ice-cold water blasts over them, the men separated. A glance passed between the two for a heartbeat, then another and another. Nestor D. gasped for air and rubbed his neck. Breathing heavily, Rooster Rowley eased a few paces away. He said, "I shouldn't have grabbed you. Dangerous. I shouldn't have done that."

"Hell, son, it was my fault. I was spoiling for a fight, and you were close. Damned sorry myself." He shook hands with Rowley, nodded to the ladies, and followed in Skeeter's footsteps.

Willi sighed. "Thank goodness. Now, what seems to have caused his outburst?"

Rooster Rowley put his glasses back on and blinked. "I couldn't say, ma'am, I couldn't say."

"But, he told you about something," Kenzie said, with arms akimbo. "We heard the last there . . . something happening that Nestor D. and you saw tonight."

"Exactly," Willi added. "Somebody's personal business."

"Could have been," Rowley said, brushing his hair over the eyeglass earpiece. "Could have been." He walked off behind the azaleas. By the time the darkness swallowed him somewhere near the giant oak, Willi had arms akimbo also, a mirror image of Kenzie's stance.

"Men," she said.

"Men," Kenzie concurred.

Willi turned toward her left. Probably Doretta had a similar pronouncement. "Where'd she go?"

Kenzie yawned big enough to suck in the Grand Canyon, blinked, and said, "Probably for some shut-eye. What do you say, girlfriend?"

Willi's bottom lip trembled a moment, and she frowned to cover up her watering eyes.

Kenzie said, "Come on. Being this late, Quannah's going to stay on the mainland. You'll get to see him in the morning. Isn't this place great? Since we got the Microsoft card explained, I feel completely safe. And it's good to see everyone else going through some problems. I'm not alone in having them; I just have different ones. Yeah, the balance is coming back into my life. It's wonderful. Thanks for being such a friend and coming with me."

Willi let Kenzie lead the way down the trail, marked only here and there by halogen lights high in the trees. The night heron sat on the porch rail of their pagoda. His wise eyes shined brightly in the moonlight. Hells Bells and damned feathered ones. She couldn't tell Kenzie about the call now, the possibility that Jerry jerk-face Cormack might have discovered their island haven. Kenzie walked inside. Thunder boomed and dry lightening seared the sky. Willi screamed, slammed the door shut, and leaned against it. Her heart pounded like pistons revving for a big race.

Kenzie opened her eyes wide. "What is the matter with you, girl?"

"Uh, guess I'm not as calm . . . as in balance as you."

She grinned a few minutes later as she entered her private chamber—a small raised bed and a lamp table with a glass of lemon water resting on it—a retreat more suitable to a Victorian setting than a pagoda. She climbed beneath soft sheets. "I'm sure things will be better in the morning." She drifted off and dreamed:

Beneath a lacy umbrella, she smoothed her sleeveless white ankle-length sheath. Red painted toenails peeked from the straps of her white sandals. Pearl Harbor's beach and sea embraced her. Sailors in wet and bedraggled uniforms wandered aimlessly, their dogtags clinking out as if breezes wafted through the bodies to stir the pieces of metal into musical chimes. Two Native American earrings weighed her earlobes down with tiny replicas of silver and turquoise hawks with coral eyes. As if she were standing beside herself, she leaned over to admire them, saying, "They're bringing messages. Better watch. Better watch." Self-admiration complete, she returned to a single body state. Her table companions—a jovial set of chaps—joined her. Charlie Chan bowed over her hand before saying, "Wise man say not good to believe eyes all the time; the truth is in the eye of the divine. Must look most deeply."

Hercule Poirot laughed and with his cane for support seated himself beside Mr. Chan. Hercule twirled his mustache. "Indeed. Indeed. In each heart is a secret to be brought to the light. Oh, and that can be frightful, most frightful, mon ami." *With a second twist of his mustache, he metamorphosed into a nighthawk, one of pure white plumage.*

Startled, Willi jumped up. The pristine hawk dove into lush azalea bushes some four feet high and nearly as wide. He swooped back around and toward her, claws open, eyes narrowed, diving, heading right for her head. A silent scream escaped her, but her legs were frozen. She looked down and her lacquered toenails bled droplets upon the patio. She gasped and peered up to Charlie Chan to beseech him for help. But she just kept screaming when droplets from his mouth matched those from her toenails. The great hawk, now close with a wingspan of five feet, lay his wings flat along his sides for this final kamikaze blaze. The bird of prey ripped her jewelry away; pain pierced her earlobe.

Nonsensical babble escaped her. She stood in numbed shock. Charlie Chan, with crisp napkin, wiped the droplets from his chin. When he glanced up, it was with three eyes, the third in the middle of his forehead. He blinked it. "The eye of the divine reveals all when the three bells ring. Must beg pardon now. Must leave lovely companion. Most sincerely regret the necessity."

"No problem."

"Hey, girlfriend," *Kenzie said, beside her.* "Here's Jerry's Bible. Can you believe he has a Bible? Maybe he ought to read it."

As if it made complete sense, Willi nodded. "That's where his secret lies."

"I thought," *Kenzie said,* "it was in the eye of the divine."

Willi sat down in her chair across the table from Kenzie, who wore the same outfit as she, down to the lone right-lobed earring. Willi said, "We better watch them, or the hawk will dive, the hawk will dive." *Around their table on the Pearl Harbor beach, sailors walked in wet and bedrag-*

gled uniforms, their dogtags clinking out as if a breeze wafted through the sailors' bodies to stir the pieces of metal into musical chimes. The white hawk squawked and dove into the blood-red azaleas.

Thunder clapped. Willi sat up in bed. Lightening flashed and a man's shadow flickered on the wall. Willi opened her mouth to scream only to have a tight hand clasp around it. She reared back and nailed her assailant on the nose.

CHAPTER
5

"Damn you, Gallagher."

"Oops."

She twisted her legs, wrapped herself in the sheets, grabbed her assailant's arms, and tried to budge him from the grasp he held. Hot breath blew against her neck.

"*Winyan,*" Quannah whispered. "If you keep fighting me, you'll wake up your tipi mates." He loosened his hold on her. She playfully slapped his arm as he turned her face toward his lips. After a few breathless moments, he released her from the kiss.

"You ornery, infuriating man."

"I missed you, too, Gallagher."

"Hmmm, maybe you did at that. Did I bloody your nose?"

He turned on her bedside light. "I don't think so. Just grazed the side of my face."

"I'll have to work on better aim." She turned over to really study him. She had to quickly catch him up on the do-ings and deeds of Serenity Island. "I have to tell you a few things. There are two couples here who are weird, really. The Pates—Preacher Halliwell and his Juna Marie—who, by the by, isn't really *his* Juna Marie. Then there's Banjo Joe Skeeter and his cousin Doretta Cameo. You are not, un-der any circumstances, to take her on any lone trail drives. Well, for that matter, not Juna Marie, either."

"Nope . . . no Cameos in June." His arm fell heavily against her chest; his snores warmed the curve of her neck.

She brushed back his dark hair, pulled his ponytail, and said, "Hey, Lassiter, this next is important. Listen."

He yawned, sat up on his elbow, and mumbled, "Got to get that info about the ranch sabotage . . . yeah . . . get into the pagoda."

"Here you are mouthing in your sleep, and I'm trying to tell you we found a dead body." She waited for his reaction and realized he was literally asleep while sitting up. She shook him.

"Yes, the IODD men; yeah, I'm going"—he yawned big enough to rival the force of hurricane Claudette—"to check that angle out."

"Would you stop mumbling. Wake up!"

"I'm listening. You found a dead body. Squirrel? It'll go to the Star Nation, too; don't fret, woman."

In the next cubicle, Kenzie stirred, turned over, and gen-tly snored. Willi whispered more frantically, "Not a squir-rel. A body, as in human—Mr. Yataro Yodo. But it wasn't him. I mean, his body wasn't dead; it just seemed like it was, because when I looked into . . . Lassiter? Lassiter?"

Groggily, he crept out of the bed and toward the win-dow. "I'll go the way I came. Catch up with me tomorrow on the trail ride if the rain doesn't drown that activity out."

She blew him a kiss and sighed. The trail ride. Oh,

great. One more terror to think about. That was one of the reasons she'd not wanted to come with Kenzie to this retreat. She, a born Texan, and she had that cross to bear. Never, never had she shared her phobia with anyone, not even Kenzie, and they'd been through childhood mumps, teen acne, college ski trips, and more. They'd shared a long history together. She and Quannah were just beginning to share. How could she tell him her secret?

Riding horses. Over a rough trail. Yippy-ki-yi-hell.

Her mouth grew dry and she lay back to gasp in air. She peered out the window. Rain slashed downward.

Yes, yes, yes. Thank you, Lord, keep that rain falling.

She pulled her hair, twisted her pillow into impossible shapes, and finally settled into a dreamless sleep.

The clang of loud cymbals rooted her out of bed. But the horror of the day that lay before her made her dive back under the pillows. At her remembered encounter with Quannah, she sat bolt upright, every strand of steel wound tightly around the cable of her backbone. Damn that man! That ornery . . . oh, there weren't enough words. She slammed her fist into her pillow. "How am I going to get through the day with all these monsters hanging over me?"

Kenzie, towel wrapped about her head, peeked around and said, "Shower is all yours, girlfriend, as soon as you take care of that Dacron varmint . . . and . . . uh, all those monsters. By the by, may I use a tiny bit of your perfume? I didn't bring any, and I just thought . . ."

"Yes? Thought someone might like a little sniff? Someone by the name of Rooster Rowley? Cocka-doodily-doodily-doo." Willi offered a possum-grinned face.

"Girlfriend, did I mention any guy? I just forgot mine, and I feel . . . undressed without a dab of perfume."

"That's your story and you stick to it, Kenzie. Sure, you can use anything of mine."

After Kenzie finished spraying, Juna Marie walked through, sniffed the air, and said, "Ooh, smells good. May I?"

Willi nodded, and Juna Marie doused herself with Elizabeth Taylor's Passion scent before heading out the door again.

Finally, with just her and Kenzie there Willi said, "You aren't going to believe what happened last night."

"Quannah used the natural knack of his ancestors to sneak into the pagoda to see his Indian princess."

"How did—?"

"I, being the best friend a girl ever had, turned over and snored so as to give you all the impression of privacy. And I did such a good job, I really fell right to sleep. So I guess I missed you two cooing doves."

"No. He did the same thing."

Kenzie looked up from rubbing her champagne-blond curls. "What?"

"Went to sleep."

"Ouch. You bored him with the island's night tales, didn't you?"

Willi jumped out of bed and threw the pillow at Kenzie. She kept the bathroom door closed enough for privacy, but open a little for conversation. Hot water steamed over her shoulders. Vanilla Fields soap created an invigorating miasma.

She answered. "I merely tried to get him up to speed about Mr. Yodo's collapse. Didn't even get to the fight between Nestor D. and Paul before Big Chief Lassiter started snoozing."

"So that was one of the monsters that you can't face today? The fact that Quannah fell asleep while you were putting the moves on him?" Kenzie yelled, while dressing, "You said there was something worse than that. I ask again, what?"

Willi rinsed shampoo from her hair, added conditioner to stroke through her black tendrils, far below her shoulder blades when wet, and raised her voice above the roar of the water. "I knew he gave in too easily." Finished with her hair, she reached for her shaving cream.

Kenzie crowed. "I would not call that a problem. Whoo hoo. Good thing I went to dreamland. So your moves were smooth! You go, girl!"

"You idiot." Willi threw a handful of her shaving cream around the shower curtain and in Kenzie's general direction.

"You missed! I take it, girlfriend, I also missed something."

"Yes." Wrapped in an oversized towel, Willi exited the shower. She rubbed lotion on her arms and legs. "Yes, you missed something. He gave in too easily to coming to Serenity Island for the retreat."

Kenzie peered up from tying her Lady Adidas. "Run that by me again."

Willi stepped behind her cubicle to dress. "He already had reason to be here on the ranch. Boy, did this retreat work in well for his plans—plans which he didn't share. Do you understand? He didn't tell me."

Setting aside her regular footwear, she brought her new Click see-through tennis shoes out to the lounge area of sofa and chairs, sat beside her friend, and pulled on cotton socks. "He was so tired, he dozed off and mumbled in his sleep. He's here in the line of duty. He's investigating some sort of ranch sabotage and checking out the IODD men. That's what he's doing here."

"Maybe he was just having a bad dream." Kenzie stood, fluffed her curls, and said, "Let's talk on the way to breakfast."

Outside, cardinals seemed intent on providing an air show as Willi sauntered beside Kenzie toward the Mimosa Teahouse. "It wasn't a dream," Willi said. He was muttering and had no idea of what he'd said. Why didn't he tell me the night I informed him about the trip?"

Kenzie took Willi's wrist and squeezed it. "Do you tell him everything? Do you trust him with everything?"

Willi's face turned as bright red as the cardinal's wing. She peered up at the sun in the sky. *Oh, God.* The rains had stopped.

The ride on the trail. Yippy-ki-yi-hell.

No, she hadn't shared something important with him or with Kenzie. Willi pulled her wrist from her friend's touch and patted her own heated cheeks.

Kenzie said, "Ah, girlfriend. Maybe it takes time. It's worth the effort with Quannah. He's not abusive in any way, in fact he seems to watch over you in such a manner as to deflect any worries possible. You said he wasn't used to sharing work things, even when you helped him on his cases. You're not bound by job ethics in that situation, girlfriend, but Quannah is, right?"

"Right. There are things he can't tell me. And never will be able to about some concerns of his work." Willi sighed down to her kneecaps. "But he could have said he had to gather info for a case. Just that would have been better than not saying anything."

"Tell him what you just said to me. My bet is he'll try to do that next time."

"Maybe."

"No maybe about it, girl." Kenzie laughed. "Boy, how the tables turn with us. Good thing we're not both down at the same time. Yesterday me, today you. So what was the other monster you couldn't face today?"

Willi avoided, with the help of two furry friends, Kenzie's glance and question. "Look at those little rabbits. They're in the brush. Awww."

She dropped a foot or two behind Kenzie on the trail. Let's see. Okay, she could get through the day—only twenty-four hours in one of the dang blamed things after all—so she could get through without revealing that Cormack might very well be stalking underneath the ferns. Sure, she could manage not to reveal that her stomach felt like soured pudding every time someone mentioned the day's activity: *the two-hour trail ride*. At the bottom of the stairway entrance to the Mimosa Teahouse, a monk hit the six-foot cymbal, a last call for the morning's pre-breakfast item.

"Ooh, I forgot," Kenzie said. "We have fifteen minutes of silent meditation to contemplate the *koan* of the day."

"Oh, yes. Those unanswerable riddle things." Willi's stomach protested with growls indicating empty. "This is truly an ungodly hour to get festivities of the day started."

Kenzie glanced at her wristwatch. "Six A.M. is early, but we've a lot to pack into one day: The koan meditation and breakfast for everyone. Then the men get to go off for about two, maybe three hours for that all-men's Inipi ceremony. I hope we get to do that before the week is out."

"Oh, yes, we will. Quannah is going to lead a mixed group ceremony mid-week."

"Great, girlfriend. So let's see, now. After the men get back, we all go on a trail ride and late picnic lunch. Yip-pee-ya-hoo, huh?"

"Yes, it's shaping up into quite a day." She'd suddenly lost her appetite. "Quite a day. Hope I survive it."

"Don't be silly, Willi. It's not like we're doing water sports where you might get dunked, or something dangerous like bungee jumping."

Willi swallowed back bile. Had Kenzie ever seen those

western movies with horses rolling over every third person regardless of Indian feathers, army uniform, or trapper's leather? What about hooves? Banjo Joe might write a ballad about her. She trudged slowly behind Kenzie.

Nestor D. and Rooster Rowley were already on rugs on the soft grass. Banjo Joe Skeeter and Doretta Cameo, good as their word, were off for a few hours in their boat. They said they'd return for breakfast. Preacher Pate and his Juna Marie arrived. This morning Juna Marie seemed as composed as any swan nestling down for a quiet float, her short white-blond hair arranged elegantly. A proprietary hand upon her elbow, Halliwell Pate assisted her onto a rug right next to Mike Toru. Nara Inoshi, on the same row as Willi and Kenzie, nodded his head. Hmm. Guess Mr. Yodo was staying in the cool pagoda to rest up. She couldn't blame him.

Samdup, his orange headband in place, serving as protection against dripping sweat later in the day, greeted each of them. He waited until all rustling, shuffling, and rearranging had ceased. Twittering birds broke the silence. He delayed a few moments longer until all Willi could discern was her own heartbeat revving at ninety miles a minute, but gradually slowing, getting into sync with some beat coming through the very ground—a slow comforting rhythm, a womb-balanced cadence.

Willi shut her eyes. She smiled. Quannah's voice came to her: Unci. Maka. *Two words for Grandmother and Mother Earth. We are all within her womb, all experiencing her strength if we will but listen to her heartbeat, which is within us all; answer its healing call. It's a gentle call, but we must still our bodies, focus our minds, and calm our spirits so* Unci *and* Maka *can help us.* Hmmm. Interesting where the mind will go when completely relaxed.

Samdup must have thought all were in that state when

he clearly offered up the koan for the day. "When walking—walk. When sitting—sit. But don't wobble!"

Willi took a deep breath. Hmmm.

Samdup repeated the koan and asked them all to say it aloud and to consider its meaning until the gong sounded.

Willi dutifully repeated. "When walking—walk. When sitting—sit. But don't wobble! When walking—walk . . . sit . . . don't wobble . . . don't . . . wobble."

In her long white sleeveless sheath, she smiled as she rode atop the horse. The roan rocked beneath her. Willi looked some eight feet down to smile at the nests in the trees. Hmmm. Above the trees. Well, that was okay as long as she didn't wobble. Cardinal fledglings gaped at her and spoke. "That's one way to sit, I guess. Either way, you're going to fall."

"What do you know?" she asked, "Your wings aren't even dry."

She rode on, a handful of horsehair wrapped tightly around her hand. If she didn't run into that savage Indian chief, she'd be fine. She frowned, but she wanted to see him. Didn't she? No, no, not like this.

Charlie Chan, his white suit rumpled, bent at an odd angle to walk beside her in the air. "Pretty lady with curiosity must be one's self first. Be most natural."

Her heartbeat escalated as the roan broke into a canter. "Oh, dear. I must sit. I must not wobble. Oh my granny's garters, this is too fast!"

"Nice lady must hurry, though. Mother Earth will reveal the truth to you if you ride." He brushed at his suit, all covered with leaf mold. One sleeve was torn away entirely now. He waved a prayer wheel in front of her face.

"Oh, horsey, slow down!" she screamed.

No matter how fast the horse ran, Mr. Chan kept pace with a sedate stride. Her heart ripped along with the ca-

*dence of the roan's hoofbeats, fast then faster, then up in
her throat, turning into fear grasping at her so that all that
jolted through her were the beats. Pulses of warmth over-
powered her, made her mouth as dry as a scarecrow's.*

*An Indian warrior, bare-chested, hair flying loose, rode
beside her. "Turn around, Winyan, turn around, then we'll
ride side by side."*

*Too frightened to even look at him, she grasped the
horsehairs more tightly. The brave thundered past her. The
only thing she discerned now was a roaring in her ears and
then she fell, and fell, and continued falling, arms like
frantic windmills. She crashed by the fledglings that piped
up. "What horse wouldn't buck you off? You shouldn't ride
holding on to the tail, lady."*

"I'd appreciate that," a voice above her said. Willi
blinked and stared into Quannah's warm eyes.

"Appreciate what?" she managed while he helped her
stand.

"Your not pulling my ponytail. That was what you said,
right? Hmmm. Were you daydreaming again?"

With her nose in the air and with her best raised-
eyebrow teacher's expression, said, "I do not daydream. I
was meditating upon the koan of the day. Can you not see
that everybody . . . ?" Her voice trailed off as she glanced
at the empty grass verging the Mimosa Teahouse.

"They picked up their blankies about five minutes ago
and headed for breakfast. So . . . you were doing what,
Gallagher?"

"I . . . well, I was having a more in-depth spiritual experience than others."

He grinned, leaned down, and kissed her with that curl
and twist of the tongue that tickled her ninety ways to
nothing. She shivered and blinked.

Before she could retort, he said, "Best be heading for

the grazing yourself. It's going to be a long steamy ride in this humidity, even if for only a couple of hours. I've got to go get the rest of the horses saddled. Then I'll be leading the men in the Inipi ceremony for a few hours. The horses will be tied over there if you want to warm yours up before we ride. In about four hours." He turned his broad back. His black ponytail hung below his summer Stetson.

"About that trail ride."

"You can't wait. I know, Gallagher, but curb that anxious bent you have, and go eat."

"Really, I may not—"

"I insist, Gallagher. Don't go stubborn on me this morning. I've been looking forward to riding side by side with you. Don't want you fainting from hunger or the heat. Bring an extra water bottle." With that, he disappeared in the direction of one of the wooden carvings with a quaint barn and horse depiction. "Oh, yippee-ki-yi-hell and spittin' spittoons."

She raced up the steps. Maybe the monks would serve sushi for breakfast. She imagined she was highly allergic to sushi; they might have to air-vac her out to an air-conditioned hospital with cool white sheets. With that happy thought in mind, she approached her breakfast. Now, with a few moments to herself, she'd be able to think of a way out of going on this trip of hoofed horror. She settled down on a pillow at a corner with a low table. Doretta Cameo, in a Dixieland pink-and-white half T-shirt and polka-dot shorts, joined her. Banjo Joe Skeeter scooted himself into a comfortable position among the pillows like a bearded sultan awaiting the administrations of slaves and harem. Rimshi served scrambled eggs, biscuits, and cantaloupe slices. So much for the sushi scene. All three dug in.

In the middle of a second helping of cantaloupe, Willi gulped. Oh, great stars, where was Kenzie? Some kind of bodyguard she was turning out to be. Rooster Rowley's laugh cockadoodle-doo'd through the room. Willi glanced in his direction, where Kenzie also laughed and pulled his glasses off to clean them for him. Maybe the perfume had given Kenzie a little feminine lift and playfulness. Rooster never seemed to mind that bit of attention, either. Hmm. As any decent bodyguard, Willi scanned the huge rooms for a sign of a lurking ex. None at hand, she tried to pay attention to the Texas cousins and plan, her strategy.

Skeeter eyeballed Juna Marie across the way. "She's a mighty classy lady. Real pretty."

"Well," Doretta said, "she was none-too-pleased with your attentions this morning."

"Humph. Not so. She didn't seem to mind, but that Preacher Pate was downright rude. Just flirting a little with her. Hell, her husband was right there; they's bound to know I meant every word in a complimentary way."

"Preachers are different, and seems like he's very possessive of her, so don't be a mule and keep kicking in that direction."

"Fine. To this other, now. I tell you we're gonna have to go slower. We'll take the binoculars out tomorrow to try and sight some of them landmarks."

Doretta leaned toward him. "Keep your voice down, cuz. Nobody's business but ours, and you know how folks eavesdrop." Both cousins glanced up at Willi.

"Well, I'm sitting at the table with you. Jeez." She wiped cantaloupe juice from the corner of her mouth. "So, you all really are looking for . . . ?"

Skeeter and Doretta exchanged a look. Skeeter said, "Hell. Me and my big mouth. Probably pie in the sky stuff, but me and Doretta here each got half the family map."

"Might still be a hoax," Doretta said, opening up her

huge purse to locate a purple CD holder. Inside, folded neatly, was half a sheet of paper. She pulled it out. "This ain't the original. I got better sense than to bring that. It's a copy, but not a complete one. An item is missing from this that's on the original."

Willi nodded. "Treasure?"

The dark-haired Venus of a woman said, "Of a sort."

"Smart." Willi said. "Smart not to have every detail on the map." She tried to glance at it over Doretta's shoulder. But her ample endowments blocked all view of the sheet. Willi repeated. "Smart."

Skeeter dug into a second helping of scrambled eggs. "Doretta, she's the one that's smart; and bless her heart, she's damned honest, too, despite her working in them nudie bars."

"You keep telling folks that," Doretta said, "I'm gonna slap you six ways to nothing and back, I tell you what."

He ducked his head and grinned. "Anyhoo, she's honest. She made me do the same with my half of the family map; locked the original sucker up and brung this drawing." He patted a small medicine bundle that he pulled out from his shirt neck. "I left one item off, too, just like she said to do. That's up here." He tapped his forehead where the Buddha's third eye was always depicted.

"So, what exactly is this treasure supposed to be?"

"Missy Curious One. Missy Willi. Uh-huh. That's what all the monks call you." He stroked his beard. "You keep the lid on this little side activity, and you can go with us this morning."

Willi sat straighter, with a broad grin on her face. *Thank you, Great Spirit.* She had just found a way out of going on the trail ride. A reason not to have to approach a snorting beast of stone hooves. A relaxing way to spend the day. Great Spirit had provided her with an escape.

"We'll tell you all about it. Know you're honest, so if you give your word it's a done deal."

"How do you know I'm honest? I am, but how do you know?"

"Lots of ways, Missy Curious One."

"Just your gut feeling, huh? That's okay with me."

Skeeter set his fork and knife down. He stared into her eyes. "The way your friend there—that cute little Kenzie— talks about you; and the fine things that sweetheart of yours has to say about you. He and me, we had a right long talk about you, in fact, us sharing the same pagoda and all. Him being a horse lover, it means something to say how you're the only lady he has great respect for other than his mama. He thinks you're right smart, too. And brave. Said there ain't nothing that scares off his Miss Marple of the Range."

"He said all that?"

"Yep, darn tootin', he did."

Well, Hells Bells and guilt tagging along. He wouldn't have any respect for her once he discovered she'd never mounted a horse other than the one in front of the super-market. She'd loved that old thing and rode it every time her mama would part with a quarter on grocery day. Yes, Quannah would definitely pull her off the pedestal. Her bottom lip trembled. She grasped it with her teeth and frowned, gradually letting it come back to shape, as she calmed herself.

Doretta chimed in. "But we really don't want everyone to know. Might be a hoax, considering our crazy ancestors. We don't want to look stupid if it comes out that there's nothing but hot air and an old joke involved."

"No problem. My lips are sealed. I don't even know what you're looking for."

She considered the dilemma as she tucked into the last of her scrambled eggs. If she went on the trail ride, in all likelihood her secret would be revealed to the one person, Quannah, who would despise her for her weakness—her fear of getting on top of a live, breathing monster of a horse. Hell, she wouldn't only wobble; she would wonk her butt on the damned ground in front of God and everybody.

She took a bite of egg and set her fork down. To stall for time, she rang the table bell and had Rimshi bring her another serving of cantaloupe. On the other hand, if she went with Skeeter and Doretta, she'd have a day of interesting conversation with good company, a relaxing meal out on the lake, and a day free of fear. But she'd still drop from that pedestal. Quannah would be disappointed, at the least, and perhaps even a bit wounded, that his Miss Marple of the Range didn't meet the day's challenge.

She finished the cantaloupe and told the cousins she'd meet them in ten minutes by the boathouse. If she wasn't there by then, they were to go on, and she'd go another day.

"Oh, you'll be there, honey," Doretta said. She opened up the basket of food. "Fried chicken. Corn on the cob. Potato salad. Chocolate cake in the cooler, and a case of Dr Pepper."

Willi's mouth watered even after the hearty breakfast. "Dr Pepper?"

Doretta nodded. "On the boat in the cooler. Not a word, though, about anything. We'll leave about the same time the trail ride starts, so just come on down to the dock."

As Skeeter got up and pulled the napkin from his neck, he said. "We need to check with the monks, too, remember, cousin?"

"Oh, about someone messing with our boat last night?"

Willi's ears pricked up. "What happened?"

"Aw, nothing big. We could just tell someone took it for a spin because I keep a close eye on the gasoline usage. They must have gone around the island a couple times,

maybe made a trip to the mainland. One or two things out
of place in the bow, too. Stowed at the same place, same
knot tie-up. Don't mind if it were an emergency of the
monks, but we need to find out."

Skeeter and Doretta wandered out. Willi stared around
at the empty room. Everyone else was in the front of the
Mimosa Teahouse. Quannah, leading Nara Inoshi, Mike
Toru, and some of the monks, sauntered by the window
and waved.

Willi quirked up one side of her mouth and raised a
hand. She couldn't quite manage an enthusiastic wave.
When he had passed, she put her head between her hands
and bawled.

About forty-five seconds into her pity party, she snif-
fled, dried her eyes, and squared her shoulders. God, how
she hated to disappoint Quannah, how she detested what
she knew would be a look of disdain when she told him she
was opting for the boat ride or worse, opting for a headlong
throw because she didn't know squat from buttermilk when
it came to riding a horse. She hugged herself and shook her
head. No, she just couldn't do that. She just couldn't. And
by damned, she wouldn't. No one could make her get up
on a four-legged beast, no matter how beautiful the animal.

Willi stood tall, raised her chin, and passed by Samdup
on her way out the door. His Sharpei features broke into a
hundred wrinkles when he smiled.

"Just visited with the IODD gentleman, Nara Inoshi. He
is sending Mr. Yataro Yodo back today to the doctor to
make sure all is fine with him."

"That's good. Glad he's feeling better. Hey, does he
need someone to go along with him, to sort of keep him
company or anything, because I can—"

"No, sorry, I got my tenses mixed up. Mr. Inoshi and
Mr. Toru already *took* him across to the mainland, just as

daylight peeked out. They have returned. I believe they came in time to participate in a men-only sweat lodge ceremony, which they had asked Mr. Lassiter to prepare."

"Ah, yes, that."

"Missy Willi, you got much from the morning koan, I hope. When walking—walk. When sitting—sit. But don't wobble!"

She tilted her nose in the air. "Yes, indeed. I don't intend to wobble!"

CHAPTER
6

Quannah breathed deeply as he shed his shirt atop the cliff. He prayed to be able to lead spiritually and well. How was he supposed to do that, and still be a lawman? Good grief, he'd have to struggle damned hard not to peer at each man as if he were a criminal with a secret to hide. The sweat lodge was as sacred to him as the confessional was to a practicing Catholic. The rub came because he'd never learned to totally turn the lawman off, and he didn't really know if he should. He bowed his head.

You come to Wakan Tanka *as you are; he will lead through the difficult steps if you allow access to heart and mind.* Ah, yes, thoughts from his mentor from the rez, old Coyote Singer. He whispered, *pilamaya yelo* in thanks for the words to come as he needed them. He pulled off his pants, folded and placed them with his other garments. His ceremonial breechcloth of soft red blanket material brushed against his legs. The monks and the IODD businessmen wore short towels. Rooster Rowley and Nestor chose swimming trunks. Quannah had only led a half dozen such ceremonies, and each one had been different in some way. He was particularly pleased that the Buddhist monks chose to participate.

As if reading his mind, Samdup, who had just walked up the hill, said, "The sharing is good, both to savor the differences and to confirm the similarities. This will be a beneficial experience of your cultural roots. Such an opportunity to stretch our spiritual lives is always welcome. I apologize for us slowing down the ceremony with so many questions, but all is intriguing."

"Not a problem."

Out of the corner of his eye, Quannah discerned movement in the circle of trees. He blinked and squinted, raised his head to breathe in deeply. A furry critter, no doubt, out for a mid-morning forage, perhaps a badger or a skunk. Both could foster good medicine for the Inipi ceremony since the badger would offer unusual ways of healing and never give up; the skunk would allow each person to invite others into their spiritual space or warn them off if they overstepped.

So to whatever four-legged creature that skittered out of sight, he said, *"Pilamaya yelo.* Thank you."

Preacher Pate, the last participant, arrived, stripped down to his royal-blue Speedos and stretched. He slapped his firm abs. "Got to keep what the Lord gave me in good shape. One of the best ways to keep my sweet Juna Marie happy as the Lord intended her to be. Beautiful day for this bit of Indian lore."

Quannah narrowed his eyes. "Yes, it's a beautiful day to live and learn."

He checked the fire blazing before the sweat lodge. With the eyes of nine men—Pate, Rowley, Tulsa, Toru, Inoshi, Samdup and three other monks—upon him, he said, "In the

most traditional ceremonies, a woman who is a personifica-
tion of White Buffalo Calf Woman takes tobacco, goes around
the fire, and leaves a trail of this offering up to the lodge opening. She would also circle the stone pit inside and leave the
last of the tobacco there. Then the lodge would be open to
the participants. However, many times a senior member of the
men's group offers. Samdup has honored us by performing
this sacred task." Quannah nodded at the old monk.

Nara Inoshi, as tall as Quannah, asked, "This White
Buffalo Calf Woman is the one who brought the Sacred
Pipe to your people?"

"Yes, along with instructions for all our ceremonies."

Quannah pulled back the lodge flap and nodded to a
young monk, Rabten, who had been assigned the outside
work of the fire tender and the doorkeeper. "Everyone follow and sit in a circle." Once all were seated and indicated
they were comfortable, Quannah signaled to Rabten. Darkness enveloped the men until Quannah sensed all had
slowed their breathing and had come more in rhythm with
the heartbeat of Mother Earth. He and Samdup brought in
the four glowing stones, stones that seemed to embody life
force so strongly, Quannah greeted each one with, "Hello,
friend—*Hau k'ola*." Softly Quannah gave a brief explanation of the rocks.

"Long ago these were made by the Creator. The images
they reflect within the fire are placed there for your percep-
tion at this moment. Each of you may see images offered
by the Stone People. These stones have been watched over
by Father Sky, energized by the fire from the Standing
People—the trees—that received energy from the sun, a
part of Father Sky. They have rested on Mother Earth; they
are a representation of our oneness with all. Again, there is
purpose here specifically for each of you, which means
each is a recipient of power during this sweat lodge cere-

mony." Quannah touched the water bucket. He poured four full dippers, and steam shot upward.

"And I suppose," Halliwell Pate said, "this is where we ingest peyote to bring about these . . . uh . . . visions."

Quannah had to swallow back anger a few times and remember that such was a widespread misconception. When calm, he said, "There are some tribes who are by law allowed to use the peyote, but the majority of Native Americans never needed such to get in touch with the Creator and the magic and beauty and the many-faceted ways he has of communicating with us Two-leggeds."

"I'm sorry. I truly meant no offense. Really, I did think that's how you would see the spirits within the spirals of steam or smoke or whatever."

"Preacher Pate, I welcome any opportunity to help clarify. You might just open your mind and heart to Great Spirit's messages, just as you would within your church of bricks and cement, stained glass, and padded carpet. Here we are more humble, but just as reverent."

"I'm ready to learn," Preacher Pate said.

"As are we." Nara Inoshi pointed toward Mike Toru with his chin.

Quannah said, "First, we will pray toward *Wiyopeyata*, the West, to thank Great Spirit for the life-giving rains that the water represents and ask that these same droplets flow through to cleanse and refresh us. As our lifeblood—sweat— flows out from us, we shall pray sincerely and ask helpers of Great Spirit to enter the lodge to give encouragement for our prayers and messages for our hearts and minds."

As he spoke, Quannah and the others perspired, giving up symbolical lifeblood. After singing an opening prayer and explaining it, Quannah said, "You will each now introduce yourself to *Wakan Tanka* and the spirit world, beginning with Paul Rowley to my left."

"What do I say?"

"Speak in this womb of Mother Earth as you would to a most trusted loved one. Speak with your heart. Tell Great Spirit—God—who you are, what you want, hope, dream. It might be one sentence; it may be a long discourse. In here there are no church bells to tell you when to start and stop. That is up to what is inside you, what the spirits gathering around us impel you to say."

The steam seemed to gather force. Quannah's ears pricked up to discern Inoshi's slight rasp on his right. Rustling from somewhere outside the lodge directly behind Quannah made him frown. The firekeeper was supposed to stay by the door, not wander around the Inipi lodge. The rustling subsided. Quannah sighed and focused again upon the men in the circle of darkness. Toru's deep breaths seemed to end in a ripple of low growls. Quannah stared at each man, trying to pierce through the outside armor of everyday living, to see beneath the mortal skin, beneath the wary eyes, beneath the bones, to the very heart and inward, further and further to the soul. Was one of these men the honored monk? Was one of them the one who wished that divine personality harm? Quannah swallowed.

No, no, he'd not dissect these men. Not now, not if he could help it.

If Great Spirit demanded he use his lawman's lessons, then so be it, but he would wait for a sign. Otherwise, these men were children and seekers of loving wisdom, of answers to pain whether physical or emotional didn't matter. They had a right within the Inipi to learn as the ceremony opened to them and they to it.

Of course, one side of his mind told him that men had been known to relax and let inhibitions fade while in the darkened womb, and would let out secrets never before shared.

At last Paul Rowley spoke. "*Rooster* Rowley. That's me.

Didn't like that name until these ladies on the island used it. Not proud of its origins, so I guess I'm asking . . . I'm hoping to forgive myself for my temper . . . yeah, my temper. In the past, I've done terrible things. I keep quiet. Bottle up. Most shameful thing was I made a real serious play for this lady in a local bar. Well, that wasn't shameful . . . uh . . . let me see here now."

Quannah said, "Take your time. We will not go on to another speaker until you've told us you are finished. If you pause, it merely gives us time to digest and offer up prayers in between."

Rooster snapped his fingers. "All right. Not a dive, a neighborhood place. We dated. I was real smitten. One night she just up and danced with another cowboy, and right there in front of my friends, said horrible things, and was gonna go home with him. I hit her, knocked her over the bar into a keg of Coors Light. Can't blame the drinking 'cause I hadn't ever cared for the stuff. They called me Rooster. Guess for the crowing and throwing my weight around. Sure wasn't because I got to keep the hen."

The stones sizzled against water as another dipperful added to the steam swirling above them.

Rooster Rowley waved the heat away as if the cowgirl's ghost stood before him. "I broke her nose. Only reason I didn't see the inside of a jail was because she *had been* drinking, had a couple of outstanding tickets, and didn't want to call the police. I came away with a strong distrust of all females. But . . . there are a number of stories I'm not proud of where I lost my temper and had horrible fights with men, usually over some woman . . . yep over some woman. Almost killed a man once. Name stuck with me through near thirty years, and finally someone pointed out Rooster could also be the one that protects. They said I protected all the American ladies here when I served in

Vietnam. Never did touch another lady in anger, and just did my duty in the rice paddles. Anyhow, I sort of like the name now. Guess all females aren't out to be mean and hurtful."

"Ahh." The voice came out as a soft coo and directly behind Quannah.

Samdup nodded his head. "Even the doves outdoors sense what you say is true, Mr. Rowley."

Quannah frowned. *Doves? Right outside the lodge?* He strove to keep his voice calm and had to fight visions of Willi hunkered down doing one of the things she most favored—eavesdropping. Surely not during the ceremony. He'd have one little hen's neck to wring, if so.

He said, "Samdup could be right. The animal world—the *Wamakaskan*—does signal us in unusual ways. It could be as he said. If so, you'll receive more messages from the same animal in the next couple of hours or days. Please continue."

Rooster took a deep breath and pulled the moist air into his lungs. "Gotta fess up something else. I came here because I'm of an age I don't want things gnawing at me, giving me nightmares, making me less than I can be. I've . . . I've hated the Japanese since my dad died at Pearl Harbor. Just see red every time one is near."

To his right, Quannah felt Inoshi shift his weight and Toru's breathy growl grow more intense.

Rooster cleared his throat, reached for his glasses, which he wasn't wearing, and put his hands back in his lap. "After Vietnam, I didn't like being around any person of oriental descent. I want that hate inside me to die. Wars were fought with the political countries, not the individuals. So . . . so that's who I am for now, and what I'm working and praying for while here—peace of mind, yeah some peace of mind. Guess that's a pretty windy tale for someone supposed to be so quiet."

Quannah signaled for the doorkeeper to open the flap
for a moment, to take out the cold stones and return with
four red hot ones. When the flap was closed and water
steamed upon the rocks, the atmosphere now was as hot as
a sauna. Swirls of steam danced about the room, forming
into figures, faces, animals, and signs. At one point he distinctly saw an ephemeral hummingbird that flitted and dissipated as fast as the momentary thought of Willi. Quannah
smiled. At least the vision wasn't one of a dove with head
twitching to hear every word.

He cleared his mind and focused on his duties as leader.
"I offer you each a dipper of water to pour over your head.
This *minne mitak oyasin*—water for all relatives—will take
your sweat into all parts of the earth to all those you wish
to touch." He closed his eyes against the fog.

"Now we offer songs and prayers for the Second Endurance given toward the North, toward *Waziya*. At this
time, we also beat the drum. This represents the heartbeat
of Mother Earth and all our relations upon her. We sing for
courage during this endurance."

Samdup passed out the sage he and Quannah had prepared in small bundles.

"Chew this or just hold it," Quannah said, "as it represents healing and fortifying to help us have the courage to
overcome the evils in the world."

Preacher Halliwell Pate intoned, "And there is much
evil here." As if standing in the pulpit, he allowed his voice
to rise, full and stentorian. "Oh, that the divine eye be upon
us this day, know our deeds and lead us toward his fold.
Lead us toward righteous action. Action *must* be taken
against evil." He drew the word *evil* out as if singing the
word in the Lord's Prayer.

Quannah swallowed and took deep breaths. Each man
had to be allowed to express himself in his own vernacular

within the Inipi. Quannah had the duty to keep all as comfortable as possible. He hoped Preacher Pate was not going to make this ceremony, so unlike that of his Protestant practice, a soapbox to preach about differences rather than an opportunity to embrace the similarities and strengths derived from different cultural expressions.

As the heat grew more pronounced, each person spoke as Rooster Rowley had done. When Mike Toru's deep voice filled the lodge, Quannah sat up straighter.

No, back down. Let the man have his moment of peace within the womb. Just listen. Listen with your heart, not as if you had a hidden microphone among the rocks.

Toru's dialog was clear and well modulated but simple. Like Rooster, he didn't seem used to words. "I understand Mr. Rowley. But, please remember, my family has been Japanese-American for five generations, with the stress on *American*. We, too, hated the Japanese for Pearl Harbor. We hated them, but yet my grandparents were imprisoned here in the United States. Enough said. I seek balance. I want to touch The Eye of the Divine. I want to be blessed."

Quannah frowned and wondered why Toru uttered the Divine Eye as if it were more than a spiritual idea, as if it were something tangible to be perceived with a touch or something to be seen. Could he be the one searching for the honored monk? Quannah shook his head.

Stop it. Don't analyze. Just listen as the lodge leader and nothing more. The badge means nothing here.

At the Third Endurance, a new bucket of water arrived, newly heated stones again transfered carefully by the fire tender. Quannah spoke while quietly beating the drum. "This time we consider the East—*Wiyoheyapa*. During this time we say our prayers for the things we talked about wanting and needing. We say individual prayers out loud. For each member of the lodge, we send power through lifeblood flowing out to all living things, we offer power back to Mother Earth and upward to Father Sky and to the Great Creator himself by presenting them as a child would, earnestly and in good faith. You will end your prayer with *hecatu.*"

"*Hetch Ah-too?*" Nestor Tulsa asked in a raspy voice.

"Yes," Quannah answered, "*Hecetu* simply means *it is so* or *it is done.*" Or you may choose to end it with *Aho*, meaning *Amen.*"

"Each one of these . . . endurances," Rooster said, "makes us dig a little deeper in our gut, get it out there clear for man and God."

Quannah chuckled. "That's one way of putting it. Another might be simply communicating with the Creator, maybe touching souls with others in the lodge."

This time around, Nara Inoshi asked to begin. "I have seen in the swirling vapor a viper weaving back and forth, keeping me back from The Eye That Is Divine."

Quannah sighed. Guess that speaking in capitals about the Divine Eye—the third eye the Buddhists considered within the forehead as a direct connection to the highest spirit—was simply part of the Japanese-American upbringing for those who practiced the religion.

He reminded himself to tell Willi of this idiosyncrasy. She loved details like that. Again she intruded upon his mind in a most pleasant way. He could swear for just a moment that above the smell of sage, above the growing odor of cleansing bodies and the scented steam, he smelled her perfume. What was it called? Intensity? No, that wasn't right. Passion. Yes, but as soon as he'd identified the scent it was no longer there.

Stop it. Stay focused. These men are depending upon you to lead them through this ceremony so they all come out with a sense of community, a sense of personal power, a spiritual experience of cleansing away the vagaries of everyday life, and what was he doing? Rolling around in his own personal emotional knapsack and thinking about Willi's perfume. He allowed one more curlicue of steam to evaporate along with the sweet scent and concentrated on Nara Inoshi's prayer.

Inoshi continued with the viper metaphor. "I would ask help against any such vipers which keep me from the Divine One. To be given the courage and the conviction to do whatever is needed to attain this goal is my request today. On this path of enlightenment we are all warriors. Make me fierce, strong, and successful." He paused a moment before saying "*Aho.*"

Hmm. Quannah wiped sweat from his eyes. *A lot of focused anger in that particular offering. Good thing we're coming to the Fourth Endurance.*

In a soothing voice, he said, "The *itokaga,* or endurance of the south, concentrates on healing and growth. Most of you have already offered ideas that this is what you seek here on Serenity Island. Nestor D. Tulsa, you have not spoken yet. Do you wish to offer something during this last endurance?"

"Yep, I got a thing or two to offer, as you put it. Like Rooster, I daggumwell got issues with the Japs after having watched my mates go down at Pearl Harbor. Scenes like that don't erase with time. My mind tells me these fellers here are straight and okay as they had nothing to do with that era."

He paused to suck in a breath in the laden air. " 'Course, on the other hand, my bet is they still, even after five generations, have relatives over there. Hell, research shows it's true. Also, can't be any healing when they're sneaking around and doing land deals detrimental to the American people, and that's a lot of what that IODD company is up to. Ain't that right, you fellers? Didn't I see you all snooping and digging around near the waterfalls the other day? Care to explain that?"

Mike Toru growled. "That is none of your business."

"We thought," Nara Inoshi said, "you were not going to be reporting."

Rooster rubbed his eyes. "Nestor D., you did tell us you weren't going to be printing nothing in black-and-white, not going to be taking pictures and all the rest."

Quannah said, "Nestor, perhaps a discussion of that type might be better served outside the Inipi."

"Right. What I meant to say was I want to heal, but I'm one that's got to have straight answers. I'd like to have a calm sit-down with you two fellers, if you were of a mind to answer some questions like why you been out at night on the island digging in certain places, things like that. You looking for minerals? You making tests? You planting bombs? A little honesty might lead to a little healing, if you get my drift."

Quannah's ears twitched. *Digging?* Great Spirit, what was going on with that?

Samdup's voice broke into the darkness of smoke and steam. "These gentlemen have permission to take a few of our garden specimens back to their IODD rooftop garden. It is part of their sharing this week of healing and balance with all of the hundreds of coworkers who could not attend."

"Humph." Nestor D. folded his arms. But, the ornery newshound that he was, seemed content now that he'd dropped a dynamite blast among the group, and he remained silent.

When Quannah looked around, almost all held the same body stance, except for the monks, whose hands rested with palms up on their legs.

Samdup offered a closing prayer in Tibetan, Inoshi offered one in Japanese, which got a ruffled response of "told you so" from Nestor D.

Quannah offered up a prayer similar to one he'd heard Eagleman, Ed McGaa, a friend and shaman, give many times. "May Great Spirit's light surround us. May the love of *Wakan Tanka* embrace us. Let the Creator's power protect us as God watches over us. Wherever we are, the Great Spirit is. *Han Hecetu. Aho.*"

All repeated the end of the prayer, and despite Nestor D.'s digs, seemed content and renewed as they left the lodge in a clockwise manner, beginning with the first person to the right of the entrance, Samdup.

Each man washed in water the monks had prepared, then they changed into clean clothes. Finally, Quannah led them in a shortened version of the pipe ceremony before allowing them to replenish their bodies with coolers and mineral water. As the last act, Quannah placed a bowl of food and a bowl of water some distance from the Inipi hut as an offering to those spirits who made their presence known.

When he made a final circle around the hutch, he again caught the distinct scent of Passion perfume. Almost immediately, the odor drifted away on the breeze. He shook his head. Was the scent real or imagined, one sent by the totem spirits as a message? And what possible message could that perfume scent have that was important to this gathering? He shook his head, his mind already filling with the duties of the trail ride, which lay ahead for the next couple of hours. He grinned. By Great Eagle's tail feathers, he was of a mind to enjoy the heck out of the day, seeing as how Willi would be riding by his side at least part of the time.

CHAPTER
7

Twenty minutes later, Quannah grinned from ear to ear. He tilted his summer hat back to reveal a red bandanna around his head before he patted the neck of Willi's paint pony. "Pretty little thing, isn't he?"

"Pretty."

Willi slurred the word. Most communication had been made in monosyllables since he'd held her foot to help her into the saddle. She studied the moves of Kenzie and Juna Marie, both who seemed to be accomplished western riders. Hopefully, she could just follow their lead today even if she were atop a muscle-bound animal, a creature with shoulders that rippled underneath her now, legs that could race and could throw her off like a bothersome piece of fluff.

Quannah patted her knee and tickled it. "I have to go up ahead awhile to break through and lead. We men at the front will jaw and let you ladies have a little morning time together. Unless . . . unless . . . you'd rather ride up front

with me; we'll ride like *T'ate*—the Wind. We might have
some considering the way those clouds are gathering."

"The wind . . . uh . . . no . . . no. Here. I'm fine right
here." Willi loosened her stranglehold on the reins and kept
as still as she possibly could atop the hoofed beast.

Quannah touched knees with her, bent over, and gave
her one of those toe-curling kisses. For a moment, she figured she could just float above the saddle for the day,
but . . . he broke the connection and sighed. She again perceived tough saddle leather beneath her, cushioned only by
a bright blue and red blanket.

He said, "Sweetbrier may be a small horse but he's one
of the fastest and the most sure-footed."

"Fastest?"

"I want only the best for my lady."

"Thanks, Lassiter, not that I need any special care."

"Absolutely not. Knew from the moment I saw you, you
were an animal person."

"Really?"

"Sure, *Winyan.* All animals are drawn to you. Children,
too. That's a sign that you're basically a good person, despite all the rumors to the contrary."

She smirked at him. "Oh, you ornery man. Get on with
you."

Well, yeah, sure, she was an animal lover, but that didn't
mean she had to be in close proximity to each species to
love it. Crocs were good at a distance, sort of like snakes.
She considered the ground far below her. Smallest mount,
right. And fast? Not good.

To Sweetbrier she said, "Just slow and easy today. Pretend you're a turtle, okay, a slow and pokey turtle." As if
she were in the store commercial and using her hands to
say, "Open, open," she made the motions toward the horse
while mouthing, "Turtle, turtle."

"Girlfriend," Kenzie said from a few inches above her. "Horsy, horsy, not turtle, turtle."

"I know *that.*"

"Hey, you could have fooled me."

"Kenzie?"

"What?"

"Kenzie . . . oh . . ."

"Oh my gosh. Are those tears in your eyes? You and Quannah have a fight?"

"I can't . . ."

"Can't what?"

Willi wiped at her eyes and squared her shoulders. "I can't ride."

"Ah, you don't know how to . . . why didn't you tell Quannah?"

Willi sent Kenzie a quelling look. "Duh-uh."

Juna Marie sidled up to them. "Couldn't help overhearing. Of course, you couldn't tell him. You'd feel like you'd failed him when this is his forté. You want to shine in his eyes. Is that it?"

"I gave up a day on the motorboat and . . . and . . . Dr Pepper!"

Kenzie said, "Got to be true love. Okay, we'll help you. Guys are going to be up front most of the morning, anyhoo; right, Juna Marie?"

"Yes, and no time like the present because we're about to start off. These are well-trained horses, so you don't have to do anything but give them a hint of what you want. So right up there we're going to take the left side like the men, so you'll first of all look left, which will turn your body that way, then lay the reins over the neck toward the left. Gently does it."

A few moments later, they were to pass through slow-moving water of an arroyo. Seeing that, Willi's heartbeat picked up speed as if she were closer to facing a typhoon.

Kenzie on one side, Juna Marie on the other, the latter said, "See, the men are going three abreast, so we'll simply do the same. Don't change the pace. The horse will pick out where to step as needed. Trust Sweetbrier."

A few more twists and turns and Willi smiled. "Thanks, ladies. I might actually survive this day."

As the swanlike Juna Marie moved off, she said, "Of course, you will. And if you don't feel like cantering, just say so. Men are generally pretty good to us on the trails and will accept any little tale, no pun intended. Let them assume away, and keep a slow, steady pace with which you're comfortable."

For some time, Willi rode beside Kenzie. In a meadow, she bent down along Sweetbrier's neck and hugged him. "The one thing I do like about this are the smells of the leather, the horse scent, the breeze."

"Well, girl, we're going to be getting wet with that breeze before long. Look at those black clouds. Must be why Quannah turned us around on that last curve. We've only gone half the ride. Come on, or we're gonna lose them, and I don't want to miss whatever Jamyang brought for lunch."

Just as they got to a Y, the left leading toward the others, the right to who knew where, thunder boomed. It didn't frighten Sweetbrier, but it did scare the bejesus out of Willi, who jerked the reins and tightened her legs, which sent Sweetbrier on the right side path, and at a full run.

"Ahhhh."

She leaned forward and grabbed hold of the saddle horn and some of Sweetbrier's mane. Her legs seemed to have a life of their own, flapping up and down in the stirrups. Behind her—far behind her—Kenzie's yelps rose up. Some other sound drowned her instructions out. Probably the rush of blood through Willi's ears, the pounding of her heart choking her esophagus, the thunder and dry lightening searing the horizon.

Some instinct told her that lying down and outward over the horse would tell it through body language that she wanted it to go forward fast. Somehow, she had to straighten up and put on the brakes. And quickly! A monster waterfall was coming up ahead. Jerking like a marionette, she managed to sit up straighter. Frantically, she grabbed for the twisted reins, pulled backward, and yelled, "Whoa, whoa, Sweetbrier, whoa!"

Sweetbrier obeyed her commands, as he had all day. He didn't completely rump it down to the ground, but pretty close. Kenzie drew up alongside. Through clenched teeth she said, "Girl, are you crazy?"

Quannah reined up beside them. "Willi, what a ride! Saw you two just as you took off. Can't blame you for wanting to race the wind. Wow!" His eyes were bright, his bronze cheeks flushed, and his ponytail loosened so his hair flowed outward as the wind whipped it around his face. "You were magnificent, Willi."

"Magnificent . . . uh-huh." Did that equate to scared shitless? "Uh . . . thanks."

Kenzie said, "Hey, guys, what's that?"

"That," Quannah answered, "is the old causeway they used to drive across from the island to the ranch mainland. It's still passable in good weather, but has had too many mudslides during floods, so it's off limits. Also, through the years, the Guadalupe has eroded into separate areas, so there's really no connection to the mainland even if you get across to the waterfall side. Only way to get to the island is to dock on the far side, where you all did."

"Looks overgrown, but still four lanes of paved way, though a bit marked with potholes," Willi said. "Jeeps could probably still traverse it. The waterfall to the side is beautiful."

"More than likely why they had the causeway there in the first place. It made for such a lovely entrance. See, there's the remains of the old gate on this side of the crossing." Sure enough, the red paint of the intricately designed wood peeled and blistered, but yet held to some spots.

Nara Inoshi reined in beside them. "The waterfalls in Tibet and Japan are considered powerful energizers, convectors for great spiritualism, if you will. The history of this island since the monks have been here indicate that that is why they first had the entrance there."

Willi peered at his serious face. "So that when you entered, you were immediately in a holy setting?"

Inoshi nodded. His only concession to western wear was leather boots. Black tapered riding pants, not jeans, and a white shirt completed his day's ensemble. Around his neck he wore a gold medallion. He smiled as he caught Willi's glance at it. Taking it off, he showed it to the three. "My great-grandfather received it from his father who passed it on down until now I have the symbol. It is the Buddhist symbol for enlightenment."

Kenzie sighed. "It is mesmerizing and . . . and comforting."

Willi and Inoshi said, "The medallion?"

Kenzie shook her head. "Oh, it's very beautiful, but . . . I meant . . . the waterfall. Looks like there's a cave back behind the fall."

Inoshi's eyes narrowed as if trying to see what she did. "Not according to the island's history. There's only a backdrop of stone, no cave." Yet, like Kenzie, he continued to stare with quiet intensity at the frothing curtain. He shook himself and smiled, a gesture that gave his face charm and approachability. "The moving water and its importance in life has been carried down through many cultures, more recently coming to the United States as part of the feng shui philosophy. For many years our IODD Corporation has decorated offices with the ideas of feng shui in order to ensure productivity, success, and harmony in business."

Willi said, "Yes, it's made inroads into many homes and businesses. I guess that's why the stone waterfalls at entryways and chimes above stairs and such have become the mode of the day."

"Exactly so, Willi Gallagher."

"I have to fess up," Willi added. "I've used some of those ideas at home. For example, months ago I couldn't sleep well, happened to have read a book on some weekend changes to be made in your home environment with feng shui, and . . ."

"You don't have waterfalls, do you?"

"Not yet. But . . . I had my radio, CD player, and electric clock in one of the shelves in the headboard of my bed. The book said all those negative waves would interfere with sleep and to place them farther from the bed and facing away from it. I also moved the bed so that it wasn't facing the open door."

"And did that sweeten your dreamtime?" Quannah asked.

"I still have my nightmares sometimes, but I can sleep a whole night through without getting up, fidgeting, checking doors and windows. It really has made for some kind of balance, even though I don't understand it."

Inoshi, eyes still trying to pierce the curtain of noisy water, raised his voice and said, "The changes allowed the *chi,* the life force, to flow through in a way that cleanses and renews the energy of the room. Therefore, you feel more at ease and can rest better."

"Hmm. Interesting," Kenzie said, soaking up every word up with bright lights in her eyes. "Could I borrow—?"

"My book on feng shui?" finished Willi. "You bet."

Quannah reined his horse around. "Best be getting back to midday camp. At least there's a covered picnic area if we have to stay due to rain. 'Course we'll move out in light rain; have to be a gully-washer to keep us off-trail."

Willi hugged Sweetbrier and turned him around. " 'Gully-washer'? I've heard that all my life, but it never had much meaning before now. Wouldn't be a pretty picture if that causeway gave, right?"

"Not if we're caught out in the open. It'd flood the lower part of the island, but not the monk's pagoda areas; those are on high ground like the mainland over there."

"Yeah," Kenzie said, "I see what you mean."

Willi rode between Quannah and Kenzie back toward the campsite. "If we got a lot of rains, wouldn't the Guadalupe River cover most of this island like it did some years ago?"

"Sure." Quannah sat so easily in the saddle he seemed an extension of the horseflesh beneath him. "That has happened . . . oh, some five years ago, but you have to have a combination."

"Combination?" Willi asked.

"Lots of heavy rain for many days without a break."

"And that's not a usual scenario."

"Nope. Not usually." He twisted in the saddle and grinned at her. "Of course, strange things happen around you, *Winyan*."

"Around me? Ha! Case of the pot calling the kettle black!"

"Good thing we trust each other, huh?"

Kenzie shrugged her shoulders and moved beside the

two. At last Inoshi finished his scrutiny of the waterfall to follow along behind.

Willi frowned, "What do you mean by that trust thing?"

Quannah halted his bay. "I mean, trust is good, and I trust you. How about you, Gallagher?"

"Well, yes, I do . . . but I don't know how you can say you do after . . . after last night!"

She jerked Sweetbrier around. He snorted at the rough treatment. "Men."

Quannah raised an eyebrow as he easily cantered the bay past her. "What's going on?" He directed the question to Kenzie, too.

Kenzie took a deep breath, opened her mouth, closed it, and shrugged. Peering at both, she tried again. "Maybe . . . maybe a little time together . . . sharing. Yes, sharing, would help clear the air."

Quannah loped back toward Willi. "*Winyan,* I know there are uh . . . balance . . . issues we must face. Be easier were we to face them together. I know you're not used to that, maybe even afraid of trusting." He tapped her nose. "Know what?"

"What?" She moved her nose higher in the air.

"I'm afraid of that, too. Only one promise I can make." He took hold of Sweetbrier's reins and pulled Willi's left knee to his right. "I'll make this promise." He allowed Kenzie and Inoshi to move past them.

When they cantered by he repeated, "I'll make one promise. Anything, any part of you that you share, any idea that you entrust to me will be handled with care and thoughtfulness. I will never, ever on purpose abuse any trust you place in me."

"Or think less of me for anything I tell you about past or present. Sure. Right. And jalapeños don't exist in Texas."

He didn't say a word, just took her chin and tilted it until their glances locked. For a half minute, he held that one finger in place. Her heartbeat slowed, the flush left her cheeks, she calmed and sighed.

At last, he murmured above the wind, "If we are to be together, it is to be a melding in some ways. In others we will be totally apart, but never *alone* as far as support goes. And, yes, Wilhelmina Gallagher, anything and everything."

"Then maybe we'd better start with—" Lightening seared across the sky, striking a tree in the far distance, the boom ricocheting in the electric atmosphere.

"Gallagher, Kenzie, ride for the camp! Inoshi, come on!"

For once, Willi did as asked without more questions. Just as they tied the horses underneath a copse of live oaks and limestone outcropping, Father Sky emptied the water flasks above. Must have been big ones and lots of them. A limestone fireplace backed the enclosed picnic area so they were dry. While they chowed down on Jamyang's salads, fresh fruits, and crusty bread, Willi considered the participants and their reasons for wanting mental and spiritual balance in the hectic modern world.

Rooster Rowley sat beside Kenzie and both talked with Mike Toru. What a good sign. Rooster wanted to stop his feelings of hatred toward the Japanese for his father's death; he seemed to be truly trying to reach out. Maybe, he'd be able to give up some of his Vietnam angst, too. *Bless him and help him.* She offered up a heartfelt prayer for him and all those who'd fought in those wars. Willi sidled closer to listen unabashedly. She was not eavesdropping; she preferred to believe she just simply had an intense and sincere concern for her fellow folks.

Rooster spoke around a bite of fresh peach. "Yeah, I

was a hellion in past days. Lots of fights. Into bikes and bikers and biker bars."

"You?" Kenzie asked. "You're so calm, so . . . non-aggressive."

"Learned my lesson, I guess. Lady down in Schertz, Texas, decided to play me the fool. I really fell for her; figured she was the one I'd be with the rest of my life. We went in a Mexican restaurant in the town over, New Braunfels, believe it was called."

"You proposed to her over fajitas and guacamole?" Willi jumped into the conversation and edged closer.

"No. I proposed to her like any good biker some nights before while we were underneath the neon lights of our group's hangout—Bandits and Boobs."

"And," Willi added, "guzzling Coors?"

"No ma'am, not me. Never did care for the beer. Nope, never did. Never even been drunk. I was sober when I proposed. She'd said yes."

"Back to New Braunfels, feller." Kenzie prodded.

"Dadgum fool two tables over from us kept trying to make eye contact with her. Finally, he did, and she winked back and said, 'hi sugar,' to him. To *him,* she said 'hi' and 'sugar'." Rooster stretched. "I shouldn't be going over this old stuff. Happened years ago. Yeah, years ago."

Willi and Kenzie both leaned toward him as did Mike Toru, who said, "No, man, you have to finish. Don't leave us hanging like that. Is this like a different episode than the one you shared in the Inipi?"

"Yeah. That was right after Vietnam. This time was only a few years ago."

"Well, go on. Might help someone else handle life if you tell how you made it through a hard time." Toru seemed embarrassed by his words and became silent. Willi figured not too many disobeyed Toru's requests.

Rooster sighed, took off his glasses, and pinched the bridge of his nose. "If that would have been the end of it, it'd been fine. But, the jerk starts making real lewd remarks, real personal remarks that let me know he'd been with Larisandi, remarks that tell me she'd been and still was with other guys. Didn't believe one word of it. Hell, I called him out for it. Idiot that I was. Yeah, I was a damned fool."

"You mean you busted his ass, right?" Mike Toru slapped Rooster on the shoulder.

"When I stood, he threw the first punch. People say there are times you just see red, the color red, when you're out-of-control angry. That was the time for me. I must've used my hand like a sledgehammer. Hit him once in return, but . . ."

"But?" Kenzie asked, gently taking his glasses from his knotted fist. She wiped them clean and set them back on the bridge of his nose.

He straightened them. "He died right there. Luckily, twenty witnesses testified that he had thrown the first punch, or I'd be wearing Texas's orange prison jumpsuits and cleaning the side of Highway 281."

"Afterward, what then?" Willi asked.

"Found out the truth about Larisandi. Why, she'd even been with someone the night I had proposed to her. Well, it changed me. I don't . . . won't use my fists to fight. I don't care too much for womenfolk, present ladies excepted."

"I imagine," Willi said, "we're a handful for you to stomach after such an experience. Trust is hard to earn again." She looked at Quannah, who winked in her direction, and she smiled back. How lucky she was. Now, if she could just learn to trust *completely* and not end up with this relationship in a psychiatrist's blender.

Willi snapped her fingers. "Was that what you talked to Nestor D. Tulsa about last night?"

Now it was Mike Toru's and Rooster's turn to sit up straighter. They eyed each other. Both of them glanced over at the Pates and back down at the table. "It was nothing," mumbled Rooster. "We got everything explained today."

Toru pushed himself off the stone bench of their picnic table. "Think we're to saddle up in about a quarter hour and try to beat the next row of clouds home." He nodded at Willi. "You did some fierce riding there before lunch. No wonder Quannah calls you that name."

"Miss Marple of the Range?"

"Yeah, because of your skills on horseback, right?"

Kenzie laughed and punched Willi's arm. "Ha! Not likely, the truth be known. He gave her that name because she's like Agatha Christie's Miss Marple, always snooping for clues and ghosts and such."

"I do not snoop. I have more important things to do right now. To put it delicately, I'd better find a bush somewhere before riding back."

"I'll go along," Kenzie said. Willi tramped off behind the granite outcropping and some hundred yards behind before finding adequate cover. Kenzie took her turn, and trailed behind Willi on the way back. She said, "Wrong way."

Willi grimaced. "I hate when I get turned around. Now we'll have to fight our way out of these brambles." She scrambled over jutting stones, exposed tree roots, and sticker patches. She held a branch back for Kenzie, misjudged, and turned it loose too soon. Like a switch, the branch sliced across Kenzie's head and knocked her down. Twisting about to try to correct her action, Willi lost her balance, ended up sliding down backasswards until an anthill loomed up to cushion her fall. She stood, doing a foot-stomping routine Quannah would have said was *lila waste*. She sat on a rock, raised her jeans leg, and scratched faster than a dog's hind leg dealing with fleas.

Kenzie, her hand over a welt above her eye, sat beside her. "Oh, yeah, this is in balance with nature. It doesn't get any better than this."

"I know you really meant to say *worse,* and I agree. Look." Willi pointed to what showed beneath some of the rocks her tumble had knocked away. A white shoe, similar to the dress shoes Mr. Yodo wore with his white summer suit, lay crumpled as if the Wicked Witch of the West had waved an avalanche wand over him. On hands and knees, Willi crept closer.

Kenzie shied back. "Don't touch it. It could have, you know . . . inside it."

"A rotting foot. No doubt." Willi sniffed. "You can smell that sick-sweet stench. Hmm. Ought to be stronger than that, and seems like all the creepy crawlies would be making high trails this way. Hmm."

"Ooooh." Kenzie took several steps away. "Is it Mr. Yodo, again?"

"Looks like his shoe. But . . . Samdup said he was transported back to the mainland this morning. Someone lied."

"You think?"

"Go get Quannah. I'm not leaving this time until someone sees this."

A half hour later, after removing the rocks from all around, all that was discovered was a second shoe—white and scuffed and with a sickly smell upon it—but nothing inside it, human or otherwise. Everyone, including Quannah, stood with hands to the small of their backs, and then stretched. "Okay, no mystery here, folks. Just a pair of shoes, probably floated down in the last high river water and got stuck in these rocks."

Willi, with hands on her hips, sighed. "No mystery? Did you say no mystery? I think there's a mystery. Look at what's drawn on that shoe." She pointed to a depiction of the third eye, one similar to those on all the brochures they'd received about the Zen retreat, one exactly like the Eye of the Divine painting in the Mimosa Teahouse.

Quannah slapped the shoes into her open hands. "Those are just scratches made by the rocks. You're letting that wonderful imagination of yours stretch a bit, maybe?"

"I don't think so. These seem deeper and deliberate."

Kenzie and Rooster studied the shoes. Both shook their heads. Kenzie said, "I think Quannah might have a point, but . . . it wouldn't hurt to keep the shoes, just in case something else shows up."

Willi had to be satisfied with that. She allowed Quannah to help her back in the saddle, tied the shoelaces, and hung the white dress shoes across the pommel. Out of the corner of her eye, she swore she could see in the shadow of the trees now and again the flitting round figure of Charlie Chan . . . or . . . Mr. Yodo. Okay, she knew that *was* her imagination, but the eye *drawn, etched, depicted on purpose* on the left shoe was not her imagination. A talk with Samdup or Jamyang might be in order when they returned.

A discussion of the day's koan, along with an explanation of many of the accoutrements of Buddhism—the prayer wheel, the cloths, the cymbals, the incense—took up their evening session. Quannah went to see to the needs of the stock and to prepare for the individual rides planned for tomorrow. As he turned to leave, he quietly asked Willi, "What exactly does this Harry Cormack look like?"

"Jerry. It's Jerry Cormack, and why do you ask?"

"One of these days, *Winyan,* you will not answer a question with a question."

She described Kenzie's stalker of an ex. "Now, the reason you asked?"

Quannah shook his head. "Oh, just thought I saw someone near your pagoda last night, thought about what you'd said concerning his obsessive behavior and figured he'd be the most likely candidate except for—"

"Except for—?"

"The tight security at the ranch on Serenity Island."

"Part of the security which you helped install, set up, and such?"

"Yes." His eyes narrowed, and his tone of voice warned her, but she stepped over the hot coals anyway.

"Even though you are the best of the bestest, feller—and I mean that sincerely, Lassiter—couldn't there be some tiny flaw overlooked, or one instance a security guard might have had a head turned at just the wrong time? Isn't there a possibility that Jerry Cormack could have slipped onto the island?"

Quannah's shoulders slumped and he sighed.

Willi sighed in turn and wished she'd not added to the weight on those broad shoulders. Then again, she seemed to breathe a bit easier. Her bunched neck muscles relaxed. "Guess, it's only fair to let you know that Kenzie and I found Jerry Cormack's business card down by the boathouse." Willi explained how she'd told Kenzie the card had probably just stuck to her luggage; nothing more sinister than that.

Quannah bent down nose-to-nose with her. "You're a good friend, Willi, to take that worry on and to ease Kenzie's mind. We'll both watch out for her. After all, it could as easily have been Preacher Pate or that Skeeter fellow or anyone, for that matter, and they might not have been sneaking around. They could have simply been trying to see their lady, just like I did the other night. Until we know, just be on orange alert, okay?"

"You got it. You, too."

He huffed. "Uh. Goes without saying for me."

She put her hands on her hips. "Yes, right. I just wanted to say it, you know?"

He grinned and shrugged his shoulders before pulling her into an embrace, planting a kiss on the top of her head. "Gallagher."

"What?"

"It's nice to hear it . . . in your voice."

"It?"

"The concern."

She snuggled in closer. "Any time, feller. Hmm, you smell like horse and hay, zing of mixed sunshine and rain."

"These are a few of your favorite things, I hope, as you'll be smelling them a lot through life."

She smiled and hugged him hard. "Through life. Ahh. I like that." After a few moments of properly punctuating their cooing with kisses, they parted.

A quarter hour before suppertime, willi sauntered away from the others. She wandered down toward the boat dock while she used a scarf to wipe off the perspiration. How she wished she had one of Sheriff Brigham Tucker's huge bandannas right now. He had insisted she take some, but they were in her suitcase. She could at least use one to hold back the soaked bangs from her forehead.

The night heron, generally still during the daylight, swooped in front of her. She twisted around. He landed on an eye-level branch and cocked his head. Into her mind came Quannah's words: "Be on orange alert." For Quan-

nah, orange alert involved being aware of the animal
world's messages, too.

"Okay, Mr. Heron. What's up this path more important
than what I might discover around the boathouse? I'll bite
this once. Better be something. Best not be anybody hearing this one-sided conversation, either. They'll leave me on
this island forever." She glanced over her shoulder and
clamped a hand over her mouth.

As she stepped around a bend, the daylight disappeared,
blocked out by a grove of giant oaks—venerable ones. The
night heron perched on a branch that brushed the edge of
the wooden walkway surrounding all four sides of the rock
garden. What late afternoon light came through the trees,
reflected off the thirty-by-thirty-foot raked ocean of white
stones. Raked in such a way that there were swirls, circles,
straight rows, angled levels . . . and not one footprint to
give a hint of the beginning or the end of the design. At
three different areas, giant stones stood in proud groupings.

The texture of wood banister beneath her hand, the
sense of looking out at sea as she moved along the five-foot-
wide covered walk, the sight of the wise night heron, gave
Willi more balance than she'd had in the whole of her full
day on Serenity Island.

An absolute sense of oneness with all life surrounded
her for a few precious moments. She emptied her mind of
everything—the boat capsizing, finding Mr. Yodo passed
out, the visions, the quarry entry by the waterfalls, the koan
of the day, Cormack's card, Juna Marie's liplocks with
who knew whom, the purpose of the IODD businessmen,
the treasure hunt. . . . all and everything faded, passed her
in a miasmic cloud and drifted to another realm. Her mind
and heart were at complete peace.

She sat on one of the low wooden benches where she
leaned her head on the top of the banister and looked be-

tween the wide rails at the calm sea, the great islands of landmasses here and there. All was as it should be there, so all was as it should be in the world as well. She sighed down to her toes and smiled.

Wait a minute. *What . . . what was that?*

Slowly, she rose, put her foot on the bottom rail, and stood with both hands holding the banister, elbows locked. None of the other rocks . . . glowed. Yes, *glowed* was the word. Some of the rocks did glisten with a bit of the dampness of recent rains, some of them had minerals in them that gave off a shine, but this rock, somewhere in the middle of those giant islands to the left, definitely *glowed.* Green. She frowned.

"There wasn't really such a thing as kryptonite right?" She eyed the night heron still quietly considering her. "Talking to the damned birds and wondering about kryptonite. And I thought I was in balance. Oh my God."

She shut her eyes. No reason whatsoever for her to *have* to find out what that was. Probably it'd turn out to be nothing more than something else blown hither by the storm. Well . . . well . . . it could be a piece of jewelry, something important to someone. Yeah, so she should try to get to the object. Why, it was practically a civic duty. Okay, so that's what she'd do. She got up on the wide banister, one knee balanced there, and reached out with the other leg and foot.

"Shoot fire. The actual garden is three feet below. Well there has to be a way in there. How else can the gardener or artist or whatever they're called do that design in the stones?" She glared at her feathered friend. "Don't suppose you'd show me the entryway?"

The night heron's eyes blinked, he turned his head now to search for prey. Soon he sighted some morsel and off he flew. She struggled upright to run down the steps to the right. There had to be an opening . . . and a rake . . . the best instrument needed to find out why one rock among all others started glowing green just as darkness set in. She opened the gate that allowed her to move into an enclosed tool area beneath the above walk around.

Perfecto.

Once inside, she could peer out the wood latticework toward the garden and also the opposite side. On the side facing the land of pebbles and stones another small door allowed access to the sunken rock garden. Well, Hells Bells, she couldn't just stroll out there and grab whatever glinted. She'd mess up the raked pebble design, which would alert others to her maneuvers. With hands outstretched she located two instruments, one a rake, the other a long-handled claw.

Doble perfecto!

She cracked open the gate on the garden side. With muscles taut, she stretched to her limit with the grabber in hand. A couple feet short! Damn it! She tiptoed two steps outward while trying to stay in the narrow raked ruts. One heel came down on a row to leave a small imprint. Shoot! She eased the claw over to the rocks where the green shined, used the pressure handle three or four times before finally grasping the shining rock, brought it toward her in a tight grasp, backed carefully out of the garden area and back underneath the walkway before loosening her hold.

Oh my gosh. A cell phone.

Of course, the LCD light showed up at darkfall. Somebody just didn't want to do without communication even though phones were banned from Serenity Island. Well, to hell with that. What was good for one was right for all. The turkey, whoever it was. As the phone had a flip-down lid, she slid it into her jeans' pocket. Wait. What if it rang while on her? Everyone would think it was hers. She grasped it, opened the front, and pushed the power button off. She blinked at the depiction on the screen just before the green glow disappeared: a drawing—scratched into the silver surface—of the third eye, *The Eye That Is Divine*. She shook her head and repocketed the phone. Hmm. Weirder and weirder.

Oh, jeez. Why'd she have to see that eye? Before that moment she would simply have taken the phone to Samdup and turned it in. But . . . but what if it were tied to the strange happenings on the island? For example, the unexplained presence roaming around the pagodas at night, the fainting spell of Mr. Yodo, his subsequent disappearance—maybe permanent, if those were his white shoes they recovered. And what about the emotions seething beneath the sincere attempts to regain spiritual balance, strength, and tolerance? Something going on with Rooster Paul Rowley, and obviously the Pates—Preacher and Juna Marie—had some issues. And Quannah hinted that the Japanese-American men might have a hidden agenda, too.

So, what to do? Turn the phone in? Keep it? For what purpose?

She stumbled over a tree root, righted herself, and realized she'd been in a miasma since she'd pocketed the cell phone. Good grief, had she put the rake up, the claw, and shut all the little gates? Surely, she had. The night heron swooped in front of her nose so closely his wings created an air lift.

"Okay, okay. You led me to the dang thing for a reason."

She peered over her shoulder. All she'd need now would be Preacher Pate jumping out from the bushes and hearing her talking to the night fowl. Fine. Fine. Every damned thing was damned fine. She would keep the phone, maybe discuss it with Kenzie—and Quannah, sure Quannah, eventually—and see what they could come up with before handing it over to Samdup. It wasn't like anyone was going to be able to use it in the meantime. What could it possibly hurt?

With that settled, she headed toward the Mimosa Teahouse and the wonderful smells of steamed vegetables and wild rice wafting outward. A fig tree's leaves, whipped up by a sudden wind, lashed out at her just as she reached the pagoda steps. A sharp ozone stung her nose, driving away the enticing aromas and making goosebumps curlicue down her neck. She rushed up the steps. A good girl talk was what she needed now.

Kenzie pulled her into the circle at a table with Rowley and Nestor D. Tulsa. "Girlfriend, you look like ghosts are chasing you."

Willi nodded. "Sort of seemed that way, too. There's a strange nip to the air."

"That's 'cause we're in for a heavy thunderstorm tonight," Nestor D. said.

Willi leaned over and whispered to Kenzie. "We need to talk."

Kenzie seemed not to notice the urgency in Willi's voice and said with a hand lightly touching Rowley's shoulder, "Rooster said the same thing. Guess you Navy men have an eye for the weather."

Rooster and Nestor D. grinned. Rooster said, "More like a nose. Willi's right. There's a sharpness to the air and the pressure is falling, has been all day." He frowned through clean lenses.

Kenzie had been up to her magic. Willi sighed. Maybe Paul Rooster Rowley was working a bit of magic, too, if the glint in Kenzie's eyes was an indication. Oh, well, they'd talk as soon as the meal was over.

Willi asked Rooster, "So, a little storm shouldn't worry a fellow like you used to the sea and the elements, right?"

He squinted at the huge picture windows. "Don't particularly care to face a huge storm on this island. That Guadalupe River has been known to travel some mighty powerful ways."

At that moment, Father Sky chose to unleash upon Mother Earth a torrential blast of water, a silver sheet of rain, a killing tempest of a downpour. Lights flickered. Three monks skittered to each table with humongous foot-wide candles along with individual votives. The front door opened. The wind literally blew the Pates inside. They had on matching outfits again, this time in baby blue with white-and-blue striped sweaters that they held up to tent over their heads.

Preacher Pate nodded and asked, "Two more places available for me and my Juna Marie?"

Everyone scooted around on the pillows to make room. Juna Marie seated herself beside Rooster. Their shoulders touched. Juna Marie flashed a winning smile his way and he grinned back. "Ma'am." He inched back as if wanting to say, "Keep your distance, now, keep your distance."

She patted his arm. "Don't 'ma'am' me. Juna Marie's the name. We talked earlier today. Don't you remember? When you ladies went gallivanting on those ponies, and Halliwell talked with Nestor D., Paul Rowley kept me fine company."

Halliwell Pate narrowed his eyes, reached around his wife's shoulder to pat Rowley on the back before he said, "Right neighborly of you. But, she's got her feller here now, yes, indeedy."

Although the words were right and seemed like light banter, Willi shivered. Something about the tone of voice seemed threatening. And what in Hades was wrong with Kenzie? She'd put a full pillow's width between her and Rooster, pulled a face longer than a giraffe's reaching for the last nibble of grass, and frowned.

Thunder roared like an Amtrak through the teahouse,

shaking the walls. Juna Marie screeched and reached out
for Rooster's arm on one side and Halliwell Pate's on the
other. "Oh, I'm sorry. My nerves are just too fragile for
these kinds of storms."

Mike Toru and Nara Inoshi came in alongside the
cousins, Doretta and Banjo Joe Skeeter. All were fairly dry
underneath a huge plastic tarp Mike and Nara held over the
group. They sat at the next table over. Jamyang took the
yellow plastic to the back of the room and draped it over
one of the round tables to dry. He then returned to set out
the steamed oriental vegetables and, to Willi's delight, an
American classic—onion-filled cornbread pones—for an
accompaniment. A side dish of chilled green salad with
ranch dressing made for a few minutes of appreciative silence. This was another one of those moments when Willi
felt in balance, as if the world were truly a peaceful and
giving place and as if she truly lived for this moment. She
was not *wobbling*.

Kenzie broke into her thoughts. "Like the Eye of the Divine is upon us."

"What?" Willi asked.

Kenzie pointed to the beautiful etched third eye depicted upon the shining wood of the wall. "We're in the
here and now. Don't you feel it? The Eye of the Divine is
not just there on the wall, but right here." She tapped the
middle of her forehead. "At this moment we're part of each
other, one with the storm, at peace with this minute in
time."

Willi eyed Juna Marie carrying on a conversation with
Rowley and with Nara at the next table. "Hm. Really? For
a minute there, I thought maybe that green-eyed monster
rather than the divine had taken over."

"Nope. If he wants to make a fool of himself over someone else's wife, then that's his business. I'm worth more than serving as a side dish to someone else's entrée. Speaking of which, this is delicious."

Willi grinned. "You don't fool me with that cool act. Bet you'd like to slap one silly, flirtatious Juna Marie upside the head."

"How can you say that, girl? Especially after her helping you with the riding today?"

"I didn't say she hasn't had her sincere and nice moments. She's being sweet right now, trying to include a shy man in a conversation. But I don't think it's totally for nice. Partly, it's just what she probably does as a preacher's wife, but in this case, I think the overtures with Rooster are a cover."

"Girl, you officially lost me."

"I mean," Willi said, "she's trying to seem friendly with everyone. Every lady here, sure, but also with every man. Maybe . . . maybe to cover up her being friendly with one in particular. And I don't for a minute think that's your Windex-needy man."

"He's not my man. There's twenty years difference between us."

"Age doesn't matter, Kenzie."

Lightening lit up the darkness outside. Every head swiveled to check the slashing onslaught against window and wood. In the moment of illumination, treetops stirred like giants disturbed suddenly from a sound snooze, angry at the interruption of deep sleep. When the flash ended and darkness engulfed the pagoda, all considered their plates again with only the candle light.

"Got to admit," Kenzie said, brushing her champagne curls out of her eyes, "Rooster doesn't seem to be encouraging her."

Willi took another bite of buttered corn pone. "Exactly. He's only answering direct questions; just trying not to be impolite."

"Well, you . . . *could* be right."

"I am, and you know it."

Kenzie smiled and started to scoot back to her original position. Willi grabbed her arm. "Wait. Two things."

"What now?"

"Where in heck is Quannah?"

"You know his part of the job is to stable the horses. Remember last night? It took him a couple of hours even with the help of one of the monks. I bet he comes sneaking into the tipi again tonight. Woo-hoo."

Willi tilted her nose in the air. "Don't know what you're talking about now."

"He adores you, girl. He'll be there to say goodnight."

Willi hefted a forkful of veggies. "Well . . . you *could* be right."

"I am, and you know it." Kenzie brushed again at her wayward curls. "You said 'two things.'"

"I found something."

"Uh-oh. Out sleuthing again?"

"No. Maybe. Yes, but not intentionally. As soon as supper is over, we're skipping the evening meditation, and—"

"No way, girlfriend. We're going to have them here, together, while in front of us Samdup makes a sand painting prayer. You don't want to miss that, right?"

"No, but this is important, Kenzie, and—"

"What are we here for, Willi? For what purpose did we come to this island?"

"Okay, okay, okay. But afterward, you and—"

"You've got my word, girlfriend." She inched back over toward Paul Rooster Rowley and between questions from Juna Marie, inserted a few of her own.

As everyone around both tables seemed intent on conversation and food, Willi stared out the window. Only small bolts of lightening now and again lit up a small part of the grounds surrounding the Mimosa Teahouse. Fine, she'd have to wait a couple of hours before going over all the details gleaned so far. She'd not feel the need to get her thoughts organized if this niggler of panic, this sense of doom, would leave her alone. The horrible idea that Yataro Yodo had truly met his end would not recede. At this point, her instincts would demand he walk right in front of her to prove otherwise.

What? What was that? She opened her eyes wider and tried not to blink. Again a small flash and a figure dashed across her field of vision.

A crouched man? A deer? A coyote?

Goosebumps danced along her arms. She squinted and waited for the next illumination. Her heartbeat cantered. The desire to move between Kenzie and the window made her stretch and stand. She acted as if she just wanted to check out the storm. Study the shadows as she might, she could see nothing but the increased force of the rain. Someone touched her elbow. Willi yelped and twisted around.

Willi grabbed her elbow and blinked. Jamyang smiled. "Did not mean to disturb, Miss Willi. Would like more tea? Made hot. Thought would be more comforting with bad weather, yes?"

"Thank you, Jamyang. Did you . . . did you see some-one . . . just then? Outside the window?"

Jamyang peered out at the maelstrom. He faced her and smiled before shaking his head. He pointed to a pile of plas-tic bags. "For guests when you go to pagoda for evening." With that last thoughtfulness, he slipped toward the back and only Rimshi, the silent monk, kept them company. Af-ter a few more moments of almost willing Jerry Cormack's nasty frame to appear, she sighed and sat down again. Folks had shifted places, and no one was at her table.

Nara Inoshi folded his long legs beneath him as he seated himself beside her. "We've not gotten to visit, other than the few moments at the waterfall. My fault entirely," he said. "Please forgive me."

"Nonsense." Willi pushed her dark tendrils over her shoulders.

Good grief and granny's bloomers, up close he was one good-looking man. No wonder Juna Marie might be attracted. Still, it did not excuse her behavior, but at least she had good taste. Willi gulped. And this mental degrading of the woman for no more than an embrace and a kiss was beneath Willi. Juna Marie might not have instigated that gesture, and it could very well have not been Inoshi on the other side of that endearment.

"Nonsense," she repeated. "Between koans, meditations, lessons, horseback rides and such, we've not had time to talk with every participant."

"Ah, but I've heard much about Miss Willi."

"Uh-oh."

"From the monks, from Quannah Lassiter, and all good."

She smiled. Might be a perfect time to clear up a few facts. Facing him with her best smile in place, she asked, "How is Mr. Yataro Yodo?"

"He is in good hands. Just exhausted."

"How do you know? I mean, since he's on the mainland, and we have no communication . . ."

"That is very true. When Mike and I took him across late last night, we made sure to talk to the doctors before we returned. Yataro was simply exhausted. One of the reasons our IODD Company sent us here was to get some rest, some peace from the rigors of business that causes high blood pressure and ulcers and, of course, stress, which leads to many ailments." He sighed. "Yataro should have taken off months ago."

"Please give him my regards next time you see him. I always admired his 'look.' "

"Excuse me?" Inoshi stroked his neatly trimmed mustache.

Willi rolled her eyes. "He dressed like one of my favorite characters, Charlie Chan. The white suit and shoes."

"Ah, yes. You are the one who is so interested in snooping."

"Snooping?" Willi knit her brows and flattened a palm on the low table. "I do not *snoop*. When the authorities call upon me from time to time, I help with investigations."

"Ah, yes. A bad choice of words on my part. Forgive me. You are . . . *curious* about people."

"Curious is acceptable, yes." Willi tilted her nose in the air, but nodded. "Yes, I am curious. I think that's a healthy bent, don't you? I like to know about those with whom I share island space with, for example. When we found Mr. Yodo, it really upset me to think he was dead. In fact, I got down on the floor and peered very closely. Could have sworn his hand was already swollen and purple from . . . uh . . . well, he wasn't dead, so that's neither here nor there. And I guess since he was able to write things on a notepad, his fingers were functioning."

Inoshi leaned his long frame in close to her. Another inch and their noses would touch. He swallowed so hard she heard the gulp. His spearmint-scented breath piqued her senses. She kept as still as a rabbit caught in dusk-time headlights.

He swallowed again and said, "Notepad?" He rubbed his mustache as if trying to wipe it off.

"What about it?"

"You said he wrote on a notepad?"

"Did I?" Willi stalled for time. "It was a horrible moment. I remember getting down on all fours to study the floor, and I saw a really wet, slimy spot running from his swollen hand to somewhere behind the altar of candles and prayer display." She sighed. "I'm so embarrassed. The notepad may have been something I daydreamed. Not that I do that often."

Inoshi leaned back and produced a smile that would sell a million tubes of Crest. "Yes, Quannah mentioned your daydreaming."·

For once Willi let that assumption lay. She'd held herself so rigidly until he moved back, that now she trembled. No way would she get to her legs for a few minutes. And worse, she didn't know why. Nor did the reason for her not telling about the note, the pencil, and the prayer wheel come to mind. She grabbed at the hot tea as if she'd been deprived of beverages for days. After a few gulps, she rang the tiny bell for a refill.

Finally, she met Inoshi's eyes and said, "This is so absolutely silly. You'll begin to believe Quannah and every crazy thing he tells you—half of which is not true."

"He says all things with a touch of humor. No backbiting to worry about there. He seems quite smitten with his Miss Marple of the Range, and I can see why."

"You're just like I like my friends, Inoshi."

"Oh?"

Willi grinned. "Very, very kind and a little bit blind."

He laughed with true appreciation, and Willi relaxed. Obviously, just the rank weather and her overactive imagination got the better of her for a few moments. Sure, that was it. He was gracious and sensitive. Candle light flickered off his enlightenment medallion. He was also a man sincere about his beliefs.

He asked, "And your *silly* question?"

"When you and Mike Toru took Mr. Yodo to the mainland of the ranch and on to the hospital, did you notice any part of his clothing missing?"

Inoshi again wiped hard at his mustache, so hard that Willi figured he'd come away with half of it rubbed out. He tried to smile, but this grin seemed strained to her. "Anything in particular, Miss Willi?"

"Yes, a pair of white shoes."

"No."

"No?"

He shook his head. "No. He had everything with him, really. You ask because of your find on the trail today?"

"Yes. Kenzie and Quannah said it was just shoes that could have been from anywhere and had washed up during one of the high water seasons."

His jovial smile returned, and he patted her on the back. "And you were hoping for a mystery. Ah. I see."

She shrugged and held her hands palms outward. "Guilty."

Mike Toru signaled a let-up in the rain and nodded in Inoshi's direction. His muscle-bound frame moved purposefully, like a samurai, toward Willi's table. He said, "Perhaps this would be a good time to go back and check out that—"

"Quite right!" Inoshi's sharp tone and angry look silenced Toru, who closed his eyes briefly and toyed with an identical medallion around his neck. He backed up a few steps. "I'll go prepare . . . prepare things."

In a softer tone, Inoshi said, "Yes, that would be great, Mike. Thank you. Be right there."

Willi's eyes widened. She raised one eyebrow.

He said, "We do an evening meditation ritual after . . . after a special tea. To that, he refers, Miss Marple of the Range, nothing more."

She nodded. Sure, that's what they were up to at this time of night. Right after having tea here. Sure. Inoshi had never stumbled over his words before either. Nor was he a very good liar.

"The company has been delightful, Miss Willi. We will have to talk again." He rose to his full height and walked away. With a smart about-face, he snapped his fingers. "Oh, yes, exactly where did you find the mysterious shoes?"

"See? You're curious, too!"

With both hands raised, he nodded. "Guilty."

She said, "About six, maybe seven hundred feet behind our picnic area."

But she didn't tell him she had saved the pair. In fact, she left him with the idea that she'd thrown them down right there on the ground after Kenzie and Quannah had convinced her they were very old shoes.

Hmm. Maybe that's what Inoshi and Toru were really going to check out. Perhaps the body that goes with those shoes lies rotting there, and that's what they're searching for—for Mr. Yodo's remains. They themselves professed to be the last to see him before he *left the island.* Of course, they just didn't bury him deeply enough. She shook her head. No, no. That didn't quite ring true, either. There seemed something so essentially good about those two men; she really had a problem seeing them as murderers, but what other possible answer could there be?

An hour later the storm unveiled a nastier and stronger wind. Even the IODD men—Inoshi and Toru—had returned to the relative warmth and more secure walls of the modern structure. Banjo Jo Skeeter brought out his namesake instrument and Doretta opened a guitar case.

"All right," Nestor D. Tulsa said. "Now I could handle a couple of good old country songs. Grew up with music of Hank Williams, Hank Thompson, and Patsy Cline. Shoot, they were newcomers when I was at Pearl Harbor. They were winners, yep."

Mike Toru sidled up to Skeeter. "You all mind if I pipe in now and again?" He drew a harmonica out of his pocket and tapped it on his pants leg.

Skeeter said, "The more the merrier. Ain't that right, cousin Doretta? Hell, she's used to all kinds being as she tended bar and no telling what else in our Texas honky-tonks."

Doretta slapped him on his shoulder. "You keep telling those tales, I'm gonna take your Ben Gay muscle rub away, you ornery excuse for kin."

Skeeter chuckled through his white beard and shook his head. "Get her riled up enough, she might belt a Loretta Lynn song or two."

"I'm gonna belt someone, I tell you what."

All the while the cousins fussed, each one helped the other set up two mikes, a couple of amplifiers, and a stand for Doretta's guitar. She brought icy cold tea glasses over and set them on a low table so they could easily reach the drinks.

With gentle hints, Willi had tried to get Kenzie's attention from Rooster, afterward reverting to silly antics behind his back like crossing her eyes and making a slicing motion with her finger across her neck. Kenzie simply deftly turned Rooster away into a farther corner. Okay, fine. Just dandy. Now they would be a couple of hours with the Skeeter family's hoedown. Willi stuck her bottom lip out. Said hoedown would be just great if one particular ponytailed, rough-riding horseman were to amble through that door and whirl her into the "Blue Skirt Waltz" the three musicians were using as a warm-up song. Her bottom lip trembled and her eyes teared up. She sniffed and coughed to cover her concern.

She peered past the Pates, who had finally joined the circle everyone had created with pillows and rugs around the entertainers. Behind the trio, the monks were kneeling around the sand drawing and putting some finishing touches on the beautiful depiction for the day. Two of the silent brothers moved to the bright circle of the audience. Their grins attested to their love of the music and joy in the room.

Who was she to take away from this serendipitous moment with unshed tears and a hangdog mouth? Some good music might just take her mind off all the mess sprouting in her head, growing as fast as the vines in the gardens outside, blossoming and falling in disarray around the base of the trees—in this case her neck. She rubbed some of the tension away and sat cross-legged between Kenzie and Juna Marie. Looking from one to the other, she grinned. Hells Bells, sort of like being between the regal queen of swans and the chirpy, bright-eyed little hen. Said hen—Kenzie—fluffing her feathers all sorts of ways for one Rooster Rowley.

Mike Toru played a haunting rendition of "I'm So Lonesome I Could Cry" and grinned sheepishly at the applause.

Rooster said, "There wasn't anything wrong with that. You can handle that harmonica. Yep, you know how to do it right."

Kenzie and Willi grinned at each other, a silent message passing between them: *He's healing. They're both healing. This is a good thing, this singing tonight.*

Kenzie nodded. With that, Willi sat back into a plumped-up pillow and truly relaxed. Maybe she should just chill out and watch folks—something that always piqued her curiosity—and take some joy from one of her two favorite types of music—country oldies, the other being her golden oldies rock 'n roll of the 50s, 60s, and 70s. Music in some cases before her time, but still she loved those old songs more than many of the modern.

Rooster leaned over after Doretta sang Buck Owen's song about not caring if the sun shone or the bells chimed just as long as his lady loved him. "Why, she's good, too. I could listen to this all night long. Yep, until morning hours would suit me fine. Think they'd take a request?"

"Probably," Kenzie said.

"What song you want?" asked Willi.

Rooster sat up. "Uh, don't know, just wondered. Yeah, I just wanted to know."

Kenzie said, "Let's see. Doretta, do you know Connie Smith's 'Ain't Had No Lovin' ?"

In her whiskey voice, Doretta sang the first lines to the strum of her guitar, an old Martin's: "Ain't had no loving . . . ain't gonna get no loving 'til you come home." Skeeter and Toru joined in on their instruments.

Through his white beard, Skeeter smiled at Juna Marie. "You like this kind of music, ma'am?"

Before she could answer, Preacher Pate responded, "We love most the music of the Lord, of course, but—"

Juna Marie stiffened her back, turned her head on her elegant neck, and interrupted him. "But I grew up listening to many of these songs that were favorites of my parents. I like them, and you all are wonderful."

"Just what I was about to add, sweet angel of mine. You all get the toes to tapping. That's a good thing."

Skeeter said, "Some old country songs tell about the joyful moments in life, others touch on trials and tribulations, and some ditties are just purely sad and mournful comments on our human conditions, them not always being of the highest caliber. Guess that's why we need a few old gospels now and again, right, Preacher Pate?"

Everyone smiled and nodded at Skeeter's smoothing of the waters. Well, everyone but Halliwell Pate. He had his lips tightened in such a thin line, Willi figured he suffered from constipation of the heart. He patted Juna Marie's knee and left his hand there. Juna Marie grimaced and yelped. "Sorry, darling, didn't mean to pinch that pretty lit-tle knee."

Willi frowned. Sure he didn't, right. And *Dos Equis* beer never got guzzled in a Texas *taberna, amigo.* She rubbed her temples. Just one more detail to sift through when she and Kenzie could really talk about all the things going on.

Skeeter jumped into a rendition of "Milk Cow Blues" followed up by Doretta's song about her and Jesus having a good thing going, a lively one that had everyone smiling, even Halliwell Pate. She then switched to a couple of he-done-her-wrong songs starting with "Satin Sheets."

Toru kept pace with the slow ones, the fast ones, and all those in between. Preacher Pate got up to make use of the men's room at the tail end of a harmonica solo. As soon as Mike Toru finished the final strains, Skeeter grinned and said, "I just about got a song for every lady I meet."

"Oh, Lordy," Doretta said, "Yes, he makes a point of collecting songs with women's names, but not everyone gets an exact match, so watch out ladies, especially if he dedicates 'Marie Lebeau' to you."

"Naw. This one is pretty. Let's get going on it, and you'll know just who I'm a-singing it for. The first line is . . . let's see . . . 'You were a lady when I married you.' Wait a minute. 'Are you something different than you ap-pear to be?' Okay, okay, I remember. Here we go."

Surprisingly, he plucked his banjo in a soft accompani-ment to a sweet melody about Jeannie Marie and the sto-ries they were telling about her and other men. In one of the beautiful renditions of the Tommy Overstreet song's chorus, Skeeter winked at the preacher's wife and sang, "Juna Marie, you were a lady this morning when we kissed good-bye, you were a lady."

Juna Marie grinned from ear to ear at his working her name into the song.

Willi glanced up and over her shoulder. In the shadows leading from the bathroom hallway, Halliwell Pate stood with his hand slapping the wood of the wall. He knotted up his fist, reared back, caught her looking, and shook his hand like he was trying to get the circulation going in it. Willi's heart made a sluggish flip-flop. Another millisecond and the teahouse's hallway wall would have had a hole in it. She turned back around to peer at Juna Marie's blushing face.

Doretta said, "Overstreet was a collector like Skeeter. Cuz, isn't he the one that had 'Gwen, Congratulations' and 'Ann, Don't Go Runnin' and . . . uh. . . . 'Sue'?"

"Believe you are right, Doretta, hon."

Willi stiffened at the slight movement of air as Halliwell walked behind her to reseat himself beside Juna Marie. He put his arm around his wife's shoulders. "Why don't we end this evening with some sing-along type songs?"

Mike Toru started with "Down in the Valley," segued into "Careless Love," which he followed with "Side By Side." Another half hour and everyone decided it had been one of the best Hallmark moments they had had together on the island.

Willi enjoyed every moment—with the exception of the interrupted *punching* scene—but she desperately needed to talk with Kenzie. She glared at her friend. Well, by dangnab, there *was* a song named for her—"Hard-hearted Hannah." How dare Kenzie ignore the pleading looks, the tweaks on her elbows for attention, the clearing of Willi's throat. On the other hand, Willi grinned. How good it was to see Kenzie enjoying herself and purposefully showing a little orneriness, which Willi knew was not meanness, just Kenzie asserting her will a bit. Good for her!

Time to get serious, though. For some reason, Willi imagined a clock tick, ticking away with a nasty surprise bomb on that third click of the hands. With strong strides she approached Kenzie, only to have her elbow grasped by Preacher Pate who turned her around. He walked her over to the large sand painting area. Two monks now sat, one on the north side, one on the south, their hands in the palms upward position. They both seemed to be in a deep meditation, neither one acknowledging Willi's nor Halliwell's presence.

She pulled her elbow from his grasp. "What's going on, Halliwell?"

His eye twitched at the use of his given name. She grinned. So, he didn't like it, huh? Preferred the preacher title. Well, too bad. Willi sighed. Okay, she had an ornery streak through her, too. It just seemed to be stronger tonight where Halliwell Pate was concerned, and she wasn't quite sure why, other than what she thought was his ridiculous reaction to a song sung to Juna Marie.

He said, "We attended the same university, you know."

A strange opening, but Willi nodded. "Really? University of Texas at Arlington?"

"Yes, indeed. A fine school. And obviously some excellent graduates . . . such as yourself."

"Thank you, and likewise." She tilted her head. "I wasn't aware it had a religious or theological degree program for ministers."

"UTA didn't, but my scholarship was in biology, and my folks couldn't afford much more than a little spending money back then."

"So how did you make your way from UTA science to the pulpit?" Willi truly was curious, as she always was about folks, another strange legacy left to her by her parents. "Must have made for some interesting tales."

Rubbing his hands, Halliwell Pate warmed to his subject. "You might say that, yes. Worked hard, I did, at lots of different jobs. Gas station attendant, dog-sitter, valet at the Carriage House Restaurant."

"Oh, but that's such an elegant, upscale place. Must have been good tips for a college boy."

"Indeed, there were those." He nodded toward Juna Marie in conversation with Kenzie, Rooster, and Skeeter. He frowned momentarily and made a move to go over.

Willi grabbed his arm. "And the other jobs?"

"Pardon?" He tightened the sweater about his hips.

"The Carriage House, and then . . . ?"

"That's where I met Juna Marie and her family. Parked her daddy's Caddy, and this goddess stepped out. I must have stopped breathing; she was so . . . so radiant. 'Course then, me being a poor kid with nothing to offer, I kept silent." He cleared his throat, positioned himself to more easily see his wife, and said, "Best job I had was through the science department."

"Ah, a lab assistant. Not bad."

"No," he said, "No, they got me a position with the Ft. Worth Zoo's herpetology department. Of course, you know what that means in Texas."

"Well, I know what it'd mean for me. Take this job and do a Johnny Paycheck number on it."

Juna Marie's laughter floated across the room. Skeeter's old cheeks crinkled up and he slapped his knee. Kenzie and Rooster joined in.

Willi said, "Good to see everyone enjoying themselves tonight. Your wife must be a gracious hostess and help in your work."

"Yes, indeed. I love to see my Juna Marie happy." His glare seemed to put lie to his words.

Willi shrugged. Maybe he was just one of those people who, due to poor eyesight, seemed to always be frowning when in actuality they were merely focusing to see more clearly.

With a deft two-step to the side, she blocked his view of

the laughing group. "Anyhoo, I wouldn't have wanted to work with snakes, even as a starving college student. And what exactly does working with them entail in Texas?"

He licked his lips. "Means you learn to milk rattlesnakes. Well, you milk all kinds, but lots of rattlers."

Willi shivered. "Oh my gosh. That's sounds like a job for either the very brave or the very foolish."

"Guilty on both counts. I thought I was brave, but once I proved to be very foolish."

"Oh no. You were bitten?"

"Couldn't have picked a worse time . . . or a better time."

"Halliwell, you lost me."

"Behind a glass plate so the public could watch, we did a short fifteen-minute demonstration once a day. Another assistant brought in two or three rattlers in one glass cage and set it on the table. I was to take out one at a time, milk it, and place it in a second glass cage, pull another one out and repeat the process until the trio had been completed. All normal and routine. Except . . ."

"Except?" Willi cringed.

"The other fellow didn't slide the glass top of the case all the way closed after I drew out the first snake."

Goosebumps raced along her arms. "And?"

"On the other side of the window, Juna Marie and her girlfriend walked in. Swear to Almighty God as my witness, my heart flew up in my throat, my senses flew out my ears, and I just laid that milked snake back in the case. Never took my eyes off Juna Marie, didn't even feel the second rattler slither around my wrist until he bit my thumb."

"He hadn't been milked?"

"Nope. I got a full dose. 'Course we had the anti-venom on hand, but the mind panics at such moments. All I thought of was, here I was facing the one beautiful creature

I wanted for mine, and she was going to have to watch me die. I fainted. Right then and there on the concrete floor. I still remember darling Juna Marie's screams. Talk about a moment of complete horror and absolute sweetness rolled into five seconds."

Willi shivered. "You poor man."

"They rushed me to the hospital as a precaution, even though they immediately gave me the anti-venom. As soon as I was out of danger, they filled me with Demerol. Good stuff."

"Yes, I've had a few Demerol moments myself."

Preacher Pate's eyes glistened. "Guess what I awoke to?"

"The realization you needed a new part-time job?"

"Juna Marie's lovely face. As the Lord is my witness and everlasting sustenance, he sent that sweet angel to hold my hand. Her daddy took a liking to me, supported me through the change from UTA to the seminary, and helped me get a posting with one of the best churches in the metroplex. I may have been bitten by the viper of the Garden, but an angel saved me for His glorious work. The devil could have taken me to the depths of Hell before I found a lifemate, but no. No, the Lord, in His mercy, stepped in and blew back the brimstone blasts of loneliness and frustration."

Willi gulped. Okay. Now, he seemed warmed up and ready to lay a sermon on her. Although she loved Brother Farmer's homely sermon's from Nickleberry's First United Methodist pulpit, she didn't think she'd come away with a warm fuzzy glow from one of Preacher Pate's more fire-and-brimstone renditions. Not a happening thing this late at night. She made signs of yawning, acted embarrassed at her need for sleep, and made a quick getaway.

CHAPTER
9

In the women's pagoda, Doretta, Kenzie, and Juna Marie helped Willi close the door. The plastic bags, so thoughtfully provided as cover, had blown out of her tenacious grasp long before she reached the sleeping quarters. One look at the bedraggled roommates showed the same had happened to them.

Juna Marie collapsed on the floor to take off her mud-encrusted Reeboks. "I do not believe this storm. Whatever will we do if the Guadalupe does flood? It gets to that rolling stage, it'll be days and days before they can send help." Her eyes glowed. "Why, bless my soul, it'll be like we were on Noah's ark."

Doretta stripped off her clothes, threw on a robe, and dried her hair. "Noah's ark, the Toucan's back leg. He'd be missing and a couple thousand other of the good Lord's creatures not represented on Serenity Island. I hadn't seen a donkey one, and I'm right partial to those little burros."

Kenzie took a band to round up her hair in a one-inch ponytail. "That really would be a horrible scenario if only those on this island were left to people the earth, no offense to you all. But I don't think I'm worthy or strong enough for that kind of emotional, spiritual trip."

As the esoteric talk continued, Willi showered, dried her hair, and quietly drew her curtain around her bed. From underneath, she pulled out the shoes. For a long time she considered the one with the divine eye, but came up with no revelations—spiritual or otherwise. One leg beneath her, she leaned over and pulled the curtain back.

Trees became physical beings. Their branches, like the proverbial metaphors, truly resembled limbs stretching to pull away from the trunk, and twisted in anger at the impossibility. A roof tile that hit the side of an oak gouged a wound into the bark. Willi cringed at the imagined pain, and she put her fingers over her mouth so as not to cry out. Her roommates might not understand her close affinity for the Standing People—the Trees. Within a quarter hour, the slashing monster lessened its ferocity. Now the foliage seemed to welcome the calmer deluge. Perhaps the steady downpour was akin to a full body massage for a willow or pine or oak.

Hmm. She punched up her pile of pillows. In her mind's eye she reviewed when Kenzie, Rooster, and she found Yataro Yodo. She'd bent down beside the body. She *knew* in that moment he was dead, even above the fact that Rooster had not found a pulse. She *knew;* now how did she know? Willi sighed. Rivulets of rainwater swam down the pane like a nest of disturbed snakes, sliding and slithering over and under one another. Well, maybe she'd sleep on it, and figure it out. She really didn't want to go to bye-bye land until she got to say good night to Quannah and make sure he'd had a hot meal.

Someone knocked at the pagoda door. Willi fluffed her hair and sat up to pull open her curtain. Yes! Thank goodness! She stuffed the box underneath her bed, just as Kenzie opened the door for Rimshi. He smiled. Those monks always smiled.

"Missy Willi?"

Willi's heart cantered. "Good Lord. He talked. It must be something awful for him to break his silence."

"Sorry for late notice. Mr. Quannah had no other way to reach. I break silence to deliver this message."

Willi jumped off the bed. "What's the matter? Is he okay? I'll be dressed in two minutes."

The monk looked at the ceiling to deliver the message in his quiet voice. "Horse bad sick. Going to pump stomach. Mr. Rowley help. Be up most of night. Not worry."

"Why, he's had no supper. He's working himself to death just so I could be here with Kenzie, and the man has had one sit-down meal. This is—"

Rimshi raised a hand. "Hot meal delivered, and repasts for evening. We check him, Mr. Rowley and horse all night. He say you sleep tight." A fleeting frown visited the monk's features. "He say . . . uh . . . *please* and—"

"Yes?" Willi tapped her bare foot. "Please what?"

"Ah, yes. Please stay put."

"Stay put?"

"Stay put."

Doretta, Juna Marie, Kenzie, and Rimshi stared at her.

"What?" Willi pulled her curtain around her bed. "As if I'd have any intentions of getting out in this again! To what purpose? To check on his ornery hide after telling me to *stay put*. I don't think so."

Doretta said thanks to Rimshi and then yelled out. "Ought to be happy to have a feller to care enough to send a message, and then send one meant to protect you. Don't tell me that doesn't please you no end of ways and back again."

Willi peeked out. "Well, yes it does."

Kenzie threw a pillow at her. "You are such a ninny, girlfriend. Nose in the air like you don't care. You aren't fooling anyone."

Everyone doused lights, said good-night and, lulled by the now gentle rain, snoozed away. A wall separated Doretta's and Juna Marie's curtained cubicles from Kenzie's and Willi's, so Willi could only hear her friend's light snores. About an hour into a sound sleep, something awoke Willi.

She lay listening in the dark for a rustling, a snore from Kenzie, but all was quiet with the exception of the backdrop of the rain's lullaby. Her heart beat faster, though, so there had to be something. Her senses were telling her to be on alert, and yet she could detect nothing. She pushed the knob on her lamp that allowed for a night light glow. Ahh, she'd forgotten to pull the window curtains together. That was the problem. As she leaned out to do so, her hand froze.

By Great Spirit's lessons, she *knew* how she *knew*.

For a long time, she lay in contemplation with the night light glow washing over her. Her heart did not lessen its pace with the confirmation but rather escalated to a tremor up into her throat.

From her makeup bag, she pulled out the prayer wheel, then quickly pushed it into hiding again. She pulled the curtains closed and sat up on the side of the bed. Okay, she couldn't talk to Quannah, but Kenzie had promised a late-night talk, which had never happened. Willi desperately needed some serious conversation time to bounce these wild musings of hers against someone she trusted.

Quannah being out of the scene for the moment, she

would have to awaken Kenzie. Willi let her chin drop to her chest and shook her head. Waking Kenzie had never been an easy chore. Didn't matter. Willi had to have her help, and she had to have it now.

After shaking Kenzie's shoulder, pulling her hair, tweaking her elbow, and a few other things, Willi sighed. Okay, the only thing to work in the past was to tickle her feet. She applied that knowledge; Kenzie kicked out, hitting Willi's chin. Champagne hair glowing even under the soft night light's shimmer, Kenzie glared at Willi down on the floor.

"Girlfriend, do you have a death wish? What the hell?"

"Quiet. Get up. Get dressed. No questions. Hurry."

Years of friendship held sway over the moment, and without a word, Kenzie donned jeans and tennis shoes while Willi did the same. In a straw shopping bag Willi shoved the shoes, the prayer wheel, and the cell phone. Kenzie grabbed a flashlight and raised an eyebrow in question. Willi nodded and added it to the straw bag along with tiny pouches containing rolled-up raincoats and hats. The rain, merely drizzle at the moment, didn't seem worth the effort of putting on the raingear. Willi led the way down the winding path toward the Lotus Pagoda schoolhouse. At the Y going to the left toward the Mimosa Teahouse, Samdup ran into them.

"Ladies?"

"Evening," Willi managed.

"Hi and howdy," Kenzie piped up around a stifled yawn.

"Such a late hour to be going . . . where did you say?"

"Yeah," Kenzie said, "where did you say?"

Willi grinned. "Such a clown, my friend. It's her fault we're up and about. Go ahead, Kenz, tell him why you practically kicked me out of bed."

"Well, I'd just love to tell him, girlfriend, but—"

"It's a true sign of our friendship, Samdup, that I, without question, came along with her to . . . to . . . get a midnight snack."

"Midnight snack. So that's what I—"

"Yes, that's what you said, 'Get it moving, girlfriend,' for."

Samdup nodded. "No curfews here, but don't lose your way, ladies. Looked like you were about to go to the right down the wrong path, Missy, Willi." He bowed toward the left lane. "That is the way. Rimshi will serve whatever you like."

"I don't suppose," Kenzie said, "since this is my desperate midnight munchies attack, that there might be a couple bags of Doritos or Lays potato chips hidden in the kitchen?"

Samdup smiled. "You are such a funny lady, Miss Francis."

Like a nervous maître d', he hovered, so Willi kept her grin in place and pulled Kenzie toward the right branch. A couple of yards along, Willi said, "Is he still there?"

Kenzie bent down as if to tie her shoe. "Wait up, girl, or I'll be tripping all over the place." When she straightened and caught up to Willi she whispered, "Yes, he's actually following us, but at a very slow pace."

"Damn."

"Guess I'll get that midnight snack I wanted so much, huh?"

"Looks like. Damn."

"You said that, girlfriend. What is going on, really?"

Inside the eatery, Willi chose a corner table and closed the floor-to-ceiling curtain section nearest so they could not be easily observed from outside. With only two of them there other than the two monks praying beside the sand art pits, it seemed like the pagoda was even grander and hu-

mongously overpowering. Willi swallowed hard. Perhaps it
was just a bit of a panic attack on her part. One little crisis,
she could handle, two maybe. When three and four items
were stirred in the trouble pot, she tended to panic and seek
answers.

So she had a hard time getting Kenzie out of bed, so
there had been a tiny change in location for a few minutes
because of Samdup. Still, nothing altered her motives for
the wee hours. In fact, a quick vitality-packed repast might
well prepare her and Kenzie for what lay ahead. Right. She
knew what she wanted. There remained just this small
problem of figuring out how to get from *A* to *C* without
having to climb over, out-maneuver, or fight something
with a capital *B*. Like *boys* of the muscled variety, aka
IODD's Mike Toru, like bolts of lighting, like bullies by
the name of Bubba Jerry Fartleberry Cormack.

Small things.

Over a hot bowl of onion soup accompanied by slices of
broccoli quiche, Willi explained in a low voice. "I forgot
about having the prayer wheel until I visited with Nara Inoshi tonight."

"Girl, I thought that was in the meditation room with
Mr. Yodo. You took it?"

"Well, yeah. Along with a pencil stub and a small notepad."

"So, no big deal. I've seen those prayer wheels in every
room of the Lotus Pagoda."

Willi sipped the steaming soup. "Yes, but this one was
beside Mr. Yodo when he died."

Kenzie swallowed her last bite of quiche. "Whoa, Miss
Marple of the Range. He didn't die."

"Yes, he did." Willi rubbed her temples. She had to convince Kenzie to listen and to help.

Kenzie said, "Mike Toru and Nara Inoshi took him to the mainland. You saw him yourself in the IODD pagoda after his collapse."

Willi waved that detail aside. "I thought I did. Certainly there was a shadow that moved as if it were him, twirling a long mustache. But it was just a sillouhette that could have been made by anyone who wanted folks to think Mr. Yodo still walked the earth."

"Okay, girl, I'm gonna stay with you. Let's for the moment allow you to have your *moment of mystery*. What's so important suddenly about the prayer wheel?"

"There's a note inside rolled up like a tiny scroll."

"All of them have those. That's a prayer sent up to heaven each time you twirl the rattle—the prayer wheel—contraption. It's called a *chos-kor* or *khorten*."

Willi nodded. "Yes, but look."

She peered around the room to check that Rimshi sat with head bowed over the sand painting while he patiently waited for their next ring of the service bell. Willi unwound the prayer from the hollow, cylindrical body. Inside the thin paper was a yellow torn strip, obviously from Mr. Yodo's notepad. On the yellow sheet was that depiction of the third eye. One sentence scribbled and smudged stood out beneath the eye.

"A jewel shall not be sacrificed to the dragon."

Willi frowned. "Was this some special invocation, some particular mantra of Mr. Yodo's? Is it important to what happened to him?" Surely, Kenzie could see that this was out of the ordinary, that it held some significance, and that they had to do something about Mr. Yodo.

"Assuming, girlfriend, that he's dead, you mean."

"Yes, Kenzie, keep on the same page with me, okay?"

Kenzie studied the yellow strip curled inside the parchment prayer. She finished unrolling the parchment. "Hm.

This prayer has a tiny dragon in the corner. Perhaps like a patron protector of the prayer or something."

Willi snapped her fingers. "Samdup told us that on prayer banners and such that pictures in each protected the four corners: a tiger, a lion, the mythical bird—the *garuda*—and a dragon. This looks more like a snake."

Willi snapped her fingers.

"What?" Kenzie asked.

"I'm not exactly sure what each item by itself signifies. Just let's keep an open mind as we go through these things and see what comes to mind. For one thing, I got confirmation tonight—twice—and now a third time from you that Mr. Yodo is dead, and I know *how* he died."

"From me? Girlfriend, you've officially left me at the last river bend."

"Remember when I knelt down beside his body?"

Kenzie shivered. "Lord, yes. Goosebumps are going all over me now just thinking about you nose to nose with him."

"I saw a wet rivulet on the slate, almost but not quite dried, leading from his sleeve toward the back of the altar. The rest of him, leg and head and neck, were ashen, not discolored, but his hand . . . his hand was purple, blotched."

"Bitten by something?" Kenzie gasped. "Oh my gosh."

"Yes. I think a snake. When we find his body again, that can easily be proven with the autopsy."

"Not sure, girl, but I bet the powers that be frown down on performing an autopsy on a walking, breathing person." At Willi's sigh, she added, "Okay, on the same page. For discussion purposes, he's dead. Got you. And what was it that confirmed this idea for you?"

"The rivulets of water running down the windowpane tonight."

"Uh . . ."

"Like snakes, Kenzie. Quannah has taught me to read signs the universe offers up and to trust those signs no matter how weird they may logically seem. If your instincts tell you that's the right interpretation, trust your senses. And that's what was brought home to me, what woke me up tonight, made me look twice at the water rivulets. Then you again confirmed by pointing out that the picture in Mr. Yodo's prayer—the last thing he touched—had a representation of a snake on it."

"Girlfriend, ever consider you might have a paranoia about snakes, especially after your encounter with what the papers called the 'Snow Snake' in your last case with Quannah?"

Willi shoved her soup bowl back. "Quannah would say they keep showing up because I have lessons yet to learn from them."

"Scary."

"Sometimes."

Snapping off the rubber band holding her tiny ponytail and ruffling her blond curls, Kenzie said, "Okay. So, a snake kills him. Accident, right?"

"No, not accident. The monks are constantly cleaning—they're like a team of Martha Stewarts—all the time, inside and outside on the grounds. *Someone* brought that snake up to the manicured area of the Lotus Pagoda. *Someone* made sure the snake struck while Mr. Yodo was at his meditations. *Someone* then escaped through a back door, which we heard slam just before we walked onto the death scene."

"And the killer reptile just slid away?"

"Could be, or they could have retrieved it when they recovered Yataro Yodo's body."

Rimshi sidled up to their table. Willi and Kenzie gasped. Willi slid the choskor into the straw bag. Rimshi smiled before refilling their drinks. He moved quietly away, as if on silent skates.

Kenzie leaned over. "Sometimes, he's a little scary."

Willi grinned. "That's just because you can't get him to talk whenever you want."

"Maybe. Okay, what else is in that bag?"

"The shoes. Look at this one with the eye etched into it. Doesn't that look deeper, a lot deeper than all the other scratches on the white surface?"

After a few moments of careful scrutiny, Kenzie said, "Yes, yes, you can actually see where someone has gouged out part of the leather in a curve, not a shape that would probably—*probably*—occur if the article were just thrown and tossed among the rocks."

"Thank you. I'm not crazy."

"Girlfriend, I don't think we've established that yet."

"Funny."

"So?" Kenzie asked for the umpteenth time. "Where does all this get us?"

"Not sure. I saved the best for last." Willi pulled out the cell phone.

"Damn, girl. You're going to get us thrown out of the program. We aren't supposed to have those. How did you sneak it past the check out at the ranch mainland?"

"Didn't."

"You're holding it in your hand. Right there. A cell phone. Right there in your hand."

Willi tilted her head. "And what do your instincts tell you? That this is mine? That I snuck it onto Serenity Island?"

Kenzie pushed out her bottom lip and shut her eyes a moment. "Okay, okay. That doesn't feel right. You wouldn't do such a thing. Nope, you're good and true, and wouldn't have jeopardized this week in any way for me."

"Exactly."

"So, whose is it? Where did you find it?"

A lightening bolt seared the sky, and even through drawn curtains it created a light blast that shone around the drape's edges. Thunder rumbled ominously like a ground-out alternator, coming in short bursts of sound, never quite working up to that sudden expected roar.

"I found the phone in the rock garden, the serenity garden."

"For real?"

"For real. The green light caught my attention where someone had hidden it in the pile of larger stones. You know, the ones that represent the islands in life?"

"So whose is it, Miss Marple of the Range?"

"Well . . . I have this theory."

"Uh-oh. I don't like that glint in your eyes."

"Come on. While the rain's let up. I'll explain on the way. I think it's one of the IODD men's cell phone." Before Kenzie could blink, Willi grabbed her wrist, the straw bag, and asked Rimshi for two flashlights. He nodded and went to get it for her.

Kenzie said, "Girl, what do we need two flashlights for?"

"It's dark out and . . . inside. Might be best if we both had one."

"Dark *inside?*"

"Uh-huh."

"I'm not going in that spider-infested, snake-crawling boathouse even with two flashlights."

"I wouldn't ask you to do that, Kenzie. Good grief."

"Well, you better not, girl, because I draw the line at that. Lightening flashing, those boats rocking in the dark, worms crawling out of those buckets. Nope, not a happening thing."

"Not to worry. I would never put you in that kind of jeopardy or myself either." Willi tilted her nose in the air.

"Okay."

"Okay."

A few minutes later, after a frantic race up the curving pathways, Kenzie gasped. "You wouldn't ask me to . . . but you'd want me to go . . . in *there?* Words fail me, much as your brain must be failing you now."

"Don't get ugly. I've reasoned this out."

"Do tell. And I mean that literally."

Willi pulled her into undergrowth facing the imposing pagoda, with a lone light and a single figure highlighted at a table. "Okay, someone is fibbing bigger than Pinocchio. One: We found Yataro Yodo dead. *Dead.* Period. Just accept that for a few moments. But, what if, due to some nefarious business dealings, the IODD men did not want to have to leave the island? What if they carted him away from the death scene? What if they were in contact with uh . . . superiors via *the cell phone* who told them to dump the body and stay on the job? Huh? What about that? What if they used the boat in the early morning hours, not to take Yodo to the mainland and medical help, but around the island and buried—"

"Oh, Willi, I love you, but your imagination—"

"*Buried* him in a shallow grave where the four-legged furry critters grabbed his shoes, pulling them away in order to get to more delectable portions."

"*Puh-lease.*"

"Sorry. Got a bit carried away there." Willi shoved her dark tendrils back behind her neck. The humidity again created a sauna around them, almost making her wish for another downpour. "That was pretty graphic."

"Indeed," Kenzie said.

"Notice anything odd yet about the IODD pagoda?" Willi asked.

"Some idiot is staying up at crazy hours like the Lucy and Ethel duo here?"

"Sort of. Anything else?"

"Girlfriend, I'm not into the sleuthing scene, and I'm usually brain-dead at this time; hell, I'm usually into deep REMs at this time."

"He's Mr. Yodo."

"Willi, Willi, Willi. What have you done with your medications?"

"Cute. When I followed Samdup last night, I stood right here and saw Mr. Yodo through the window just as he is at this moment, now minus the mustache. Ah, see? He's moving his arm out for the tea. Again. And wait a few moments and he does it another time. See? There!"

"That is a process we earthlings call drinking, imbibing, partaking of refreshments."

"Yes, Kenzie, oh friend of mine, but that's not an earthling. That's an automated dummy. Its arm goes out every twelve seconds, the hand grasps a cup and takes it to his lips in three seconds. It takes another five seconds to put it down and retract the hand. Start counting now. One-Mississippi, two-Mississippi . . ."

After the demonstration, Kenzie sighed. "You're right."

"Of course."

"So now I'm totally confused. What does this have to do with . . . with anything?"

"The IODD men are not in their pagoda at night. By day, they participate in the lessons on Buddhism, but often they get Quannah to take them on special trail rides all over the island. They seldom come to the meals, or if they do, stay only long enough to eat; that's probably when they grab a few z's. What better way to scope things out?"

"What things?" asked Kenzie.

"That's what we're going to find out."

"Uh, I ask you again. Do you mean for us to go inside their pagoda?"

"You're so smart. It's one of the reasons I like you, Kenzie Francis."

"No, no, no. Not smart. I'm with you. Actually following you through this mud. God knows I'm a sick woman and need help."

Willi grabbed her by the arm and scampered through the underbrush, raced up the steps, and knocked loudly on the door.

"What are you doing? You're the sick woman. You're the one that needs help," Kenzie said, turning to leap off the porch.

Willi knocked again. "Just in case someone is in there."

"You warn them? What are you going to say when that bodybuilder clamps his hands around your little neck?"

"I'm going to feign tears and worry about not being able to find Quannah, and how turned around we got, and can he help us find the stables. You are to flutter your lashes over those big baby-blue eyes. Got it?"

Kenzie patted her on the back. "Not bad, not bad. Of course, since there's a sign right outside the Mimosa Teahouse pointing to the stable path, he'll think we're country dolts, but I guess we can live up to that."

Willi knocked once more, just before a competing roll of thunder crashed around them. She tried the door, which swung open, and she pulled Kenzie inside. One of the floorboards creaked. When she removed her weight, another sinister creak followed. From the light behind the cardboard figure—not a three-dimensional mannequin—Willi viewed the large pagoda. Two full bedrooms here, with bath between, as well as the front sitting room. Scents arose around her—expensive colognes, lavender soap, crisply ironed cotton. Sandalwood incense also.

Kenzie guided her to a niche in the wall set with a small Buddha, candles, two prayer wheels, and rolled-up prayer rugs. Old candle stubs and fresh flowers also lay alongside the small meditation altar. Really sweet bouquets of red, white, and blue blossoms.

"Hmm." Willi scratched her head. "They really are sincere about the practice or else are excellent about the details of their cover."

"Are those prayer wheels like Mr. Yodo's?" Kenzie asked.

"Here. Use your flashlight and let's see."

Willi bent her head toward Kenzie as they twisted Mr. Yodo's prayer wheel this way and that. "Yes, it has the same designs. Maybe their company gave them similar ones before the retreat?"

"Could be."

"Let's see," Willi said, "if the messages inside are alike."

"They're supposed to be holy prayers. Should we disturb those?"

"Kenzie, the one in Yataro Yodo's didn't seem right somehow as a prayer. If they are similar, then maybe I've just interpreted incorrectly. If not similar, well, maybe that will tell us something about what really happened to Mr. Yodo and what he was trying to tell us in his message."

Kenzie held the light steady, with her fingers splayed over the lens so just the needed illumination aimed right at the prayer slips. The first one was in Japanese.

Willi sighed. "Not a lot of help there." She opened the second one. "This one, too, is in Japanese."

"Everything feels legit," Kenzie said. "Except for . . ."

She stared at the cardboard figure in front of the window. Willi, too, peered at the moving apparatus—a simple thing a junior high schooler could have set in motion. Certainly not a difficult device for the caliber of minds the IODD Company boasted.

Willi repeated Kenzie's thoughts. "*Almost* everything is legit. *That's* not. And something else. I just can't put my finger on the problem." She glared at the choskors. "These look very ancient, and yet . . . Toru and Inoshi are . . . are very modern." She shook her head.

Kenzie said, "Okay, let's see what else we can find. There's some other reason they are on this island besides being practicing Buddhists. Something more. You've convinced me, girl, or rather . . . *he* has." Kenzie pointed to the figure with the flashlight.

"Don't move it around," Willi screeched, clicking the flash off.

In the glow of the light a soft shadow appeared at the corner of the window in front of "Yodo." Kenzie must have seen it, too, because she grabbed Willi's forearm. Gently, Willi pulled her back toward the bathroom. She inched her way around the tiled room and into the black glass enclosure of the shower. She eased her legs over the shower edge and leaned down to help Kenzie do the same. With a fingertip, she slid the door shut and draped towels over the top. Then, like mice caught between the trap and the corner, she and Kenzie stood with hands clasped.

CHAPTER
10

Willi shivered despite the closeness and humidity. Fine hairs on her earlobes twitched as did her nostrils, trying to take in scents and sounds to determine who had just opened the pagoda door and stepped across the telltale creaking board.

Thunder boomed loud enough to evoke visions of a dynamite blast, Kenzie yipped and grasped so hard, her nails dug into Willi's arm. With teeth gritted, Willi loosened each finger's hold.

"Sorry," Kenzie whispered in her ear.

Light came on in the outer bedroom. Nara Inoshi's? Mike Toru's? Creak of bedsprings. Drawers being opened and shut. Maybe the snap of a suitcase. Now a brighter light shone directly within the bathroom. As long as they didn't move, Willi figured they couldn't be seen behind the black glass and all the towels. But enough light filtered in for her to see the corner of the tub and shower.

Damn!

A snake with a rat, half in its mouth, half out, the muscles working the furry creature down into its stomach, was in the tub with them. Guess the IODD men kept a little pet. Aww, jeez. Willi swallowed, but was proud she hadn't screamed out. It looked to her like a king snake. She'd come a long way concerning her paranoia of all snakes since Quannah had insisted she learn about them and pay attention to the messages brought.

She and Kenzie were safe as long as the scaly one concentrated on swallowing, and that could take a while, if *Wild Kingdom* and Jeff Corwin could be trusted. Outside the bathroom door, drawers banged. A trash can popped open and shut. The toilet tank top was removed and replaced with a clank, and then came the unmistakable sound of someone relieving himself. The flush of the toilet carried the sound away. First thing after getting out of the reptile-infested shower, would be to declaw one MacKenzie Francis.

"Shit."

Who said that?

"Shit." It was a gravelly voice speaking low on the other side of the glass. Willi cut her eyes toward Kenzie. If she said something about *not literally, thank you very much,* Willi would have to kill her, right there and then. Kenzie opened her eyes wider, and drew in both her upper and lower lip. She'd certainly been thinking it, darn her hide.

The light flicked off, and in a few moments the moan of the floorboard and a difference in the air announced the door opening and shutting. Inoshi or Toru were back to night prowling. As soon as that happened, Willi flicked on the flashlight and kept it on the languid reptile while she and Kenzie stepped out of the tub. They shut the sliding door.

"That's two things," said Kenzie, finally relaxing her death grip. "The cardboard trickery and the snake. Guess they took it away after it killed Mr. Yodo. If that's what happened. I'm not 100 percent, but ninety-seven point six is pretty close, right?"

"Yes. But that snake isn't poisonous. It didn't kill Yodo. It's just a pet, I guess. Let's get out of here before the other fellow comes in."

Willi's foot slid from underneath her. She balanced herself against the doorframe. A piece of paper stuck to her foot. Kenzie picked it off and unfolded the one-inch square.

"What's this?" Kenzie frowned.

Willi studied the crude drawing on an eight-by-eleven sheet of notebook paper. "It's a map . . . or part of a map." She snapped her fingers. "Oh my gosh. I know who was just in here."

"Inoshi or Toru?"

"No. Banjo Joe Skeeter."

"You really do deserve that name, girl."

"Huh?"

"Miss Marple of the Range." Kenzie eased toward the front door. "How do you know that's his map? Couldn't it belong to the IODD men? That might explain the other reason they're on the island. Or maybe it belongs to the Pates?"

"Nope. Skeeter and Doretta told me about the family map."

"People do confide in you, girlfriend. I suppose now that I'm your breaking-and-entering partner, you might do a little confiding in me."

"I've been trying all evening, but we had to have some hands-on learning for you to stop long enough to listen to me." Willi stepped over the creaking floorboard. Kenzie shut the door behind them.

"Okay, Willi, where to now? Our pagoda or the teahouse?" Lightning flashes grew more intense. Another wave of the storm system was moving in.

"Mimosa." Willi said. "We'll take a look at this cell phone. You're better at mechanical thingamajigs than I am."

At the path where dense foliage rose above their heads, Willi was struck from behind and knocked to the ground. A hand came over her mouth.

"Don't make a sound." Kenzie said, and she pointed toward a break in the copse of trees, where feverish dancers were whipping their limbs in chaotic cadence. A figure flew past. There and gone in a blink of an eye.

Kenzie gasped. "It's *him.*" Trembling, she rolled off Willi's back and collapsed into a weeping heap.

"Kenzie, don't."

"Girl, I'll never escape. He's always going to find me."

"Not so."

"I want him gone, gone. Damn it. The son of a bitch."

Kenzie rocked back and forth while a high-pitched, unearthly keen rose from her throat. "He's going to ruin everything. Finally, I felt at ease with some new folks with no ties to that ass."

"It was a mere shadow. Could have been—"

"I even sort of had . . . had a romantic crush on . . . well, on someone. But I don't dare care for anyone, don't dare try to have a private life, don't dare bring any joy into my life."

"MacKenzie Francis, that's not true. Now, stop it!"

"He'll just touch it, taint it, and ruin it over and over and over for me."

Willi sat up and pulled Kenzie's hands away from her face. "Don't do this to yourself." She ground out each word and squeezed so hard she must've been cutting off Kenzie's circulation. "You are stronger than he is. You have good folks in your corner. That was not him, anyway."

"What do you mean, girl?" Kenzie withdrew her

hands, shook some feeling back into them, and repeated, "What?"

"Both the IODD men are out wandering around the island, Skeeter pops into a private pagoda to take a pee, and here we are cowering beneath the azaleas. Hells Bells, every one of the twenty-plus folks could have been the figure we just saw."

Including Jerry Cormack.

She just wasn't going to add that to Kenzie's paranoia package right now, considering what just the possibility did to her each time something happened.

"Girlfriend, I'm such a wuss."

"Not so."

"So. How do you put up with me?"

"Because I like excitement in my life? Dunks in the lake, facsimiles of dead bodies, knockdown dragouts beneath the Texas azaleas? What can I say, you add to my life."

Kenzie grinned. "Thanks." She helped Willi up.

Before reaching the Mimosa Pagoda, they peered out over one of the many cliffs and down at the Guadalupe, which frothed like mocha with cream swirls, just a pleasant confection hiding the possible caffeine roils beneath the surface.

Kenzie said, "Seems like it's risen some, doesn't it?"

"A tiny bit, I guess. By sunshine time in the morning, it'll dry out faster than an armadillo's carapace."

"Anyone else would have just said *hide.*"

With nose in the air, Willi intoned, "*Carapace* is a more correct term."

"Yes, ma'am, Ms. Gallagher, ma'am."

At the pagoda, two of the monks sat at each end of the artistic sandbox, seemingly practicing in unison an intricate and silent type of mantra using only hand signals.

"Like a ballet of prayer," Willi said, taking in each nuance of their movements, holding her own breath in her intense need to understand what each flicker of hand and wrist meant. "Beautiful."

As the sand shrine took up the middle section before the floor-to-ceiling windows, they had a choice of the regular seating to the left or the floor cushions and low tables to the right. Rimshi lit tinder in the fireplace along that side, so Willi took a seat on the warmed rugs and cushions. It was to his credit and training in equanimity that he didn't seem the least put out that they'd been customers every couple of hours all evening. After asking for and receiving hot cups of green tea, Willi eyed Rimshi until he moved into the kitchen area. She drew out the phone but kept it down beside her hip. She handed it to Kenzie. Grabbing a pen and paper from her bag, she said, "Okay, turn it on. I'll write down any numbers or names we can get from the thing."

Kenzie raised an eyebrow.

"Okay, anything *you* can get it to divulge."

With nimble fingers Kenzie opened the cover, switched the power button, and stared.

"Uh, Willi?"

She played around with the buttons, seeming to zip from one menu to another on the phone. "Willi?" she repeated.

"What?"

"You get one guess and one guess only about the ownership of this electronic wonder."

"Huh?"

Kenzie held it so Willi could see the lighted information in the window as Kenzie scrolled through every single menu.

"IODD men? Nara or Toru?" Willi asked.

"That would be my guess, and everything's in Japanese, so it's useless to us as far as identifying the owner."

"But"—Willi tapped the end of her nose with her pen—

"Isn't there a toggle switch to change it from Japanese characters to English?"

"Maybe, but I don't know what it is, girlfriend. I'm not that good with thingamajigs either."

"Damn. So I almost broke my neck getting to that green-eyed monster, and it tells us nothing."

"Tells us the IODD men aren't conscientious guests about abiding by the island's request of no cell phones. That, coupled with the fact that they've somehow rigged a dummy to mislead folks about their whereabouts, gives me reason to wonder about them and their motives."

"Right you are, Kenzie, right you are. And I've been a dummy. When they discover this missing, they'll know someone else knows *something*. So, what to do, replace it?" She sipped her tea and tucked the phone back in the depths of her bag.

Thunder boomed so loudly, even one of the monks by the window yelped. Willi spilled tea across the table. Rimshi came out of the kitchen, closed the curtains where the monks kept on with their silent hand signals, and then cleared the spill. Less than a half minute later, hail started coming down, the large pellets blasting against the metal roofing as if an army marched overhead. A torrent of rain streamed down, too, from what Willi could see of the skylights.

She shivered, goosebumps rising along her arms. If that damned Jerry Cormack were out wandering the island, he ought to be pelted skinless. No one deserved it more. She glanced at her watch and the date and said, "I can't believe it."

"What now?" Kenzie asked.

"We got here Sunday afternoon, right?"

"Yeah, girlfriend, one fact we can check off. Oh boy."

"It's just that by late Sunday night, we'd found Juna Marie Pate in the arms of someone other than the devoted Preacher Pate, discovered Yataro Yodo's body, and witnessed the aftermath of a fight between two Navy veterans."

"It was a full day, even by Texas standards."

"Now, it's not even eleven P.M. Monday and we've got a possible flood situation building, located Yataro Yodo's shoes and last messages in the prayer wheel, found out the IODD men have idiosyncratic night habits and cardboard cabin companions, rode runaway horses on a trail ride, and found an illegal cell phone. Jeez."

"Don't forget the map."

"Right. The map." She unraveled it, but could make no sense of it no matter which way she turned in on the table. "Great. Doesn't even look like this island. What gives with that?" She folded it into tiny squares again and tucked it into a side pocket of the bag.

"Not exactly living up to the name 'Serenity Island', is it?" Kenzie asked.

"Nope. More like a modern-day Payton Place cum Smallville."

"And you left out a few things, girl."

"What?"

"The Inipi ceremony." Kenzie's cheeks pinked up beneath her freckles.

Willi said, "You're right. But that was men only for today, right?"

"Right. Right." Kenzie wiggled between the pillows, punching one this way, another that way.

"Okay, okay," Willi said, "Give it up."

"Huh?"

"You're dying to tell me. You know something about the Inipi ceremony." Willi used the universal hand signal of pulling her fingers toward herself in that give-me, give-me gesture.

"I've done such crazy things lately."

"Yes, yes. So? What did you do, Kenzie?"

"Probably been around you too long, that's why."

"Don't blame whatever this is on me."

"Well, I was just wandering before the trail ride started, you know. Heck, we had a couple of hours to kill. Uh, that may have not been the best choice of words."

"Come on. Come on."

"And the smoke from that tent smelled so good."

"The Inipi lodge?"

"Yeah, girfriend, that place. So, all the men had gone inside. Well, all except one of the monks, and he stayed by the tipi flap."

"Lodge door."

"Like I said, by the lodge door, so I may have crawled—"

"Crawled? Oh, I love this." Willi grinned.

"Anyhoo, in one part of this ceremony, the men tell something of their past, and it was interesting. That's all. Can't imagine what made me do that."

"No, no, no. Back up. You know very dadgum well. Who are you talking to here? Particulars, please about—oh, let me see—one Paul Rooster Rowley?"

Kenzie put her splayed fingers over her mouth and closed her eyes. When she opened them, she giggled. "He doesn't think all women are mean, like he did before, because I used his name Rooster in a different way, and so I'm responsible for him thinking better of himself and not like he did when, you know, those women were putting him down and he was getting into fights where he used to lose his temper, which explains why he didn't want to lose his temper in the situation with Nestor D. last night, and so I just thought that was sort of neat that he is ready to . . . well . . . to . . ."

"To be interested in some special lady like you?"

"Well, maybe, I don't know, but—"

"No maybe about it. I feel so sorry for you, Kenzie."

"What?"

"Crouching behind an Inipi lodge, eavesdropping—for heaven's sake—*tsk, tsk*. I do feel sorry for you; you *have* been around me too long."

Kenzie giggled. The sound lifted Willi's spirits. "Well, for some this may not be a serene island, but it's definitely a healing island. There must be something magical and powerful about it."

Kenzie yawned. Willi did, too. Eyes watering, she said, "Since we're both talking in yawn, maybe we'd best table the decisions about what to do about whom until the morning. Rain's let up, let's make a run for some true shut-eye."

"Works for me, girlfriend."

It would really have worked better for Willi if, as she left the pagoda, both monks had not turned a hateful stare in her direction. The intensity was like a quick turbo blast of fire sprayed outward then sucked into an airless vacuum. She blinked, and the duo held their heads bowed in prayer.

CHAPTER
II

Willi woke to the sound of droplets of rain making the final trip off the pagoda roof to plop in the many pools scattered around the housing area. Sunshine flowed through the window, a precursor, she hoped, for a fun day outdoors. She must have been the slug-abed, because everyone else had already left. She considered each cubicle while getting ready. Kenzie always made her bed, even at hotels, for heaven's sake. Her blanket neatly folded, her pillows plumped, but there Miss Neatness drew a line. A pile of dirty clothes lay heaped beside the bed, and her makeup cowered in nooks and crannies on the lamp table, the edge of the bed, and on the floor. And she never understood why she lost so many things. Goofy girl. Willi picked up Kenzie's dusting powder that lay open on the edge of the table where any passerby might knock it off.

Doretta's cubbyhole behind a Japanese screen indicated a frenzied search through all her luggage with bright red tops and hot pink walking shorts higgledy-piggledy on bedposts, mixed with the unmade bed covers and trampled underfoot from her private pigpen on into the shower area. Willi kicked them toward the walls to make room to pass.

Just before she stepped into the shower, she came back to peek into Juna Marie's curtained bedchamber at the opposite end near the window. Everything was pristine with military corners. Good grief, the woman even carried a can of Pledge furniture polish and paper towels in her luggage.

"Got to be some reason to be that . . . anal."

As clean and neat as the room was, it seemed sad somehow, as if the swan's nest had been ransacked by a cleanfreak. Each pair of jeans, shorts, and every shirt or sweater had a particular type of hanger suitable for that garment. The suitcases, closed and probably locked, sat in the corner, stacked in order of size with the makeup case on top.

Willi's glance fell on one item that lifted her spirits. "Ah! Nice, that, really nice."

The only thing out of place in the whole cubbyhole was a bright red, yellow, and blue bouquet of wildflowers stuffed in one of the tea glasses used by the Lotus Pagoda crew. Willi smiled, picked up the vase to sniff the fragrance, and inhaled greedily. At least, Preacher Pate was attentive to his Juna Marie. Why was the fool woman making kissy face with anyone else?

Willi shook her head. "Withhold judgement. Might not have been her instigating the embrace, remember," Willi whispered to the Japanese screen.

By the time Willi got out of the shower, into her clothes, and outside, she changed her mind about the fun day. Good God, the humidity would bring a bull elephant to his knees. The moist heat slammed against her on her walk to breakfast. Mud encrusted the sides of the walkways, and downed tree branches covered some areas. She moved the smaller ones to the side.

"I'm so sorry, Standing People. So sorry."

The larger ones she maneuvered around, usually to the detriment of her sneakers, which slid in the wet puddles, the mud slime. and drowned flower blossoms.

Hmm. Must've been too wet to meditate upon the koan of the day outside the Mimosa Teahouse. When she tramped up the steps and inside, she pulled her soaked blouse away from her heated skin. So much for freshness.

The participants, in a triple semi-circle around three sides of the sandbox, reclined on their meditation rugs and stared out the glassed windows on the fourth side of the picture. Willi tapped Kenzie on the shoulder, unrolled her mat, and sat beside her.

"What a lovely alternative to the lawn."

"You bet, girl, especially since it's still soaking wet."

Kenzie took a handful of napkins from a nearby table and wiped her forehead. "Does no good to wear makeup in this weather."

"I know what you mean. Here's a bandanna. Old Sheriff Brigham Tucker insisted I'd need a half dozen and forced them on me. I finally dug them out. Glad I did."

"Me, too." Kenzie grabbed one and followed Willi's instructions about how to wear them. "Samdup isn't here yet. Not the Pates, either. Everyone seems tired today."

"And surely you know why," Willi said, "when half of them were traipsing over the island most of the night." She peered over Kenzie's shoulder. "Where's Quannah?"

"Oh, Rimshi said he went over to the ranch mainland in the motorboat this morning. Must've been a rough trip with the water swirling the way it was. Scary."

"And he didn't even stop to say good-bye?"

Kenzie patted her arm. "He told you he'd be busy. Remember he's working; we're not."

"Keep reminding me."

"You really miss him, don't you, when you don't see him for twenty-four hours?"

"Does it show?" Willi sniffed and squared her shoulders. No pity party today. "I'll tell you what I saw that was sweet and thoughtful."

Before Kenzie could ask what, Juna Marie settled to the left, almost facing them in the semi-circle. She smiled.

Kenzie said, "Gosh, she really does glow like an angel."

"Yes," Willi said, "she looks like a happy woman and with reason, because Preacher Pate brought—"

Halliwell Pate burst through the door in his Dockers and blue sweater about the hips. In his hand he carried a bouquet of posies. Red, yellow, and blue. Just like the one in Juna Marie's chamber.

Willi, with mouth agape, stared. Hmm.

"Brought her what?" Kenzie asked.

"A bouquet."

"Girlfriend, I'm not blind. I can see that, but Juna Marie sure doesn't seem too happy about them."

"Here you are, my Juna Marie. Nothings too good for a sweet, virtuous one like you, my darling wife, no sir-ree. The Lord has blessed us both. Can't find devotion and fidelity so easily in these times. What a pleasure it is to have this gentle soul as my own."

Juna Marie peered up at Halliwell. Her face turned crimson, then white. Juna Marie mumbled a thank-you and took the flowers. She sat them between her legs crossed in front of her and stared out into the room, across the sand artistry, into what must have been the depths of hell, judging by her expression. Not a muscle moved; she didn't blink; she became like a human statue. Even when Samdup took his position on a prayer rug in front of the artistic offering of the day, Juna Marie's lips remained parted as if she wanted to speak but couldn't.

"What is going on, girlfriend?" Kenzie asked.

"All I know is there's another bouquet just like that one—and I mean absolutely and totally alike down to the last leaf—in Juna Marie's room. A fresh bouquet. So why would he bring her another only a few minutes later?"

Kenzie whispered, "Maybe the first wasn't from him?"

"Had to have been, because no two men would pick the very same combination of flowers, arrange them alike. Would they?"

"Okay, girl, perhaps he saw the other one and copied it?"

"That's scary."

"And might account," Kenzie offered, "for the barely breathing woman before us."

"We'll talk to her after the koan meditation," Willi said, while pulling her legs to the side in a more comfortable position.

Samdup's benign smile bathed them in a glow as soft and gentle as a baby's glance. "Today we use an old haiku by Master Basho for our contemplation." He paused and looked deeply into each person's eyes, a significant time allowing each to calm, each to focus: "The old pond. A jumping frog—Plop!"

Oddly enough, the sand painting depicted a frog on a lily pad with dragonflies and butterflies and mosquitoes—of all things—flying around its head. Must amount to a veritable flying feast for a frog.

"Ah," intoned Samdup, "to be the child, to experience the wonder of all around you as a neophyte of the world. Hmm. To feel, hear, see as a little one again the wonder of the present moment such as this magic one." He repeated the koan.

Willi and Kenzie smiled at each other. It was nice to share this moment, to remember their own childhood and its magical moments. Yes, this was nice.

Kenzie whispered, "Recall the old tires your daddy used to rope up for us as swings?"

"Yeah, and the pumpkin cake your mama made?"

"Ooh, girl, and the times we went possum hunting with your cousins? That was the first and only time I ever shot a gun."

"Even better. Building that underground castle."

"That was the best, girlfriend, the best."

And Willi agreed. She and her cousins took shovels and hoes and first built a stairway down into the depths—some fifteen feet down in the back field—then carved out a circular hut big enough for about a dozen folks to sit. They even had a fireplace and benches cut into the walls. A magical summer experience. Truly, the best with cousins and friends.

Kenzie nudged her in the side. Halliwell Pate and the IODD men frowned at her and Kenzie.

Willi grinned. "Sorry. Just a little trip down memory lane."

They all quietly looked up at the old monk. Samdup opened his hands, palms outward to include them all in a gentle gesture of being held and protected. He said, "This day is going to be most different for many of you. Something you may never have experienced. Today, as you go about for the next fourteen hours after the gong sounds until you hear the great ring again, you will contemplate and live through the day in complete and total silence."

Nara Inoshi said, "Wonderful. A true time of introspection."

"Perhaps we will encounter the Eye of the Divine," Mike Toru said with a sigh.

Halliwell Pate said, "I always do the same thing come each Thursday, to get myself ready to write my Sunday sermon. Nothing like some vege-out time to come into tune with the Lord's will and ways. Isn't that right, sweet Juna Marie?"

Juna Marie, her white feathery hair limp from the humidity, mumbled, "Time to think. Yes, that would be great. Uninterrupted by anyone else's thoughts. Just my own. Oh, yes, I like that idea." She turned soulful eyes to Samdup. "Thank you. Thank you."

Willi, eyes wide, stared at Kenzie's horror-stricken face.

Oh, this was not good, not nice. No, no, no. Not a happening thing.

Willi tensed when she heard Kenzie sigh, a sure sign she was going to adhere to the day's request.

No, no, no, they had places to go, people to see, clues to uncover.

Samdup quailed the murmurs with a gentle downward turn of his palms, bouncing them slowly until the grumbles subsided. "As I said, unusual for you, but hopefully, you each will have much to share after the fourteen hours. If you come together at lunchtime here in the teahouse, you will be silent, having to express your wishes through means other than voice. Again, same way at the evening meal. At midnight your silent time will be ended. So, go to your breakfasts now set on the low tables. The gong will sound in three minutes."

Everyone bustled toward tables, ordering quickly. Willi said, "We can't do this, Kenzie. My gosh, I need to figure out what to do about the cell phone, and we were going to go back to the rock garden and talk over what all has happened. And what about Juna Marie?"

With her hand she turned Kenzie's face toward the al-most catatonic preacher's wife. Juna Marie sat at the next table where she stared at the flowers. They seemed to breathe more than she. "What about her?"

"Girlfriend, I know. I know. But, the day of silence is part of the process. If it weren't for this . . . this gosh-awful situation hanging over our heads, we'd not be worried about not being able to communicate."

"Good choice of words, *communicate*." Willi drank down her orange juice as if they'd been put on a no-liquids instead of a no-talking ban. "We can still *communicate*, right? You remember any of the sign language we had in high school?"

"A little. We'll work it out."

They grinned at each other. Willi said, "Okay, I feel bet-ter. This is going to be fine."

Samdup, with a small bell that he rang three times, got their attention. "The old pond. A jumping frog—Plop!"

He rang the bell for another trio of tintinnabulation. "In a half minute the gong for silence will sound. One other criterion will be followed. Only at mealtimes will you see each other. If you sight one another, you must choose a different path. Please honor each other's spiritual trail these hours, and turn aside. This day is to be spent alone."

"Did he say *alone?*" asked Willi.

"Alone, girl. All alone."

A gasp from the two arose. Willi blinked. Kenzie blinked back. They both screamed, "Nooooooo!"

Their final protest was lost in the clamorous clanging of the heavy gong as Rimshi hit it three times. Somehow, they mimed to him their need for fresh fruit, some pita-pocket veggie pies, and a couple bottles of cold tea before they parted. They had no choice but parting since Samdup stood at the meeting of the pathways and started each off in a different direction or at a different time, giving the person ahead time to chose numerous paths along the way before someone was on his or her heels.

CHAPTER
12

Willi glanced down each path in the hopes of catching a glimpse of Kenzie. Darn, they should have signaled each other or said a place or . . . well, whatever. Too late now. If Kenzie had been with her, what would she have done?

Ah, yes. She wanted to wander toward the huge rock garden where she'd discovered the cell phone. With that intention cemented, she held her head high and tromped toward the garden. Within a couple of yards, the night heron croaked in its flight—which she caught in her peripheral vision—as if to say, *Come this way, this way.*

Willi shook her head at that silly thought popping into her brain. Nope, she'd not go toward the bird, thank you very much. She eyeballed the feathered friend, and said in a low voice in case anyone was within hearing distance, "No thank you. It might be more interesting to see who else showed up at the garden. And I'm not breaking the si-

lence unless someone else hears me. At least I think that's
right."

The creature whizzed by her head yet again and dis-
tracted her for a moment, at which time she decided the
serenity garden could wait. First and foremost she needed
a quick return to the ladies' pagoda. In fact, after all that
tea, it seemed a high-priority item. Secondly, one tooth required the definite attention of her mint floss.

In her hurry, she shut the door harder than she meant
to, opened her mouth to apologize to whoever might be
there, but a glance at Kenzie's and Doretta's areas showed
both were out. As she raced toward the bathroom, Willi
glimpsed Juna Marie perched on her bed with legs crossed
yoga style.

She wanted to say, "Hiya. Sorry for the loud entrance,"
but settled for a hands up, a woebegone look, and a pat on
her chest. No sense in messing up the day of inner retreat
for others.

Juna Marie's attention remained glued to the bouquet
on the table while she slowly ripped and tore every single
petal off the posies Preacher Pate had brought to the koan
meditation. Her swanlike neck, regally stiff, did not bend
to the work; rather she plucked blindly. The bruised flowers—the white petals already turning brown—floated to
the bedspread and wooden floor. Crimson blooms and blue
curled like dried offerings across Juna Marie's shorts and
tanned legs.

Willi came around in front of Juna Marie to touch her
shoulder and gave her a look she hoped said, "Are you
okay?"

Juna Marie swallowed audibly. Without moving neck or
head, merely cutting her eyes around to stare at Willi, Juna
Marie sighed, put a finger to her lips, and continued with the
total annihilation of the wildflower bouquet. Willi backed up.

She hated to leave the woman, obviously in an emotional crisis, with what Freddy Fender would call *petals of love* in "Mexican Rose." This was not nearly as pretty as the song. Nope, sweet and beautiful was not a happening thing here.

Sadness, sure.

Hurt. Some deep, down-to-the-bone pain hurled out into the room with each torn leaf. Willi stood by for a good three minutes, but Juna Marie did not change her position among the discarded wildflowers, nor make any motion that indicated she wanted Willi to remain.

So, she took care of the flossing, checked her bag, added an orange and an apple from the bowl of fresh fruit, and left. For a few minutes, she waited on the porch while getting all the bulky things in her shoulder bag more comfortable. She didn't, for some reason, want to leave neither the shoes nor the cell phone in the pagoda.

The door behind her clicked. Well, good grief.

She tried the doorknob. Juna Marie had locked the world out. Willi clamped her lips together. No problem. Might be, Mrs. Pate figured it'd be easier to maintain the full day of silence by locking everyone out, or . . . maybe just one particular person—Halliwell Pate.

Willi wandered again toward her original destination, the rock garden, while musing about the Pates. Surely, if they had a marriage gone wrong, as two Christian folks they'd try counseling, and if that didn't work, they'd find a way toward an amicable divorce. Willi took out the orange and peeled it, throwing the peels into the woods for the feathered ones and four-leggeds to enjoy. Hmm. Reminded her of Juna Marie's silent tirade against the bouquet. The deliberate ripping asunder of the blossoms bespoke a . . . what? Long-time loathing? A hatred on the front burner, boiling over? Directed at Halliwell or was it self-loathing on Juna Marie's part?

The night heron swooped in front of her, landed on a branch in the sallow shadows, and blinked, all the time twitching a shoulder feather, indicating to Willi's mind that she should not go to the stone garden, but the Lotus Pagoda.

Nope. She directed her thoughts toward the fowl. *I'm headed for the garden, not the Lotus Pagoda, the teaching area. And why are you out flying around within sight of the sun, anyway, you night bird, you?*

The heron leaned his head to one side and blinked.

At the Y, she rubbed her nose and wiped a sheen of morning perspiration away. She rubbed her temples. Okay, right now, she was so confused. So, what the hell. She breathed deeply and repeated the koan. Fine, the heron wasn't a frog, but . . . but, of course, the poem was meant to convey the wonder and magic of all nature, not just the frog. What the hey. So, wasn't this just like her luck, to get a nosy bird plopped in front of her instead of a beautiful butterfly or a cute little bunny or a thousand other magical creatures?

She eyed the fowl. Not wanting to break the silence, even for the bird, she nodded at him and mentally informed him his name from this moment on was Botherbutt.

Okay, Night Heron, Night Bird, Botherbutt, maybe . . . maybe you know something I don't. Well, I'm going to feel really stupid doing this, but fine. I'll do what you seem to be trying to tell me. I'll deny to my dying day, you winged wonder, that I did, if anyone should ask. So . . . so there.

Okay, maybe old Botherbutt did know something she didn't. Like it might be cooler on that side of the island where the Lotus Pagoda stood. As soon as she made the corner toward the teaching pagoda, the heron disappeared into the deep foliage, no doubt to garner a little shut-eye in a cooler bower.

By the time she reached the Lotus Pagoda, sweat

soaked every cotton fiber of her jeans and T-shirt. So much for cooler. Obviously, that wasn't the reason she felt bound to come in this direction. Oh well. From that drenched state, a plan had materialized. Quiet time might be just the ticket to get things categorized, arranged in some pattern. What better place than one of the meditation rooms? First, she went into the ladies' room, rinsed and wrung out the bandanna, and ducked her head underneath the faucet. Ah. Welcome coolness. A cricket chirped in the corner. Willi smiled. She quoted the koan silently. "The old pond. A jumping frog—Plop!"

She bent down to scoop the cricket up and place it in the vestibule rather than the ladies' room. She peered up toward heaven.

Yes, Daddy, I know. Don't throw a cricket out of the house; it'll bring bad luck. I'm not. Simply going to put Jiminy's cousin in another room.

Scrunching down into the corner to maneuver better brought her ear close to the wall next to the men's room. A strange clicking and the low rumble of a deep voice, though muffled, came through the partition. Hmm. Not fair. Somebody was breaking the silence. Or maybe there were two since generally one assumed you needed someone else to talk with, right?

Unless a person chose to talk to a winged creature.

Or perhaps, in this case, they conversed with a second cricket. What the heck was the clacking sound? Maybe a problem with the plumbing.

Nah. The noises were too random. She peered upward as if she would know what rhythm bad plumbing would produce. She shook her head, bumped the pipes underneath the sink, grabbed the cricket, and tiptoed out to the vestibule. More than likely her imagination running wild again. Everyone had taken the vow of silence for the day.

Must have been the pipes or water dripping or something mundane but nothing of the human variety creating the strange resonance on the other side of the wall.

Now, to find a place where no one would intrude while she collected her rambling herd of thoughts, corralled them into some sort of rational ramuda, and got them branded— meaning, got them written down on paper. After all, she had Mr. Yodo's notebook to use. The door to what she considered his last resting place swung lazily in a draft created when the AC kicked into high. Well, what better place to sort. Sure, why not?

She stepped in and gently closed the door behind her. Ah, this room was on the other side of the men's room. With her back to that, she faced the shrine with the Buddha statue, this one of wood with red and gold paint. She took up a flame lighter, thumbed it to life, and lit a dozen candles. The flames created shadow dancers on the walls and floor. One flitted grotesquely across the ceiling. Goosebumps rose on her arms as she peered over each shoulder. As she intuited a presence behind her, she twisted around only to face the bare wall.

Despite her uneasiness, she grabbled within her bag to draw out a pen and Mr. Yodo's notebook. She listed each of the participants and tried to come up with a reason any of them might want Mr. Yodo to seek a higher realm of being before his allotted time.

Paul Rooster Rowley, by his own admission, disliked anyone of Asian blood. Perhaps he was working toward more tolerance, but no one changed such thinking in the matter of two days. Ditto that reason for Nestor D. Tulsa. He didn't even seem to be hiding his hate of the Japanese-American businessmen.

Again she heard the faint clacking and clicking, but no

deep rumblings. She shivered. The drying perspiration merely felt clammy, not truly cooled by the AC drifting over her. She tapped her pen on her retroussé nose.

Hatred of the Japanese contingency. Which brought *them* to the forefront of possibility. Certainly, there might be rivalries between three such highly placed men in the company. Maybe one of them wanted a shortcut to the next position—Mr. Yodo's spot. Made sense, being that he was the most senior. It might be necessary to move him out before someone else could take his place. Good gosh almighty, surely that didn't have to be an out-and-out murder. Might even be something as screwy as one lower down in the pecking order, killing him, not for his position, but for the job that would be vacated upon the next guy moving up the proverbial corporate ladder. Okay, she could check out that angle if she confided in Quannah. He'd have the means to find out those details. She made a notation.

How about the Pates? Halliwell and Juna Marie. Willi frowned. Try as she might she couldn't come up with a— Whoa. Oh, yes, there might very well be a strong motive on both sides. Willi scribbled furiously now, trying to get the rampaging thoughts down in some manageable order.

Sure. Halliwell Pate would hate anyone who dared look at his Juna Marie. Hells Bells, hadn't he almost shoved his hand through the Mimosa Teahouse's walls last night? If he showed such jealousy over old Skeeter playing a song for Juna Marie, what might the ordained one do if he saw, as Willi and Kenzie had, his Juna Marie in the embrace of one of the IODD men? Yeah, definitely, he belonged on the list of suspects.

Now, Juna Marie.

As Willi pondered the gracefulness of the woman, a large book or something akin dropped on the floor behind her. Willi jumped up and twirled around. Nothing there. No plumbing could have made that sound.

Scrabbling on the wall beside the men's room drew her closer. She leaned her ear against the dark paneling of the room's wall. A distinct snap burst upon her eardrum. She leaned her head to one side. Someone flushed. Ah, okay. Guess the snap was one of those sliding locks. Willi grimaced, swearing to herself not to share this second "potty moment" with Kenzie. Great balls of fire, she'd think Willi was one of those bathroom perverts discussed on that Jerry Springer show. Plenty of creeps around listening to others in the most intimate and disgusting moments, not to mention the video pirates who invaded privacy. Willi shook her head, shoulders, and arms in revulsion and backed away.

Jerry Springer.

Jerry.

Jerry Cormack. Oh, how she wanted to lay this at his feet. No way. Wouldn't wash. He didn't know any of the participants. Wait just a skipdeedoodah. What if Jerry had been discovered breaking in by Mr. Yodo? Nah. That would have worked if Yataro had been hit on the head or bludgeoned to death with one of the really big candleholders. But . . . there was that hand gone purple, filled with a snake's venom if she were right. If she were a betting lady, she'd lay odds Jerry Cormack would pee his BVDs and wear them backasswards before he'd touch a viper.

Writing pad in hand again, she wrote down the cousins' names—Doretta Cameo and Banjo Joe Skeeter.

Motive, motive, motive.

Willi shut her eyes and tried to envision what might set good-hearted Doretta and sweet old Skeeter on a hunt for Yataro Yodo's skin. She wrote two words underneath both their names. She sighed. Damn. Could be, could be.

Treasure Map.

She drew curlicues around the word *map*. That idea was a real mustang leap—completely wild and not likely to be caught. Why did her mind have to work this way, even about the most pleasant of folks? She waved both hands in front of the candles. Rhetorical question, that which she'd never been able to answer in all the years before, and probably never would. Just simply the way her brain processed ideas. Period. Accept it. Move on.

"The old pond. A jumping frog—Plop!"

She smiled and nodded as the koan eased into her written musings. The outside door closing—a sound she recalled from nights ago—echoed. A yawn, bigger than the Guadalupe's breadth, attacked her, leaving watery eyes in its wake. Time to stretch. She wandered down the hallway, opened the outside double portal to see the backside of Nestor D. Tulsa sauntering away, and quietly shut the door. Guess he'd been making use of the facilities.

A small lizard, no bigger than her thumb, scrambled down the hall. Now that critter she *could* catch and put outside. He wiggled his tail at her, and when she overreached she grasped air, and fell against the men's room entry. The wily reptile scooted into the male domain. Well, Hells Bells and damned bats. Why did she always have the strangest encounters with God's critters? She lay sprawled on the floor under the sudden weight of that question, and an answer flashed into her brain so fast and with such clarity, she gasped.

Ohmygod, ohmygod, my gosh.

Botherbutt made her change directions. Noises kept attracting her attention. The small lizard led her into an area she'd not ordinarily enter. Something important lay here in the Lotus Pagoda's men's room. As if to confirm the idea, the lizard stopped running, turned around, and faced her. His nasty little tongue darting out made goosebumps dance over her arm. She wrinkled her nose.

Her breathing had slowed until she somehow imagined she moved in slow motion. Getting up to her knees, then onto unsteady legs, she simply stood in the middle of the paneled bath. If not for the three cubicles and the two men's urinals, the room was identical to the meditation rooms. The tile on the floor—a beautiful jade green—glistened as did the deep polished wood of the walls. What in the heck could she hope to find here? Had she had a brain bubble?

She peered down at the floor. The lizard was nowhere—not under the sink, inside the stalls, or by the toilets. What kind of fantastical brain poop was she creating, for goodness sake? She almost turned to walk out, but . . . but the feeling engendered by the moment of intense *knowing* translated into a core lesson, one that brought tears to her eyes.

Trust.

Oh, yeah. Great. And she had to have her epiphany inside the men's room of a teaching pagoda on an island where no one spoke. Yep, okey dokey.

Trust. How many times had Quannah begged her to trust her innermost feelings? She couldn't go through a week in Nickleberry without the Kachelhoffer sisters telling her to have faith in the universe.

Trust. She had to trust herself; her instincts, the crazy critters that sometimes, pushed, goaded, and maneuvered her into strange circumstances. If she didn't learn to trust herself, there'd be no hope of offering that most precious commodity to another like . . . like Quannah.

She had choices. There were always those dangblame choices, some cool as the proverbial cucumbers with ranch dressing and some hotter than a vine-ripened chili pepper.

Choice *número uno:* Walk away and don't look back, don't trust her instincts, turn against all the teachings of

Quannah and the Kachelhoffer sisters, set her back against . . . trusting herself. She hung her head. That would lead to a worse morass of conflicts.

And *segundo?* Stay. Snoop . . . well, *look.* See what she could find. And what was there to lose with that scenario? Not a dangblame thing. Three stalls, a linen closet of supplies, and a changing bench couldn't take too long.

She searched behind the sink, around the toilets, into every dark corner of the cubicles, even stepping atop the urinals to push up the ceiling panels. At last, she bent down as she had been on the opposite side of the wall when she heard the strange clacking sounds. On hands and knees, she inched along, shoving the changing bench out from the floorboard, tapping the wood paneling. She was about to open the linen closet when strong footsteps stomped down the hall.

A man's tred.

Caramba and double-damn Aunt Jenny's penny. Hiding in bathrooms was fast losing its fascination. She entered and locked the last cubicle before perching precariously atop the toilet. At least she didn't have Kenzie's nails digging into her skin. Good thing, as said skin at the moment sported goosebumps the size of prize-winning eggs.

Luckily, he chose a meditation room on the other side of the hall, if her hearing could be trusted. At the moment, she wasn't sure of that, but she got down off the seat rim, back down on hands and knees. Just as she shoved the wooden changing bench into place, an oddity caught her attention.

A piece of wood or cloth stuck out perhaps less than an eighth of an inch, just enough that at the present angle, she could tell it wasn't smooth wood. She scrabbled at it with a fingernail. At last, she worked enough of the soft cloth out, and she pulled on it. That motion dislodged a two-by-six-inch section of the back of the changing bench. Willi bent

down to peek inside. A cloth bag lay there; in fact, that's
what she'd been plucking. She swallowed. Ah-ha, another
cell phone? What was wrong with these people? Did they
have no respect? Were none of them serious about the Zen
retreat? But when she looked inside the bag, she discovered something entirely different. One of those flip-top,
handheld mini-computers beeped when she pressed a tab
on the side.

Why that old newshound! Nestor D. Tulsa lied. He *was*
writing a story. Somewhere in this micro-mess he had
tapped in their stories. Wait. Don't jump to conclusions.
Might just be a diary. They'd all been told to keep one, but
not an electronic daily entry, rather the old-fashioned written type. Could simply be that Nestor D., being set in his
reporter ways, wasn't willing to give up the ease of the
keyboard. Willi touched the end of her nose. She'd sure
like to believe that he hadn't lied about not doing any jour-
nalistic work while here.

The meditation room door creaked. Willi held her
breath so long she grew dizzy.

Please. Please go outside, not in here. Please.

Someone above must have been listening. Whoever
came out of the room went straight down the hall and out
the front door.

Willi quickly turned off the palm computer, stuck it inside its protective bag, and replaced it in the opening back
of the changing bench. She broke out in another sweat
while pushing the bench back, a more difficult task than
pulling it away from the wall. No reason to add the contraption to her purse. After all, she knew where it was.
Maybe she'd figure out a way to get Nestor D. to own up to
having it on the island. Perhaps he'd tell her the purpose
was something entirely innocent.

Of course, as soon as she opened the men's room door

numerous ideas raced around the inside curves of her brain track. He could be keeping notes on each and every person on the island for a later exposé. There was a possibility he even had something to do with Mr. Yodo's disappearance. Could be he worked for a group against the IODD businessmen. Maybe he was an operative, here to let "them"— whoever they were—know what and where each of the men would be at a given time of the day or night. Good luck on that one! He'd better have snuck in a tracking device to hook to their tennis shoes if they wandered as much as Kenzie and she had seen so far.

Willi retied the bandanna around her head and strode outside and toward her original destination and purpose. The rock garden might draw the owner of the phone there, and she'd be present to intercept when they discovered it missing. Ha! See if they felt like talking then.

Maybe the cell phone—the other electronic device not allowed on the island—was Nestor D.'s also. She stumbled over a tree root grown out into the path. Nope, nope, ix-nay on that idea. Nestor wouldn't be caught dead with a phone using only Japanese characters. What was she thinking?

The canopied walkway on four sides of the garden offered a cooler respite than even the teaching pagoda. Large oak trees further buffered the encroaching heat waves. She opted for a wooden bench tucked beneath a frothy overhanging weeping willow tree. Ah-ha. A wonderful nook from which to see the entire garden while remaining hidden from anyone else. She sank down and crossed her legs in the dappled gloom. In a few moments, she jolted awake from a nap. What the hey? A line of ants traipsed across her foot. One must haven bitten her. She brushed the hordes off and scratched like a cat with fleas. A change in the air pressure alerted her to another presence. She rubbed the sleep from her eyes.

Nara Inoshi strode around the perimeter with shoulders squared, head back, breathing in the humid air. She pulled her legs deeper into the shadows and away from the ants' main route, she hoped. He marched the entire length and breadth three times before halting. At once he squinted his dark eyes as if peering through the leaves of her bower.

Willi swallowed bile, which rose and rose again. She never realized until that moment just how much noise the human body could make doing a simple thing such as clearing a throat. When she finally managed to choke the mess down, her temples throbbed with the effort required to do it without making a sound. At last, Inoshi seemed satisfied that he was alone. He turned his back on her and leaned much as she had the night before upon the railings where he could look upon the huge stones depicting landmasses. He bent down and peered between the rails.

Ah, so. Willi grinned. Maybe he was trying to see the green glint of an electronic beam.

Too bad, so sad, and way too late.

Inoshi peered over his shoulder, then straddled the railing, also much as Willi had tried to do. His long legs and well-honed physique made a much better job of it than she had. He was going to jump directly down into the stones. Oh my gosh.

Willi covered her mouth with her hands. Stings attacked her ankle and she had to move both hands to scratch. Another task not accomplished with complete quiet. Damned ants!

Inoshi, rather than jumping, merely dangled his long legs on the other side of the railing, put his elbows on his knees, and seemed to settle in for an impromptu meditation while contemplating life's ebbs and flows within the rock patterns below.

She pinched another red marauder from her leg. Well,

Hells Bells, that one had relatives on the warpath—a warpath leading straight to her right knee. Just as the second and third cousins arrived, Inoshi pulled his lanky frame back over the rail and headed down the boathouse path. Twenty seconds after he sauntered out of sight, Willi came out from the willow's branches and executed an Apache stomp Quannah would have praised.

Well, shoot fire and piddle piss, as her granddaddy used to say. What a waste of time. Time wasted checking on Juna Marie and the bouquet destruction, time lost in the meditation room and the men's room. Now, her hunch about the cell phone proved unfounded. Obviously, the phone wasn't Inoshi's. Hmm. Hold it, hold it. Might be he simply didn't feel right about getting it in the daylight. Might just have been checking. He'd not worry about the green light not showing in the sunlight. So . . . still . . . time wasted with nothing learned.

She hobbled down the path, stopping every few seconds to scratch her ant bites. After bending down for one of her itching sessions, she straightened to discover Rimshi on the path. He bowed, pointed to her ankle and then to one of the many potted plants along the walkway. She shrugged her shoulders.

He pulled off a few leaves from an aloe vera plant and smeared a thick liquid onto the bites on her knee, indicating she should do the same for the rest of her right leg and ankle. Willi smiled and mouthed a silent *ahhhhhhhh*. Oh, and it did soothe. She nodded her thanks. Rimshi inclined his head and retraced his steps along the path.

A breeze wove its way through the trees, wrapped around her in a cooling embrace, and drifted away. In its wake, the zephyr left a comfort zone around her, her shoulders relaxed, her mind floated, and she chose to lie flat on her back on the grassy knoll. The grass rose a good three feet around her, but all she cared about was the panorama above her. Idly, she opened herself to the pictures created by the fluffy clouds, for the moment devoid of rain and lightning. They could have been marshmallows or cotton balls or jet airstreams. Peaceful, so peaceful.

A hand clamped over her mouth and eyes so hard she couldn't utter a sound.

"*Shh*. Shush." Kenzie tapped Willi's cheek with one manicured nail. She pointed to Willi's right.

Kenzie removed her hand and Willi cut her eyes to the right, expecting to see at the very least a snake slithering through the grass or a rabid skunk, tail lifted in a powerful salute.

For a few moments, her vision blurred from the pressure of Kenzie's hold. When she blinked, it cleared enough to see only the figure of a crouching man some twenty feet away.

CHAPTER
13

Only denim-clad legs could be seen as the man crouched behind an outcropping of native cacti scattered here and there in the deep grass.

Kenzie mouthed silently, "Jerry?"

Willi shook her head, but swallowed hard against the facts. Same size, dark head of hair. From this distance it was difficult to judge the height of a man in such a position. By dang creeping crawdads, she *would* find out. Something had to be done about this piece of refuse.

He zigzagged from one hidey-hole to another until he disappeared over the edge of the hill. A few more moments passed. A distant underfoot crunching resounded when Willi stood still and listened. She crept forward with Kenzie right behind her until they reached the first cacti-hiding place. Kenzie peered down and gasped. Two or three well-chewed toothpicks lay on the ground. Willi didn't have to break the silence to fathom the idea roiling in her friend's mind.

Jerry Cormack and his damned toothpicks.

Disgusting as it was, Willi used two fingernails to lift the pieces, place them in a Kleenex tissue, and tuck them in her ever-growing bag of clues.

The man disappeared into the heavier foliage. Willi allowed him to go a hundred more yards before blurting, "We have to talk."

Kenzie's eyes teared up. "I had so wanted this day of silence . . . but . . . *he's* ruined this, too!"

Willi snapped her fingers. "No, by damned, he hasn't, not unless we allow him to do so. Right now I think we should follow what Quannah calls *antelope medicine.* Come on." She grabbed Kenzie's wrist and hightailed it toward the woods surrounding one low-life Jerry Cormack. "I want to get to the bottom of at least one mystery on this so-called Serenity Island."

Kenzie dug in her heels. "No! Willi, are you crazy? What the hell is antelope . . . whatever. I'm not going anywhere near that sorry—"

Willi tightened her grasp. She jumped over a protruding root. "Watch it!" She peered into the dense bushes. "Ah, there he goes!"

"Stop!" Kenzie grabbed the edge of Willi's blouse. "I will not—"

"Exactly," Willi said, making a quick turn to face her friend nose to nose. "You will *not* take this cowering any longer. Antelope medicine refers to proper action in a tough situation. Is it good for you to cower in fear? No. Is it fair this damned weenie of a man has taken power from you, made you feel afraid at his shadow? Absolutely not! Is it right that just the thought of his presence makes you feel like a mistreated kennel mutt? No, no, and double-damned no."

"So . . ." Kenzie faltered, her glance darted upward, around, and back to the ground. She trembled. "So what do you expect me to do?"

"Come on." Willi held tightly to Kenzie's wrist and pulled her alongside him.

When they were both loping at a steady pace and had again caught sight of the denim, Willi paused a moment to put her hands on her knees, the better to suck in needed air.

"I expect," she said, "for you, MacKenzie Francis, to be the confident, competent person you were before his insidious mental abuse. I expect you—*you*—to speak up for yourself. Now."

"Now?"

"Now."

As Willi scrambled through the brambles, the noise alerted Cormack. He put on speed, but Willi increased hers, too. She took it as a positive sign that Kenzie kept pace without a wristlock. He crept into a dense scrub area up against a craggy mountain pocked with small caves. Just as his left leg was about to disappear into the dark void, Willi reached out to grab the ankle beneath the jeans.

"You jerk! Wait! Hold it right there!" He stopped kicking and Willi nodded for Kenzie to close in. She said, "Now."

At first Kenzie's eyes flooded, and spilled over as she trembled. Willi was pretty sure her friend's mouth had grown a prize crop of cotton. Kenzie squeaked out one word. "Fine."

"Try *jerk* for starters."

Kenzie gulped. Chest heaving, she yelled. "You damned jerk. You sorry creep, you will stop following me. You . . . you low-life excuse . . . for a man. I will not . . . *will not* . . . live in fear of you, you worm."

As the words tumbled out, Kenzie transformed. She

raised her head, squared her shoulders, and spread her feet. She helped Willi pull on the protruding leg. "Yeah, yeah, you big man, you, sneaking around in my mailbox, my checking accounts, my workplace. You know what? People laugh at you. Yes, you silly excuse for a human. You haven't got the balls, you've got . . ." She looked toward Willi for help.

"He's got," Willi yelled, "damned *cacahuates* for *cajones,* is what he's got."

Kenzie frowned. "Exactly, damned—uh—"

"Peanuts for balls," Willi translated.

"Ah. Yeah, girlfriend, you are so right. I can't believe I've let his childish, stupid shenanigans bother me for one minute." She dropped his leg. "Hell, he can't even come out and face me. He can't face *me.*" Kenzie laughed and pulled her blond curls away from her pinked-up cheeks. "What have I been afraid of? A worm."

Willi grinned. "A nasty, bothersome fly."

"A cockroach." Kenzie snarled.

"White trash."

"A maggot." Kenzie kicked at his leg. "Come out and get off this island, now. I bet Quannah would love to escort your ass across the water."

Willi brushed her hands together. "And I don't think maggots can swim."

He crab-crawled backward out of the narrow den, got to all fours, then stretched to his full height and turned around. He stood in a belligerent stance with arms folded in front of him, a toothpick dangling between his lips.

Willi peered upward into his eyes. "Uh-oh."

Kenzie blushed even harder. "Oh, shit."

"We're sorry," Willi said, "We thought you were—"

"Someone else," Kenzie finished.

Nara Inoshi placed a hand over the Buddhist medallion

around his neck and two fingers across his lips. He smiled, but refused to break the sacred silence. His eyes lit up with the humor he alone was enjoying. He waved and left them contemplating the cave, the mountainous area, the cacti, and the egg on their faces.

Looking at a particularly large cactus, Willi said, "Perhaps we could impale ourselves upon it."

With a stern voice, Kenzie answered. "You think?"

"Now, now, don't get your drawers in a wad. We both thought—"

"Girlfriend, do you know these kinds of things only happen to me when I'm with you? What do you think about that? And what do you think that poor man is going to say after our day of sacred silence is ended? Huh? Huh? Tell me, girlfriend."

Willi, in a prudent move toward her left, got out of arm's reach before answering. She continued to walk out of the brambles. "I think, he'll have one of the more interesting tales to tell and enjoy the heck out of the telling. I don't think I've seen such a grin on Nara Inoshi's face since our arrival."

"Ooooooh."

"And . . . and I think he's going to be able to tell a certain cock-a-doodle-doer that you are one brave and straightforward young woman who isn't going to let the world run her into the ground."

"More likely tell about my mud-mouth." Kenzie pushed her sweat-soaked hair from her blue eyes.

"Well, yes, he might mention that. I've told you not to use such colorful language. If you were one of my students, I'd have to assign you detention."

"What? But . . . you . . . you were the one going on about cacahooties or whatever."

By then Willi was running full-tilt across the field, which

was good, since the dried tree branch launched at her head missed by a good three feet. By the time they got to the next craggy cliff, they were both laughing and out of breath.

Between gasps, Willi said, "Where are we?"

"Can't you hear it, girl?"

"Huh?" Willi raised her head. "What?"

"The waterfall. The one we saw on our trail ride. Must be that direction. Maybe half a mile."

"Didn't realize we'd run so far. Want to go see it again?"

"Yeah, girl, but could we take it at a slower pace?"

"Sure thing. If you'll stop this spate of bad behavior. Naughty language, throwing things. *Tsk. Tsk. Tsk.*"

"I'll try to curb that. I may have to stop seeing people who influence me in such a negative way."

"*Moi?*"

"Duh-uh, girl."

After a few minutes of quiet walking, Kenzie said, "Willi?"

"Yeah?"

"Thanks."

"Anytime."

"Damned maggot. Won't ever be afraid of him again. You're a good friend."

"Yeah, I am. You're lucky."

"Oh, you ornery—" She grabbed Willi's arm. "That's not Nara Inoshi up ahead, is it?"

"No." Willi squinted. "I think it's—"

"Why's he on his hands and knees crawling?"

"Get down," Willi said. "And be very, very still. Now is the time to practice true *silence.*"

Quannah leaned down close to the ground. since sighting the old monk over two hours ago, he'd lost visual contact, but had used his considerable tracking skills to continue his quest. He shut his eyes a moment and took a long drink from his canteen while he reviewed his morning.

At early light, Samdup had met him at the Inipi site where they sat at the edge of the precipice overlooking the rising Guadalupe, now rolling with the recent rains. Already, the day promised bone-deep heat. Quannah pulled out the stopper of one of his two canvas canteens, took a deep drink, and offered the other to Samdup seated cross-legged in front of him.

The monk declined. Hands on his crossed legs with the palms up, he said in his calm voice, "You've looked over the notes?"

"Yes, sir. Nothing much there, really. Each person seems to be exactly what he says he is. Of course, someone undercover would have all the *t*'s crossed and the *i*'s dotted. It might be easier were you to introduce me to the one referred to as the *Divine Eye*." Quannah held his breath. He needed one smidgen of direction, one tiny clue of where to look, or who to scrutinize more closely.

Samdup merely shook his head. "Many secrets are in people's hearts. You've just not uncovered the right ones."

Quannah persisted. "Might be *he* could tell me if someone has been following him, asking the wrong types of questions, such things as that. Those might give me a thumbs up on a possible threat."

Samdup smiled. "The ancient one will reveal nothing that would be of help to you in that manner. Guidance, yes. Benevolence, assuredly. Blessings in abundance, always."

Trying not to narrow his eyes and cross his arms in what Willi called his Big Chief stance, Quannah changed position and peered downward at the tumultuous waterway below. This case resembled that muddy maelstrom with a momentary glimpse of possibilities—clear waters sliding past—suddenly sucked under and replaced by debris. He sighed. There had to be some way not to have to go at this blindly. He was about as much use as that piece of barbed wire caught in the washdown of the river. Prickly and tightly impaled, but without a way to get clear of the rubbish around him.

Samdup said, "I thought perhaps you learned valuable details within the Inipi ceremony."

Quannah swallowed. "My position was one of leader. I could not—*would* not—let myself probe for clues in that setting."

Samdup nodded. "I also thought that." He smiled and his Sharpei features crinkled kindly. He seemed to search carefully for each of his words. "We profess to live in the here and now. In this moment, what you have is what you have." His glance became intense.

So intense that the goosebumps rose on Quannah's arms. Okay. A message there, but what?

Samdup continued. "What is a part of you is a part of you in the present second. If it is part of the whole, it is useable in this perfect time." With that last pronouncement, Samdup rose with a grace that belied his years, nodded, and left Quannah considering the indentation left in the grass.

He emptied his mind. Sometimes that was the only way he could open himself to the messages. But the harder he tried to relax, the more his mind churned. Images of Willi, bandanna tied on her head, horseback riding at breakneck speed toward a great wall of water, jolted him. He blinked. He did a mental rundown of what he knew of her schedule today. Ah, yes, Samdup had said that today would be a day of silence and contemplation. He grinned. Oh, he wished he had placed a bet on how many minutes that would last with Willi.

Okay, okay. Anyway, she wouldn't be on horseback and

certainly not anywhere near a dam of water such as he saw. He shook himself. Might be his mind conjuring up a pleasant picture of her because he'd missed her so much the last few days.

He cleared his mind again. Just as he was in that completely relaxed state akin to the warmest moments before waking, something drew him back. Why in Great Spirit's name could he not let go? This had never been difficult. Ah, best search out the reason. Had to be one, of course.

The left side with the writhing Guadalupe did not hold a clue. Without moving more than his eyelashes, Quannah scanned the area in front, and to his right. His breathing stilled. This time, he didn't allow his glance to swoop, but rather to focus on the edge of the woods and only on a tiny portion at a time. For a full five minutes, he scanned slowly and repeated the process.

At last, his patience bore fruit—a minute flicker of movement caught his attention. Perhaps a buckskin colored tail lifting in the breeze. There again. The brownish stir among the green leaves riveted his attention. His skin tightened around his eyes, and hairs on the nape of his neck rose. In the literal blink of his eye, the creature bolted from sight like a quail flushed from its nest. Just as quickly, Quannah sprang up and dashed for the pinpointed spot.

He was rewarded by the sight of a pair of browned legs disappearing from view. Old, gnarled legs, the veins thickened like vines wrapped around an ancient oak. Had to be. By Great Eagle's tail feathers, he'd finally caught sight of the Divine Eye. And come high Guadalupe or an army of protective Buddhist practitioners, he was not going to lose track of the old monk.

Now, miles farther along, he listened. Ah, the waterfall was close. Even the air was tinged with a sweeter breath because of its nearness. He frowned at the indention on the ground. One was the bare heel mark of the gnarled one, the other a tennis shoe pattern that Quannah recognized. The two IODD men wore the same brand, same make. The difference was the weight. This print was left by the taller and lighter of the two, Nara Inoshi. Was he the one after the Divine Eye? Quannah stayed low to the ground, leaning his head to one side. Which way? Which way did they go? Both in the same direction? Hmmm.

Willi kept her hand on Kenzie's shoulders until Quannah stood and strode off in a purposeful manner, glanced down here and there, and finally loped off toward the waterfall.

Kenzie groaned. "Now? Now may I get up? What was with the karate chop, girl?"

"Sorry, didn't realize I'd grabbed and knocked you down so hard, really."

Willi sat on her haunches, head only above the rocks and cacti that dotted this part of the island. She pulled in her bottom lip while watching Kenzie strike a similar pose.

"So?" Kenzie smirked. "Ah, does antelope medicine cover this situation? Huh?"

Willi frowned and pulled her bottom lip in another half inch. Each blade of grass seemed to make her skin itch, each cactus offered up a prickly warning of danger, and even the clouds overhead began to turn from marshmallow puffs to more ominous dark wisps.

"I want to follow and see what he's doing, see if it ties in with any of the other crazy things happening on this retreat."

"Do you, perhaps," Kenzie said, opening her baby blues wide, "need to face Quannah about anything? Refer to his cacahooties in a rant and rave?"

Willi sighed. "It would be nice to know what, or *who,* he's out hunting. That's exactly what I wish I could do, just ask him what his task is here other than the trail rides, find out why he keeps wandering around like . . . like right now."

"Hmmm. So this . . . uh . . . right action antelope medicine . . . uh . . . just how do you determine what is the correct step here?" Kenzie sat all the way down and crossed her legs. She used the bottom of her shirt to wipe perspiration off her forehead.

"I suppose . . ." Willi blew out a long breath of frustration. "I suppose—"

"Yes?"

"You have to consider both sides, and—"

"Let's see, girl. Those two sides in *my* case were—"

"Cormack's immoral and illegal stalking behavior versus your right to stand up for yourself and demand not to be followed without your knowledge and permission."

Kenzie chewed on a grass stem. "So, in *your* case, you have to decide what's right before racing after a certain investigator?"

"Oooh."

"So at what conclusion have you arrived? Do we mind our own business, or do we go dashing after Quannah just to find out what he's doing?"

"Well—"

Kenzie interrupted her. "Even though we are supposed to be silent this day, supposed to go in opposite directions if we meet up with others, supposed to be contemplating the koan of the day, whatever in heck it was . . . uh . . ."

Willi peered at her feet and in a woebegone and resigned voice quoted: "The old pond. A jumping frog—Plop!"

She quirked her mouth to one side, finally peered into

Kenzie's eyes and said, "I wouldn't expect you to go and get into more mess along with me. I mean, if I decide to follow."

"Girl, you aren't going without me. If you decide that, I'll be there. Whatever you deem as . . . as good antelope medicine."

"I should trust that he knows what he's doing."

"Yes, absolutely."

"I know that he's on some sort of assignment, and . . . he can't tell me every detail."

"Yeah. We've covered that before."

"I really don't have the right to stalk him, even though it wouldn't be anything like what Jerry Fartleberry Cormack was doing to you."

Kenzie nodded. "I concede there is a difference. I believe it's merely one of curiosity on your part, but—"

"But that doesn't mean I've the right to do whatever I want in the name of curiosity." Willi stood up, dusted off her jeans, adjusted her bandanna, and with her hands in her hip pockets said, "Okay."

"Okay?" Kenzie rose and copied the pose. "So? Curiosity wins out and off we go in your Big Chief's steps?"

"Don't make this harder than it has to be." Willi peered in the direction they'd last seen Quannah. "He's out of sight doing whatever it is he was doing. He may have completely circled back around in another direction by now."

"True."

"So, let's go ahead with our walk to the waterfall. We can enjoy eating with beautiful scenery surrounding us. Maybe that will make up a little for my blundering in and disrupting your day of silence."

"Nonsense. That was meant to be. I feel so good, and I thank you again. So, what else did we need to talk about?

You mentioned you'd been trying to get my attention since last night."

Willi grinned. "Lots. For example, I got trapped in the men's room."

"Men's room? Where?"

"At the teaching pagoda, the Lotus."

"Only you, Willi, only you." Kenzie shook her head. "Do I dare take a quantum leap here and assume something got you curious, and you went there in search of . . . of?"

"A strange noise, actually."

"So, explain while we walk."

"I suppose to be completely honest I'd have to tell you about the cricket and the lizard."

Kenzie nodded. "Sure. Yeah. I'm gonna love this; I can tell."

Willi sighed. "Uh . . . first I need to explain about—"

"Yes? About?"

"About Botherbutt."

CHAPTER
14

Unlike when willi had approached the waterfall head-on while on horseback, coming upon it this way was definitely harder going as she and Kenzie had to walk literally up the steep mountainside. When Willi peered over the cliff edge to her right, this branch of the Guadalupe swept by only a few feet down from them at the moment. On a whim, she started a hop, skip, and a jump down the incline toward the river.

Kenzie followed. "What's going on here?"

"Just curious," Willi offered over her shoulder.

"Do tell."

"No reason we can't tramp along down by the river's edge and reach the bottom of the waterfalls. I'm sure that's just as pretty."

Kenzie huffed as she scrabbled over a particularly sharp rock. "Be careful. I don't want to fall in that swirling mess.

Looks nasty, like maybe there's a water medusa down there having a bad hair day."

"Medusa with a bad hair day and her PMS acting up."

Kenzie laughed. "And her without any Valium. So, watch your step. Let's not socialize with her today."

"Agreed. No dips in the river until it calms down." Half of an hour passed, and there was a stronger hum of cascading water. Willi said, "Must be close."

Around another three bends, Willi said, "Aww."

"This," Kenzie said, "is more like it. Isn't it strange, though? We can't hear the waterfall at all within the fold of these canyon walls."

The Guadalupe divided into reservoirs and inlets, numerous lateral waterways with a calmer surface. Among the overhanging stones above, the cave they were standing within had the appearance of a shallow grotto. Willi pointed around them. "Lots of them through here."

"And yet the main Guadalupe keeps rolling on by, barely upsetting these side venues."

"At least," Willi said, "not on the surface. Probably dislocating all kinds of fishy homes deep underneath." She set her bag down. "I know we're close to the falls, but why not sit in this shadowy, cool place for a bite. It's so . . . so . . ."

Kenzie nodded. "It's so calm. We need a little serenity."

"Considering we're on—"

"Serenity Island. Oh, yeah, girl, this is a good spot. We can see across the river into all those other inlets, and the way this part curves, we'll have a view of the wildlife on half of this side, too. Sort of like an amphitheater *au natural.*"

Willi laid out the sandwiches, fruit, and water along with a couple of bags of hard candies. While they ate, they practiced the silence, despite Willi's desire to talk out all the happenings on the island. Another five minutes and the wildlife seemed to have accepted them as harmless. The buzz of a wasp sounded nearby. The trees—breezes riffling their leaves in a lazy three-count movement—really did play the waltz of the winds, visually and musically.

This moment of quiet and companionship with her friend could not have been improved upon other than to have Quannah along beside her, too. She took a deep breath, and as she gazed out upon the hundreds of twittering songbirds, the water herons, and a couple of circling turkey buzzards, she offered up a silent prayer of thanks for all the wonderment and for Kenzie and Quannah in her life. For this hushed moment—this moment stilled to human voice—all was right with the world. When she peeked sideways at Kenzie, she noted her friend's similar composure. Yes, they had both finally found some of the promised balance of Serenity Island.

Willi considered the daytime water heron, so different from Botherbutt in its white coloring and long legs. A gangly second or third cousin removed, no doubt. But it was not gawky when it swooped for a fish in the inlet opposite. Delight at the sight brought the koan to the forefront: "The old pond. A jumping frog—Plop!"

No sooner had she experienced her close encounter with an enlightened state, than she pricked up her ears. Something was wrong. She glanced sharply at Kenzie. She, too, sat in a more alert posture, her bite of sandwich held at bay before her lips and finally lowered to the napkin.

"Listen," she said.

"Yes, from over there." Willi pointed to another dark cavern, through which the Guadalupe detoured, one of those on the same side of the river, within the curving nook Kenzie had earlier noted.

With silent but tacit agreement, Kenzie copied her

movements as Willi scooted back farther underneath the shadowy rock. She pulled her bag out of the bit of sunlight that slanted off their perch.

Willi whispered, "Even the birds got quiet."

"Probably more of us humans messing around."

"Obviously, Kenzie, considering the sound of that . . . uh . . . ?"

"Electric wood saw?" Kenzie finished off her momentarily forgotten sandwich. "Maybe the monks are out doing a firewood run?"

"This far away? Nah. Maybe . . . maybe it's a motor-boat."

"There." Kenzie pointed to one of the shadowy grottos.

"Where?"

"Eleven o'clock. You might have to lean out a bit to see it."

On hands and knees, Willi eased forward and peeked around their rock outcropping. "Must be Skeeter and Doretta."

"On their treasure hunt?"

"Yeah. I guess so."

The boat idled down after swinging into the side inlet. There it sat, now with the ignition off, the rear end of the motorboat with raised sun umbrella in place. "Guess they had the same idea for a quiet luncheon."

"Just one of them," said Kenzie. "Doretta decided to participate in the silence for today. Said she needed some time to herself. Skeeter kidded her about the upkeep on her *bazookas* and *big hair* and took the picnic basket and his banjo and guitar aboard just as I chose the path where you and I met up."

"Hmmm."

"That was a loaded *hmmm* if ever I heard one. Give it up, girl."

Willi frowned in thought, took a last bite of crisp apple, and pursed her lips.

Kenzie prodded. "Something about Doretta? Okay, Skeeter? Their treasure hunt? And why are we still whispering?"

Willi snapped her fingers and pointed her forefinger at Kenzie in that you-got-it mode.

"The treasure hunt? What about it?"

"We're whispering because sound can carry in such an . . . an acoustical place. The hunt doesn't make sense, Kenzie."

Willi rubbed her hands together. "We didn't exactly have to drag the fact from them that the hunt was why they came to the island. You would keep that secret, especially if it'd been in the family interest to do so for so many years. Why all of a sudden start blurting it out?"

"Maybe," Kenzie said, "they truly didn't believe there was any treasure."

"Huh?"

"Maybe they just used that old map as an excuse to connect, seeing as how they are the only two cousins left in the family. And don't say they aren't cousins. They could be twins."

"True. No doubt they're family."

Willi cleaned up the scraps and threw them out toward the bird populace. "Perhaps it's that innocent, but maybe they just used the map as a cover-up for . . . something else."

"Hey, slow down, Miss Marple of the Range. Everything doesn't have to be wrapped up in a mystery. Most of us lead pretty ho-hum ordinary lives. Some of us *would like* to live ho-hum ordinary lives."

"Not you, Kenzie. You'd be bored."

"I won't have to worry about that with you as a friend."

"I shall take that as a compliment."

"Hmmm."

"Now that," Willi said, "is a loaded *hmmm*."

Music—a lilting song accompanied by very accomplished guitar picking—drifted from the direction of the far grotto. A Latin melody. Willi tilted her head.

Kenzie leaned out of their shelter to hear better, too. She said, "I didn't know Skeeter could also play the guitar like that. Sure glad he chose not to be silent today."

"Beautiful, isn't it?" Willi finally recognized the tune. "My parents loved that song. I think Jerry Vale sang the rendition they preferred."

"What is it?"

" 'You Belong To My Heart.' "

Skeeter's tenor rang out. " ' . . . you belong . . . now and forever . . . we were gathering stars . . . ' "

Kenzie sighed. "Oh, what wonderful lyrics."

Willi nodded, " 'Darling, you are the one.' " She grinned and swayed with the rhythm. " '*Una vez, nada más.*' And he knows the Spanish version, too. Oh, Kenzie, listen. The birds are actually twittering in time to the music."

"Oh, girlfriend." Kenzie rubbed the goosebumps rising on her arms. "This is definitely a Hallmark moment."

"Guess we've had a lot of *frogs plopping* today."

"Yeah."

When he sang it the second time through, they sang in whispers along with him. In the middle of the line, "We were gathering stars while a million guitars played our love song," there was a strangled gargling of the word *guitars* while their voices finished the line. It took them a few heartbeats to jump up and peer outward in time to see the boat rocking and hear grunts and curses reverberating through the canyon.

Willi yelled, "Hey, what's going on? You okay, Skeeter?"

The only answer—a pinched-off yelp. The boat gave a

last heave as if someone had either jumped into or off the vessel. Skeeter's guitar flew out and crashed into splinters upon the canyon rocks. Quiet reigned.

Willi scrambled over brambles along the edge of the river while hollering, "We're on our way. Skeeter, hang on. Hang on!" Kenzie grabbed their belongings and struggled after her.

Quannah, squatting, scrutinized the ground yet again. He turned his back upon the gorge with the Guadalupe flowing and with the waterfall now sluicing down on the far side, creating a roar of the elements as the stone and water crashed together below. This area boasted far more rocks than soil, more cacti than grass. Sweat poured between his shoulder blades, soaked his forehead and hair again, and trickled down his chest.

He took out one of his Uncle Brigham's borrowed bandannas—yellow and green stripes. He wiped his face and neck and tied the bright cloth there. A moment's thought made him decide to untie and fold the bandanna and put it away. No sense announcing his approach if someone happened to look back along the trail. A few feet farther along he found a heel mark. An inch of a treadmark print showed. Inoshi's, no doubt. A half hour passed before he came across another sign, this one in the form of a winged friend from above.

A turkey buzzard swooped slowly downward, spiraling out of the sky to dive at a lizard. His return trip to the air crossed over Quannah, shadowing him for a moment in the comfort of the wide wingspan.

"Brother Buzzard," Quannah said, "is that a message? Lizard is the sign of shadows, one who represents the dreamtime and what can be learned through dreams. That doesn't seem right for this scenario."

Back on his haunches, Quannah closed his eyes and allowed the breeze to dry the sweat on his brow, to lull him into a semi-relaxed state, and to bring him face to face with the correct information. His mother had taught him to be aware of the animals—the *Wamakaskan*—and their messages. What had she told him about Lizard Medicine when it was bright daylight, not the dreamtime? Another reptile scuttled over a rock, slunk into the shade between a crevice, and disappeared. Quannah nodded. A lizard ran from his shadow; he ran from his fears, but those fears only followed behind him.

Hairs on the nape of his neck rose, a sure confirmation that he had finally garnered the correct tidbit from his mother's teachings. No sooner had that realization hit, than Quannah glanced quickly behind him. There, behind that farthest outcropping and dropping down toward the edge of the old bridge, the tattered ends of the Divine One's robe disappeared. Glance glued to the spot, Quannah rose in one fluid motion.

"Ahh!" A startled voice behind him yelped. Quannah, on his toes, ready for headlong flight, twisted around, bent, and with one leg struck out at the intruder.

Suddenly, Nara Inoshi was on the ground, rubbing his shin.

Quannah sucked in air, two and three times to calm the adrenaline rush. He put out a hand to help Inoshi to his feet. "Sorry. You startled me. What are you doing here?"

Inoshi narrowed his eyes and backed away. A cornered muskrat would look no less angry. In that primordial response, his reaction mirrored Quannah's own fight-or-flight stance as he assumed an offensive karate position.

Quannah narrowed his own eyes. Great Eagle must be laughing at him right now. How did he miss the signs of Inoshi circling back around him? "Again, Mr. Inoshi. I'm sorry."

Without speaking, Inoshi swallowed, brought his legs together in a relaxed stance, and lowered his arms. He waved a hand and shrugged his shoulders in the universal what-gives-with-this-action signal.

Quannah scratched his head. *Obviously, taking my beginner's course in tracking skills.* Out loud he said, "The monks wanted me to check out the . . . the . . . gopher populace. One or two have shown up close to the enclave. They wanted to avoid any influx by using controls if needed."

Inoshi peered around the field, a field with no gopher holes in sight.

"Uh . . . as you can see," Quannah said, brandishing his bandanna before wiping his forehead, "there just aren't any out this far. Of course, I've still got a lot of island to check. Probably three days worth of walking, and I have to do it in bits and pieces."

Inoshi nodded.

While refolding the handkerchief, Quannah asked, "And you?"

Nara Inoshi patted his chest.

Quannah pushed for more. "Out here for some particular reason?" Like trying to abduct the old monk, maybe.

Hanging his head down, Inoshi sighed. "I was trying to stay away from people so I would not break the silence." He patted his Zen medallion around his neck.

Quannah said. "My fault. Not yours. You go back into the silence. One sentence won't be held against you. It will be as the wind took the words away. I should have remembered and honored your day. Your speech was my fault, not yours. I'll continue in this direction and not bother you again."

Inoshi glanced toward the falls, frowned, but finally without another word, made an about-face and headed toward the compound. Quannah waited until he had gotten out of sight. Maybe Nara Inoshi practiced his beliefs with sincerity and dedication. Maybe, and then again, perhaps not. Just as easily, he might have been on the same hunting trail as Quannah, the path leading to the Divine One—the ancient monk so many in the world wished to control or worse, to destroy. Nara Inoshi, IODD manager, would not be the first nor would he be the last to hide behind a façade of religious fervor in order to gain nefarious ends. A good three minutes passed before Quannah breathed deeply and tried to hone in on the spot where he'd last seen the Divine One.

A new awareness seemed to ripple through him as he got nearer to the falls, now a beautiful cascade of floating silkiness on the far side, a powerful representation of the grandeur Mother Earth could display. With every cell on alert, he scanned the edge of the precipice where the bridge attached to concrete beams. Even after many years of abandonment, the pilings of steel and concrete seemed strong. Only the two-lane span across the river seemed weather worn. Pitted with potholes here and there, chips off the edges at other spots, the crossing begged for repairs.

Quannah shook his head. *Focus. Focus on the minute details. Make a mental grid of this tiny spot where the Divine One was last seen and scan. Scan carefully.*

Sure enough, his patience, like the ant's persistence, was rewarded. A few strands of the coarse monk's robe entwined among the brambles. He pulled them loose, and as if they were a great treasure, he stowed them in one of the plastic bags he kept in his shirt pocket. He grinned. This was turning out to be a great day.

Nothing more fulfilling than being under Father Sky, the heat of life-giving sun upon his skin, the scents of the earth open and revealing many paths, many stories to him. His task, to narrow down all the possibilities to one clear sign leading toward his quarry, proved challenging. With squared shoulders he accepted that opportunity, acknowledging his ability to meet all obstacles.

At last, he was closing in on the elusive old monk. Finally, he would know the identity of the person he was supposed to be protecting. To end the day with tangible proof in hand that the Divine Eye, the most honored of all the monks, did exist on the island, gave him an adrenaline punch almost as heady as his first sight of the old man.

Nothing, absolutely nothing could stop him now. He opened his eyes widely and took the first step across the causeway. His nostrils flared. Closing in. Oh, yes, closing in was the best of all three parts of a pursuit: *First sight. Tangible confirmation.* The *knowing*—the innate knowledge he followed the correct path—sent trembles of anticipation through him.

Even in his moment of warm exuberance, he peered up at the sky. "*Pilamaya yelo, Wakan Tanka* for sending helpers. Thank you, Brother Buzzard and lizards—both the one who gave his life to get my attention and the reptile that slunk into the shade to remind me to watch the shadows behind. *Pilamaya yelo.*"

He tiptoed until he broke into a smooth gait halfway across the metal and concrete span. His hair flew back like the Indians of old, on foot, on the hunt and enjoying the natural elements against the skin each length along the way. As he leaped over a pile of broken concrete debris in the middle, a scream rent the air. He stumbled, hit the ground hard, and screamed in pain as he heard the telltale pop of his rotary cuff snapping.

"Damn."

He rolled to the side of the trashed area, ripped his shirt, and skinned his shoulder on the edge of a jagged pothole before he finally hugged the cold bridge. Had it been a scream or a gunshot from afar? Its intensity still rang against canyon walls below. He peered over the edge of the causeway down into the frothing, fast-flowing water below the falls. He blinked his eyes at the sight, and his heart stopped for a millisecond, for a lifetime.

"Gallagher. No, no. Great Spirit, no."

Biting back the pain now coursing down his shoulder to the elbow, he raced toward the bottom of the canyon toward the flowing Guadalupe.

Willi stumbled across the rock-strewn area edging the Guadalupe. Behind her Kenzie struggled with both their bags. Skeeter's screeching followed by choking and gargles made her sick to her stomach.

Dear God, let them reach him before . . . before . . . she didn't even want to finish that thought.

A flash of Yataro Yodo on the pagoda floor zipped through her mind's eye, and her throat constricted. Reaching the spot where Skeeter had docked the boat, she jumped into it and leaned down. He clutched at his chest. A sickly sweat soaked his white beard, and he trembled.

"Heart attack?" asked Kenzie over Willi's shoulder.

"No, someone struck him, Kenzie. You saw. Might have given him a heart attack, though."

Willi lifted him to a sitting position and told him to cough. "Yes, Banjo Joe Skeeter, you cough as if your life depended upon it, and that may well be the case." Okay, stay calm, she told herself. Help couldn't come to him, not if it depended on them going for someone and bringing assistance back across the island on foot. No, they—she and Kenzie—had to get him to help.

She said, "Keep coughing. It keeps the heart and lungs pumping."

His eyes fluttered, and the pain coursing through him was obvious in his features, but he breathed on his own, at least. He tried to say something.

She leaned close to his white beard. "What?"

"In the . . . inside . . . the . . . guit—"

"What'd he say?" Kenzie said, busying herself in trying to make him more comfortable. "What'd he say?"

Willi repeated his words. To him she said, "Just lay back. Relax. You can get another guitar. We're going to get you to medical help quickly. Shut your eyes and relax."

"Maybe he thought his . . . uh . . . copy of . . . you know . . . was taped inside the guitar?" Kenzie hazarded a guess.

"Maybe so, if he didn't realize he'd lost it the other night." She said this low enough he could not hear.

"What else do I need to do for him, girl?"

Willi said, "Now, get his knees over those pillows there; prop him behind his back, too." She studied the controls. "We've got to get him to the pagoda compound."

"Or to the ranch mainland, girlfriend?"

"No, no, that's beyond our capabilities," Willi said. She grabbed hold of Kenzie and whispered. "Just driving this back to the dock may be more than we can handle. Unless . . ."

"Unless?"

"Unless you know something about boats?"

Kenzie shook her head.

"Or navigation, or—"

"Nope, girlfriend. Not me."

"Or river currents."

"Uh-uh. Not a happening thing."

"Damn." Willi said. "Well, it starts like a car. See? Here's the key in the ignition."

"Well, let's go. He's passed out." Kenzie wiped Skeeter's brow with one of a couple dozen clean wipes. "Oh, these are handy on a boat, I guess."

Willi frowned, sucked in her bottom lip, and tried to calm her own heart rate, which at the moment could have taken her three times around the Indianapolis speedway in front of the lead racer. She turned the key; the boat motor roared to life. The vibrations scissored throughout her limbs.

The commotion roused Skeeter, who pointed to a throttle before his eyes rolled back in his head. He again said, "Guitar. Tied inside."

Willi stared into Kenzie's eyes. She copied her friend's shrug and hands in the air. "Folks say strange things under stress and fear of their lives."

A few false starts and maneuvers got the boat finally backed out of the small grotto, but something was wrong.

Kenzie grabbed Willi's arm. "Shouldn't we be going that way?"

"You're right, but we seem to be caught in the eddies created by the waterfalls. Even with the motor, I can't get it to—"

A horrible screeching like metal on stone rent the air and the sudden demise of the motor froze Willi to the spot. "I don't know what to do, Kenzie."

"You don't know what to do? I always depend on you to know what to do. Of course, of course you . . . you . . . know. Get us to the edge, and we'll figure something out as soon as the boat is secure."

"Right." Willi located a pair of oars locked into the side. "For emergencies, I guess."

"This would be one, girl."

"Here. We'll try."

Their bit of training with Jamyang, Rooster, and Nestor stood them in good stead for about five minutes. "We're still going in the wrong direction," Willi said, "but maybe we'll be okay. Skeeter and Doretta said they'd been *around* the island many times, so we'll just go around it this way."

"If it doesn't get any rougher than now, sure."

Willi took a deep breath. "Sure. We can do this. Trained by the best Navy men, that's us. Old pros at this."

Kenzie struggled with her oar. "And she tells me to get a grip on reality. Right."

As they swerved on the edge of the outcropping and came around the curve, Willi peered at the enormity of the waterfalls cascading down upon them. "Uh-oh." She studied the eddies swirling between the rocks, which they were rapidly approaching. "Oh, my God."

"What do we do?" The panic in Kenzie's voice matched her own.

"Row like hell, and try not to smash on these rocks. Won't take us long to get . . ." The remainder of her sentence evaporated in the roar of the insistent impact of water and stone. Her bag flipped open, spilling its contents underneath one of the fold-out seats. "The cell phone!"

"Let me try," said Kenzie. "Maybe we can get somebody." The bow of the boat tipped upward and came down with a sickening drop. Kenzie dropped the phone and got a stronger hold on her own oar.

Willi's heart did a flat out flip, catapulting her into pure panic. She fought it down and took a death grip on the oar, pushing on a stone here, rowing like a crazed Olympian in the open spaces—spaces few and far between the rushing froth hiding unforgiving rocks. Adrenaline coursed through her veins; she screamed out her rage against the elements as her butt smashed down again and again. On her knees now, she fought a quick curve and backturn that sent the boat spinning for a few stomach-lurching moments. A huge fall of water sluiced over the side of the boat at the same time it contacted with relentless stone, pushing the boat dangerously to the side.

Ohgod, ohgod, ohgod. God, no.

Out of the corner of her eye, she caught sight of Kenzie. The tilt had caught her while she stood, thus upending her, knocking her beneath the nasty river surge.

Oh, dear God. "Kenzie!"

The boat swashbuckled back to the other side, scraped between two monstrous outcroppings, and Willi pushed with all her might against one side. Her oar broke in half.

"Kenzie!"

Behind her Kenzie coughed and sputtered up a Guadalupe cocktail. Skeeter, one leg over the gunwale, would be swept overboard any minute. Willi leaped upon him the same time as Kenzie to pull him back to safety. The boat righted itself and hit the calm area of river, floating fast, but not into any sharp rocks. Willi gasped for air. The current carried them past a bend and the onslaught of noise against her eardrums disappeared as quickly as it had earlier manifested itself—in seconds.

Peace.

Quiet.

Only the struggle for air could be heard, and . . . someone yelling.

Willi croaked out the words through her abused throat. "Who? Where is that coming from?"

Kenzie pulled herself up to her knees. "There. I can't make out who."

Willi pulled her plastered hair from her eyes. Sure enough a man on shore yelled to them and then dove into the fast flowing water.

"Hand me your oar."

"What?" Kenzie threw the battered piece to her. "Why?"

"Why? He's come to finish the job. Knows we've saved Skeeter. Oh, dear Lord, he's going to finish the job and include us."

"What do I do, girl?"

"Try to get the motor to kick over."

He reached them, struggled over, and had one leg inside the boat. His black hair swam around his head. Willi screamed. "Oh, no, you don't." She pounded on his chest with the piece of oar, the motor came to life, Kenzie throttled, and he landed in the swirling Guadalupe.

"Gosh," Kenzie said, "He's a strong swimmer."

"Well, he won't catch up with us now."

In the boat's wake, she thought she heard him say, "Damn you, Gallagher."

Kenzie stood up straight and looked her in the eye. They both gasped. In the distance, he climbed back on shore.

Willi gulped. "Oops."

He disappeared up the hill, clutching at his mid-section and holding an elbow close to his side, obviously heading back across land to meet them when they docked. Willi trembled and tears streamed down her face.

Kenzie put an arm around her. "It'll be okay."

"I know. Just my reaction to the aftermath of all the adrenaline and knocking the stuffing out of the man I love above all others. Oh, yeah. Everything will be just fine. I must have hit his shoulder. Oh my gosh. Will this go any faster?"

"Doing the best I can. It won't shift or whatever. Guess something got messed up in the rocks."

"Yeah," Willi said, "We should be thankful the motor started at all." She propped Skeeter up as much as she could on torn cushions. His eyelids fluttered. He even had color in his cheeks.

He whispered, "Didn't touch me. Nope, the son of a bitch."

Kenzie said, "That's what he thinks."

Willi hazarded one question. "Skeeter, who? Who was the son of a bitch?"

He licked his lips, coughed, and lay back exhausted. His lips moved, but she could not hear any intelligible words.

To Kenzie, she said, "Just stay close to the bank until we sight the dock. Ohmygosh." She shielded her eyes with one hand and pointed with the other to a high mesa on the waterfall side of the canyon. "See that?"

"Right at the edge of the smallest water cascade? Yes, I do. But, I thought all the monks—"

Willi snapped her fingers. "That's him. That's the Divine Eye, the ancient monk Quannah mentioned in his dreamtime moment. I bet you anything."

"Can't bet on that one, but I can offer confirmation, girlfriend."

"What do you mean?"

"Uh, well," Kenzie hedged while turning the wheel. "When I accidentally overheard things the men said inside the Inipi, someone else—not Quannah—mentioned he was here *to touch* the Eye That Is Divine. I thought the person meant to get closer to a sense of spiritual balance, but I guess—"

"He meant to actually *touch* him—the person?" Willi asked.

"Right. Of course, words were sometimes muffled what with them pouring water over the stones and all that hissing steam, not to mention the prayers they sang."

"Right. Not that you meant to listen in closely."

"Exactly," Kenzie agreed.

Willi pointed. "There. I see the dock. Oh, thank you, Great Spirit."

"Girlfriend, that would be an *amen*."

CHAPTER
15

Within an hour of their arrival, the monks had some-how signaled to the ranch mainland, a medical helicopter had arrived, and Skeeter along with Doretta had been air-lifted away. Nara Inoshi and Mike Toru shook their heads.

Kenzie shivered and pointed at the latter. "Do you see what he's carrying around with him?"

"Good Lord, that pet . . . that . . . snake . . . we shared shower space with the other night."

"Creepy to have a critter like that around all the time. Uck. No wonder he's not engaged or married."

Willi said, "Maybe, maybe not. Lots of women like them as pets, too. Just because we have a problem with the legless ones, doesn't mean others don't . . . uh . . . love them."

"Okay, girlfriend, if you say so."

Willi whispered, "Seems they're the only ones not to have broken the silence." She stretched and yawned. "I must have lived two lifetimes today, and every muscle and bone is complaining about the double abuse. I want a bath, a nap, a sweet reconciliation with one most-probably-angry special investigator, and an end to this day. No more flopping frogs, slinking snakes, or roaring rapids for me. Inoshi and Toru can win the honors in the silence game."

Kenzie raised an eyebrow and indicated with a pointed look the three men—Rooster, Nestor D., and Preacher Halliwell Pate—staring at the whirling blades until the helicopter became a speck in the sky. "Guess those three also kept the silence," she whispered back.

Willi peered over her shoulder across the island with such intensity she wondered how the trees dared not move so she could see when *he* first came into sight. Having seen him ascend the bank, she knew he was fine physically, but whether he would yet be miffed or downright angry over the oar whacking, she hadn't a clue. Either way, she couldn't blame him. Poor man had taken his share of discomfort since knowing her. Could he stand a life of such abuse? She hoped so, because she couldn't imagine breathing without him.

Kenzie grinned. "Best hope the walk takes him a while. The better to cool down."

"*Humph.* Am I that easy to read? Actually, with Big Chief, that pressure cooker might go either way. The man has been known to be hardheaded from time to time." Willi headed toward the women's pagoda. "I need a bath."

"Ah," Kenzie said, "a bubble bath. A *hardheaded* woman could do worse."

"With a soft pillow to lean back on, and a cool piña colada in hand or—translated to the amenity level for Serenity Island—an icy glass of tea," Willi added, choosing to ignore Kenzie's barb. "Then it's serious time for going through this mess and deciding what's what." She patted her hefty and soaked bag. "I've got to have some answers, or I'll go crazy."

Jamyang approached them with a finger to his mouth. "Emergency over. Mr. Skeeter on way to hospital. Now, honor silence. No talk until evening meal, please." His sweet smile took the sting out of the words.

Willi gave the "okay" hand signal and nodded.

Kenzie opted for a right-handed thumbs up.

But their look to each other promised otherwise as soon as they were out of earshot of Jamyang and the men on the pier. On the porch of the pagoda, Willi tried the doorknob.

"Come on, girl."

"It's locked. Told you. Juna Marie bolted it this morning."

Kenzie tromped off the porch and around the corner to Juna Marie's window to stand on a box frame of lavender and azalea.

Willi followed. "Good grief," she said, "Juna Marie hasn't moved a muscle since this morning."

"Long time," Kenzie said, "to sit cross-legged in one spot."

"Not if you've got a lot of heavy thinking to do."

Kenzie shivered. "Must be a load bigger than an eighteen-wheeler with a tag-along."

"Both filled with quarried stone." Willi shoved a discarded apple core aside with her toe. "Look at this."

Kenzie said, "Well, seems like someone set up a little nest out here. One guess as to who sat here watching Juna Marie's every breath."

"Preacher Halliwell Pate. Can't really blame him. She isn't exactly forthcoming today."

"Maybe she has reason not to be. He is a tad on the jealous side. Sort of stifling," Kenzie insisted. "At least, we know where *two* people on this island were all day."

On one hand, Willi raised a finger. "More than two. The Pates kept the home perches staked out. Three: Banjo Joe Skeeter on the Guadalupe near the waterfalls. Four: Nara Inoshi on the same basic paths as we were for a while."

"Please," Kenzie said, "don't remind me."

"Five." Willi held up a second hand to count. "The ancient monk stood behind the waterfall."

"Mustn't forget one wild swimmer. You know, the one you whomped with your oar."

"Don't remind *me*." Willi groaned. "Now, the question remains of where were—"

"Nestor D. and Mike Toru?" Kenzie asked.

"And, one other," Willi added. "Rooster Rowley."

"Don't forget Doretta. I suppose we're to believe that one of them jumped into Skeeter's boat?"

"Come on." Willi strode to the other side to where her cubicle was. She easily raised the window, but was too short to climb onto the windowsill. "Up to you, Kenzie."

"The things I do for you in the name of friendship." Kenzie grabbed hold, swung up to the sill, teetered on the edge, and said, "Push."

Willi did, perhaps a bit too hard, if the crash and the ensuing, "Damn you, Wilhelmina Gallagher," were indications.

She met Kenzie at the doorway and said, "Wish folks would stop cursing my name, and don't use *Wilhelmina* again, or I'll have to tell your mother about the time you smoked marijuana right there in your granny's house."

"Girl, that was fifteen or more years ago. And it was *not* marijuana. Just some old tobacco of my granddaddy's we thought was marijuana. And, that's not funny. Tell Mama now, and she'll have a stroke. Wonder if that's what happened to Banjo Jo Skeeter."

"A stroke?" Willi stifled a yawn, made circles with her shoulders to remove some of the absolute tiredness from overtaking her. She could not succumb to the needs of mere mortal flesh now. Answers. By damned, she wanted answers before she slept this night. She repeated, "A stroke?"

"Well, yeah, because he couldn't seem to talk or move much, but was—well, his eyes were focused; he understood what was going on around him."

"Kenzie, the man was attacked. He had a blow to the head from his assailant."

"We never actually saw anyone with him in the boat." Kenzie's voice faltered.

"Stop it right now, MacKenzie Francis. Don't you dare start treading water on this one. You saw the boat shift as someone jumped into it; you heard the scuffle. What about his song cut off in mid-phrase? If he had a stroke or heart attack, it was due to the initial attack, and perhaps from going through the rapids, hearing his boat being torn asunder with two clowns at the helm. That would give him a stroke, but that's not what his attacker intended. No, not at all."

"Who . . . who had a stroke?" Juna Marie, as pasty as a Dairy Queen vanilla cone, approached. She moved her limbs as if they were as frozen as the ice cream, and blinked. "Who?"

"Juna Marie," Willi said, pulling her closer. "Skeeter had an accident. Didn't you hear the helicopter come and pick him up?"

"Accident?"

Willi rubbed Juna Marie's icy fingers. How could she be so frigid in this humidity? "Let's get the blood flowing here. You've sat too long. How about you hopping in for a hot shower. We can wait a few minutes." Good heavens and Hells Bells, had she said that? Her own body protested with a knee creak and ankle pops as she sat on the floor to take off her wet outer clothes.

Juna Marie's cheeks developed two tiny circles of heat. "What kind of accident? Where?"

Kenzie pulled off her wet socks and tennis shoes. "A boating accident. Near the waterfalls."

At that tidbit, Juna Marie sighed. "Good. Out on the water . . . then it couldn't have been . . ." She blinked again, this time rapidly over and over. "Everything will be fine." She put both hands over her mouth. "Oh, I forgot."

"Not to worry. The silence has been broken many times, and after supper we get to talk, anyway," Willi said.

"The Divine One won't mind; that ancient old water sprite is pretty forgiving and gentle," Juna Marie said.

Willi exchanged a look with Kenzie. In unison they said, "Old water sprite? The Divine One?"

Juna Marie headed toward her curtained-off area, came out with a change of clothes, and entered the bathroom to turn the water spigots on full blast.

In her panties and bra, Willi scrambled up from the mass of soggy clothes. "Wait. Explain, please, about the old water sprite."

Juna Marie said, "He lives behind the waterfalls. Must be the oldest of the monks. In his nineties, at least. We found him."

"You and . . . ?" Willi quirked an eyebrow upward.

"You and Halliwell?" Kenzie asked.

"No. Mr. Tulsa. Nestor D., you know." Juna Marie put a hand across her heart. "But Halliwell was there, too. Thank goodness. Wouldn't have wanted anything to happen to one of our World War Two vets."

Willi guffawed. "Not likely. He's a tough old bird himself."

"Actually, I owe Mr. Tulsa my life. I slipped on rocks

near the falls, and if he'd not caught me and held me until Halliwell could help him pull me up, I'd have fallen head-first into the rapids below. I don't want anything to happen to Mr. Tulsa. He's a good man."

"Skeeter is a good man, too. He and Doretta only have each other for family. I hope he pulls through the effects of the attack."

"What attack? I thought you said accident." Juna Marie looked at her as if Willi were the one confused. "That's an entirely different scene. I have to think about this." Juna Marie shut the door, through which she said, "Everything is fine. I was right here all day long. Yes, so nothing could be too wrong."

"What?" Willi did another duo-in-unison word with Kenzie.

Kenzie shrugged out of her own nasty rags. "She needs some blood flowing to the brain. Too much thinking and too little action for her today, obviously."

Willi pulled out clean clothes and lay them near the bathroom door. "I'm next."

"Calm down, girlfriend. Not a problem." Kenzie, with a blanket around her, sat on the pagoda floor and toed Willi's lumpy bag. "So, now, we finally have a few minutes with-out stalkers, attackers, or boaters bent on bruising us. What all *is* in there?"

Willi pulled the curtain close around the area and brought out items one at a time. "Here's Yataro Yodo's notepad and pencil along with his prayer wheel."

"Read what was written on that little paper inside again."

" 'A jewel shall not be sacrificed to the dragon.' "

Pulling her feet underneath the light summer blanket, Kenzie yawned. "Strange. I remembered it being some-thing about a snake."

"Don't you dare, MacKenzie Francis, go to sleep right now. See? Here's a strange mark on the prayer sheet that looks just like an etched Buddha symbol for the third eye in the middle of the forehead, signifying enlightenment. And, hey, you're right. Each corner of the prayer is protected by an animal, and the corner that should be a dragon is a snake."

Kenzie stifled another yawn. "Isn't that the third time that critter has shown up? Weren't you telling me if the universe keeps giving you the same idea, there's a message or . . . what? . . . a lesson or whatever?"

"Whew," Willi said, "Right you are." She tapped the end of her retroussé nose. "The one when I landed in the lake."

"And the pet in the IODD men's shower." Kenzie shivered.

Willi frowned. "The rain snakes on the window, the one in this prayer *choskor.*"

She put Yataro Yodo's shoes beside the first items. She and Kenzie said in unison. "Who knows?"

Willi pushed the shoes back. "We'll consider them later."

Kenzie said, "What's that?" and pointed to a folded sheet of loose-leaf notebook paper.

"That's Skeeter's hand-drawn map—his treasure map—with one part missing. The one he dropped in the IODD men's pagoda." She twisted it this way and that, shook her head, and handed it to Kenzie.

After a few minutes, Kenzie held the map up to the light to see it better and straightened the wrinkles out. She started to put it down, frowned, and held it up to the light again. "Hey, look here. When I hold it up and look at it from the *wrong* side, it makes more sense. There's the dock and then coming around the island to the left is the cliff where the Lotus Pagoda schoolhouse sits. His dotted line stops there."

Willi squinted. "But there's another line drawn from the pier to the right and going around the island that way. Obviously, a much safer route than the one we took today."

"Sure, girl, and here—these little triangles he's drawn in. What are those?"

"Maybe places they stopped to check landmarks, marked off as they moved around the island."

"Oh my goodness, Willi, guess where there's a big circle of them?"

"Right where we were at the grottos and near the waterfalls. So today wasn't his first trip to that area?"

"Evidently not." Kenzie's stomach growled audibly, reminding both that sustenance would be needed soon, even though they were hours away from suppertime.

"Put a little hurry in your get-along, Juna Marie. We're starving," Willi yelled.

A muffled "Almost done," came back in answer.

Kenzie shook the purse. "What else? Hurry."

"The useless cell phone." Willi sighed.

Kenzie grinned. "Girl, it's still got power. See? Green light's blinking."

"So?" Willi tapped the silver-shelled phone. "Maybe, we can't tell what numbers are hidden behind all those Japanese—"

"Or Chinese—"

"Or Chinese letters, but maybe we could just scroll down and—"

Kenzie leaned forward. "Yes, and punch it in and see—"

"Who we get," Willi finished. "What do I say if I reach someone?"

"That, girlfriend, might be a moot point unless you speak one of those languages. Play it by ear."

"Okay, by ear. Here goes." She scrolled up and down the five or six lines of gibberish on the screen.

"Just do it, Willi. Hurry, before Juna Marie comes out."

"I'm going to. Don't yell at me."

"We're whispering."

Willi glared. "Well, it was a whispered yell."

She punched the SEND button and held the phone to her ear. There was ringing at some distant end—perhaps Okinawa, maybe Singapore or some Thailand enclave. At last, the receiver lifted and a voice spoke. Willi froze for a moment, then her mouth opened in shock as she shoved the phone into Kenzie's hands.

"What the hell are you doing, Will—?"

Willi covered the mouthpiece with her hand. "Don't say my name. You talk to him; he doesn't know your voice."

"Huh?"

Kenzie grabbed the phone and tentatively said, "Hello. Yes, I suppose I may have the wrong number. Just what town have I reached, sir?"

At the response, Kenzie's eyes grew round. "Really? Nickleberry, Texas?" She grimaced at Willi and shrugged her shoulders in that what-in-great-wonder-do-I-do-now gesture. "Yes, sir, well, really, I was lost. Yes, lost, and . . . I was trying to reach a . . ."

Willi whispered, "A relative . . . some relative, whatever."

"I was . . . was trying to reach a cousin. You know most folks? Really? Oh, as sheriff. Oh, bless you, sir. Hope that cold gets better."

Willi nodded. Yep, that was definitely Quannah's uncle, Sheriff Brigham Tucker of the oversized bandannas, Benadryl tablets, and Luden's cough drops.

"Name of the cousin? Well, yes, sir, I'd be glad to share that name with you."

Willi wrote on Yataro's notebook. *Coggins Self*.

Kenzie dutifully said the name, then held the phone so

both she and Willi could hear the sheriff's answer. "Yes, ma'am, we got a lot of those Self folks roundabouts in these parts. Lots of Selfs and Wests connected by marriages and blood in Nickleberry. Let's see now, Tiffany West I believe lives off of Licorice Lane, and Coggins, even though he's one of the more eligible bachelors of the clan, stays in a double-wide on her place, them being first cousins. Nope, nope. I misrecollected. Coggins and Shaw Self share a double-wide. Both them young men are good folks, honest and hard working."

He sneezed again, and after a blessing from Kenzie, he said, "Coggins just got back from a visit to San Miguel de Allende, Mexico. He speaks Spanish real good. 'Course, I guess you know that, being cousins and all. Now, what'd you say your name was young lady?"

"Oh, my goodness. I guess it's showing on your phone ID there, so you can see I'm . . ." Kenzie improvised.

Willi crinkled paper, hoping it sounded something akin to static on the line.

"Didn't catch that. Guess you're phone connections going bad. The dang ID just says UNAVAILABLE. Surely, you ain't Unavailable Self?" Sheriff Tucker laughed at his joke.

Willi smiled. She pictured him tugging at his earlobe as if he had a tick bothering him. Damn. She missed old Sheriff Tucker and all the rest of the Nickleberry buddies. At a sharp jab from Kenzie, she wrote, *Shwartzy Self from Abilene.*

"Oh, yes, Schwartzy. I recollect you from a tiny little bit of nothing. Quietest young lady. Right nice like all the rest of you Selfs and Wests, though, right nice. Used to run around with another skinny-legged little girl I'm right fond of. Do you remember Willi Gallagher? Why, we're practically relatives now."

A few more minutes spent in learning about the budding romance of his nephew, one Quannah Lassiter, and Miss Willi, then getting directions to Coggins Self's mobile home, and Kenzie said good-bye. "Well."

Willi nodded. "Well, indeed."

"What do you think?" Kenzie said.

Tucking the cell phone out of sight, Willi said, "Guess we know who the phone belongs to now."

"Uh-huh."

"So, I'm going to have to go put it back."

Kenzie nodded. "I'll go with you after supper. Quannah will be busy with the stable duties then."

"I certainly hope so. Last thing I need after whacking him with an oar is his discovering I took his cell phone." She squared her shoulders. "Know what?"

"What now?"

"I feel better. We solved two mysteries today."

"Two mysteries?" Kenzie asked, bunching and pinning her short curls on top of her head.

"Yes, first, that idiot Jerry Fartleberry Cormack is *not* a force to be reckoned with, for one thing. Guess I'd better tell you about a phone call received just before we left for the island." Willi told Kenzie, but before Kenzie could react, she added quickly, "He'd hoped we'd worry ourselves to death about him, planned that we *think* he was here and all-powerful and frightening, supposed that we'd react by not enjoying the retreat. He had just enough to know you were at a lake somewhere and that's all. Our own dread of his presence did the rest of the work for him."

"Until today," Kenzie grinned, obviously remembering her "cacahooties" tirade against innocent Nara Inoshi. "Do you truly think he's not been slinking around? Just because . . . because I'm not afraid of him anymore, doesn't mean I'm stupid and going to let my guard down totally, unless I'm sure."

Willi grinned, handing over the cell phone. "It shows UNAVAILABLE."

"Okay, I'll do it." Kenzie dialed the jerk's home number, and again she leaned over ear to ear with Willi. On the fifth ring, one jerk-face Cormack answered. She let him get into a cussing rage against the silence that met each of his requests to know who in the damnsamhill was this, before she disconnected. "Ha. He's not on the island." Kenzie's eyes lit up and she squealed, raising her arms in a victory air-dance.

"So," Willi continued, "Two items are off the list of the storm-swept debris swirling around my head." She paused, then frowned at Kenzie's intense stare. "Excuse me?"

Kenzie grinned, "Just trying to see through that mess." She thumped Willi on the head, zipped up and into the shower just as Juna Marie came out.

"Wait a minute. It was my turn. I'll remember this."

From the other side of the door, Kenzie mouthed. "I'm shaking."

As the shower spigots burst forth with steam on the bathroom side, a torrent rushed down from the sky to attack Mother Earth in a blitzkrieg of lightning and hail. Willi and Juna Marie both ran to the door and opened it.

"Not yet five o'clock and look at that sky," Juna Marie said, toweling off her white-blond coif.

Willi said, "Blacker than the inside of a viper's gullet and twice as deadly. Get inside. That hail is as big as golf balls." She put her hands to her cheeks. "Quannah's out in this."

Juna Marie ran to the window on her side. When she turned away, she sat cross-legged on the bed again, the towel dropped to the floor, her hair in feathery tufts around her regal head. Willi leaned into her space to hear her say, "Halliwell's out in this."

The whispered words so similar to her own, held an entirely different vibe. She was worried about Halliwell being out in the storm, but . . . not worried *for* him. What then? For whom was that fear felt? Willi trembled from the suddenly chilled air. Sure, that was what caused her skin to prickle.

"Oh, Quannah, be careful. Please get back soon. Please."

CHAPTER
16

When Kenzie stepped out of the bathroom, Willi went inside, but instead of the leisurely bath she'd promised herself, she rushed through a hot shower and shampoo. Hairs on her neck prickled even though wet, creating an antsy feeling, which made her want to rush through her bath and quickly locate Quannah. Might his chest have been hurt worse than they had at first thought? Why hadn't he come by to let her know all was okay? He knew—he had to know—she'd not realized who he was as she had struck out. When she came out to towel-dry her hair, Kenzie and Juna Marie were both sitting cross-legged on Willi's bed and staring out at the storm. As if the celestial stage crew kept getting their cues mixed, the curtains of rain came and went, leaving space in between each drawing back for an encore.

Juna Marie was saying, "Yes, Willi is lucky. Quannah was just really thoughtful and nice today."

Willi said, "Huh? When was he here? Was he all right?

What did he say? Come on. We'll go meet him at the Mimosa Teahouse."

Kenzie held her hands palms out. "Stop. This was earlier, much earlier in the morning. Take a minute to calm down; chill out a second, girl. You might want to get dressed before we do go hunting one Indian brave."

Willi pulled on pink bobby socks and then her plastic Clicks. She also opted for warm jeans—denims worn down to that velvet touch—along with an undershirt and a frothy pink turtleneck. Sprayed liberally with her Passion perfume, she figured she was presentable for even an out-of-sorts special investigator. Trying for more calm, she repeated, "When was he here?"

Juna Marie answered. "This morning, not long after you left. Talked to me through the window. Real quiet and gentle like. No wonder he's good with horses. Finally, I leaned out and chatted a while." She closed her eyes and her lashes brushed against pink cheeks. "I know I broke the silence, but he even got me to laughing. *Laughing*," Juna Marie repeated the word like giggling was a wondrous accomplishment, as well it might have been considering her early morning condition.

Will brushed her hair out, deciding to let it air dry. "He has his moments with animals and with folks. Kind of hones in on how best to approach. He teases me a lot. I love it. And he has this maddening wink, and—oh, I wish he were here. Now. Right now. I'd take any teasing he'd care to dish out."

"Guess," Juna Marie said, "he knew kidding would've scared me right off today. I just needed a real slow, quiet voice of reason. He'd almost talked me into coming outside and said he'd not tell anyone I'd broken the silence; said it probably didn't count until I got out of the pagoda, anyway. Trying to make me feel good, like I told you.

You're real lucky, Willi. You hang on to him. He's always working sweet things about you into the conversation, too. That's real nice because . . . he's sincere."

Willi patted her hand. "At the moment he may be sincerely and royally pissed at me, if he's okay. If he's not out there with a broken rib."

Juna Marie giggled. "Yes, Kenzie told me about you whacking him good and hard with that paddle. You two won't ever have a boring day together. You all saw him walking up the incline. He's fine. You know that."

. "Hope so. Outside your window, huh? So that's whose apple core we found."

Behind Juna Marie's back, Kenzie shook her head and waved her hand as if to say "don't go there," but Willi couldn't take back the words.

Juna Marie sighed. "No. I was leaning out the window like I said, enjoying his gentle talk, hearing the birds twitter, and even welcoming the humid heat, but . . . Halliwell came along. I was in a fine mood, would have come on out and gone down a trail with him, but he . . . oh. He can be so embarrassing sometimes. And after the . . . incident this morning, then him yelling like he did at Quannah, I just clammed up again."

"Incident?" Willi asked.

Kenzie tied her own tennis shoes and said, "The bouquets. The two flower arrangements."

"Oh, right," Willi said. "The one from Mr. Pate and the other from—?"

"Mr. Inoshi."

"Oh?" Willi frowned. "Oh, okay."

Juna Marie bent her slender neck and ducked her head. "I thought he was paying me a compliment, making a . . . a . . . move on me when he first brought the bouquet—Mr. Inoshi, I mean. But he just wanted information. He thought

Yataro gave me his prayer wheel, of all things. Why would he think that?"

Willi exchanged a glance with Kenzie. *Maybe because he witnessed a certain embrace between his coworker and the preacher's wife? Perhaps because he thought something vital about the ancient monk—the Divine One—resided in the sacred object?*

"So . . . why exactly were you angry at Halliwell?" asked Willi. "I'm confused. Sorry."

"Not at all. I'm rambling," Juna Marie said while pulling on her blue sweater. "He just . . . won't let me breathe and sometimes goes overboard to be protective or to let me know he's being protective. He went out and made up the same flower arrangement. I guess it's just his way, but it didn't sit right with me. By doing that, he took a sweet and innocent gift from . . . from a friend and made it into something else entirely."

Kenzie said, "I can understand that. Oh, yeah. Turned a Hallmark moment nasty."

"Definitely," Willi agreed. "So what happened when he talked to Quannah?"

"That was awful." Juna Marie's cheeks reddened. "He acted like Quannah had . . . been inside the pagoda here with me, not just stopping by the window and passing the time. Said all the right things but all the wrong way, if you know what I mean?"

"His perspective turned another friendly moment into one fraught with innuendoes?" Willi asked.

Juna Marie nodded. "*Innuendoes,* yes. The perfect word. So, I shut the window, and didn't talk to anyone until you all came. He sat out there all morning. Guess he got tired or really hungry an hour or so before lunchtime. When I got up to scrabble through my purse for a candy bar he was already gone. Poor Halliwell. He's so attentive, so proud of my being by his side, but sometimes . . ."

"Sometimes," Kenzie said, "you need a little space. My former husband never gave that to me, and doesn't yet. That's one of the main reasons we're divorced. He was a compulsive control freak."

Juna Marie bit her bottom lip. "I shouldn't tell anyone this. He'd be so upset with me, but Halliwell has seen doctors."

"Doctors?" Willi asked.

"For anger management," Juna Marie admitted, with her chin touching her chest. "He's really trying to overcome some of the problems, and has sought the Lord out many a time in prayer." She sighed even above the wind soughing outside. "I've spent years in such prayers with him. I'm weary. *We* might not weather this storm." She peered outside at the rain, abated for the moment as if the audience were gone and it made no difference that the bare and darkened stage offered no entertainment.

Willi, knowing Juna Marie did not refer to the literal weather around them, shook her head. "I'm so sorry."

"I'm not without blame in the battle this time," Juna Marie said, raising her head and looking at both Willi and then Kenzie. "I purposefully pursued a gentleman . . . just to see if . . . if . . ."

"If you were still attractive to the opposite sex other than your husband?" Kenzie asked. "I thought about that a time or two myself. I think it's a normal reaction to such abuse."

Juna Marie bridled. "Oh, Halliwell isn't abusive. Well, he doesn't mean to be. He's just got a temper and is attentive in a way that, after all these many years, is beginning . . . oh . . . to wear me down, to have a toll on my mental health and my physical well-being. But, it was wrong of me to encourage Yataro Yodo the way I did."

Curiosity getting the better of her, Willi said, "You two met for the first time on the island the other night?"

"No. Yataro helped our church board and Halliwell purchase new land for our youth center, and helped us locate an excellent and reasonably priced contractor. Sometimes, Halliwell had me carry papers to his office."

"And then?" Kenzie asked, leaning forward.

"I came in once during a quick lunch he'd had brought in and he asked me to share and we talked and we . . . didn't do anything. Nothing. But he told me about the retreat, and he'd already told Halliwell and the church board members. They're the ones who wanted us to come and bring back the experience to share."

Willi and Kenzie both nodded their heads.

"I guess I flirted with him; he may have read too much into that and the fact that we did come to the retreat. I admit when he held me that first night we arrived, and . . . well I didn't back off from his kisses. I'm quite ashamed of myself for the action."

"Don't beat yourself up over a stolen kiss, Juna Marie," Kenzie said. "That's just what keeps you stuck in the same old, same old. As long as you didn't take any other action."

Willi smiled at the question implied. Juna Marie understood it, too, and shook her head. "No, no."

As Willi listened, she rested her elbows on her knees. How the tables had turned. Kenzie had arrived at the island as a basket case afraid of her own shadow and in terror of encountering Cormack's. Now she doled out healing to another who was hurting and needing guidance through an emotional upheaval. Willi sighed. She wanted only blessings and healing for the Pates. Be nice to leave the island with two happy endings: Kenzie strong and balanced again; the Pates in sync in their marriage once more.

Juna Marie's stomach grumbled, and she grabbed at her middle. "Guess that candy didn't last long. You all want to go while the rain's slowed a little?"

"Finally. You bet," Willi said, pulling a yellow hooded poncho over her sweater. "Maybe the best place to encounter these men is where we can feed them . . . and there's lots of other folks around."

Kenzie laughed. "Witnesses are always good."

Juna Marie frowned. "Yes, and I'm a bit worried about . . . Halliwell being out in this. He's proud of keeping in shape, but he's not really an outdoorsman type."

A few minutes later, they'd reached the Mimosa Teahouse, which welcomed them with the promising odors of noodle soup, spinach salads, and hush puppies redolent of onions. Two monks, sitting on the perimeter of the sandbox, added the finishing touches of sand to a beautiful lush hillside, a waterfall gently cascading over stepping-stones. There on one stone sat a weary traveler, obviously enjoying the twitter of a trio of bluebirds in a nearby bush while washing his dusty feet in the flowing silver of the water. The monks' backdrop behind the plate-glass windows—a royal purple sky with sparks of distant lightning—added an eerie element to the tableau of the religious men and their work.

The monks wore deep frowns and constantly glanced across the room at the diners. Juna Marie said, "I suppose we're considered very crass to be talking before the eleven o'clock gong sounds."

Kenzie shrugged. "They'll have to understand we're neophytes, and just too much has happened today. It's not like we're trying to engage them in conversation."

Samdup materialized at Willi's elbow so stealthily, she

never noticed until his voice announced quietly but with a resonance that reached every cranny of the large pagoda. "Today you had much to learn with the koan, but it is true, many events—worldly events—took place, which had to be tended to as well. We will count this as a half day of silence, and practice another half day later in the week, if you all wish to continue the exercise. For now, relax, rest . . . and . . . *chat,* if you so desire." With some hand signal, he changed the artists' demeanor, and they bowed and smiled. All was well.

Juna Marie sighed and said, "Thank goodness. I didn't need a larger load of guilt today. Oh, I'm so hungry. Maybe getting things clear and thought-out today did something for my appetite. I've got to discuss things with Halliwell."

Willi said, "I'm starving, now, too, but not so much for food or the ambiance of the lovely sand pictures, but for sight of one Quannah Lassiter, even if he's in a rage."

The outside double doors burst open.

Kenzie and Juna Marie announced, "Ta-dah! Your prince has arrived."

Willi jumped up and ran into the curve of the arm he held out. The other one he kept close to his chest. She said, "Yum. You smell so good."

"Yes, *Winyan,* after a bath in a shower . . . with *soap,* probably much better than when the Guadalupe barfed me up onto the bank. Have the other men come in yet?"

"You're favoring that arm. I'm so sorry. I didn't know it was you, an—"

Quannah pulled her close and rubbed noses with her. She immediately calmed down. He said, "It's all right, Woman-with-Tweetybird-Medicine, and—"

"Hummingbird, thank you very much, and . . . and what?"

"And this was an earlier injury of the morning; you

merely set back the healing by a couple extra days. Some
bruised ribs. Not a biggie. So where are Inoshi, Toru,
Nestor, and Rooster?"

"Not a biggie? Not a biggie. You come right over here.
Sit. Yes, I'll get more pillows. There. Is that better? You
need another one underneath that arm?"

"Stop fluttering, *Winyan.*"

"Please," Kenzie said, "let her fuss a little. It's the least
you can do to appease her guilt feelings after whopping
you off the boat. She's been worried sick. And I'm, like
you, wondering where all the guys are. Surely, they'd not
let rain keep them from this feast."

Willi glared at her friend. "Worried sick? Me? Where'd
you get such an idea? I was merely concerned we might
have to go traipsing out in the dark and the rain to find his
happy warrior's ass if he'd happen to have gotten lost.
Concerned about getting wet and muddy again. Worried?
Not on your life."

Quannah rubbed the edge of her right cheekbone with
his index finger. "Not even a little?"

"Maybe . . . maybe a smidgen." Suddenly, with fire in
her eyes, she stared at him as if he'd just broken all five of
her classroom rules at once. "What possessed you to jump
into the water and try to board the boat in the first place?"

Quannah frowned. "At the time it seemed like the right
thing to do. A man sees his lady in distress, he goes to
save her."

"Save me? I was doing just fine."

Kenzie choked, "Ha!"

Willi, with nose in the air, continued. "Save me? Oh my
gosh."

"Looked to me, Gallagher, you were about to dump over
in the rapids. Didn't seem you had any great mariner's
skills. But,"—he paused to hold his hand up in a protective

palm outward gesture—"I bet you could make any sailor walk the plank. No doubt about that anymore."

"Well, Lassiter, I'm glad *you* were worried about *me*." Willi smiled and peered up at him through her long lashes.

"Worried about you? More concerned for the boat and Skeeter. Did you knock the wind out of him, too?" The glint in his eye and the smile tugging at the corners of his mouth took any bite out of his question.

"Oh, you don't know."

Willi and Kenzie filled Quannah in on the accident. While they informed him, Preacher Halliwell Pate arrived, greeted all, and took his Juna Marie to a more reclusive table close to the sand painting. Juna Marie, with her spine straight and regal, started talking as soon as they sat down.

Even though Willi shushed Kenzie and Quannah so she could lean over and hear better, no sound drifted across the room. But the way Halliwell pulled back from his wife, the manner in which he tightened the blue sweater around his white shorts, and the method he used of putting his hands across his own mouth, proved a testimony to his shock over his sweet Juna Marie speaking her mind to him.

"Gallagher, stop that," Quannah said, while enticing her with a spoon of hot soup. Peering around as the door creaked against the wind, he spilled the spoonful and had to wipe her chin off. He repeated, "Stop that. It's rude."

"What?"

"Eavesdropping."

"I was merely enjoying the stillness for a moment, attempting to calm down, trying to arrange these floor pillows more comfortably. Don't know why you two are always picking on me about such things as if I would ever, actually, on purpose, listen in to a private conversation. That would be . . . *uncivilized*."

"Ah," said Quannah, "So that's how your savage Indian side comes out."

He and Kenzie did a high-five.

Willi rolled her eyes, then scarfed down her meal. When all three were finished, she said, "Guess I'd better fess up to something that might be . . . well, it might be important." She had developed a load of guilt heavier than the ozone pressing around the pagoda about not informing him of the cell phone.

Quannah folded his napkin and told Rimshi he'd come back later for the dessert—a hot peach cobbler. "I need to get going. Maybe we can touch base later on your transgressions, *Winyan,* if they can wait. Something's not right, and I have to—"

Willi huffed. "You've been so preoccupied. What's the matter? What do you have to do? Is it something we can help you with? I hate to think of you working with the horses tonight with your ribs hurting. Kenzie and I can—"

"No, I just have to see the old monk. A lot of questions could be answered if I can manage to get him still for five minutes. I'm too antsy to sit, Gallagher. Do you . . . would you try . . . to understand? I've got to do this now."

She smiled at him, placed a warm hand against his cheek, and bent toward him to give him a lingering kiss. "I *do* understand. I know there's something more than the horses and trail rides on your mind. When the mood strikes to share that, well, I'll be ready to listen. And I also understand about being driven to do something in the immediate moment. I've accomplished my share of crazy and weird things today. Wish I'd known you needed to speak with Samdup. He was here right before we sat to eat."

"Samdup?" Quannah's hooded eyes scanned the torrents of water now slashing against the floor-to-ceiling windows.

"Yes, Lassiter, the old monk . . . the old monk you needed to see right now?"

"Right. Sure. Yeah, well . . . don't wait up or anything, and don't worry. After I've talked to . . . *him,* I'll bed down with a couple of Aleve painkillers."

"An early night might be a good call for all of us," Willi said, taking a big helping of the cobbler and placing it and a fork in a tinfoil wrap Rimshi brought at her request. In her best Mary Poppin's singing voice, she half said, half sang, "Here, this'll help the *medicine go down in a most delightful way.*" She kissed him on the nose. "Don't talk too long. Get some shut-eye, Big Chief."

He winked at her. "Not that you're worried."

She grinned. "Absolutely right, One-with-Arrogant-Head."

He whispered in the soft shell of her ear. "Love you."

She licked her lips and said, "Ditto, kiddo. Love you, too."

His broad back disappeared as the double doors opened long enough to give entry to a sledgehammer of rain along with a boom of thunder that vibrated Willi's teeth, and then the doors slammed shut.

Kenzie laughed and patted Willi's hand. "You two look good in love."

"Thanks. Sure feels good. Ornery feller, though."

"But Willi, he has to be. He's got the most ornery Miss Marple of the Range to take care of for the rest of his life."

"Hope so. Hope so."

Kenzie finished her last bite of peach cobbler. "Uh-oh."

"Uh-oh?" Willi peered in the direction of Kenzie's glance.

"She's at it again."

"No kidding. Must not have gone well, her telling Halliwell she needed some space."

"You think, girl?"

Willi, with Kenzie behind her, approached the swanlike figure, perched as if sailing on a languid lake, rather than in the middle of a raging flood of emotions. "Juna Marie?" Willi placed a hand on her fragile shoulder.

Juna Marie ruffled her feathery white-blond hair. "I'm just so confused. So many questions are floating in here." She tapped her forehead. "I'm going to pull a Scarlet O'Hara and just figure that tomorrow is another day, and I'll worry about all these questions tomorrow. You all have anything for a headache?"

"Sure," Kenzie pulled out a packet of ibuprofen.

Juna Marie took them, rose, and, without benefit of pulling her poncho over her, went outside.

"Sweet dreams," Kenzie said in the wake of her hasty departure. "Everybody is at sixes and sevens, as the saying goes. What's happening, girlfriend? Do we call it a night, curl up with Dean Koontz's and Earlene Fowler's latest and hot tea, or try to figure out why everyone is so *antsy,* as Quannah said? Warm bed sounds good; lots of pillows piled high; extra blankie against the chill tonight. Works for me."

"Work. That's exactly what we need to do."

"No, no, no, Willi. No work. Rest. Chill-out time, girl. Let's veg. We've had a full day."

Willi tapped the end of her nose.

"Don't go doing that, girlfriend, please."

"What?"

"What? Tapping your nose, like you're thinking up mischief. Lucy Ricardo opened her eyes wider than daisies. Samantha the witch wiggled her nose. Your nose-tapping always preceeds us getting into trouble."

"Kenzie, Kenzie, Kenzie. I'm trying to clear up the unanswered questions. We'll sleep the better for it. Right now it's not even eight o'clock. Far too early for beddy-bye."

"Silly me."

"I should think so. Now, why was Quannah worried

about the other fellows not being here? Men don't do that worrying-mama routine for each other."

"You have that right. Yeah, odd."

"Very odd. The menus are posted. Would any of those men willingly turn down peach cobbler?"

"Oh, my."

"Oh my, is right. Quannah might not have known the exact reason he was concerned, couldn't put his mental finger on the cause, but he had the inner *knowing* they should have been here."

Kenzie's eyes teared up. "You don't suppose . . . you don't suppose something has happened to Paul . . . to Rooster, do you?"

"No, no, no. I don't get that feeling, but there's some piece of business keeping him from a good supper and a good woman. He would not have missed this unless something very important came up. We have to figure out what."

"What . . . or who?"

"Kenzie, not to worry. There are no females to worry about. Doretta, who never showed an interest in him, is off the island with Skeeter. Juna Marie, who did flirt with him, is not truly interested, and admitted she'd only kissed one man on the island. Both of us know it was Yataro Yodo, may he rest in peace."

"Girlfriend, he may not be dea—"

"Dead. Yes, he is."

"So, what can we do about all this while the storm is making nasty out there?"

"First," Willi said, counting on her fingers. "We go to see if Nestor D. or Rooster are in their pagoda. Might find out what they saw the IODD men doing that caused them to fight the first night we were here." She blew air out her mouth, which fluttered her bangs. "Secondly, we go see the old monk."

"Samdup? What for?"

"Ah, well, that I'm not sure of yet, but . . . but it's not Samdup we have to find. It's the Eye of the Divine."

"Huh?" Kenzie's bewilderment showed in wide eyes and mouth hanging open.

Willi lowered her voice, even though she knew the two artist monks could not hear her across the cavernous room. "The *old* monk."

Kenzie snapped her mouth shut so hard her teeth smacked together. She winced. "As in the one behind the waterfall?"

"You are so smart. That's one of the reasons I love you, Kenzie. You get there before the crowd, yes you do."

"Well, Miss Marple of the Range, you are not going to drag me anywhere near that damned Guadalupe again, much less in the dark, much less—are you listening to me?—much less while a torrential spate of devil's spit is making it roll over the banks. Just looking for victims. Idiots to come out in inky nightfall and stumble in. Are you listening to me? Don't pull my arm that way. I can put my own damned slicker around me."

"Hurry, before others get the same idea."

"Willi, you don't ever have to worry about anyone figuring out what goes on behind that heart-shaped face and blue-green eyes. But whatever it is, I'm saying *stop* to it tonight. Not a happening thing. Uh-huh. Don't push me down this way."

At last, they stood on the doorstep of the men's pagoda—the one housing Quannah, Skeeter, Nestor D., and Rooster, since the IODD Company had paid extra money for their executives to have the separate men's rooms farther down the pathway.

"At least, we won't encounter cardboard cut-outs crafted by IODD ingenuity," Willi said.

"Crafted by IODD ingenuity to mislead and confuse," Kenzie added. "So what do we hope to accomplish here?"

CHAPTER
17

Will pulled her yellow slicker hood back to her shoulders and knocked on the door. That same edginess, the mental nervousness suffered by Quannah, must have spread to her. Dang, she just *knew* time was important here. Hell Bells, she could almost hear the tick-tock vibrating up through *Unci*, Mother Earth, insisting she get answers before another person was placed in danger.

Paul Rooster Rowley, drying his hair with a towel, opened the door. With only a pair of black jeans and socks on, he clearly wasn't expecting company. From the stifled comment from behind her, she gathered that Kenzie appreciated his still fine physique, the tufts of dark hair etching a trail down his chest, the way his jeans fit across muscled buttocks.

He said, "Now, wait just a moment, now, just a moment. Let me find a shirt. There's one right over here."

When he vacated the doorway to gather his clothes,

Willi edged inside, pulling Kenzie along with her. "Kenzie was concerned about you."

Blue eyes narrowed, Kenzie placed a well-aimed elbow in Willi's side. "As was everyone," she added.

"No call for worrying, ladies, none at all." He grinned after pulling on and tucking in a striped short-sleeved shirt. " 'Course it's sort of nice being missed . . . by someone . . . uh . . . by ladies and all. Yeah, that's what I meant to say." He pointed to the one loveseat against the wall that faced the four cubicles. "You all make yourselves to home; yeah, get comfortable, won't you?" He sat on a bed and laced up his tennis shoes. "Something you ladies need help with?"

"Pardon?" Kenzie asked.

"Maybe a little training on motorboats and the things they can and can't do in the river?" He chuckled. "I tell you, you all don't need anything that way. A miracle, that's what you worked today. Yes, ma'am. My hat's off to both of you. Fine job. Real good job, you did."

"Aww, thanks," Willi said, "Kenzie did most of the hard work, really."

"That so?" His eyes lit up and he grinned at Kenzie while nodding his head. He even forgot to repeat himself.

Taking advantage of the cozy, warm feelings melting around the room, Willi said, "Got one question we need a simple and honest answer to."

"Bet I could provide that. Sure."

"The first night on Serenity Island when all of us met in the Mimosa Pagoda, you recall?"

"Yes, ma'am, I do; yes, indeed, I do. Pleasant that was. Better than I first experienced on the lake."

Willi grinned, taking the ribbing in good grace. "You won't get an argument from me. Well, that afternoon or evening you and Nestor D. saw the IODD men doing something, something that caused a fight between you and Nestor. What was it you all saw?"

Rooster ran a hand down his face, sucked on his teeth a moment, and then wiped his features again. "I'm not sure I can give you your honest and simple answer. Why would that concern you ladies, anyhow? How could that possibly be important to you two?"

Kenzie got up to sit right beside him. With a hand on his shoulder, she peered into his eyes. "Trust me on this. I don't know, but when Willi gets one of these scorpions of rampaging worry attacking, the only ones that get stung are those around her if she doesn't get answers. Please, please, appease her curiosity. She's just trying to eliminate certain worries from other happenings on the island. This could well be one incident she could just scratch off her list of concerns. Please?"

"Oh, well, I'm not partial to scorpions, real or otherwise. Guess it won't hurt as long as you just simply forget it, once told, if it's not important. Deal?"

"Deal," Willi said.

"Deal," Kenzie brushed her champagne curls out of her eyes. "You bet."

"Okay, we—Nestor D. and me—were walking out the kinks of the rowing. Near black as midnight in some of the more forested areas. There, in a really heavy growth of bushes high as your eyes, were that Inoshi feller and the muscled-up one, one that played the harmonica."

Kenzie said, "Mike Toru?"

"Yeah, Toru, that's the one. Both them were covering up a shallow hole. Nestor D. figures the worst. Gotta be digging up gold or artifacts or something illegal, of course. Then, they did something surprised us both."

"Oh?" Willi leaned forward.

Kenzie clutched at his sleeve; he pulled her hand on through and rested it atop his arm. "Surprised you both?"

He patted her hand. "Yes, ma'am. Sure did. Hell, they weren't after any treasure or artifacts I'd want. They had a trap of some kind to catch snakes."

"Snakes?" Kenzie asked, leaning back.

"So what was in the ground in the hole? The trap?" Willi asked.

Rooster shrugged. "Maybe. Or they pulled it out once they caught the snakes; I suppose they pulled it out."

"Nestor D. agrees?" Willi asked, peering around the corner of the next cubicle over.

"Oh, he ain't here. Isn't here. Went to meditate at the Lotus Pagoda, the schoolhouse place."

Yeah, right. Willi tapped the end of her nose. Meditate my hind foot and the donkey's tail. He's there typing all our sordid little stories into his mini-computer, looking for that sale to *Time* or *U.S. News* or worse, *People.* She said, "So, he didn't think the covered hole was part of the snake trap?"

"Naw. He figured he'd go back and see later about what they buried. Insisted they *buried,* not *exhumed,* anything. His mistrust will not die."

"Yes," Willi said, frowning and concentrating, trying to make all the tidbits in the swirling maelstrom still for one moment. "Where in the world on the island was this?"

Rooster described the exact turn taken off the yellow brick pathway along with the huge azaleas surrounding the area. "Oh, I know where," Willi said. "It's a beautiful spot.

"One," Kenzie said, with a pointed look, "we won't be needing to visit, seeing as how it plays host to crawling critters."

Rooster said, "To be fair to Inoshi and Toru, the monks gave them permission to dig up and take home some of the native plants and small animals to propagate. I suppose that could include the reptiles. I think that's why they got a pagoda to themselves. Tanks in there of lizards, turtles, and such."

"Ah," Kenzie and Willi said together. "And flowers."

"Possibly. Well, nice as the company is, I've got to get going. Got an invitation."

"Oh?" Kenzie said, unwrapping her hand from his elbow and clasp.

"Yeah, that nice man, Preacher Pate, talked the monks into a small cookout, yeah, a cookout for just us guys. Preacher Pate ain't that much for the outside activities, but he came through on this."

"That's why everyone missed the peach cobbler."

"Skeeter was gonna sneak us in some Dr Peppers, but guess we'll make do with the tea, as usual."

Willi said, "Nonsense. His boat's in dock. Probably will be until some big repairs are made. There's two locked-down coolers the size of small cars. The drinks are bound to be in there, but . . ."

"But," Rooster said, putting on his glasses and frowning.

With a sigh and a smile, Kenzie pulled them off and took a soft tissue to them. "Here."

"Sure glad you keep those clean for me. I can see lots of pretty things through them now." Like a lapdog, he grinned at her.

"Oh, you." Kenzie ducked her head.

Loudly, Willi repeated, "The drinks are there, but where are you all going to have a cookout in this storm?"

"Preacher Pate found us a real neat cave out near the waterfalls today. He's to have everything set up. Well, Nestor D.'s going to be doing a lot of it and that feller— why can't I ever remember his name?"

"Toru?" chimed in Kenzie.

"Him, yeah. Toru's building the fire and all; yep, he's setting up the food. Now we'll have drinks instead of tea; even better. Nestor D. came in early and popped six or seven bags of popcorn he'd brought." He hung his head. "I got the manners of a rhino. Shouldn't be talking all this up with you all seeing as how you're not included."

"Not a problem," Willi said. "We girlfriends like to have ladies-only days, too. Quannah is a big believer that bonding with the same gender allows us to freely express concerns and get feedback in a manner easiest for us to understand. Even the *wamaskaskan*—the animals—have times when like genders stay together and away from the other."

"You sure it's all right, because if it were upsetting to you—" He faced Kenzie. "Well, I wouldn't go; that's what I'd do, I wouldn't go."

"Really?" Kenzie asked, a finger touching his cheek.

"Right real."

"I appreciate that, and I might even hold you to it on occasion, but you go and enjoy and have fun this evening. This day has been a stressful, rather than the comfortable silent one it was supposed to be. Go. Do a detox on the day."

"Okay."

Willi stepped outside to give them a moment of privacy for which Kenzie thanked her when she joined her. "That was nice."

"So," Willi asked, "Is he a good—?"

"Perfect. Yes, yes, yes!"

The clouds chose that moment to rip asunder, letting loose a driving hard rain along with wind that whipped a dead tree branch across their path. Willi retreated underneath the porch.

"Just where did you think you were going, girl?" Kenzie yelled.

"To the old monk."

"No, not in this." At Willi's yelp of protest, Kenzie held a hand up. "Can't we wait a few minutes? You know Texas weather. Give it five and you'll see sunshine."

Willi grimaced and nodded her head toward the men's pagoda door, before cupping her hands and raising her voice. "Guess we could ride out the worst inside, but then we're going. No question I have to let that stubborn, closemouthed Big Chief Lassiter know about all the clues—"

"Or garbage—"

"*Clues* that might help him with whatever he's after. They do all seem to lead to this . . . this oldest monk."

Inside, Willi shook out her poncho and hung it on a peg. She did the same with Kenzie's. "Let me ramble a moment here, okay? I've tried to find secluded spots to sit and think things out, and that's not worked any better for me than it has for Juna Marie. Maybe having a sounding board would—?"

"Call me plywood four by eight and sound away." Kenzie perched on Rooster's bed with military corners and pulled his pillow in her lap. Willi smiled and chose to tease her at a later time.

"Okay, we found Yataro Yodo dead in the Lotus Pagoda. A possible means of death was snake bite."

"Because of his right hand?"

"Yes, and . . . Kenzie, exactly . . . his *right*."

"Yeah, we noted that, girl."

"No, no. I've been stupid, and not noted that. He was right-handed; the IODD men knew he was, hence the cardboard figure moving the appropriate hand forward for the tea."

"So?"

"So . . . I'd been thinking that the prayer sheet inside the *chos-kor* had been written by him. What if his killer had written it? Some sick message left to explain *why* he murdered Mr. Yodo."

"All killers do that?"

"No, Kenzie, but a lot do. Now how am I going to get handwriting of Mr. Yodo's to compare?"

"You already have it, don't you . . . uh . . . in that spiral you used?"

Willi grabbed for her bag to pull out the prayer wheel and the notebook. Kenzie held out the prayer while Willi flicked through the pages to lists, koans written down, and some calculations. Taking them to the lamp table, they spread the papers out side by side.

"Can you tell, oh English teacher?"

"As a matter of fact, yes. The prayer has spiky printing. Quite neat and meticulous letters. Written with one of those Precise liquid fine points some of us don't allow students to use. They're generally too messy. And if you deny it to some—"

"You have to deny it to all to be fair. Understood. You are good, girl. I can see now that you've pointed it out. Cool."

Willi tapped Yataro's notebook. "This is of a heavier hand, larger letters, and although precise, not slanted like the other one at all. In fact, Mr. Yataro probably got *A*'s in printing in the third grade. And he must have liked pencil, because that's all he uses in his notebook, and that's what was found. No pen."

"So . . . so someone else wrote it?"

"No doubt. And the monks said they were personally placed, meaning put in the prayer wheel by the individual."

"So the monks would not have written out prayers for someone else's *chos-kor?*" Kenzie retrieved the pillow and sat back down. "You know, I'm beginning to believe Mr. Yataro *is*—"

"Dead?"

"Yep, dead. However, our Miss Marple of the Range,

there's no reason that info can't wait until morning and the
storm has cleared."

Willi hunkered down on the sofa after carefully replac-
ing the valuables in her little Zip-Lock sandwich bag.
"Yes, there's a reason. I can't put my finger on it yet. Willing to take some more hammering?"

"Yeah, I'm a Home Depot top-of-the-line type of plywood, girl. Go for it."

Willi shook her head then her hands out. "Okay, okay.
Quannah, in his sleepiness, mumbled that he was here to
check out the IODD men about sabotage or something.
Certainly, that's somewhat corroborated due to the cell
phone. He had a way to communicate if problems arose.
Oh my gosh, Kenzie. He can't call for backup. We've got
the damn phone!"

"Whoa. Calm down. He didn't look like he needed any
cruisers with blaring lights. He wanted to talk to the old
monk. That was all. When we locate the old feller, there
will be Quannah, and you can hand the cell phone and all
these worries over to him."

As if the phone sensed their conversation, a loud rendition of "*La Cucaracha*" broke forth from the confines of
Willi's tied bag. Her eyes opened so wide, Kenzie laughed
and the moment of tension broke. Willi scrabbled inside
the bag, and punched the RECEIVE button. "Hello?"

"Miss Willi, is that you?" Sheriff Brigham's voice
wrapped warmly around her.

"Yes, yes, it is."

"Smart of my nephew to let you help him. I told him
you wouldn't mind even if you were dedicating this week
to your friend Kenzie."

Willi held the phone where Kenzie could also hear.
"Right. Uh . . . did you have something special to . . . to
report?"

"Well, now, you're sure Quannah has told you everything? I don't want my boy taking a tomahawk to my old scalp when he returns."

Kenzie dutifully got paper in hand. Willi said, "Oh, yes he told me about . . ." Thunder boomed outside, which helped Kenzie's offstage antics. Willi said, "That about covers it. This storm is bad and we might lose contact. You know cell phones."

"Right, right you are, Miss Willi. Tell him I did go to the hospital and checked on those cousins—the uh . . . oh, dangblast. Where'd I leave my notes?"

Willi said, "The cousins? Doretta Cameo and Banjo Joe Skeeter? Is he all right?"

"Yep, but poor feller has had a battle, I tell you. What with that snake bite and all. They got to him in time, but he's gonna lose his pinkie finger. Bless him. Said weren't no never mind. He didn't use that one on banjo or guitar. Horrible accident, I guess . . . except—" The cell phone did a dead space mambo where a few disjointed words danced between sky and earth before it finally disconnected.

"Except? Except?" Willi kept yelling into the vacuum. She replaced the phone in her bag. "Snake bite."

"Oh, poor old Skeeter." Kenzie's eyes teared up.

"He'll be fine. Doretta would yank his beard out if he wasn't."

"Girlfriend, I apologize."

"For what?"

"For not believing in this innate ability you have to see things as they are, not as most of us who look at the surface and turn away. Too many reptiles crawling around not to be some connection, huh?"

"You figure?" Willi sighed and paced the floor. Adrenaline, not fully active, was still doing a slow drip through her system. "Someone came in or merely snuck the snake in through the open window of Yataro's meditation room."

She snapped her fingers. "Skeeter kept trying to tell us something. Ah, yes. *It* came out of the guitar. Maybe *it* was the snake that bit him."

Kenzie dug her nails into the pillow. "What about the that one we shared a shower with in the IODD men's pagoda." She shivered. "You said it wasn't poisonous."

"Oh, I don't know. I tried to believe that for the moment, but I could have been mistaken. No expert here, but they—the IODD men—obviously are. Everyone but us knew they were collecting reptiles and plants."

"Why would they kill their own man, though?"

"They may have been, as Quannah mumbled, into some sort of corporate sabotage, some nasty thing to buy the island due to underground riches or something. Might have been doing testing during all those nocturnal forays. Could be that he wasn't going to go along with the plan at the last minute. Might be . . . might be someone else killed him, and they just buried him. Literally covered the murder up to stay on the island until their dirty deeds were completed."

"Cold."

"The corporate world is an iceberg, Kenzie."

"Glad you're in teaching."

"Oh, that kind of mentality is everywhere. Plenty of frozen-hearted headhunters in teaching, too. Most so incompetent, the only way they can look good is to get someone else over a barrel. Education isn't a pretty world when turned belly up."

"Jeepers, girl. I'm sorry."

"Not a concern at the moment. The storm has withered. Right now we have to find that special spot off the yellow brick road near the tall azaleas and dig up whatever's there. I'm laying two stashed Snickers bars on it being poor Mr. Yodo."

"Naw, I don't think they'd chance putting him right in the middle of all the pagodas. I'll take that bet and up the ante by two packages of Mrs. Fields oatmeal cookies."

"You hid those from me, your best friend? Gee, Kenzie." She threw the now dried rain poncho at her and put on her own.

"Yeah, Miss Marple, and when did your integrity fly out the window . . . somewhere with the candy bars. So, what else you got? Huh? Huh?"

"Nothing, nothing. Yah ha ha."

"Yeah, girl, that's your story, stick to it."

This banter allowed Willi to keep up her courage long enough to get outside on the porch where Kenzie said with a smirk, "We can't do it."

"Oh, yes we can."

"No shovels, girl, not even a trowel."

"I know where they are. We shall leave no stone un-turned."

After getting the tools from the under-stairway shed of the stone garden, and making a slippery trip across the now muddled bricks, Willi parted the tall azaleas by the simple expedient of shoving her back against them. "My gosh, these are thick. Here's the place. Grass hasn't covered it yet. Barely enough room between these plants to bend an elbow to dig."

Kenzie glanced at her wristwatch. "About seven o'clock. But with this overcast sky we're going to lose light soon. God, the things I do for our friendship." She shoved the heavy shovel into the mud and slung it to the side. Rumblings from the sky constantly urged them to hurry before another cloudburst caught them with only the garden flowers for protection.

About a quarter hour later, sweat and renewed raindrops poured off Willi. She studied the determined face of Kenzie. Moments like this had to be the pivotal ones in life. A friend standing beside her in the worst of circumstances, not laughing at her less-than-normal beliefs, but helping by doing something she found so disgusting. Not one word of reprimand, not one word of whimpering. Willi leaned on her shovel. "Thanks."

With perfect understanding, Kenzie smiled back. "Not a problem, kiddo. I like Snickers."

"Yeah. Well, I love you, too."

"Ah, Willi, we've been sisters of the heart since we were eleven. Love you, too. So, does this mean you're gonna let me take a bubble bath first from now on, sissypoo?"

"If you call me 'sissypoo' again, I'm gonna give you your first mud-wrestling lesson."

"I'm shaking, girl." Kenzie sighed. "We can't put this off any longer. Did you see it?"

"The piece of cloth sticking out? Yes, I see it. Go easy scraping now."

Willi finally got on her knees and used her hands. "Guess I win my bet."

"Looks like, girl, looks like. Damn."

The body, with the clothes completely muddied and stained, not much white left to the shirt and pants at all, lay face down. Willi said, "They just threw him down, no burial at all, just garbage covered over. Help me turn him over."

Kenzie grunted alongside Willi. Willi hesitantly whipped off his face.

"Uh-oh."

Kenzie on bent knee, hung her head. "Oh my God."

"Guess . . . guess you get the Snickers."

"I've lost my appetite. I may never eat again. Oh my God," Kenzie repeated.

CHAPTER
18

Willi, along with Kenzie, used the ponchos to cover the body, and then they scrambled out of the dense shrubs. "The men," Willi said, "should be gathered at the grotto or cave or whatever soon. How about we rush to our pagoda, change into warm and dry clothes, and along the way find one of the monks to direct us to where they are. Don't believe we can wait to tell Quannah now."

"Agreed."

Inside their warm room, Juna Marie got the hair dryer out and as each one came within range, she tried to help them dry their hair. "Are you sure he's . . . he's passed?" Juna Marie asked for the seventy-fifth time.

"Positive," Willi said.

"No doubt," Kenzie said. "He had that kind of soft plastic look."

"Please," Juna Marie said. She also donned warm clothes. "I'm so glad I didn't . . . didn't know him well."

Willi stopped at mid-calf with the jeans she was pulling up.

"Oh," Juna Marie said, "That sounded crass. But if you don't know someone, you don't have to feel guilty."

"Guilty?" Kenzie asked, pulling on a turtleneck.

"Well, about . . . uh . . . anything causing his passing."

"Girl," Kenzie said, "why should you feel guilty? Unless you were the one who killed and buried him. Somehow, I don't see that. What I'm thinking is one of the monks just went bonkers. The life might be too constrained year after year. Hey, it happens in all beliefs and sects."

Juna Marie looked as wilted as the dried petals around her pristine bed. She began to clean them up. "Oh, Halliwell would hate this. He likes things neat and in place."

"He'd get upset by a couple dozen flower petals?" Willi asked.

"Yes, but I meant all this turmoil on the island."

"Definitely," Willi agreed, "not in the neat-and-in-place category."

"And now a death. Oh, Halliwell will be very upset. I believe he bonded with all these fine gentlemen in the Inipi ceremony. Oh, he takes things so hard."

"Two deaths." Kenzie and Willi caught her up on the happenings.

Juna Marie sighed. "Oh, yes, let's go and turn this over to your fellow. I feel badly that a veteran of the wars had to end up in such an awful grave. And you two believe it has something to do with the electronics and land development gurus, the IODD CEOs?"

"Yes, but we don't know the details, either," Willi insisted. "We've got to reach Quannah."

"And he's really a special investigator for the Texas Rangers?"

"Yes, and I see no reason not to let that tidbit out, seeing as how he's about to be knee-deep in mud and corpses."

"Oh, poor Halliwell. He'll be beside himself about how this will look for the church, him being on an island where . . . these things happen. And he doesn't like the outdoors, really. Oh, this storm, the mud, eating in a cave. No, it's not his scene at all. I shouldn't have insisted we come. All this is my fault."

Willi pulled her hair outward with both hands and yelled, "Oh, get over your daylong pity party, lady. Everything doesn't revolve around you, and you are certainly not responsible in any way for this catastrophe." In a softer voice, she added, "Life just happens, death being part of that—even if premeditated murder—but it's not your fault."

"Right you are." Juna Marie lifted her regal head, pulled a pink sun hat over her feathery-white cap of hair, and said, "What do we do?"

"We have a dangerous killer on the island. We have to get our happy butts to the other side, find the men, and get them to view this body—Nestor D.—before *he* disappears."

Kenzie wiped at her eyes and cleared her throat in such a way so as to seem like she was just getting last-minute touches made.

Willi wasn't fooled. "You okay?"

"Yeah. When she said 'veteran' I thought how easily it could have been Rooster instead of Nestor D., and—"

Juna Marie hugged her. "Our men, for better or worse, are a big part—not all, but a big part—of our lives. We don't want to think of any of them in harm's way."

Willi hugged her, too. "And, not to worry, sissypoo. Rooster wasn't the one so vehement and vocal in his dislike of Inoshi, Toru, and Yodo. In fact, he healed many wounds by working with them."

"They're killers. Would they really care?" Kenzie's face blanched, but determined, she stayed on her feet and swayed a moment.

Willi said, "Don't you faint, Kenz; don't you dare."

"Let's go find them."

Each of the monks shook their heads when asked where the cave cookout was. None of them had heard anything about the activity. Samdup, calm and serene, stood before the sand painting.

"Quannah was going to see the *old* monk, the one behind the waterfall," Willi said, feeling her own face drain of color. *Nobody knew about a cookout. Ohmygosh.*

"Ah, yes. One of our retirees—Shining One—who opted to stay on the island. A good and gentle soul. He's so quiet, we forget he's here. If you run into him, realize he is eccentric, which is why he prefers the English name, but he suffers no dementia. Quite alert and aware and active, he is."

"So? Could they have meant his pagoda or—"

"He lives in a beautiful cavern. It is the old gift shop underneath the falls from when the island opted for less spiritual clientele. Beautiful hand-painted ceilings, electricity, and even plumbing to the old bathrooms."

"I suppose there were more day visitors when the bridge was in use and the island had not separated from the mainland?" Juna Marie asked.

"Exactly, Mrs. Pate, exactly."

"Okay, we'll do more history of the island later," Willi said, her vision growing blurry with her growing anxiety. "Could one of your monks accompany us there?" She glanced at the three disappearing into the bowels of the cavernous kitchen environs. She sniffed, expecting the scents of onions and rice, steaming broth, and vegetables. The air remained pristine, clear of all culinary diversions.

"I am so sorry, but no, for your own sakes. Not in this

weather. You all *must* return to your pagoda. The men will be fine. I've sent Rimshi and Rabten to take care of Mr. Tulsa. Our one cell phone, unfortunately, due to the storm, has only intermittent use, but I will continue to try to contact the authorities."

He ushered Juna Marie and Kenzie out by the elbow. Willi, who followed in their wake, glanced at the three monks with heads bent over the sand drawing. Again, she caught them with looks of pure hatred crossing their features.

Her heart skipped a couple of beats. What were they in, some Buddhist Pagoda of No Return? Every nerve in her came alive with fear, and her heart jumped a foot and lodged in her throat to beat so erratically, she feared *she* rather than Kenzie would faint.

Something was terribly wrong.

She licked her lips and actually got them unstuck by the time Samdup had maneuvered them onto the Mimosa Pagoda's steps.

She said, "Could one of you perhaps come and stay at our pagoda with us?"

Kenzie, who knew her so well, raised an eyebrow and opened her eyes wide.

Willi repeated her request. "We'd feel so much safer."

"Please, ladies, lock your doors. We cannot spare men right now as matters stand, but at intervals we will come and check on you, truly. None of you are in the picture as intended victims, I assure you. Now, off you go. Follow the yellow brick road. You have your flashlights? Good." That said, he swished his robes and disappeared into the Mimosa Pagoda.

"Did you hear that lock click?" Juna Marie asked.

Kenzie said, "They never lock us out; meals are twenty-four seven. What gives, girl?"

Willi grabbed her arm. "Don't know. I counted more monks on duty—at least six—than we usually see all day long. And there's nothing cooking—literally—nothing cooking in there. Why didn't they have one person to spare for us? Why is this place locking up like the Bandidos gang just hit town and this is the Fort Knox of beer joints?"

"Are we going—?" Kenzie asked.

"Head toward our rooms, but once we get there, make a quick trip behind and to the side and back on that yellow brick road. We're going to find Quannah, come hell, high water, or a grave zombie."

"We could have done without that last one, girl."

"Sorry. Hurry, let's go."

An hour later, they'd sloshed through a completely different world than the one encountered earlier in the day. The field of prickly cacti, now a sliding mud flat, offered no traction as they stumbled up the hillside. At the end of the paved crossover they paused. Willi peered over her shoulder.

"You keep doing that," Kenzie said. "Is there something special you're looking for?"

Willi rubbed her arms and peered into the dark shadows surrounding them. "I thought . . . nothing."

"You thought what?" Kenzie searched the area, too.

"Just . . . had that feeling someone is out there watching our every move."

"Oh, great. Guess we're all to be on orange alert, girl."

Willi shivered. "Let's make it red. That's a long span of road now that I see it up close. Lots of jagged edges, pot-holes. We'll have to stay close to the middle and together."

Kenzie linked elbows with Willi on one side and Juna Marie on the other. "Together. Sounds like a plan to me."

Willi took a few tentative steps and pulled the others along. Wind soughed through debris along the road, small cairnes of stones piled hither and yon, and the trees brushing the attached edge of the bridge.

"What'll we do if Quannah's not there?" Juna Marie asked. "Even if he's at the shop behind the waterfalls, he may not know where the others are holding their cookout."

Willi paused and with flashlight probing studied the cracked concrete bridge. "Careful here. The surface is eaten away. No telling how weakened the foundation is." She loosened her tightened shoulder muscles. "As for your question, I don't think there is a men's food fest going on."

Kenzie asked, "What'd you mean?"

"Think about it, ladies. None—not one—of the monks knew about the outing. Usually, they're really good about preparing baskets of food for special things, so they would have for this if anyone had told them."

"Girl, I'm sure we're supposed to deduce or whatever at this point, but I guess my brain is too waterlogged."

"Someone set a meeting up, a meeting to get all the men in one place. Two are already dead. Does that suggest something to you?"

A rebel shaft of wind rippled across the bridge, caught some of the lighter loose steel wires, and scraped them like raunchy, rough fingernails on a new car finish, jarring every nerve in Willi's body, instigating a shivering she could not control.

"Let's turn off the flashlights," Kenzie said.

"Good idea," Juna Marie said. "We'll just go slower."

"That gibbous moon won't provide a lot of light," Willi said, but flicked the switch, stood still a moment to acclimate her eyes to even more darkness, and then moved steadily onward. "We're only about one-fourth of the way over. So, I ask again: Doesn't that scenario give you the idea that someone wants all the men in one area for a reason? Maybe has designs to hurt others. The stupidity that is done in the name of corporate takeovers and other schemes is . . . pure evil. You're right, Kenzie. They are murderers, and if someone maybe even guessed that they had killed Yataro Yodo and Nestor D., they would have no compunction about removing such an annoyance."

"Willi?" Kenzie's voice wavered. "Willi?"

"Yes?"

"Uh . . . there's another reason to get all the guys in one spot. And they might very well have the food and fire and everything else, just to make everything seem normal."

"What reason?"

"I think I know," Juna Marie said.

"Okay, ladies, now you've lost me. Ouch! Damn. Watch it, there's a deep pothole here. God, I scraped the whole side of my ankle. Even with the sock, I can tell blood is seeping." When Kenzie bent to check it out, Willi said, "No, no, not that badly. I'll tend it later. So, what other reason would someone have to gather all the men at one end of Serenity Island?"

"So we—" Juna Marie said.

"So we would be alone and vulnerable," Kenzie finished.

Not halfway across the cement span, Willi stopped. Her shivering turned into tremors with the realization she'd been a fool. Like an IV drip of ice water, blood seemed to only reach her heart in painful drops, to be squeezed out even slower. She shut her eyes, and vertigo blasted her so hard, she had to hold tightly to Kenzie to keep herself upright.

She said, "Ohmygosh, my God, you all are right." She could barely get words past her constricted throat. "I . . . I think . . . panic . . . attack. Can't breathe."

"Sit down a minute," Kenzie said.

Juna Marie took her extra powder-blue sweater from around her hips and threw it over Willi's shoulders. "Moments of epiphany hit us like that sometimes. Knocks the ever-loving Lord's wind out of us."

"Thanks. I'm so angry at myself. My insatiable curiosity has finally placed me and you all in the gravest danger, and I never saw it coming. Of course, they know I was the one who insisted Yataro was dead. Inoshi pumped me for information about his *chos-kor* and notepad, then questioned Juna Marie. So, she's suspect. He knows one of us had to have taken it. He wanted to know specifically where I found the shoes, and I if I still had them. I lied and said they were left at the scene. I'm sure he and Toru went back to search. Oh God, oh God, they know I've got them. If we saw them snooping around at night, there's no reason they might not have seen us and assumed we knew more than we do."

Juna Marie and Kenzie raised their heads, each pivoting to search in all directions. Atop this monster span of steel and concrete, the elements of wind and rain, the fear of primordial man beasts on the hunt, sent them into protective crouches, protecting of one another and alert to all sounds. No coven of mother wolves could be more attuned to the nuances of metal creaking against stone, of water ripping away below them, of the constant splash and churn of the waterfall becoming louder and louder.

Their surrounding body warmth lessened Willi's chills, her self-loathing brought more heat, and finally she rose upward. "We've got to find Quannah. Inoshi and Toru will be after us. Quannah will know what to do; how to set a trap to backfire on them." Her urge was to run with abandon, lope at full speed, scurry to the safety of the cavern behind the waterfall, and reach Quannah, get in sight of one so blessed as the old monk—the Eye of the Divine.

She wanted to propel her friends to safety, and pulled them both harder than she should. She'd never ever be able to live with herself if she let something happen to Kenzie. A second wave of dizziness hit her at that impossible thought.

"Slow down, girl. It'll be okay."

With tears rolling down her cheeks, she grabbed Kenzie by both shoulders. "Today, we thought we were being stalked by your ex, but it was Inoshi who kept us in sight. Maybe wanting to listen in, maybe just wanting to know where we'd go on the island. He was there—"

"Yes, there when Skeeter was attacked."

"Yes, yes. Oh, it all fits."

"So," Juna Marie, out of breath, asked, "You think they'd . . . kill . . . us?"

"Think about it. They can't be sure what we know, but they can make sure we don't let anyone else in on the news. So . . . perfect scenario tonight. The storm bursting in; the planned get-together with the men. The Guadalupe roiling below us already up to the banks and now swirling onto the beach areas. Perfect place to have three accidents occur while all the men just happen to be doing some more in-balance bonding and reaching out to the divine. They hope by morning light to have us floating down the Guadalupe as drowning victims. Who knows what story they'll concoct, or even if they'll need to."

Willi took a deep breath and tied the arms of the blue sweater tighter around her neck. "Come on," she yelled over the increasing roar of the falls. "We have to hurry now."

After trampling over shards of ripped-up concrete and metal, tree limbs and entire bushes torn asunder by the earlier fierceness of the storm, Willi stood at the far side of the bridge, directly in front of a path leading up to and through a section of the falls that looked like two glistening curtains, pulled aside enough that the elite could wander through before the main show began. She sucked in air. Signaling to the other two, she started forward. Sure enough, after passing between the two cascades, they were sheltered by nature's own stone above them, a portico of the island's stronger rock elements. Farther along, two wooden doors greeted them. They stepped inside. Immediately, the roar of the falls became subdued. Soft, fluted lights lit up the ceiling to leave the lower regions in soft but comforting shadows.

"This must have been the main foyer at one time, with those display cabinets to hold souvenirs and such," Juna Marie said. "Other rooms are off each side; looks like lecture rooms, but the lights don't even work in them."

Kenzie explored more, going around a curve. "Come this way."

Willi followed, but a third attack of the vertigo hit her. She swayed and kept herself from falling by simply sitting down.

Kenzie ran back to her. "Willi, I've never known you to do this. You're always the strong one who has her act together. You never fall apart."

Juna Marie also knelt beside her. "True. You're the one that's pulled us together. Why, we might be dead now if you hadn't got us out of the sleeping quarters. We'd have been like those proverbial sitting ducks."

Willi licked her lips and finally spoke. "Don't know what's the matter. Each time these ideas flood in tonight, they are so . . . so . . . overpowering, they bring me to my knees."

"Literally, girl."

"Yeah, literally."

"What horrendous horror have your brain cells come up with now?" Kenzie asked, helping her to her feet.

"I just kept seeing those monks."

"We need a little more, girlfriend."

"Twice. I caught them, when they were by the sand paintings, giving me the most malevolent looks. Those were not gentle, compassionate glances of concern; no, those were absolutely angry piercings of the flesh. Tonight was the second time, just before we left. Maybe, Kenzie, maybe you're right. Could there be another explanation for Nara Inoshi's and Mike Toru's actions? I mean, could one of the monks have gone off the deep end, like you suggested? If so, perhaps we're walking right into the killer's den."

Kenzie sighed and shivered. "Like which monk would have more right to turn a bit more sick than the recluse, huh? Oh, great. This is not good."

Juna Marie stood and wrung her hands. "I don't like this. I want to find Halliwell."

"And Rooster," Kenzie wailed.

"And Quannah," Willi said. "I'm okay now. Boy, I hope that doesn't happen again."

"What'll we do? Go back?" Juna Marie asked. "Perhaps we could hide in the Lotus Pagoda—the teaching pagoda—until daylight."

"Yeah, girl, what do we do?"

Willi pushed her hair behind her ears. Jeez, she had to brace herself and get her act together. Folks were depending on her. "We don't hide out; there's no guarantee no matter where we are. Let's finish searching here, but . . . maybe we can find some weapons first."

They ran back to the foyer. "Here's an umbrella," Kenzie said, plucking it from where it leaned against the corner by the door. "Hey, and here behind this counter are half a dozen stone bookends, probably for displays. Ah, here's a couple of walking canes. Surely not for the spry old monk.

Spittoons, too. Boy, these were from long ago, when smoking and chewing were allowed inside businesses."

"Maybe items leftover from the souvenir days." Juna Marie hefted the long, straight cane.

Willi opted for the shorter, twisted wooden one. "Okay, we can do this. We stay together. We fight together if need be. They—whoever they are—won't be expecting that."

Kenzie, somehow having developed a dangerous trailblazer streak, led the way again. Around a curving natural wall of stone, they came to a cluster of tiny rooms. "Janitor supply rooms, no doubt, maybe the workers' lounge. Make sense if he were to use that as his *bivouac*."

"They're all locked," Juna Marie said. "Well, there's this one last hallway. Not much light."

"No, not much light," Kenzie agreed.

"None," Willi said, clicking on her flashlight. This time she took the lead, with Kenzie and Juna Marie holding their weapons above their heads behind her. At the end of the hall, illumination flickered from beneath the one double-wide wooden door with gigantic iron hinges.

"Somebody's in there," she whispered.

CHAPTER
19

Willi again said, "someone's on the other side. Listen. Hear the shuffling."

"Makes sense, girl, that an old monk might shuffle."

"Not the active one we saw," Juna Marie said. "Through such thick doors, sounds will be distorted."

"You're right." Willi turned off her flashlight, put it in her voluminous bag, and hefted the straps on her shoulder. She gently tried the handle. "Locked. Okay, let's try." She knocked loudly once. Twice. A third time before a bolt squeaked from the other side of the door. The portal opened to reveal one wizened and brown and as hard as coconut.

"Hello," Willi said. "Are you Shining One? We're sorry to intrude, but Quannah Lassiter was supposed to come see you this evening. We're trying to get in touch with him." She glimpsed and heard a natural spring in one corner of the rounded room. Ah, it must flow back out to the water-fall. Beautiful.

A benign smile creased his face, more weathered it seemed than the ancient Black Hills. "He come. He go." Shining One pushed the door closed.

With only a sliver of space left open, Willi yelped. "Wait, please." She managed to shove a shoulder near, leaned on the wood, basically forcing him not to be rude and to open it wider.

"Thank you. How long ago?"

With each word she edged farther into the portal space. Inches wider now, the opening offered a view of a vast room. A fireplace that reached two floors in height, and could probably hold half a tree, only offered a small fire nestled in one corner of it.

"He go half hour, maybe more."

Juna Marie pushed on the door and smiled. "Hello, I'm Mrs. Pate. Mr. Pate and I met you the other day, remember? Probably Mr. Lassiter has gone to join him and the other gentlemen in a little cookout. Would you know where they might be?"

Shining One's eyes glistened, perhaps from the effects of old age, perhaps simply because he recognized a sweet and beautiful person before him.

"You go, now. Much company this day. Too many. Too many. You go, ladies. You go, now. Good evening, all. What must be, must be." As he stared pointedly at Juna Marie, he whispered, "A jewel shall not be sacrificed to the dragon." He glanced down the hallway toward a section covered by an oriental tapestry and forcefully shoved their hands away. "Below lies the divine."

Hearing the click of the bolt, Willi stared at her companions. "Trying to give us a message?"

"That'd be my guess, girl." Kenzie hefted her weapon. "My bet is someone is in there with him, but not Quannah."

"We can't leave a wizened little man to fend by himself

if . . . if it's *them.*" She tiptoed down the hallway with them behind her.

Juna Marie leaned her head to one side, exposing her neck. "When we visited the other day, we never saw this door, but we were in *that* room with that huge fireplace, and that fresh spring water flowing through."

"Where'd you enter?" Kenzie asked.

"A curved doorway, but I'm turned around, not sure—"

"Maybe that tapestry covers it at night. Could be he was trying to tell us to sneak in that way," Willi guessed. She stood still a moment while a shiver passed over her as fluffy as dusting powder, leaving a coating as light as talcum, but with a more sulfuric feel and scent.

Kenzie asked, "You having another panic moment?"

"No, no. I'm okay. What he said about a jewel not being sacrificed to the . . . the dragon, where have we heard that phrase?"

Kenzie snapped her fingers and pointed at her head. "I know. The prayer wheel."

"Yeah, but not the wheel, the prayer inside. Right you are."

Juna Marie, a puzzled look on her face, asked, "What?"

"We'll fill you in more later, but suffice it to say, this may be what the IODD men searched for every night. A precious jewel, a spiritual icon of the religion, some blessed artifact of tremendous value."

Kenzie clicked her tongue. "Of course, and what better place to keep it than with the oldest monk in the community, behind the guardian waterfall? I bet it's a huge ruby."

"Maybe an emerald," Willi said, her eyes growing wide with possibilities. "Perfect stone of some sort, and they refer to it as they do to the third eye, as the 'Eye That Is Divine' or the 'Divine One.' Oh, that's got to be it. Maybe, it's a wonderful Buddha statue with a jewel within the third eye. Good grief, that might have been the treasure the cousins hunted, too. Remember all the triangles at the waterfalls on the map, Kenzie?"

"You might be right. So many people hurt over . . . materialistic baubles."

"Not baubles, Kenzie. The monks would revere the statue or jewel or both if they were ancient artifacts of their beliefs. Only the secular minded would see the dollar signs and Swiss bank accounts."

"Whatever it is," Juna Marie said, "we can't let them hurt that innocent old man. Oh, I wish—"

"Halliwell were here," Kenzie said. "We know." To Willi she said, "What next?"

Willi wiped her hair off her forehead. "Still a good idea to stay together. Let's check under the tapestry." She lifted the edge, and found it so heavy that both Kenzie and Juna Marie had to help heft it aside. Stymied by a gated door with iron bars, they sighed in unison. Willi set aside her crooked walking cane, tried to reach inside to a lever, but couldn't quite make it. She tried with the cane, but it wouldn't bend as needed to shift the door attachment either. Sweat beaded and poured down her temples and into her eyes. "Almost." She pushed until her shoulder practically mated with the wrought-iron curlicues. "God, please." The latch merely needed a breath's movement to release. She had it balanced on the edge of the latch catch.

Behind her a yelp from Juna Marie and a scream from Kenzie, accompanied by their weapons hitting the floor, ringing out an anthem of doom, alerted her to trouble. Cold metal at her shoulder was nothing compared to the round barrel of the gun at her head.

"Ease back," Toru said. "Slowly."

Her stomach did a horrible chug-a-lug, the contents threatening an appearance, before she gulped in air and stepped away from the door. He pulled her right arm behind and up toward the back of her head. "Oh, jeez, you don't have to do that."

He grabbed her around the throat with his massive hand and squeezed. Pain shot all the way through both ears, into her temples and head. As the pressure increased, her eyes seemed forced from the sockets. She whimpered.

He said, "Shut up, Ms. Gallagher. Just shut up. You've been talking too much."

When she faced Juna Marie and Kenzie, she knew their whitened features mirrored her own. Nara Inoshi had already placed duct tape on their wrists behind them and around their arms above the elbow. He pushed them in the direction of the double portals.

Toru said, "Clean the area, Ms. Gallagher. No one else coming along should wonder about an umbrella and a couple of walking canes in the hallway, right? It's not tidy, and it's disrespectful not to leave it as we found it."

She couldn't manage to work up spit, but managed a croak. "Yes . . . you're right." She stole a glance upward at Kenzie, meaning to reassure her that she was okay, but Toru blocked her way. She tried to say a few words of encouragement, but this time her voice wouldn't come to the surface. *Oh, Great Spirit, had he ruined my larynx in that crushing hold?*

She'd faced a gun before, but not at such close range, not touching . . . oh, my God . . . touching her skin. Nothing to offer any resistance to the power, the horrible carnage-producing bullet that would take less than a second to sever her forever from friends, from dear God, no . . . from Quannah. She bent to pick up the useless weapons while he bent, too, keeping the cold steel in place, not giving her a parchment's worth of space between now and death. When she straightened up, he had to use his

other hand to support her elbows or she would have
fainted. She took deeper breaths and tried to steady her
nerves. *Think. Stall. Something.*

When the group reached the monk's door, her brain
wasn't exactly hitting any high RPMs but the pistons
churned slowly. She had limbs free, she had three weapons,
and she knew the gated door was open. Somehow, she'd
wait for the right moment and do something, anything but
lie down and let them assassinate her and her friends.

When Shining One answered the door, his eyes teared
up again. Poor old thing, he was probably so frustrated after so much turmoil—gaggles of company in one day—
and being kind and Buddhist he could not rant and rave. As
frail as he was, he stood his ground at Nara Inoshi's request
to let them in.

"No, all go. No more. Must go home. Go bed. Safer.
Buddha's blessings and . . . good-night."

Toru stuck his foot in the doorway and pushed it back
all the way. He shoved Willi into the room, keeping one
arm in a tight clasp, the gun barrel at her temple.

Shining One said, "So sorry, ladies. So sorry not reach
the divine below." His eyelids fluttered. He trembled and
stumbled as he abdicated the doorway.

Nara Inoshi said, "No apologies to them, venerable one.
They are some of those after the Eye of the Divine. We will
not allow this disrespect for our heritage."

Willi stood as tall as her bent arm would allow. Her
voice would only permit a stage whisper, but all listened.
"Excuse me, but we're not the thieves. You all are. You two
so-called IODD corporate men, looking for a quick trip to
the fast lane without benefit of old-age pensions. What better way to reach that than heist an ancient and valuable
jewel? And you call yourselves Buddhists. You think we
don't know you're the killers?" As she gabbed away, she

studied the room. Ah, yes, there behind her was a narrow hallway. That had to lead to the gated entry, the second way into the room . . . or out of the room.

"Yeah," Kenzie said, "Nestor D. was right about you all. Got too close, didn't he? Is that why you had to whack him?"

Both men froze for a full fifteen seconds, truly looking like Texas mouth-breathers with lower jaw unhinged in disbelief. "Jewel? Killers? Nestor D.?"

Toru shoved her away but kept his gun pointed at her. "We are here to revere and protect, not harm. You're the one who killed Yataro. You were the last one to see him. He'd discovered where the Eye of the Divine resided. You found out, wasted him during sacred mediation, and thought that would drive us away."

Inoshi said, "But we remained to do between us what Yataro also gave his life for—to protect the Divine One. True, we buried our friend, so as not to have to leave the island and retreat from our sworn promises one to the other, but he will get many honors in a proper internment later. You will suffer all that the law allows, Ms. Gallagher. You and your compatriots."

"Me?" Willi could not believe their accusations. Dear God, the shards of pain ripping through her throat with each syllable had to be akin to getting stitches in an eyeball without benefit of Novocain. "Why not tell the truth, you lowlifes? You know it wasn't me. You and one of your poisonous snake specimens did the job on Yataro. Shining One, please do not believe these men. I had no reason to hurt Mr. Yataro. I didn't even figure out about the statue and the jewel until a few minutes ago."

Inoshi, a quizzical eyebrow raised, pushed Kenzie and Juna Marie toward two hardback chairs, taped them under the breasts and around the ankles—one ankle to one chair

leg—and then turned toward Willi. "Why do you keep going on about statues and jewels? Just shows how materialistic *you* are."

Toru, hand shaking with obvious rage, said, "She is evil.
Let me take care of her for the Divine One."

Willi gasped, stumbled farther away from them and almost into the shadows of a plant guarding the narrow
hallway.

Inoshi frowned, put his hand atop Toru's, and took the
gun from him. He emptied the chamber and pulled out the
clip. Breathing deeply, he shook his head. "No, no. There
is something wrong. She's not evil. Too curious for her
own good, and talks too much; that is a given. At the wrong
places at the worst times, but she's not . . . she's not the
one." He went over to the spring to throw out the cartridge
and clip. "The cleansing energy of the waterfall will eventually claim them. If we are to practice our beliefs, we cannot do it with weapons of death."

Juna Marie said, "Of course, there's nothing but sweetness and helpfulness in this lady. What's the matter with
you people? You need God's gentling hand upon your lives.
When Halliwell arrives, and he will be looking for me by
now, I'm sure—when Halliwell arrives he can counsel with
you both."

Shining One spoke, this time in a whisper and as if he
were in great pain, having difficulty breathing. "I tried to
tell. Better go home, go bed. Now, too late. Not Divine Eye
in danger, but you, gentlemen . . . and now, now ladies.
May Buddha smile on you. May Buddha protect . . ." With
that, the once vigorous old monk sank into a heap of cop-
pery robes and brown limbs.

Toru rushed to him, gathered him in his arms, and wept.
"What have we done? We've given him a heart attack."

Willi said, "No, this is the way I found Yataro. You all

have to believe me, and . . . and Kenzie and I were with Skeeter when something similar happened. All these people don't just collapse. Look for a bite, a viper bite."

Toru felt for a pulse, bent down to check for respiration, and shook his head. "We've been blind and misled. There is a small discoloration here below his elbow, but that could be a bruise."

"No," Willi said, slinking one step more into the darkened hallway. "Bruises don't happen that fast. It's a snake bite, I tell you, and you all are playing some sick game. Maybe Inoshi will have one wrap around you next, Toru."

Shaking that thought away, Toru said, "Not Inoshi. I know him. And what does anything matter? It's too late for Yataro and for Shining One; it's too late."

"I wish," Kenzie said, "people would stop saying that. Could one of you take this gift wrapping off now?"

A stentorian and mellifluous voice echoed throughout the room, filing the cavernous space with what sounded like God's own last magnificent call.

"A jewel shall not be sacrificed to the dragon."

Goosebumps traversed every centimeter of Willi's skin. Her palms perspired with the flow of those rich words into the airspace. She backed into the narrow hallway.

Kenzie twisted in her chair, peering over her shoulders. "Where? Who?" The last word squeaked out and was lost in a repeat of the masterful line.

Preacher Pate strode out of the shadowed side of the stone fireplace with a cloth-covered cage in one hand. "As He turned a staff into a snake for Noah, He shall on this judgment day turn a snake to the good of his humble servant."

"Oh, Halliwell," Juna Marie cried out while scooting her chair across the floor. "Thank goodness you're here.

Tell these men. Tell them to let us loose. Tell them they
don't have to do this awful thing."

"My sweet pet," Halliwell said, peering across the room
at her. "For you, the Lord and I do this; for you I've been
on bended knee this last year."

"What? What are you talking about? Halliwell?"

"Sweet Juna Marie, beautiful Jezebel you've become,
but I love you and will protect your virtue from all of these
demons—these dragons—who tempt you."

"Oh, dear Lord and God," Juna Marie muttered while
struggling against the tape.

"Yes, call upon your Lord, my God everlasting, ever
true and ever full of strength when we ourselves fall short
of the divine image. He will help heal you. And in my hand
he's placed the skills, the instruments needed to cleanse
our lives of those who would do harm to your gentle soul."
He came over and kissed her on both eyelids.

Tears pooled in her eyes and streamed down her cheeks.

Kenzie stared at Willi, raised her chin, and nodded, indicating for Willi to run down the hallway and out. No
way was she going to leave Kenzie trussed up with that
crazy son of a bitch in there. She scrambled across the
room and behind Kenzie's chair. With her nails and teeth
she started picking and gnawing at the layers of silver
duct tape.

Toru, holding the old monk's body, carried him toward
a cot near the fireplace. As he passed Preacher Pate, Halliwell pulled the cloth from the cage—a cage full of
writhing snakes. He flipped up the top, grabbed one, and
expertly attached it to Toru's arm, holding it there while it
milked its venom into his strong muscles.

Willi could not breathe for a moment. At last, she
ripped the layer of tape that bound Kenzie below the

breasts. Now she worked on that around her elbows. While she ripped with nails and teeth, she kept an eye on Mike Toru.

He crumpled to his knees for a moment, straightened himself, and with the reptile clinging to his biceps, he laid the monk down, turned and clasped the snake off, and threw it at Preacher Pate. He easily moved aside and the copper-colored length landed in the flowing spring water.

With elbows and one wrist free, Kenzie was able to work on one of her ankles while Will tugged at the left wrist bindings.

As Toru struggled, Preacher Pate turned toward his beloved Juna Marie, who had maneuvered her chair halfway across the room, which kept his interest riveted on her rather than on the tape gnawers. "My sweetest flower, you cannot help your wandering eye when there are vile creatures to tempt you at every turn. Admiring you, flirting with you, putting thoughts into your innocent head. Trying to tempt you away. So, they get a taste of their own medicine."

"No, no, Halliwell, they didn't. Oh, please, don't do this."

"I had meant to take care of only Yataro. Yes, my beloved, I knew he had insisted you come, and I knew what dark needs he held in abeyance until this destination was reached. I saw your lustful encounter."

"Oh, Halliwell, let me explain. It was a simple kiss, nothing more, and never would have been more."

Preacher Pate smiled. "That's why I agreed to the trip. I knew that here the Lord would provide the means." He patted the cage. "But, then others . . . others began to attack you." Suddenly, he turned toward Inoshi, who had bent over to get the other cane on the floor. Halliwell laughed. "God is not with you this night, philanderer. You are one of the very dragons that he's sent me to slay. No, no, not at all with you. What did you hope to accomplish by giving *my* wife a bouquet? The Lord knows your lascivious thoughts. Say your last prayers."

"You are unbalanced, preacher. Put the cage down. Let these ladies go."

"Of course, the ladies will go. I'll make sure they get the fastest-acting venom, you know. God is not without compassion and instructs me in these things."

Kenzie's limbs, all free, looked bloodless. Willi rubbed her ankles, then her legs. When they made a run for it, she had to be ready. *Please, God, let her not stumble. Help me not to stumble.*

In his awesome confidence, Halliwell Pate turned back toward the fireplace, placed a foot upon the stone step in front, and bent to work the embers. Inoshi chose that moment to attack, running at him full-blast. Willi helped Kenzie out of the chair, half pulled, half dragged her toward the narrow hallway. As they entered it, Halliwell was laughing. He threw a log, which caught Inoshi off guard, since he was probably expecting a reptile to be arcing in his direction. His shirt caught fire; he rushed toward the stream to put it out.

"Run, Kenzie, run!" A trained guard dog couldn't have heard her warning, but the push on Kenzie's backside got the message across.

Halliwell yelled after them. "There's no way out, ladies, no way at all. Go ahead, get your blood flowing. It makes the venom go through your system much faster." He quite calmly approached Inoshi, now with reddened shoulder and chest, and without a weapon.

Willi stopped in front of the gated door and hugged her bulging drawstring purse. Oh my God, he'd padlocked the door. Her heart literally stopped for a beat. Kenzie, too, froze. "We can't give up. No, no, we can't." Behind them, Juna Marie, started singing in a sweet voice an old spiritual, "Mansion Over the Hilltop."

Willi peeked down the hallway. Preacher Pate sat on the side of the spring, holding a snake by the head so very close to Inoshi's head. The tableau froze. Pate relaxed as Juna Marie's voice filled the cavern. He said, "No reason we can't enjoy a few of the Lord's best selections before finishing the work he has set forth for this night. You ladies listening? My Juna Marie has a beautiful voice."

Kenzie ran to the end of the hall and back to the gate. Willi pulled every which way on the lock. Kenzie said, "Only a bathroom, big one. You know, for lots of tourists, which there haven't been any but us for eons. If we'd been smart . . . well."

Willi banged on the gate. "Damn it! We were so close." Her frustration came through her pitiful squeaks. She glanced at Kenzie. "Windows? Were there any windows? Anything?"

"Not unless you count the weird tile designs. All of them green lizards and crickets, can you believe? Can you believe I'm about to die a horrible death, and I'm critiquing décor? What'll we do? Go back in and both of us attack him at once?"

Willi grew quiet. She bent her head to one side. In a sing-song, she whispered, *"Below lies the divine, crickets and lizards, below lies the divine, crickets and lizards, lizards and crickets, below lies—"*

"Girl, please get a grip. What are we going to do? We can't give up."

"Of course not, Kenzie. Whoever said we'd give up?" Willi straightened her back, hustled down the hall and into the commodious bathroom. She grinned at the faded greens of the crickets and lizards. "First, let's jam that door shut."

"How?"

In the deepest tuck of her bag, she located her emergency tools, a two-inch screwdriver and a short wrench among them. They unbolted a toilet, pulled it over, and wedged the crooked cane and the umbrella into a crossed lock to hold the door handle. "It'll give us a few minutes."

"What for?" Kenzie said. "To freshen our Mabelline mascara?"

"No, to get *below*. This place—the waterfalls—is referred to by everyone as the *guardian*. Maybe that's literal. It somehow guards the jewel, the statue, whatever. But Shining One said, 'The divine lies below.' Therefore, there's a way to get to it. He said it when he looked down to the gated door . . . or toward the bathrooms. Ah-ha."

"Ah, so, Miss Marple of the Range." Kenzie grinned. "I'm beginning to have hope. Oh, no. The song ended." Sure enough, the dulcet tones quieted. But within a trio of heartbeats, Juna Marie began "Whispering Hope."

Willi nodded. "Get on the floor. Look for a section of the wall that might move, might be a different color, odd texture, anything."

"You've had experience with this before?"

"As a matter of fact, yes, which is why I *know,* absolutely without a doubt, that there's a way out of here."

"Fairest Lord Jesus," "Shake These Bones," and "Every Time I Feel the Spirit" rang through the viperous death chamber before Kenzie said, "Willi, come here." In the last cubicle, behind the toilet, the tile was set differently. "Everywhere else it's lizard, light green tile followed by a dark green, then a cricket. Right here, they're all cricket tiles."

"Sure are." She took the screwdriver and Kenzie the wrench. Only two minutes and the old grout gave way, the tiles fell and they kicked away a three-foot hole that looked like it was attached to a kids slide. The only thing that kept them from sliding through was the commode, which effectively kept them from having enough room on either side to scoot into the opening. "We got that other one up, we can get this one, too," Willi said.

At the door, the umbrella crashed. "Oh, my God, hurry. Hurry!" Kenzie yelled. She raced to each of the five basins, pushed in the old rubber-type stoppers, and turned on the spigots. Water overflowed onto the floor.

Willi's hands shook. The screwdriver skidded out of her sweat-soaked palm and slid down the chute. "No, no!"

The door handle rattled behind them. Kenzie wrenched up the last bolt. "Why won't it move?"

Willi stood to help her lift. Struggling and grunting, they moved it half an inch.

The toilet blocking the bathroom door scraped across the floor. With one mighty effort, Willi tugged, Kenzie screamed out, and they both lifted and swung. The toilet let go of ancient ties with a strong suction and gasp, catapulting one half of itself on top of Kenzie.

Halliwell broke through and roared when he saw their plan. He held a snake in each hand. Neither looked as harmless as Mowgli's Kaa. Kenzie pushed Willi toward the chute opening. He sprinted toward them, but his shoes slipped in the flowing water, and he hit his elbow on a sink edge. The pain brought him to his knees, yet he retained hold of his death duo.

"Go! Hurry! I'll slow him," Kenzie said.

She did that by somehow finding the superhuman strength to hoist half of the toilet at him, scoring a decent bleeding gash in his head. In his rage, he threw one of the vipers just as Willi slid down into a dark abyss of Hell.

The roar enveloped and echoed much louder than her pitiful whimpered excuses for screams, which she knew were erupting one after the other and could not be heard. She landed in a pile of blankets or maybe on an old mattress. Here, she was thankful to discern, were seventy-five-watt bulbs at intervals along a roughly hung line leading through a tunnel. Praying Kenzie would be right behind her, she ran on a ways. She stopped now and again, but . . . no footsteps sounded behind. Okay, she would not panic.

Kenzie was one smart cookie. Maybe after the crapper hit the crazy jerk on the head, he would be out cold. Kenzie would opt to go check on Inoshi, Toru, and Juna Marie. *Works for me. That's what I will believe. I will. Kenzie is fine. She got out. She got out and she's fine.*

Willi traveled for a good fifteen minutes. The sound of the waterfalls dissipated entirely. All was cold and quiet. So quiet. How far below ground was she? Some intervals along the tunnel were so dark she feared moving, but just as she'd be ready to give up and hightail it back in the direction she'd come from, a light would flicker up ahead.

Have a little faith. This probably would lead to the dock or something.

She'd not quit. She would survive and get out to tell one most desirable special investigator he was just that—desirable and loved and wanted on many levels forever and ever, thank you very much.

At last, through a tiny red door, which even she had to bend down to get through, she entered a dead end, a keyhole circle of a room with rich wooden floors and walls. Pictures, each in an intricately carved red frame, hung on the circular wall, photos of a monk in sepia colors as if taken many centuries ago. On closer inspection, she frowned. Not really photos, but photos of drawings from long ago, perhaps many, many centuries ago. The artistic grouping seemed to span this man's life from birth to death with his remains in state and long lines of people holding flowers and food.

Willi turned her attention inward to the middle of the room, which had a bronze fence similar to the one surrounding the monks' sand art, but larger, some fifteen feet in circumference. Within the circle of bronze was a raised dais on top of which reclined a glass case . . . no, a coffin, at eye level. The muted light played across the features and limbs if such they were still to be called. For the bones in the sarcophagus were quite ancient, she was sure.

She sighed. *The Divine One.*

The Eye of the Divine. Here lay the treasure everyone sought. A most honored and revered Tibetan Buddhist monk, thousands of years old. The history they had been taught mentioned him in passing, as if he were only a bit of lore, but this had to be him. Why not have him out where they could pray before him as the pictures on the walls showed had been done in the past?

Humming? Was that singing she heard? Juna Marie? No, no. This was a . . . a mantra, and it came from the heavens above. She glanced upward. Light flickered through an opening in the ceiling, just tiny tendrils that leaked illumination to the outward sides of the circle. She almost expected the specter of the departed monk, either this venerable one or Shining One, who gave his life tonight, to drift down on the dust motes brought into focus. The mantra grew more steady and loud as if coming not from just two or three, but from many.

She narrowed her eyes and peered back down the rough passage, empty of footfalls. She sucked in air that only left her throat dry and sore. Not one drop of saliva came no matter how many times she swallowed. She rubbed the chills on her arms.

Think, damn it, think.

Could have been a side venue she missed, which, if by chance Preacher Pate had chosen, could have led to an opening into the cacti field or perhaps even by one of the pagodas. If he weren't somehow stymied by Kenzie, there was the second path option. Hells Bells, if that were viable, then once he found his quarry wasn't there, he'd return and come down to this dead end to find her. Great, just damnblasted great, and what had she been doing? Taking a leisurely scan of the museum beneath the mesmerizing mantras.

She screamed. "Oh, dear God, Great Spirit!" What to do? The light from above and the voices were so close. There had to be a way. She scrabbled in her bag, still somehow attached around her shoulder, but nothing useful came to hand. She needed something with which to reach up and bang on the ceiling. The immaculate room offered nothing in the way of stick or shovel. She stepped over the bronze divider and leaned upon the glass coffin. The wooden scaffolding supporting the coffin was solid with no hidden drawers. Nothing there. She tapped her fingers on the glass, then whispered.

"I'm so, so sorry to be disturbing your last resting place. Really."

Once resting upon the case, the tension in her shoulders lessened. She soft-shoed the verbal offerings again. "If you have any ideas, uh . . . Divine One, I'd appreciate them about now. Kenzie could need assistance. Certainly, Juna Marie and Inoshi do . . . and . . . Quannah . . . ohmygosh what if Halliwell Pate had already gotten to Quannah just because he stopped to cheer up Juna Marie?" That notion weakened her knees, and she almost buckled.

Tears trickled over her eyelids; she licked the saltiness and added a biting sting to her wounded tissues. "I'll do anything, anything to get back safely to help him, to help Kenzie. If you could maybe give me an idea . . . anything."

For some minutes she stared at the humble bones, which we all must become, studied the lofty brow, the appendages covered by the monk's robe and shawl. Simple sandals, one laid to each side of his feet bones. The glass cooled her forehead. If she could just get some of that coolness to her burning throat. If she could just rest her own tired body, get off her overworked legs.

And then she saw the answer to her prayers. A cane. The monk must have been buried with his cane and it was well hidden in the folds of his robe.

After struggling up on the rim of the scaffolding, obviously kept well polished by the monks if her slips and slides were indications, she opened the sarcophagus. "You remember later that this was your idea and don't hold it against me in the next life, okay? Please?"

After securing the cane, she gently closed the lid, climbed atop the glass case, and stood. Thank God, it was not a rounded top, but a simple straight-level job. The *Ohms* above her had gathered force and were lengthened now into "Ohmmmmmmmmmmmmmm." With the cane, she knocked on the ceiling. Quite a few bangs and bashings later, the ceiling opened up. Staring down at her were all the monks on Serenity Island and not one looked divinely happy about their beloved ancient one being disturbed.

A great roar sent the Mimosa Pagoda door slamming open, and in seconds, Quannah, hair flowing in fifteen different directions, leaned over the maw of the space the monks used for the sacred sand paintings.

"*Winyan.* Gallagher, are you all right?"

Samdup eyed both and shook his head. He knelt down

and pressed a knob at the edge of the sandbox. Slowly, the Eye of the Divine rose to floor level with Willi kneeling upon the casket so as not to lose her balance. When Quannah helped her step off the glass case, she immediately turned and handed over the venerable one's cane. She strained to whisper as loudly as possible. "He . . . *he* told me it was the only way to get your attention. It was all his idea. I give him . . . uh . . . full credit."

Jamyang, in the first row of angry monks, grinned and giggled. "He was noted for giving clothes off his back. Not a surprise at all, then." His laughter proved infectious and many others smiled their frowns away.

Samdup caught the flow of meaning and added, "Even after many centuries, his good works continue. He also had a wonderful sense of humor. He would love this moment. You will do us the honor of allowing us to photograph you with . . . with the honored cane before we replace it. Then, you will always be a part of the Divine One's resting room."

Willi nodded and clung to Quannah so hard that he said, "Easy, *Winyan*. I'm not quite ready to go *below* yet."

"I'm so glad. Ohmygosh, why are we standing here? Kenzie! She was—"

From a corner of the room, Kenzie said, "I'm right here."

"How did you—?"

Kenzie held tightly to Rooster's hand while she said, "That hit with the toilet tank knocked one of those vipers for a loop. Struck Preacher Pate right on the head." Kenzie snapped her fingers twice. "Took that long." She hugged Willi. "What took you so long?"

Samdup said, "Underground trail take twice as much time as running above."

Willi rubbed her throat and after a painful swallow asked, "Juna Marie? Inoshi? Toru?"

Quannah squeezed her gently. "You always worry about everyone else. We're going to take care of you right now, *Winyan.*"

"I have to know."

Samdup smiled. "Our cell phone finally made connection. Toru is on a care flight to the hospital and there . . . over there are Mr. Inoshi and Mrs. Pate. The authorities are on the way."

Sure enough, Juna Marie sat quietly crying and sniffling, and no one was more deserving of a pity party at this point. Poor woman. Inoshi, upper body bruised, sat beside her, comforting her.

"So, he didn't get bit?" Willi said.

"Girlfriend, Juna Marie saved Inoshi's life with that singing. Kept that madman, *poor Halliwell,* from acting at that crucial moment. When he came after us, Inoshi got her out of the tape bindings and they ran out before I even came down. They carried Toru between them. So, really, she helped to save two lives, and . . . what a horror she's lived with, sensing but not quite knowing he was on the brink of doing something so crazy."

"Now, my Miss Marple of the Range," Quannah said, and kissed her forehead, "let's do something crazy ourselves, maybe . . . a whole night of uninterrupted sleep."

"Already that bored with me, huh?"

"I'm up to anything my little Tweetybird requests." The twinkle in his eyes promised wonderful surprises.

She rallied and as loud as she could whisper, said, "Hummingbird, thank you very much."

Like Kenzie and Rooster, Quannah and Willi walked out hand in hand. Just as they got to the steps of the Mimosa Pagoda, Quannah said, "Just wish I knew what happened to my cell phone. Thought it was well hidden. None of the monks fessed up to seeing it."

"Cell phone?" asked Willi.

"Yeah, you know something about it?"

She patted her bulging bag. "I'll see what I can come up with for you."